THE DOCTOR
AND THE PRINCESS

BY
SCARLET WILSON

MIRACLE FOR THE
NEUROSURGEON

BY
LYNNE MARSHALL

MILLS & BOON

Scarlet Wilson wrote her first story aged eight and has never stopped. She's worked in the health service for twenty years, trained as a nurse and a health visitor. Scarlet now works in public health and lives on the West Coast of Scotland, with her fiancé and their two sons. Writing medical romances and contemporary romances is a dream come true for her.

Lynne Marshall used to worry that she had a serious problem with daydreaming—and then she discovered she was supposed to *write* those stories! A Registered Nurse for twenty-six years, she came to fiction writing later than most. Now she writes romance which usually includes medicine but always comes straight from her heart. She is happily married, a Southern California native, a woman of faith, a dog-lover, an avid reader, a curious traveller and a proud grandma.

THE DOCTOR
AND THE PRINCESS

BY
SCARLET WILSON

MILLS &
BOON

Published in Great Britain 2017
By Mills & Boon, an imprint of HarperCollins*Publishers*
1 London Bridge Street, London, SE1 9GF

© 2017 Scarlet Wilson

ISBN: 978-0-263-92645-3

Our policy is to use papers that are natural, renewable and recyclable
products and made from wood grown in sustainable forests. The logging
and manufacturing processes conform to the legal environmental
regulations of the country of origin.

Printed and bound in Spain
by CPI, Barcelona

Dear Reader,

I really enjoyed writing *The Doctor and the Princess*—
partly due to the fact that I got to make up two
countries, and partly because I got to write about my
first princess doctor!

Gabrielle isn't supposed to take over her principality—
you *do* know that all made up principalities are secretly
Monaco!—but her brother has abdicated and she has
no choice. She hasn't exactly shared the fact that she's
a princess with her doctor colleagues, and the arrival of
her security staff at the exact moment she's about to get
up close and personal with her own Mr Darcy causes a
stir.

Sullivan Darcy is the perfect hero—right down to his
flaws. He's a doctor who has served in the army and
now works for Doctors Without Borders. The attraction
between him and Gabrielle is pretty much instant.
But beneath the surface Sullivan isn't as smooth as he
seems. He lost his dad two years ago and hasn't taken
time to grieve. His brain keeps pushing things away—
he's a doctor, he's a guy, he shouldn't be feeling like
this… In this day and age depression is recognised and
known. It can affect anyone, of any sex, at any age and
at any point in their life. That's what I wanted to reflect
in this story.

And it turns out that Sullivan Darcy needs Gabrielle
just as much as she needs him.

I love to hear from readers. Please feel free to contact
me via my website scarlet-wilson.com.

Love,

Scarlet Wilson

This book is dedicated to my Australian partners in crime—
Rachael Johns and Emily Madden.

Conferences have never been so much fun!
Can't wait for the next one. x

Books by Scarlet Wilson

Mills & Boon Medical Romance

Christmas Miracles in Maternity

A Royal Baby for Christmas

Midwives On-Call at Christmas

A Touch of Christmas Magic

The Doctor She Left Behind
The Doctor's Baby Secret
One Kiss in Tokyo…

Mills & Boon Cherish

Maids Under the Mistletoe

Christmas in the Boss's Castle

Visit the Author Profile page
at millsandboon.co.uk for more titles.

**Praise for
Scarlet Wilson**

'The book is filled with high-strung emotions, engaging
dialogue, breathtaking descriptions and characters you
just cannot help but love. With the magic of Christmas
as a bonus, you won't be disappointed with this story!'
—*Goodreads* on
A Touch of Christmas Magic

CHAPTER ONE

'It's an emergency, Sullivan, I swear.'

Sullivan let out a wry laugh as he shook his head and ran his fingers through his damp hair. 'It's *always* an emergency, Gibbs.' He stared at the inside of the khaki tent.

Gibbs laughed too. 'Well, this time it really is. Asfar Modarres collapsed. Some kind of intestinal problem. He was lucky we got him out in time.'

Sullivan started pacing. 'Is he okay?' He liked the Iranian doctor. He'd joined Doctors Without Borders around the same time as Sullivan. They'd never served together but he'd known him well enough to see his commitment and compassion for the job.

'He should be fine. He had surgery a few hours ago.' Gibbs sucked in a deep breath. Sullivan smiled. *Here it comes.*

'Anyway, there's two weeks left of the mission with only one doctor on site. We're at a crucial stage. MDR TB is up to worrying levels in Nambura. We need another pair of hands.'

Sullivan shook his head as he paced. 'I'm a surgeon, Gibbs. Not a medic. Last time I learned about TB I was in med school. I know virtually nothing about it, let alone the multi-drug-resistant strains.'

He wasn't kidding. Ask him to wield a scalpel and he wouldn't hesitate. As an army surgeon he'd operated on the most harrowing injuries, in the most dire of circumstances. No one had ever questioned his surgical abilities. He prided himself on it. But put him in a situation where he wasn't the expert?

'You're a *doctor*, Sullivan—and that's what I need. Anyway, there's no one else I can send.' Gibbs hesitated. 'And there's another issue.'

'What?'

'Nambura can be…difficult.'

Sullivan frowned. 'Spit it out, Gibbs.'

'The medic is Gabrielle Cartier. The two nurses Lucy Provan and Estelle Duschanel, the onsite pharmacist Gretchen Koch.'

Sullivan sucked in a breath and groaned. Four females on their own. Nambura tribes were very traditional. Some of the tribal leaders probably wouldn't even talk to four Western women.

A female colleague had reported minor hostilities on a mission a few months ago. There was no way he'd leave the four of them there for the next two weeks with no back-up. His father would never have left fellow team members at risk and the same principles had been ingrained into Sullivan all his life.

'Okay, you got me. When can you arrange transport?'

Gibbs started talking quickly. 'I'll send you our latest information and protocols on MDR TB. You can read them en route. The helicopter will pick you up in fifty minutes.'

The line went dead as Sullivan stared at the phone. Fifty minutes. Gibbs had clearly already sent the transport before he'd made the call. It was almost as if he'd known Sullivan didn't have anything to go home to.

His top-gun pilot father had died while Sullivan had been on his final tour of duty in Helmand Province. He'd flown home, watched his father buried with full military honours, completed his tour, then had signed up with Doctors Without Borders.

Three years later he'd only managed to go home for nineteen sporadic days. He still hadn't emptied his father's closets or packed up any of his things.

He flung the phone onto his bunk as he pulled his bag from the top of the locker.

Just as well he travelled light.

The music met his ears as the chopper lifted back up into the black night sky, flattening the trees all around him.

He tilted his head as he tried to recognise the tune and the direction from which it was coming. There was only one path from the landing spot leading through the trees.

He wound his way along it, the music getting louder with every step, until eventually he emerged into a clearing filled with familiar khaki tents identical to the ones he'd left a few hundred miles away and three hours ago.

He glanced around. The set-up rarely varied no matter where they were in the world. A mess tent. Bathrooms and showers. An operation centre and the staff quarters.

A flap was pinned back on the tent that seemed to be the epicentre of the noise. Sullivan's curiosity was piqued.

She had her back to him. Which was just as well as his eyes were immediately drawn to her tanned bare legs. She was wearing a rose pink T-shirt tied in a knot at her hip, revealing the curves of her waist. Her dark hair was in a ponytail that bounced along with her movements. But it was the khaki shorts that had caught his eye. Judging from the frayed edging, they'd obviously once been a pair of trousers and he'd like to shake the hand of the person who had cut them.

On her feet was a pair of heavy black army boots and a pair of rumpled socks. And those legs just kept going and going.

She was bouncing on her toes now. She wasn't just dancing to the beat of Justin Timberlake. Oh, no. She was singing at the top of her voice. And this wasn't just a casual bop about the place. This was a whole dance routine.

He dropped his bag and folded his arms in amusement as she slid from one side to the other, mimicking the movements the world had seen a million times in the dance video. She had rhythm. She had style.

And she had his full attention.

There was no doubt about it. His blood was definitely flowing through his body a little quicker now. This emergency mission had just got a whole lot more interesting.

Something sparked in his brain. Recognition. He could practically feel the hormones surge through his body. He couldn't stop the smile dancing around the edges of his lips. For the first time in a long time there was a spark. A something. If he could grab this sensation right now and bottle it, he would.

Who was she again? He filtered through the names Gibbs had given him. Gabrielle somebody? Although he'd been with Doctors Without Borders for three years, it was impossible to meet everyone. There were thirty thousand staff covering seventy countries. They saved lives by providing medical aid where it was needed most—armed conflicts, epidemics, natural disasters, and other crisis situations. There were also longer-term projects designed to tackle health crises and support people who couldn't otherwise access health care. Every day was different. He'd just spent three months covering a burns unit. The mission before that had been in Haiti, offering free surgery. The time before that had been in a DWB hospital in Syria, dealing mainly with paediatrics.

She lifted her hands above her head, giving him a better glimpse of the indentation of her waist and swell of her hips in those shorts. He couldn't help but smile. This girl knew how to dance.

If he'd seen her in a club he would have been mesmerised. Her hips sashayed to the music. Her head flicked from side to side. Her whole body was bouncing. If they'd been in a club, he might even have fought the temptation to step up behind her, press his body against hers and join in. But they weren't in a club. They were in the middle of the Narumba jungle.

Her feet crossed in the clunky boots and she spun around. It was obviously meant to be a full circle, but she caught sight of the unfamiliar figure and stumbled midway.

His actions were automatic. He stepped forward and caught her elbow before she landed on the floor, pulling her up against him.

Her eyes were wide. Her skin soft. And the scent of roses drifted up around him. The hand that had shot out to break her fall had landed on his chest as he'd grabbed her.

For a second they were frozen in time. The music was pumping around them, the heat of the jungle rising between them, and the darkness of the night enveloping everything.

Her eyes were the darkest brown he'd ever seen. They suited her tanned skin and chocolate hair. It was only a split second, but the heat from the palm of her hand seemed to penetrate through his thin T-shirt straight to the skin on his chest. He sucked in a breath just as she stepped backwards.

* * *

'Gabrielle?'

As if the stranger standing in front of her, looking like film-star material, wasn't enough, the deep throaty voice sent a shudder of electrical pulses flooding through her system that started in the palm of her hand and shot a direct route to her fluttering heart.

It took a second to catch her breath again.

No, it took more than a second.

Darn it. He was smiling at her. A perfect straight-white-teeth kind of smile.

Her palm was tingling from where she'd made contact with the firm muscles on his chest. He was tall, lean and wide. She'd bet every part of him was as muscled as his chest.

He had a buzz cut—like someone from the army. In fact, she'd put money on it that he'd served in the military. He had that demeanour about him, that aura of confidence as he stood there in his khaki army-style trousers and a thin dark green T-shirt.

He held his hand out to her again. 'May I have this dance?' he joked.

She gave an inward shudder as her brain kicked into gear. She spun to turn the music down on her speakers. What must she look like?

In this area she spent twelve hours with clothes fastened up to her neck, not even revealing a glimpse of her ankles. By the time she got back to camp she needed an instant shower, a quick feed and clothes she could relax in.

She took a deep breath and turned around, regaining her composure and putting her game face into place.

She shook his hand and smiled. 'Yes, I'm Gabrielle. But you have me at a disadvantage. We haven't met before.'

He frowned. 'You haven't heard from Gibbs?'

She nodded and put her hand on her hips. 'Oh, I heard.' She lifted her hands in the air and made quotation marks, 'You girls can't stay there by yourselves. I'll find you someone.' She tilted her head to the side. 'I'm assuming you're the someone.'

He glanced around the tent as if he were sizing up the place. Then, in a move that only reinforced what she was thinking, he turned and looked outside at the camp, checking out the surroundings. Once he seemed satisfied he turned back to her. 'I guess I am. I'm Sullivan Darcy.'

She couldn't hide her smile. 'Gibbs has sent me my own Mr Darcy?'

He raised his eyebrows as she continued. The accent was unmistakable. 'US army?'

He nodded. 'I was. Now I'm with Doctors Without Borders.'

She walked over to a table and lifted some paperwork. 'What's your speciality? Medicine? Infectious diseases?'

He pulled a face. 'You'll hate this.'

Her stomach clenched. 'Why?'

'I'm a surgeon.'

'Oh.' Her stomach sank like a stone. In some circumstances a surgeon would be great but it was not exactly what she needed right now. She bit her bottom lip, trying to find the right words.

He stepped forward. 'But if it helps I did a refresher and read all the protocols on the trip here. Just give me some instructions and a prescribing regime and I'm all yours.'

He held out his hands as if he were inviting her to step into them. For the first time in for ever the thought actually did cross her mind.

Missions were exhausting, the time off in between

short and frantic. She couldn't remember the last time she'd felt a buzz when she'd met someone. A connection. The chance to tease, the chance to flirt.

Her own Mr Darcy was pretty much looking like manna from heaven right now.

She was lucky. She'd never had the same pressure her brother had—to find the perfect partner, settle down, marry and get ready to run a country.

Sixteen years of being in the spotlight as the perfect princess in Mirinez had been enough. Medicine had been considered an 'honourable' profession and she'd climbed on that plane to study medicine at Cambridge University, breathing a huge sigh of relief. Since then she'd only returned for weddings, funerals and a few state events. Mirinez had lost interest in her. She hadn't been in press reports for years. And that was exactly the way she wanted it to stay.

His green eyes met hers again. 'That accent? French?'

She shrugged. 'Close enough.'

She pulled out a chair at the table and gestured for him to sit down before he quizzed her any further. 'Let's focus on what needs to get done in the next two weeks.'

She shot him a smile. He stepped closer. His chest was barely inches from her nose and she caught a whiff of pure pheromones. Oh, she could pretty it up by saying it was a combination of soap, remnants of musk antiperspirant and some subtle cologne, but from the effect it was having on her senses it felt like one hundred per cent testosterone.

He didn't seem worried about their closeness. In fact, she could almost bet that he thrived on it. The thin fabric covering his broad chest brushed against her arm as he sat down. 'Like I said, tell me what you need and I'm your guy.'

She pushed away the rush of thoughts that flooded her brain as she pulled forward a map. She circled areas for him. 'We've done here, here and here. In the next two weeks we need to cover this area, and north of the river. We expect to see around seven hundred people a day.'

She was glad that he didn't flinch at the volume of people who still needed to be seen.

He reached over to study the map. 'How do you work your clinics?'

She gave a nod as the hairs on his arms brushed against her. *Yip.*

'The TB regime is harsh. We split our duties. We have two nurses, a few local volunteers…' she frowned '…and only one translator.'

He waved his hand. 'Don't worry about that. My Farsi is passable. The dialect might be a little different from where I've been working but I'm sure I'll muddle through.'

Muddle through. She smiled. It was like something her grandmother used to say in private. Not quite the expression she'd expected from the muscular guy who screamed 'army'.

'You're good with languages?'

He looked amused. 'You're surprised?' There was a challenge in his words and a glint in his green eyes.

Her brain couldn't quite find the words.

He gave a little nod. 'I speak ten languages.'

She blinked. 'Ten?'

He shrugged. 'I was a navy brat. I moved around a lot. I picked up languages easily. It was the only way to fit in.'

She pressed her lips together then rearranged the papers.

Interesting. It was clear he'd hit a sore spot.

She got straight to the point. 'Lucy and Estelle deal

mainly with the patients who require treatment for their TB. Gretchen dispenses the medicines. The volunteers administer and read the tests.'

He raised his eyebrows and she quickly reassured him. 'We train them ourselves.'

She opened a laptop. A spreadsheet appeared on the screen. She licked her lips. He was watching her closely. It was a little unnerving. 'We're estimating sixty per cent of the population have TB in one form or another. Some are active, some are latent, and some...' she sighed '...are multi-resistant.'

'How many?'

She nodded slowly. He must have read at least some of the information that Gibbs had sent to him. She let out a sigh. 'Around twelve per cent.'

'That high?' He couldn't hide his surprise. He'd known that drug resistance was rising all around the world, but the figure was higher than he expected.

'Tell me what you need me to do.' He was unnerved. And Sullivan Darcy wasn't used to feeling unnerved. He was used to being the expert in the field. He was used to knowing his subject area inside out. And as Gabrielle's rose-hinted scent wound its way around him he needed to find some focus.

Gabrielle nodded and licked those pink lips again. She pulled open a drawer next to her and pulled out some kind of cool pack. He watched as she unwrapped it and pulled out the biggest bar of chocolate he'd ever seen.

She gave him a cheeky smile. 'I hate mushy chocolate.' She broke off a piece and handed it to him. He automatically reached out and took it.

'I didn't peg you as a chocoholic.'

She shrugged, her brown eyes gleaming in the artificial light in the tent. 'I have lots of secrets, you'll just need to hang around to find them out.'

He almost choked on the chocolate he'd just put in his mouth. It was almost a direct invitation.

He leaned back in the chair, stretching one arm out to press the button to restart the music. 'I can see Justin and I are going to become very good friends.'

He folded his arms across his chest and smiled.

CHAPTER TWO

GABRIELLE NORMALLY SLEPT like the dead. It was a skill she'd developed over the last six years of working for Doctors Without Borders. An essential skill. No one needed an overtired, grumpy medic.

But she'd been awake since four-thirty. She'd watched the sun rise as she'd contemplated some more chocolate, wishing she'd had a secret stash of wine.

She could swear she could almost hear him breathing in the tent next to hers. This wasn't normal. It couldn't be normal.

Most men she'd met in her life had fulfilled a purpose. She always chose carefully. No one who would sell stories to the press. No one who was secretly looking for a princess. Guys who were interested in relatively short-term gigs. Six months maximum. Enough time for some getting-to-know-you, some trust and some intimacy. But no promises, no intentions and no time for the petty squabbles and fights to set in. She'd always been the one in control.

She'd never actually felt that *whoosh* when she'd met someone. More like a flirtatious curiosity.

But with Sullivan Darcy it wasn't just a whoosh. It was a full-blown tornado. For a woman who was always used to being in control, it was more than a little unnerving.

And she was mad with herself. Being caught dancing by him had thrown her off her usually professional stride. Gibbs hadn't told her anything about the doctor coming to work with her and last night it had seemed too forward to pry.

He'd said he was a navy brat. What exactly did he mean? The guy could speak ten languages? Really? It kind of stuck in her throat. Languages had been one of her major failures as a royal. Mirinez bordered three countries, France, Italy and Monaco. Her native language was French. English had been instilled in her as a child and spending her university years and training time in the UK had served her well.

At a push she could stammer a few words in a few other languages. The same standard statements required by doctors. *I'm a doctor, can I help? Are you in pain? What's your name?* But that was it. Languages had always been her Achilles' heel.

She'd spent her life being top of all her other classes. Her brother, Andreas, had consistently been annoyed that his younger sister could out do him in every academic subject.

And being a doctor was kind of a strange thing. She'd worked with plenty of other doctors who were experts in their fields—just like she was in hers. But she'd never really met a guy who seemed smarter than her.

Mr Ten Languages felt like a little bit of a threat. It was making her stomach curl in all kinds of strange ways. She wasn't quite sure if it was pure and utter attraction or a tiny bit of jealousy.

She flipped open her laptop to check the list of patients for today. Her emails blinked up. Three hundred and seventy-six. She'd read them all soon. The sixteen-hour shifts here were all-consuming. By the time they got back to camp, washed up and had some food, she didn't have much energy left. Reviewing patient details and stock supplies was a must. Reading hundreds of emails when a large percentage of them were probably spam? That could wait.

She ran her eyes down the list. The work was never-ending. TB was a relentless disease. There was no quick fix here.

'All set.' Gretchen, the pharmacist, appeared at the entrance to the tent with a smile on her face. 'I've just met our new doc.' She winked at Gabrielle. 'In some parts of Switzerland, we would call him eye candy.'

Gabrielle burst out laughing at Gretchen's turn of phrase. They'd worked together for Doctors Without Borders for the last six years—always on the TB programmes. It had been Gabrielle's first official diagnosis of a patient when she'd been a medical student and had been her passion ever since.

'I don't know what you mean.' She smiled in return. 'I'm far too busy working to contemplate any kind of candy.'

Gretchen wagged her finger at her. 'Don't think I don't know about the hidden candy.' She raised her eyebrows. 'Maybe it's time to contemplate another kind.'

'Gretchen!' The woman ducked as Gabrielle flung a ball of paper at her.

There was a deep laugh and Sullivan appeared with the crushed ball in his hand. 'Anything I should know about?'

She could feel the heat rush into her cheeks. It was like being a teenager all over again. She stood up quickly, grabbing the laptop and her backpack. 'Not at all. Let's go, Dr Darcy, time to learn some new skills.'

She was baiting him and she could tell he knew it.

He shook his head and slung his own backpack over his shoulder. 'I like to learn something new every day.'

He wasn't joking. And Gabrielle took him at his word.

As soon as they'd travelled to their first stop and set up, she took him aside. 'You know the drill. Ordinary TB is horrible enough. It kills one point four million people every year with another nine million suffering from the disease, mainly in developing countries like Narumba. Along with malaria and HIV it's one of the three main killer infectious diseases. Drug resistance and multi-drug-resistant TB numbers are increasing all the time. Because it's spread through the air when people cough and sneeze, it's virtually impossible to stop the spread. One third of the world's population is infected with my-cobacterium tuberculosis but it's dormant in their bodies. Ten per cent of these people will develop active TB at some point in their life.'

There was passion and enthusiasm in her voice. There was also a hint of anger. She was angry at what this disease was being allowed to do to people all around the world. He liked that about her.

'We've been using the same archaic test for the last one hundred and twenty years and the test is only accurate half of the time—even less so if the patient has HIV. I hope you're comfortable with kids. We have a new test for TB but it's not suitable for kids. They need the traditional test and we have the facility for chest X-rays if neces-sary. Mainly, we go on clinical presentation and history.'

He nodded. He'd read more notes after Gabrielle had gone to bed. He was happy to do something to pass yet another long night when he couldn't sleep.

She kept talking, her voice going at a hundred miles an hour. 'You know the clinical presentation, don't you? A persistent cough, fever, weight loss, chest pain and breathlessness. The nurses will bring through anyone who has tested positive and is showing resistance to rifampicin. You'll need to check them over clinically before starting their prescription.' She pointed to a printed algorithm. 'We have a chart for adults and a chart for paeds. The new test also doesn't show anyone who has non-pulmonary TB. The nurses will bring through anyone with a history who gives concern.'

He blinked as he looked at the clinic list. 'You see this many patients every day?'

She nodded, her brown hair bouncing. It was tied up on her head again. She was wearing a high-necked, long-sleeved shirt and long trousers, even though the temperature was soaring. He was lucky. He had on shorts and a T-shirt, but even so the heat was causing trickles of sweat to run down between his shoulder blades.

She gave a little tug at her neck. 'Okay?' he queried.

She gave a nod. 'Let's just get started. We need to see as many patients as we can.'

She wasn't joking. It was only seven a.m., but news of their clinic must have spread because there was already a queue forming outside.

Four hours later he'd seen more kids in this TB clinic than he'd ever want to. Doctors Without Borders might be there to try and tackle the TB epidemic, but to the people of Narumba he was just a doctor. His surgical highlight of his day so far had been grabbing some equipment and a scalpel to drain a few abscesses. He'd also seen a huge variety of skin conditions, variations of asthma, diabetes, polio and sleeping sickness. He'd seen multiple patients with HIV—mixed with TB it would be deadly for many of the people he'd seen today. He could barely keep track of how many patients he'd actually seen. And the queue outside? It just kept getting longer and longer.

Long queues were good. He had never been work shy. Long days were much more preferable to long nights. If he exhausted himself with work, he might actually get a few hours' sleep tonight.

He kept a smile on his face as another mother came in, clutching her child to her chest.

He nodded towards her, speaking in Narumbi. 'I'm Dr Darcy, one of the team. What's your name, and your son's name?'

She gave an anxious smile at his good grasp of the language. 'I'm Chiari. This is Alum, he's sick.'

Sullivan nodded and held out his hands to take the little boy. 'How old is he?'

'Four,' she answered quickly.

He blinked. The little boy resembled a two-year-old. The weight loss of TB had clearly affected him. He took out his stethoscope and gently sounded the boy's chest. The rattle was clear and he had the swollen and tender lymph nodes around his neck. He asked a few more questions. 'Does anyone else in the family have symptoms?'

The woman's face tightened. 'My husband died last month.'

He nodded in sympathy. There was a little pang in his chest. He recognised the expression in her eyes. He'd seen that loss reflected in his own eyes often enough when he looked in the mirror. But there was no time for that here. He had a job to do.

'What about you? Have you been tested?'

She shook her head and looked anxiously at her son. 'I don't have time to be tested. I need to take care of Alum.'

Sullivan reached over and put his hand on her arm.

'I understand. I do. I'm sorry for your loss. We need to

make sure that you are well enough to take care of Alum. We can treat you both at the same time.' He glanced outside the tent. 'I can get one of the nurses to do the test. It's a new kind. Your results will be available in a few hours. We can start you both on treatment immediately.'

He sent a silent prayer upwards, hoping that her test didn't show multi-resistant TB. Chances were if she had it, her son had it too. Normal TB took a minimum of six months to treat. But if Chiari showed signs of resistance to rifampicin and isoniazid she'd be considered to have MDR-TB. The MDR-TB drug regime was an arduous eight months of painful injections and more than ten thousand pills, taking two years to complete. The side effects could be severe—permanent hearing loss, psychosis, nausea, skin rashes and renal failure had all been reported. But the worse news was there was only a forty-eight per cent cure rate.

He pressed again. 'What about Alum? Has he been eating? Has he had night sweats or lost weight?'

Chiari nodded slowly. He could see the weariness in her eyes that was obviously felt in her heart. She'd likely just nursed her husband through this disease. Now there was a chance she could have it herself, and have to nurse her son through it too.

He stood up, holding Alum in his arms. 'Let's go and see one of our nurses. I'd like to try and give Alum some medicine to help with his weight loss, and start some medicine for TB. Our pharmacist, Gretchen, will give you the medicines and teach you how to give them to Alum. Then we can arrange to get your test done.'

After a few moments of contemplation Chiari stood up and nodded. Sullivan carried the little boy into the next tent. The nurses Lucy and Estelle nodded towards a few chairs in the corner. This was the fiftieth child he'd taken through to them this morning. They knew exactly what to do.

He filled out the electronic prescription for Gretchen and left her to explain to Chiari how to dispense the medicines for Alum. The reality was that children had to take adult pills, split or crushed. There were no TB medicines ready for kids in the field.

Gabrielle appeared at his side. 'Everything okay?' Her hand touched his shoulder.

He reached up automatically and his hand covered hers. He appreciated the thought. She was looking out for him. He met her dark brown eyes. 'It's a steep learning curve.'

She looked a little surprised. 'I thought it would only take someone like you an hour to ace.'

Was she joking with him again? He shook his head. 'Maybe after the two weeks. But not on the first day.'

She tilted her head to the side. 'I heard you talking there. You really do have a good grasp of the language. How do you do that?'

'It's similar to Farsi. It was a necessary skill when I was in the army. We treated a lot of civilians as well as servicemen. It doesn't matter where you are in life—or what you do—communication is always the key.'

She gave a careful nod. He folded his arms across his chest. 'There are a few cases we might need to chat about later. Adults. They're being tested but I'm almost sure that both of them are non-pulmonary TB.'

He could tell she was trying her best not to look surprised. Non-pulmonary TB was the hardest catch. The normal test didn't work, neither did a chest X-ray. There were so many variations that the symptoms were often mistaken for something else.

'No problem. If you give me the notes I'll check them over.'

He picked up the two sets of notes he'd started to write, his hand brushing against hers as she reached for them. 'Actually,' he said, 'I'd kind of like to be there to see what you think. Let's just call it part of the learning curve.'

The edges of her lips turned upwards. She really was cute when she smiled.

'You want a teaching session?' There was a definite glint in her eye. He leaned forward a little. He could think of a whole host of things that Gabrielle could teach him.

She was close. She was so close that he could glimpse a few little freckles across the bridge of her nose. Her brown eyes were darker than any he'd seen before and fringed with long dark lashes. It was clear she wasn't wearing any make-up—but she didn't need it. He could quite happily look at that face all day.

'Sullivan?' She nudged him with her elbow.

He started. 'Sorry, what?'

Her smile spread. She raised her eyebrows. 'You were staring.'

It was a statement that sounded like a bit of a satisfied accusation. Nothing could dampen the sparks that were flying between them.

He could feel them. She could feel them. He'd been here less than twenty-four hours. How on earth would he manage a whole two weeks around a woman like Gabrielle Cartier?

He was still getting over the wonder of actually feeling... *something* again. There had been a number of women over the last three years—but no relationships. He wasn't in a relationship kind of place. But now he could feel the buzz in the air. It felt alive around him, pulling him from the fog he'd been in. Gabrielle Cartier was like the freshest air that had swept over his skin in the last three years.

Two weeks could be perfect. It was just long enough to be familiar with someone but not long enough for any expectations.

He smiled back. 'I wasn't staring.'

'Yes, you were.'

He nudged her back. 'I wasn't. I was contemplating life.'

She laughed. 'I don't even want to take a guess at what that means.'

She was right. She didn't. But he couldn't stop staring at that smile.

She glanced at the notes. 'How about we see these two patients now? It doesn't really work well if the two doctors are seeing patients together.' She took a hesitant breath. 'We just have too many patients.'

He nodded carefully. 'I get it, you don't like having to teach the rookie.' He shrugged. 'Ten minutes. That's all. Then hopefully I won't need to ask for a second opinion again. I'll be confident to make the diagnosis myself.'

He wasn't joking. He would be confident. Sullivan had never needed to be shown anything twice in his whole career. He'd embraced the doctor's motto of see one, do one, teach one.

Gabrielle's gaze narrowed a little. She gave a quick nod. 'No problem.'

The next few days passed quickly. Every time she turned, Sullivan Darcy was at her back. Or maybe it just seemed like that.

He hadn't exaggerated. He picked up things quickly. He'd diagnosed more patients with non-pulmonary TB.

He'd adjusted antibiotic regimes for patients who were struggling with side effects. He'd spent hours and hours with patients with the dual diagnosis of HIV and TB.

His only tiny flash of frustration had been with a young child who was suffering from appendicitis. They had no real surgical equipment in the field. No theatre. No way to sterilise the tools that would be needed for surgery.

The nearest hospital was four hours away across a dry and bumpy road. Finding transport was a problem. All they could do was give the child some pain relief and a shot of antibiotics in the hope it would stave off any potential complications before sending him off in the back of a worn-out jeep. As the jeep disappeared into the distance Sullivan kicked an empty water canister clean across the camp, his hands balled tightly into fists.

She watched from a distance.

There was something about him that was so intriguing. Ask him anything medical and he could talk for ever. Ask about training placements, hospitals, work colleagues and experiences with Doctors Without Borders and he'd happily share all his experiences.

But ask about his time in the army or his family and he became tight-lipped. And there was something else Gabrielle had noticed about Sullivan Darcy.

He had the same skill that she'd developed over the years—the art of changing the subject. She'd recognised it instantly. And it intrigued her.

Had he noticed the same skill in her?

It was late. The sun was starting to set in the sky. They'd stayed much later at this site. It was one of the furthest away from their camp—which meant that the people in this area rarely saw medical staff. It made sense to do as much as they possibly could while they were there.

There was a noise to her left and she looked up. The heat of the day rarely dissipated and she'd undone the first few buttons on her shirt and pulled it out from her trousers. One of the tribal leaders had emerged from behind some scrub trees and was scowling at her.

There were a few other men behind him, all talking rapidly and gesturing towards her.

She glanced around. Lucy and Gretchen were nowhere in sight. Estelle was at the other end of the site, loading their transport. In the dim light it was difficult to see anyone else. Their local translator had already left.

The tribal leader strode towards her, gesturing and talking loudly. She'd almost baulked when Gibbs had refused to leave the female staff alone on the mission. But the truth was there had been a few incidents when a traditional tribal leader had refused to allow the women access to their tribes.

It had only happened twice. But Asfar Modarres had played a vital role in negotiating access to the people suffering from TB.

The tribal leader marched straight up to her face, his voice getting louder by the second. She quickly started tucking her shirt back in. No skin around her waist had been on display, but it was clear that something was making him unhappy.

The rest of the men crowded behind the leader. She swallowed. Her mouth was instantly dry.

In the distance she could see Estelle's head jerk up, but Estelle was too far away to offer any immediate assistance. Gabrielle had never been a woman who was easily intimidated. But she'd never been crowded by a group of angry men. The others had started to fan out behind their leader, surrounding her on all sides. Her automatic reaction was to start to step backwards, trying to maintain some distance between her and them.

Any Narumbi words that she'd picked up from the interpreter flew from her brain. 'I'm a doctor. Wh-what do you want?' She could only stammer in English.

The tribal leader poked her in the shoulder with one finger. It wasn't a violent action. But that one firm poke was enough to make her stumble over her own feet and thump down onto the ground, a cloud of red dust puffing around her.

The noise came from behind. It wasn't a shout. It was a roar. She recognised Sullivan's voice instantly, although she had no idea what he'd just said in Narumbi.

All the men looked up immediately. She could hear the thuds and a few seconds later the men were pushed roughly aside, several landing in the dust like she had.

Strong hands pulled her up roughly. She hadn't even had time to catch her breath. One arm wrapped tightly around her shoulder, pulling her close against his rigid muscles. The words were flowing from his mouth in fury.

She didn't have a clue what Sullivan was saying, but it was clear that the men could understand every single syllable. The tribal leader looked annoyed for a few seconds and tried to answer back. But he was stopped by the palm of Sullivan's hand held inches from his face.

Sullivan's voice lowered. The tone changed. Became threatening. A kind of don't-even-think-about-it message emanating from every pore in his body. She could feel the vibrations coming from his chest, shoulders and arms. But Sullivan wasn't shaking through fear or intimidation. She knew straight away he was shaking with rage.

It was a whole new side of him. She'd seen the cheeky side. She'd even seen the flirtatious side. She'd seen the professional side, his willingness to adapt to a situation outside his normal expertise and practise effectively.

Now she was seeing something else entirely. This was the man who'd served in the military. This was the man who left her in no doubt about how vested he was in protecting the people he worked with. Part of her had felt a little resentful when Gibbs had told her he was sending a man to work with them. Right now, she'd never been so glad that Sullivan Darcy was right by her side.

The palm of Sullivan's hand hadn't moved. He was still speaking in his low, dangerously controlled voice.

The men exchanged nervous glances. It didn't seem to matter that Sullivan was outnumbered. His tall, muscular frame and no-nonsense approach left no one in doubt about his potential.

The tribal leader shook his head and muttered, casting a sideways glance at Gabrielle again. After what seemed like an endless silence—but must only have been a few seconds—he spun around, his cloak wide as he stamped back off into the scrub.

Her chest was tight. She hadn't even realised she was holding her breath until Sullivan released the firm grip on her shoulders and blocked her line of vision.

She jolted and gave a shudder. Sullivan crouched down, his face parallel with hers. 'Gabrielle, are you okay? Did they hurt you?'

His hands were on her, pushing up the sleeve of her shirt, checking first one arm and then the other. He knelt down, reaching for her trouser leg.

She grabbed his hand. 'Stop it. Don't.'

Every muscle in her body was tense, every hair on her skin standing on end.

His dark green eyes met hers and she saw a flash of

understanding. She was still gripping him tightly, her knuckles turning white.

He put his other hand over hers and rubbed gently. It was comforting—reassuring. The thud of other foot-steps sounded. It was Estelle, quickly followed by Lucy and Gretchen. 'Gabrielle? What happened? Did they hurt you?'

She could hear the panic in their voices.

Her eyes were fixed on Sullivan's hand rubbing hers. A warm feeling was starting to spread up her arm. She sucked in a deep breath, filling her lungs and trying to clear her head.

Sullivan seemed to sense the tension leaving her body. He kept hold of her hand but straightened up, glancing around at the other women.

'Have you finished packing up? I think it would be a good idea to make the journey back to camp now. It was a misunderstanding. A language thing. He misunder-stood something that Gabrielle had told his wife. He was unhappy and was angry when he realised she couldn't speak Narumbi. We've done all we can do here today. I'll need to file a report.'

Gabrielle licked her dry lips. She was the leader of this expedition. The decision when to pack up and go back to camp had always been hers. Normally, she would be offended but this time she didn't feel slighted at all. She just wanted a chance to get back to camp and take stock.

'We're ready,' said Gretchen quickly. 'I'll drive.'

She was decisive. Gabrielle gave a nod and walked over to where her backpack and laptop were. The rest of the staff spoke quietly to each other as she climbed into the back seat of their custom jeep. She wasn't surprised when Sullivan climbed in next to her.

She waited until the engine had been started and the

barren countryside started to rush past. 'What did you say to them? What had I done to upset him? What did I say to his wife?' she asked quietly. She wasn't looking at him. She wasn't sure that she could. She fixed her eyes on the horizon. Thoughts of the language barrier were spinning around in her head. She hated it that she hadn't understood a single word out there. It had made her feel like a complete and utter failure.

Sullivan reached over and put his hand on her leg. Some people might think it was too forward an action but somehow she knew it was only an act of reassurance. 'He was unhappy because his wife had told him you'd given her a different medicine for the wound on her leg. She'd been using something that his mother made—some kind of paste. You said she had an infection and needed antibiotics.'

'That was it?' She was frustrated beyond belief. 'That woman had a serious infection in her lower leg. If I hadn't treated it, there's a chance she could lose her leg.' She replayed events over in her head. The consultation with the woman. The altercation between Sullivan and the tribal leader.

He pressed his lips together. 'I said exactly what I should say. I told them their behaviour was shameful. We were there to help them and everyone in their tribe. I told them if the women around me didn't feel safe, we wouldn't be back.'

This time she did turn her head and narrow her gaze. He looked her straight in the eye.

'Is that your poker face?'

He frowned. 'What?'

'Is that your poker face? I might not speak Narumbi, but I don't think that's exactly what you said,' she replied carefully.

His steady gaze hadn't wavered. He was good at this. She'd have to remember that.

He licked his lips, his first tiny sign of a release of tension.

'Then it's just as well you aren't fluent in Narumbi,' he said promptly.

He lowered his voice. 'I won't allow you—any of you—to be treated like that.' He sighed. 'I understand that we're in a different country. A different culture means different people. I respect their views. But if they're hostile towards you, or threaten you…' He squeezed her thigh and looked her straight in the eye. Last time she'd been this close they'd been alone in the tent when he'd arrived. The light had been much dimmer. This time she could see the intensity of the deep green of his eyes dotted with tiny flecks of gold. '…I'd fight to the death,' he finished.

She gulped. He meant it. She didn't doubt for a second that he absolutely meant it. 'Thank you,' she whispered as she shifted in her seat. How come he could look at her unflinchingly one second and tell her only a version of the truth, then the next the sincerity in his eyes could take her breath away?

She looked down at her hands. 'I hate not being in control,' she said quietly. 'I hate the fact that things can slip so fast, so quickly.' She shook her head. 'If I could have spoken the language I could have explained.' She tugged at her shirt. 'Or maybe he didn't like my clothes.'

'Stop it.' His voice was firm. 'Gabrielle, you and the rest of the women in the team are appropriately dressed. His mother is the head woman in their tribe. He thinks you insulted her expertise.' He put his hand on his chest. 'It's a different culture. Women in their tribe aren't really treated with much respect. Maybe that bothers him?

Maybe he's more modern than he seems—so the thought that someone questions the respect his mother holds made him angry.'

He leaned forward and touched her cheek. 'You made a clinical decision. You're a good doctor, Gabrielle. If you hadn't given his wife antibiotics it's likely she would lose her leg. And I've told him that. In no uncertain terms. Give yourself a break. Their behaviour was unreasonable.'

He settled back into his seat and folded his arms. 'And I told them that too.'

For the first time since it had happened she gave a small smile. 'And a whole lot more too.'

She saw him suck in a deep breath. His gaze hadn't faltered from hers, but she could tell he was contemplating his words.

'I've grown a little fond of you. I'd hate anything to happen on my watch.'

She felt a prickle go down her spine. Was this good or bad?

Part of her wanted to smile. It was almost an acknowledgement of the mutual attraction between them. But part of it sounded a bit over-protective. Sullivan couldn't know, but she'd deliberately left that part of her life behind. Being a doctor and working away from Mirinez gave her the freedom she'd never experienced as a child. It wasn't like Mirinez was some kind of superpower. It was a small country but prosperous—mainly due to its tax haven status. But her great-grandmother had been a film star, which had put Mirinez firmly on the media map.

She glanced at the others in the jeep. Estelle, Lucy and Gretchen were chatting amongst themselves in the front. They weren't listening to Sullivan and Gabrielle's conversation at all. The jeep had moved quickly. Even though the road was bumpy they were far away from the site of the camp today. What's more, she felt safe around Sullivan. Now he was sitting right next to her she finally felt as if she could relax. She bit her lip. 'Well, I might have grown fond of you too, but I'm not your responsibility, Sullivan.'

He only smiled. That was the annoying part of him. That darned confidence. Over the last three years she'd found it common amongst the medics who'd served in the army. Maybe she was even a little envious of it. She had felt vulnerable today—and she hated that.

'I'll take that under advisement,' said Sullivan smartly. He leaned forward and whispered, 'We've only got another week to go. Then it's back to base. How long have you got before you're back on another mission?'

There was an intense twinkle in his eye. He'd already admitted he was fond of her. Headquarters were back in Paris. All staff that arrived back had a few days debrief, then, unless people were rushing back to see their families, there was usually a few days where they would let their hair down before everyone dispersed to their next mission.

She licked her lips. 'I might have around ten days. I'm not sure where I'm going next. Gibbs hasn't told me yet. What about you?'

Mad thoughts were already flashing through her head. Ten days in Paris with Sullivan Darcy? Now, that could be fun.

He raised his eyebrows. 'I haven't committed yet.'

'You haven't?' She was surprised.

He shook his head. 'I have a few things I should really take care of back home.'

She straightened up. 'What kind of things?' He'd never

mentioned a family back home. And he'd been flirting with her. Just like she'd been flirting back. He didn't wear a ring. But if he suddenly mentioned a Mrs Darcy he would see a whole new side of Gabrielle Cartier. She just wasn't that kind of girl.

He let out a long slow breath and looked away. 'I really should take care of my father's house. He died a few years ago and I've been too busy working to get around to clearing it out and sorting through his things.'

She hoped her sigh of relief wasn't as noticeable as it felt. 'Who takes care of it now?'

He grimaced. 'No one really. I've only been back for a few odd days at a time. I have someone take care of the garden, and I've made sure that the services continue to be paid. But at the moment it's really just collecting dust.'

The tone of his voice had changed. It didn't have the strength of earlier, or the cheekiness that she'd heard on other occasions. There was something wistful about his tone. Even a little regretful. It was a side of Sullivan Darcy she hadn't seen before.

This time she made the move. She reached over and put her hand over his. 'Maybe you needed to let it collect dust for a while. You have to wait until you're ready to do things. That time might be now.'

For a second she thought he might come back with a usual cheeky quip, but something flashed across his eyes and he stared at her hand covering his.

He gave a slow nod. 'You could be right.' Then one eyebrow rose. 'But I don't want you to make a habit of it. I get the impression if you think you're right all the time you could be unbearable.'

She couldn't help but grin. This was how he wanted to play it. It seemed Dr Darcy could reveal the tiniest element of himself before his shutters came down again.

She could appreciate that. Particularly in an environment like this when things could flare up at any second and you had to be ready for any kind of emergency.

He leaned towards her again, this time so close that his stubble brushed against her cheek. 'Trouble is,' he whispered in her ear, 'what can we possibly do to get through the next week?'

A red-hot flush flooded through her body. She tried not to look at the muscled pecs visibly outlined by his thin T-shirt, or the biceps clearly defined by his folded arms. Sullivan Darcy was one sexy guy. But two could play that game.

She moved, stretching her back out then straightening her shirt, allowing the fabric to tighten over her breasts.

Then she gave him a playful smile. 'Who knows, Dr Darcy? I guess we'll just need to think of something.'

CHAPTER THREE

FOR THE LAST few days they'd danced around each other. It was ridiculous. And Sullivan knew it. They were both grown adults and could do whatever they wanted to.

But he got the definite feeling that although Gabrielle was attracted to him as much as he was to her, she wasn't comfortable about initiating a relationship under the microscopic view of their colleagues.

And she was right. It wouldn't really be professional. No matter how much his brain told him otherwise in the depths of the pitch-black nights in Narumba.

He'd been furious when he'd seen those men around her. That leader *attacking* her. Anytime he thought about it for too long he felt his rage re-ignite. As soon as they'd got back to camp he'd contacted Gibbs and filed a report. Another team would replace them as soon as they left. He wanted to make sure precautions were taken to safeguard the staff.

Then he'd written another note, asking the staff to try and check on Alum and Chiari to see how they were coping with the medicine regime, and if they were having any side effects, and yet another about the tribal leader's wife, asking someone to check on her leg and her antibiotics.

It didn't matter where they pitched up. The clinics

were packed every day and he saw a hundred variations of Alum and Chiari. That, mixed in with a hundred children who'd been orphaned and a hundred parents who'd nursed their children through their last days made him realise it might be time to have a break.

He'd never contemplated one before. Never wanted to. But the desperate situation of some of these families was beginning to get to him.

He wasn't quite sure why he'd told Gabrielle about the reason he hadn't signed up yet for another mission. Maybe she'd just asked at the right moment.

Or maybe he was just distracted by the possibility of ten days in Paris with a woman who was slowly but surely driving him crazy. If he didn't taste those pink lips soon he might just decide to set up his own camp inside her tent.

Every night when they got back, she showered, changed into one of a variety of coloured T-shirts and usually those darn shorts. There should be a licence against them.

The *whoosh* he'd felt when he'd first seen her was turning into a full-blown tornado. Maybe it was just the blow-out of actually feeling something again. Maybe, after three years, his head was rising above the parapet a bit. He'd met a few women in the last three years but he'd been going through the motions. There had been no emotion involved, just a pure male hormonal response. Gabrielle was different. Gabrielle had an aura around her. A buzz. He smiled to himself. She was like one of those ancient sirens who had lured sailors to their deaths. He'd have to remember not to let her sing. Or talk. Or dance. Or wear those shorts.

It didn't matter that they were the only five people in the camp. It didn't matter that he was the only male for miles. As soon as he heard the music start to play in her tent he was drawn like a moth to the flame.

Gabrielle could conduct whole conversations while she sashayed around to the beat of the music. He'd recognised it was her *thing*. Her down time. So far they'd discussed fourteen special patient cases, numerous plans for the next day's camps, treatment regimes, transfer times and some testing issues.

It was hard to have a conversation when the best pair of legs he'd ever seen was on display.

And tonight was no different from any other—with the exception of the soul music. She smiled as he appeared at the tent entrance. 'Lionel and Luther tonight,' she said as her loose hair bounced around. 'Decided it was time for a change.'

He nodded as he moved towards her. She'd tied a red T-shirt in a knot at her waist but hadn't got around to tying her hair up on her head as normal. It was longer than he'd realised, with a natural curl at the ends.

Sullivan wasn't usually a dancer. It wasn't that he couldn't feel the beat of the music, it was just that he'd never felt the urge to rave in a dark disco. And he certainly hadn't felt the urge to dance at all in the last few years.

But as the music changed to a slower song he sucked in a breath. Slow dancing he could do.

This was private. This was just him and her. No one watching. And he couldn't watch Gabrielle much longer without touching. He moved more purposely, catching Gabrielle's hand while she danced and pulling her against him.

'I think the tempo's changed.'

He could feel the curves of her breasts pressed against his chest. One of his hands lingered at the bare skin at her waist and it felt entirely natural for his fingers to gently stroke her soft skin.

She hadn't spoken yet but as he kept his gaze fixed on hers, her pupils dilated, the blackness obliterating the dark chocolate of her irises. She reached one hand up to his shoulder. It was almost like a traditional dance position. The one a million couples dancing at weddings the world over would adopt.

'You're right,' she said huskily, 'the tempo has changed.' She started to sway along to the music in his arms. It was easy for their bodies to move as one. What's more, it seemed completely natural.

He couldn't help the smile appearing on his face. He'd spent the last few days thinking of how it would feel to be in exactly this position. Her rose scent was winding its way around him. He slid his hand from her waist up the smooth skin on her back. She didn't object. In fact, she responded, tugging at his T-shirt and moving both her hands onto his skin. He caught his breath at the feel of her soft hands. Gabrielle wasn't shy. Both hands slid around to the front. She was smiling as she moved them up over his chest. He lowered his head, pressing his forehead on hers.

'Not long until Paris,' he whispered.

She glanced towards the opening of the tent. 'I don't know if I want to wait until Paris.' The huskiness of her voice made the blood rush around his body.

He walked her backwards against the table, pressing her against it as his lips came into contact with hers. She tasted of chocolate. Of coffee. She responded instantly. Lips opening, matching his every move. His hands moved to her firm breasts, slipping under the wire of her bra and filling his hands.

She arched her back and he caught her unspoken message, moving his other hand to unclip her bra at the back and release her breasts more freely for his attention.

She pushed herself back onto the table, opening her legs and pulling him towards her, a little noise escaping from the back of her throat. She made a grab for his T-shirt, pulling it over his head.

He laid her back onto the table, concentrating his lips on the paler skin at her throat then around her ear. The little sigh she gave made his blood race even faster.

Then he felt her hands on his shoulders. She wasn't pushing him away but her grip was firm. He eased back, connecting with her gaze and rapid breathing. At the base of her throat he could see a little flickering pulse.

'Gabrielle?' he groaned.

Her gaze was steady. 'Four days,' she whispered. 'In four days, we can do this in Paris.' Her head turned towards the tent entrance again, the flaps held back onto the dark night. It really was wide open to the world; any of the other camp members could appear at a moment's notice.

He drew in a deep breath. She was right. He knew she was right. It didn't matter that he'd be much happier if they could both just tear their clothes off now. For a few seconds he'd lost his normal professional demeanour.

They both had. Gabrielle was the lead professional on this mission. He had to remember that.

The spark between them had been building every day. Right now he felt as if the electricity they were generating could light up the Chrysler Building. There was something about this woman that got under his skin. Right from his first sight of her dancing around this very tent. It had been so long since he'd felt a connection like this that he was half-afraid if he closed his eyes for a second it would disappear. He couldn't let that happen. He *wouldn't* let that happen.

Four days. He could put a lid on it for four days. He might even message a friend to ask for a recommendation for a more private Paris hotel than the one he usually bedded down in.

He stepped back. Keeping in contact with Gabrielle Cartier's skin was a definite recipe for self-implosion.

He smiled. 'Four days isn't so long.' He grabbed his T-shirt and pulled it over his head as he walked towards the tent flaps.

He turned as he reached the entrance and started walking backwards. He winked at her. 'Watch out, Paris. Here we come.'

CHAPTER FOUR

THE DEBRIEF HAD been quicker than expected. Their data collection had been fastidious. It helped correlate the numbers of cases of pulmonary TB and MDR-TB in Narumba. The data spreadsheet recording all the side effects of any of the medications would be analysed by their pharmacy colleagues, and the extra information on childhood weight and nutrition would be collated for international statistics. The longest part of the review was around the safety aspects of the team that had gone out to replace them.

Sullivan had already made some recommendations. Three of the team members this time were male and extra interpreters were available.

Six missions had returned at the same time and right now every member from each of the missions was jammed around the booths in a bar in Paris. Drinks filled the tables. Laughter filled the air. After a few months of quiet it didn't take long for the thumping music and loud voices to start reverberating around his head.

Gabrielle seemed in her element. The girl knew how to let her hair down. Literally. Her glossy dark curls tumbled around her shoulders, her brown eyes were shining and the tanned skin on her arms drew more than a few admiring glances. She was dressed comfortably, in well-fitting jeans and a black scoop-neck vest trimmed with black sequins. A thin gold chain decorated her neck, with some kind of locket nestling down between her breasts.

Maybe it was the buzz in the air. Maybe it was just the electricity of Paris. Or maybe it was the novelty of having some down time. But one part of him couldn't fully relax.

He'd drunk a few beers and joined in a few stories but the undercurrent between him and Gabrielle seemed to bubble under the surface. This whole thing seemed like a preface to the main event.

It could be it was simply easier to concentrate on the here and now than the future. The future would mean finally having to think about going back home to Oregon to deal with his father's belongings. His stomach curled at the mere thought. It was pathetic really. He was a thirty-three-year-old guy—and he'd served in some of the toughest areas of the world—but the thought of bundling up some clothes and taking them to goodwill made his blood run cold.

It was so much easier not to acknowledge it and just move on to the next job. Take the next emergency call that came in from Doctors Without Borders and head off on the next mission.

He excused himself and stood up, walking towards the men's room. The corridor here was little quieter, a little darker. His footsteps slowed and he leaned against the wall, closing his eyes for a second.

He couldn't talk about this. He wouldn't talk about this. He and his dad had been on their own for so long after his mother had been killed in a riding accident when he was three. All he could remember of her was a smell and a swish of warm soft hair. He had plenty of photographs of her but when he closed his eyes, it was the touch and the smell that flooded his senses.

It meant that he and his dad had been a team. For as long as he could remember there had been an unshakable bond. His father had refused to be stationed anywhere without his son. Japan, Italy, UK and Germany had all played a part in his multinational upbringing. There had hardly been any discipline because he'd never been a bad kid. He'd never wanted to disappoint his dad. And the day he'd told him he wanted to do his medical degree and serve, tears had glistened in his father's eyes.

The sudden phone call out of the blue had been like a knife through his heart. His father had never had a day's illness in his life. The post mortem had shown an aortic aneurysm. The surgeon in Sullivan hated that. It was something that was fixable. Something that could have been detected and fixed. His father could have had another twenty years of life.

Instead, Sullivan had been left to unlock the door on the Hood River house and be overwhelmed by the familiar smells. Of wood, of fishing, of cleaning materials and of just…him.

The house that had been full of happy memories seemed to have a permanent black cloud over it now. Anytime he thought of returning his stomach curled in a familiar knot. It was hardly appropriate for a former soldier.

There was a nudge at his side. 'Hey, you, what are you doing, sleeping on the job?'

He almost laughed out loud at the irony. She'd no idea how much the art of sleeping had escaped him in the last few years.

Gabrielle gave a smile and moved in front of him, matching his pose by leaning on the wall and folding her arms across her chest. He couldn't help but smile.

'Was I boring you that much?' she teased.

He reached out and touched her bare shoulder, running his finger down the smooth soft skin on her outer arm. 'Oh, believe me, you weren't boring me at all.'

Her eyes twinkled. 'So, why are you hiding back here?' Her folded arms accentuated her cleavage and she caught his gaze and raised her eyebrows.

He let out a laugh. It was one of the things he liked best about her—a woman who was happy in her own skin. If only every woman could be like that.

'I wasn't hiding.' He grinned. 'I was contemplating a way to get you back here on your own.'

'Hmm…' She moved a little closer. 'And why would you be doing that, Dr Darcy?'

He loved the way his name tripped off her tongue. The accent sent shivers to places that were already wide awake. Her hand reached up and drummed a little beat on his shoulder.

His hand moved forward, catching her around the waist and pulling her up against him, letting her know in no uncertain terms what his intentions were.

Her eyes widened and her hands fastened around his neck. 'I'm assuming you made good on our plans.'

'You could say that.'

'What does that mean? Where are we staying?'

In the dim light of the corridor her brown eyes seemed even darker. Full of promise. Full of mystery. The feel of her warm curves pressing against him spoke of another promise.

He wound his fingers through her hair. 'I might have booked us in somewhere a little bit special.'

Her eyebrows raised again. 'You have?'

'I have. It seems a shame to waste any more time.'

She rose up on tiptoe and whispered in his ear, 'And is that what we're doing, Dr Darcy, wasting time?'

Her warm breath danced against the skin behind his ear. He let his eyes close for a second again before he groaned out loud and made a grab for her hand.

'Let's go.'

She didn't resist in the slightest. 'Let me grab my jacket,' she shouted as she let go of his hand and weaved her way through the crowd. He gave a quick nod and headed over to the bar, pulling out his wallet and settling the current bar tab. He didn't want to wait for the flying euros as they fought over who wanted to contribute. To some the bar tab might have seemed large. To people who'd been in other countries for three months, it didn't even come to the equivalent of a night out every weekend.

He waited at the door as Gabrielle gave a few people a hug and planted kisses on some cheeks. As she leaned over the table he had a prime view of those well-fitting jeans. Boy, did they hug her curves—but right now the only place he wanted to see those jeans was on the floor of their suite in the Mandarin Oriental.

She didn't walk towards him. She bounced. It was almost a skip. He couldn't wipe the smile off his face as her gaze connected with his and she made her way back over to join him.

'Ready, soldier?' she said as he held the door open.

He was too busy watching her moves, too busy focusing on those long legs and curves, too busy watching her eyes to notice anything else.

It all happened so quickly.

Gabrielle took a few steps out of his reach. She was teasing him, taunting him, spinning around to face him, pulling down her jacket to reveal one shoulder.

One second he could see her delicious smile, the next second his vision was entirely obscured.

It happened in the blink of an eye.

Six men—all dressed in black—surrounded her.

It seemed as though time stopped. At least it did for Sullivan. He'd never really suffered from flashbacks of his time in the army, but now adrenaline pumped through him.

He might be a medic, but he'd always made sure he could give the guys from Special Forces a run for their money.

Tunnel vision. That's what some people called it. But for Sullivan it was different. It was ultimate focus.

He moved quickly. The first guy he just grabbed between the shoulder blades and flung backwards to the floor. The guys on either side took a couple of punches to the face. The guy at ten o'clock got a swift kick to the chest, the guy at two o'clock a karate-style chop.

But the man directly behind Gabrielle had more time—if mere seconds—to react. He grabbed Gabrielle and spun around, shielding her body with his own.

Noise had faded as he'd moved. He hadn't thought. He'd just reacted. It took another second to realise Gabrielle was screaming. The kick from behind took the legs from him, but the punch to the head hardly registered.

'Stop it! Stop it!' Gabrielle screamed, extricating herself from under the dark-suited man's grip.

An arm clamped around Sullivan's neck and he reached up to grab it, ducking forward and throwing the man over his shoulder without a thought. The second punch to the side of his head annoyed him.

Who were these men and why were they attacking them?

Or were they?

He gave his head a shake. Only about five seconds had passed.

He pressed his hand to the ground, getting ready to

jump back to his feet, when Gabrielle moved into the middle of the sprawled bodies. *'Stop!'* she shouted, standing with her legs spread apart and her arms held wide.

All heads turned in her direction. She turned to the man behind her and pointed at Sullivan. 'He,' she spat out furiously, 'is with me!' She pointed her finger to her chest to emphasise her words.

Her angry gaze connected with Sullivan. 'And they...' she looked around at the dark-suited men, and let out a huge sigh '...I guess are with me too.'

'What?' Sullivan shook his head. Maybe that last knock to the head had been harder than he'd thought. What on earth was she talking about?

He stood up and looked around. A few of the guys were shooting him looks of disgust and dusting off their suits.

He could sense one of them standing directly behind him. The guy was practically growling.

Sullivan stepped forward. His first instinct was still to protect Gabrielle. 'Are you okay? What on earth is going on?'

He slid his hand to the side of her waist. She was trembling. Her whole body was trembling. But he could see the determined jut to her chin. She pressed her lips tight together as she tried to compose herself.

She spun around, facing the guy who'd shielded her body with his. 'Arun, what is going on? Why are you here?'

The dark-skinned man gave a little bow. 'Your Majesty. Your brother—the former Prince Andreas—has abdicated. He left the country a few hours ago. We have to take you back to get you sworn in as Head of State.'

'Your...what?'

Sullivan gave his head a second shake and glanced

downwards for a second. Was he secretly out cold or hallucinating? The dark-skinned man had a strange accent, Middle Eastern mixed with a distinctly British edge.

Gabrielle swayed. Two sets of hands reached out automatically to catch her. Arun's and his own.

'He's what? Andreas has done *what*?' Her voice rose in pitch and she started pacing in circles. 'Where is he? Where has he gone? Why hasn't he spoken to me? He can't do this.' She flung her hands in the air. 'He can't just walk away from Mirinez! Who does that? Who walks away from their country?'

Five sets of eyes blinked and averted their gaze for a second. Sullivan felt something washing over him. Unease.

Arun kept his gaze solidly on Gabrielle and his voice low and steady. 'Princess Gabrielle, it's time to return home. It's time to come back to Mirinez. Your country needs you.'

Panic flooded Gabrielle's face. She pulled her phone from her bag and started pressing buttons furiously. 'Andreas. I need to speak to Andreas. He emailed me a few weeks ago. I told him I'd get in touch when I got back.'

Arun pulled an envelope from his pocket as he glanced at his watch. 'He's currently on a flight to New York. He left you this.'

Her hand was shaking as she reached for the envelope. She pulled the letter out and took a few steps away, head bowed as she read.

Sullivan looked around and put his hands on his hips. 'It's one of these things, isn't it?' He took a few paces, glancing towards every corner on the street. 'You're filming us somewhere and it's all a set-up—it's all a big joke.'

Arun met his gaze and shook his head, giving a few rapid instructions to the other men, who changed positions.

Gabrielle was still reading the letter. Her body was rigid, her face pale. She crumpled the letter between her hands.

Several of their colleagues came out from the bar. 'Gabrielle? Sullivan? Is everything okay?'

The shout seemed to jolt Gabrielle into action. She pushed her hair back from her face. She gave a wave. 'Hi, Connor, Matt, everything's fine. Just a little misunderstanding.'

Connor frowned and shot Sullivan a wary glance before giving a brief nod and disappearing back inside the bar.

'A misunderstanding?' Sullivan walked up to Gabrielle. 'We walk out of a bar and get attacked by six goons and you think that's a misunderstanding?'

She glanced sideways. 'Shh,' she said quickly. She stared down at the crumpled paper in her hand.

Sullivan took a deep breath. 'Are you going to let me into the secret here? What's with the princess stuff—and why are these guys attacking us?'

Gabrielle gave a huge sigh, her shoulders slumping. She shook her head. 'They're not attacking us. At least, not me. They're my protection detail.'

'Since when do you have protection detail? Where were these guys when we were in Narumba?' He shook his head. 'And princess? Mirinez? Is this all some kind of joke?'

Tears glistened in Gabrielle's eyes. 'Believe me, Sullivan. I wish it was.' Her gaze was drawn back to the six men. 'I have a protection detail now because I've just inherited the title of Head of State of Mirinez. It's a small principality—you've probably never heard of it.'

Sullivan narrowed his gaze and racked his brain. He'd lived in enough places to know most of the geography of the world. 'I have heard of it. It's in the Med. A few hours from here, in fact.' He tried to pull what he could remember from the vestiges of his mind. 'It's a tax haven, isn't it?'

Gabrielle made a kind of exasperated sound. 'Yes, yes, it is. My brother inherited the title. He was Head of State.' She held up the crumpled paper. 'But it seems he's had a change of heart.'

Sullivan felt as if he were waiting for someone to pinch him. Or punch him—but, no, two guys had already done that.

'You're a princess?'

She nodded.

'We spent two weeks together in Narumba. We were just about to head off to a hotel suite and do…whatever. And you're a princess. And you didn't tell me.' It was almost as if saying it out loud actually clarified it in his head.

For a second she looked pained. But that passed fleetingly, quickly replaced by a stubborn look. 'It wasn't important. I'm a doctor. That's what you needed to know in Narumba. And even though I was a princess it wasn't important. I didn't need to fulfil that role any more. When I work for Doctors Without Borders I'm just Gabrielle.'

In a way he could understand that. He could. But it still annoyed him. Would he have looked at Gabrielle any differently if he'd known she was a princess? He didn't think so. But it was just the fact she hadn't told him that irked.

He kept his voice steady. 'You didn't need to fulfil that role…but now you do.' He met her gaze. 'So what now?'

There it was again. That little flash of something. It wasn't horror. It wasn't fear. It was just…something. That thing that you saw in a kid's eyes when his parent made him do something he really didn't want to do. It looked almost like regret about having to be there. Having to take part in that point of life.

Gabrielle looked down. 'I guess… I guess…' She lifted her gaze. 'I guess I have to go back. I have a duty.'

Her voice shook and her eyes reflected all the things she wasn't saying out loud. The upset. The shock.

He reached up and touched her cheek, 'If you don't want to go back, you shouldn't have to go. You're a free woman, Gabrielle.'

She blinked and he could see the tears hovering in the corners of her eyes. She pressed her hand up to her chest. 'But I'm not. Not now. I haven't been back to Mirinez for the last few years.' She gave a sad smile. 'Being a doctor gave me the life I wanted. I never wanted to rule. I never wanted to be Head of State. That was always Andreas's job.'

'But he's bailed.'

His blunt words brought a hint of a wry smile to her lips. 'He's bailed.'

She sucked in a deep breath and looked over at her protection detail. It was almost as if something had just flashed into her brain.

He had the oddest feeling—like a million little men with muddy feet were stamping all over the next few hours of his life.

'What does this mean for you?'

All the warmth and fun that had been in Gabrielle's face earlier had vanished. She had that strange pallor about her—the kind that a patient had before they fainted.

He put his hand on her shoulder. Visions of the night he'd planned had just slipped down the nearest drain. The fancy hotel suite and room service he'd looked forward to sharing with Gabrielle would remain a figment of his very vivid imagination.

He could go back to the bar and get drunk with the others.

He could sign up for another mission, avoid taking that flight home—yet again.

Gabrielle squeezed her eyes closed for a second.

The words were out before he thought about them. 'Gabrielle, if you need to go home, if you're worried, I'll come with you.'

She opened her eyes. They widened slightly. It was almost as if she couldn't think straight.

She shook her head. 'Don't. Don't do that. Don't come with me. I can't ask you to do that. It's not fair.'

'What's not fair?'

She threw up her hands. 'This. All of it.' She glanced over her shoulder and lowered her voice. 'I *don't* want to go back. I can't ask you to come with me.'

He shrugged his shoulders. 'You haven't asked. I've offered.'

She paused. He could see the hesitation in her face. But she shook her head again. 'No, it just won't work.'

He hated the expression she currently had on her face. She was saying no, but his gut instincts could tell she didn't mean it. And Sullivan had always prided himself on his instincts. It was the one part of him that thankfully hadn't dulled in the last few years.

He held up his hands. 'Well, okay, then. I don't even know where Mirinez is. But I'm sure I can find it on a map. I can still get there, you know—with or without you.'

She gulped. That edge of panic was still in her eyes and they were shining with unshed tears. He could sense the emotion in her.

He didn't need to go to home. He'd put it off for three years. He could put it off a whole lot longer. It didn't matter that he'd almost persuaded himself that this time he finally would go. It wasn't like he really wanted to.

Part of him ached. And he couldn't quite work out if it was entirely for the woman in front of him, or for the recognition that once again he was avoiding the one thing that he shouldn't.

The thought kick-started him.

'I'm coming with you, Gabrielle. You don't need to say a single word. I know you're shocked. I know this wasn't in your plans.' He raised his eyebrows and put his arm around her shoulders. 'We'll talk about the fact you didn't tell me you were a princess later.' He was half-joking. He wanted to try and take the edge off her nerves and worry.

She sucked in a breath. He could tell her brain was churning, thinking of a whole lot of other reasons to say no.

He leaned forward and whispered in her ear, 'You need a friend right now. That's me.'

Gabrielle was a princess. This was the woman he'd flirted with like mad for the last two weeks, had worked alongside and he'd dreamed of exploring beneath the confines of those clothes.

Were you actually supposed to do that with a *princess*?

Part of him wondered if there was some ancient law against those kind of thoughts—let alone any actions.

She tilted her chin up to his ear. Her voice was trembling. 'Thank you.'

Every emotion was written on her face. She was scared. She was worried. She was overwhelmed.

This was a whole new Gabrielle. The one he'd worked with over the last two weeks had been confident, efficient and extremely competent at her job—even when under pressure and difficult circumstances. She had a cool head in a crisis.

This Gabrielle looked as if she could burst into tears.

Just how bad could Mirinez be?

He glanced over at the security detail, some still glowering at him as they talked in low voices. These were the people in charge of protecting Gabrielle? He wasn't entirely impressed. The only one that actually gave him any confidence was Arun.

He gave a squeeze of her shoulders. What on earth had he just got himself into? 'I guess it's time to visit Mirinez.'

CHAPTER FIVE

FOUR HOURS LATER their plane left Charles De Gaulle airport. Their departure had been a whirlwind.

One of the security detail had sidled up to him with a suspicious glare and muttered to him in French, 'Special Forces?'

'Surgeon, US Army. I've done two tours of Helmand Province and spent the last three years with Doctors Without Borders.'

The man blinked at the quick response in his own language. He sauntered off again.

Sullivan was pretty sure that his details were now being fed through every security system that they had. He didn't care. There was nothing for them to find.

The private plane was sumptuous. There were wide cream leather seats, a table in front of them with an attendant waiting on their every need.

The protection detail was on the same plane, but Gabrielle spent most of her time on the phone to someone in Mirinez, answering emails or staring out of the window forlornly.

As the plane descended for landing Sullivan leaned over and looked out. The vast picturesque landscape took him by surprise. Mountains, green fields, river and trees. As they skirted the edges of the coastline there was a huge array of harbours filled with bobbing boats and a number of cruise ships anchored in the ports. It seemed Mirinez was quite a tourist destination.

The plane banked to the left and they passed over a city, which was overlooked by a cream castle halfway up the mountain.

'This is Mirinez?' he asked. From her reactions he'd thought they'd be landing somewhere stuck in the virtual dark ages. From a few thousand feet up Mirinez looked like a playground for the rich and famous.

She nodded as she drummed her fingers nervously on the table. 'Yes.'

His voice seemed to focus her. She pointed out of the window. 'This is our main harbour. Chabonnex is our capital city. It's the most popular tourist destination.'

He looked up towards the mountain. 'And the royal family stays in the castle?'

She gave a wry smile. 'Yes. That's one thing that's never changed in the history of Mirinez.'

Sullivan spoke carefully. 'So, there's just you and Andreas left?'

Gabrielle nodded. 'Our father died a few years ago after a massive stroke.' She sighed. 'He wouldn't listen. He liked the good life. He was overweight, had high blood pressure and cholesterol and wouldn't listen to a word I said to him.' Her voice softened. 'I think, in truth, he just missed my mother.'

He felt a pang. 'What happened to your mother?'

It took a few seconds for her to answer. 'She had heart surgery. We thought it would be routine. She'd had a valve replaced due to rheumatic heart disease as a child. There had always been a question about whether my mother should have children.' Gabrielle gave a little smile. 'But apparently she'd been very determined. The heart valve needed to be replaced and she went in for surgery…'

Her voice tailed off and Sullivan didn't need to ask any more. Cardiac surgery might not be his speciality but any surgery carried risks.

He wanted to reach over and squeeze her hand but the truth was he wasn't quite sure what his role here was. He still wasn't certain why he'd insisted on coming. A tiny part of him recognised that being here was easier than going home. Was coming here really just an excuse to avoid that?

He still hadn't really gauged the strong attraction between them. Getting up close and personal with a colleague on a mission, or back home, was entirely different from travelling to a country with a princess about to be made Head of State. If Gabrielle could barely get her head around this, how could he?

She turned towards him. Her smile was nervous, but the gleam in her eye was still there.

She lifted her hand as if she were about to touch his cheek. But her hand froze in mid-air and she glanced behind them towards her security detail. Their gazes connected almost as if the touch had still happened. The buzz that he'd first felt in Narumba was still clearly there.

They'd just never quite reached the place that they'd been heading to.

She pulled her hand back, her dark eyes intense. 'Thank you,' she whispered. 'Thank you for coming with me.'

The reply was easy. 'Any time.' He leaned back as they settled back in their seats for landing.

Mirinez. Another country to check off his list on the map he'd had since he was a child. He had no idea what would come next.

* * *

Her stomach couldn't settle. All the way up the mountain in the limousine her eyes were fixed on the castle.

Sullivan seemed relaxed. He wasn't demanding her attention, just offering the occasional smile of support. She was secretly glad he'd insisted on coming but she was also confused. The intensity of Paris and Narumba and all the things she'd intended to do with Sullivan seemed so far out of her grasp. Starting something now would be unfair. She hadn't even had a chance to contemplate what her role would be in Mirinez. They'd only ever spoken of ten days together. A fling. She couldn't weigh him down with the royal duties that were about to descend on her.

All she knew was that he felt like the one solid thing around her. And that didn't refer to his muscular stance—though that wasn't exactly a problem either.

Arun had been furious that the royal security detail of six had been beaten by one unknown quantity. Gabrielle didn't know whether to laugh or cry.

She was furious with Andreas. *Furious*. She'd never known anger like it.

Her entire life it had been made clear that Prince Andreas would inherit the title and rule the principality. It had never even occurred to her that might not happen. Their father's death had been a shock to them both, but it had only moved the inevitability of Andreas's role a little closer.

She'd spent the last few hours in the plane rethinking every conversation, every contact, every text, every email that they'd ever shared.

And she was still furious. It seemed that life in Mirinez wasn't Hollywood enough for Andreas's wife. She'd made him choose. And he had.

The last few years out of the spotlight had been blissful for Gabrielle. She liked living under the radar. She liked being a doctor, thinking like a doctor, acting like a doctor. That was the life she had chosen.

As the limousine turned and drove between the stone-carved pillars and through the wrought-iron gates Gabrielle sucked in her breath. She'd loved living here as a child. It was only as an adult she'd felt cloistered by the views and opinions around her.

The limousine door opened and she stepped out. The stones crunched beneath her feet as the cold-tipped air from the mountain swept around her. The cream-coloured palace loomed above her, built on the side of the mountain, looking over the city of Chabonnex below.

The city was stunning. From here it looked like a village built for tiny people, filled with tram lines and townhouses. There were no skyscrapers or tower blocks in Mirinez.

She walked up the steps to the palace entrance. The doors were wide open and the familiar scent of pine, lemon and old oak filled the air. The palace had always smelled like this. She walked across the black and white marble floor. She'd been told that the palace in Mirinez had been based on designs of Blenheim Palace in the UK. Mirinez's was like a miniature version. Every room had high ceilings with ornate plaster designs, lavish chandeliers and wood-panelled walls.

Her father's advisor, Franz Hindermann, was waiting. He gave her the briefest of nods. 'Princess Gabrielle, we have much to discuss.'

She nodded in acknowledgement. 'Franz, I've brought a guest with me. A colleague from Doctors Without Borders, Dr Darcy. Will you show him to my apartments?'

Franz couldn't hide the blanching of his face. She

was surprised. She'd long since been an adult—what did he expect?

'Ab-bout your apartments,' he stammered as he handed over a clipboard filled with sheets of paper.

'Yes?'

'Well… I've moved you.'

'What?'

So that's what the hesitation had been for. 'Why have you moved me?'

Franz cleared his throat. 'Prince Andreas moved out rather quickly. And he took all of his belongings with him. His last instructions were to move you into the royal apartments.'

A chill spread through her. So this was real. This was actually happening. The apartments that had housed her mother and father, and then her brother and his wife, were now hers.

She'd spent years with a view that looked out over the mountain and stables. A view she'd loved.

Now it would consist of something else entirely. 'Oh, okay,' she said quickly. 'Put Dr Darcy in the rooms next to mine.'

Franz nodded and hurried away.

Sullivan appeared at her shoulder, holding his bag. 'You okay?'

She turned towards him. Right now she wanted to turn back the clock twelve hours. She wanted to go back to the bar in Paris where there was wine and laughing and a really hot guy in the corridor. She wanted to close her eyes, take his hand and let him lead her to the promised hotel suite where she could peel off the clothes that had kept them apart for the last two weeks.

She didn't want to think about being a princess. Her country. A brother who had abdicated and disappeared.

She didn't want to think about the responsibility. She couldn't even begin to imagine how this would affect the life she wanted to live.

She rested her palm against his chest, feeling his defined muscles and warm skin through the thin cotton of his T-shirt. Somehow being around this man grounded her. Focused her.

It let her think about the things she really wanted to do. Patients. Medicines. The next mission. Dark nights. Tangled sheets and so, so much more.

'No, I'm not,' she said clearly. 'But I will be.'

Sullivan's eyebrows rose for a second and his familiar grin spread across his face. 'Let me know what you need.'

He leaned forward and whispered in her ear, 'In every sense.'

The tight feeling in her belly unwound, spreading warmth that blossomed outwards. She pulled back, staring at her hand. She shouldn't have touched him. It was confusing things. For her and for him. She couldn't meet his enquiring gaze. She just gave the briefest of nods towards Franz and watched Sullivan follow him up the main staircase.

After twenty-four hours Sullivan felt as if he was having an out-of-body experience. People didn't move around this palace—they glided. The volume control seemed to be in a permanently muted state. He wondered what would happen if he went back to the main entrance, stood with arms and legs apart and let out some kind of jungle scream—or maybe even, in keeping with Europe, a kind of yodel.

He wasn't used to being around so much quietness. Quietness reminded him of a few occasions he'd been out retrieving wounded casualties in Helmand Provence and he'd had the signal from the one of other soldiers to keep absolutely quiet. Those days were long past and he had no real desire to go back there.

Or to the silence of his father's house.

Plus, he was bored. The wonder of living in a palace was for five-year-old girls in pink fluffy dresses. Not for guys used to living out of a backpack for three months at a time in places where running water wasn't always available.

He wasn't working. And if he wasn't working he had time to think.

Time he neither needed nor wanted. Thinking might take him down a road he didn't want to travel.

Someone had bought him a suit. Last time he'd worn a suit had been at a job interview long ago. There hadn't been much call for one since.

He'd picked it up, held it against himself and laughed. It was designed to fit a man of much smaller proportions. He doubted he could even fit a thigh into those trousers.

There was always a member of palace staff floating around outside the rooms. 'Why do I have a suit?' he'd asked a small nervous-looking individual.

'Mr Hindermann th-thought you might n-need one,' he stammered, 'if you were accompanying the princess to any official events.'

Sullivan raised his eyebrows. The thought hadn't even entered his mind. He wasn't here to do anything like that. That would make him—what—some kind of man candy? He shuddered as wicked thoughts crossed his mind.

'Get me a kilt.'

'Wha-at?' The man looked even more nervous.

'A kilt. I don't wear suits. I have Scottish heritage. I'll only wear a kilt.'

He was doing his best not to laugh. He had no more

Scottish ancestry than an American apple pie, but it would teach them to ask and not to *presume*.

'Do you know where Arun is?'

Redness was creeping up the smaller man's face. 'Mr Aliman will be in the security headquarters.'

'And that is?' Sullivan pointed down the corridor and took a few steps in that direction.

The man pointed. 'Down the stairs, into the west wing, take a left, another left, a right, a left and up the second flight of stairs.'

Sullivan blinked. Then smiled. 'No problem.'

The palace was bigger than he'd thought. Wings must have added on in later parts of the construction. But the directions were good. Ten minutes later he found Arun.

The dark-skinned man stood as soon as Sullivan appeared at the door. 'Dr Darcy, what can I do for you?'

Sullivan paused for a second, wondering how to approach this. Arun was the only guy in this place that he might actually relate to. He sat down in the chair opposite. 'I was wondering—' he began.

'What to do?' cut in Arun.

Sullivan smiled. He liked a man who got to the point.

'I can arrange a tour for you around Mirinez's capital and historic sites.'

Sullivan couldn't help but roll his eyes. 'Thank you, but no. That's not what I had in mind.'

His eyes caught sight of a thick itinerary with Gabrielle's name on it. He leaned forward, catching the paper at the edge and letting the pages fan past his thumb. '*This* is everything Gabrielle has to do?'

Arun glanced at the empty doorway. 'Princess Gabrielle has been gone for a number of years. There is a lot to catch up on.'

Sullivan folded his arms. 'Why do I feel as if you chose those words very carefully?'

The edges of Arun's lips turned upwards. 'Because you'd be correct. A number of issues have been...'

'Ignored? Pushed under the carpet? Destroyed?'

Arun gave a brief nod. 'It's fair to say that for the last few years Prince Andreas was...distracted. A number of trade agreements with our neighbouring countries urgently need reviewing. Some business deals on behalf of the government, some laws, some peace treaties all need the royal seal of approval.'

Sullivan shook his head. 'What on earth has been going on here?'

Arun shrugged his shoulders and lifted his hands. Sullivan got the distinct impression he secretly wanted to answer, *Not much.*

Sullivan leaned forward and put his elbows on the desk. 'What can I do?' He gestured towards the itinerary. 'It looks like Gabrielle won't have time to breathe, let alone anything else.' He met Arun's gaze and put his cards on the table. 'I don't take kindly to sitting around. Is there a hospital? A clinic I could visit? Somewhere I could make myself useful?'

Arun paused for a second then gave a careful nod. 'You understand healthcare in Mirinez is different from the US?'

Sullivan frowned. 'What does that mean?'

Arun held up his hands again. 'Mirinez is a tax haven. We have many, highly exclusive, state-of-the-art, private hospitals.'

Sullivan leaned back in his chair. 'Is this a tax haven or a plastic surgery haven?'

'Don't the two go hand in hand?' There was a wry expression on Arun's face.

Sullivan didn't even try to stop the exasperated sound coming from his throat. 'What about the citizens of Mirinez? They can't all be millionaires. Where do they go?'

Arun nodded. 'We have a few state hospitals and a few state-funded clinics. We also have a number of semi-private clinics part funded by businesses operating in Mirinez.'

Sullivan stood up. 'That's fine. Take me to some of those.' Then he realised how those words sounded and he lifted his hand in deference. 'Sorry, I'd be grateful if you could find someone to take me somewhere I might actually be useful. I'm a surgeon. My qualifications are available for anyone who needs them.'

Arun was smiling. 'Which one of my men that you punched would you prefer to take you?'

Sullivan winced. 'Yeah, about that...'

Arun nodded. 'You're right. We've rarely had any incidents. Their training needs to be reviewed and updated.'

Sullivan put his hand on his chest. He was trying not to smile at Arun's response. 'But I never said that.'

'You didn't need to.' Arun picked up the phone. 'I'll get someone to meet you at the rear entrance to the west wing—near the stables.'

'The tradesmen's entrance?' he joked.

'Exactly.' Sullivan was starting to really like this guy. His British sense of humour was shining through. 'Where did you go to school?' he asked.

'Gordonstoun.'

'That explains it, then,' he quipped.

'Oh, Dr Darcy?' Arun had a mischievous look on his face. 'Did the suit fit?'

'Not in this lifetime.'

Sullivan headed out the door as the very British laugh followed him down the corridor.

CHAPTER SIX

MIRINEZ FELT LIKE a whirlwind. From the second she'd set foot in the palace Gabrielle hadn't even had time to think.

She'd now sent Andreas seventeen emails and left six voicemails, each one more irate than the last. It wasn't the fact he'd abdicated. Well, it was. But it was also the fact he hadn't been doing the job he should have been doing for the last three years.

She looked at the carved wooden desk that had been in the palace for hundreds of years. Franz had allocated her tasks into piles. And it wasn't simple piles like urgent, important and information.

No, these piles were overdue by two years, overdue by one year. Must be signed today. Must be contacted today.

Then there were sub-piles about legal matters, countries, trade agreements and finance.

She held up her hands. 'What on earth has Andreas been doing? How have things got so bad?'

It shouldn't be like this. It definitely shouldn't. Mirinez was a small principality with a population of forty-five thousand. Her father had managed things comfortably. He'd looked after orders of state, their government, entertained visiting dignitaries, all while keeping up a whole variety of personal interests. Since she was a child, Gabrielle had known the role didn't need to be a full-time job. She'd thought that once Andreas had married his TV star wife, he would have plenty of time to keep her happy. It seemed he'd spent *all* his time keeping her happy and none at all dealing with matters of state.

Right now, if he'd been in the same room she would have wrung his neck with her bare hands.

Franz couldn't even meet her gaze. She reached over and squeezed his hand. 'I'm sorry. I'm just shocked that things have been so neglected. I had no idea Andreas wasn't fulfilling his duties. Why didn't you tell me?'

Franz met her gaze with his slate-grey eyes. 'I was forbidden.'

The words cut through her heart like ice. 'What?'

Franz was a traditionalist. He must be nearly seventy now and had been in the employment of the Mirinez royal family for Gabrielle's entire life. If Andreas had forbidden him to contact her, he would have respected the Prince's wishes. She didn't even want to think what the stress had done to Franz's health.

She was beyond angry. She was furious. Her stomach gave a little flip at the thought of what she'd brought Sullivan into.

She hadn't been upfront about being a princess. But when he'd sensed her momentary panic at returning home he'd insisted on coming back with her. Truth was, whether he liked it or not, Sullivan Darcy was a gentleman.

But the amount of work in front of her was going to consume her every waking minute. She hadn't expected this. He was her guest.

She leaned her head down on the desk as the old-fashioned phone in front of her started to ring. Franz answered it in his usual low voice but his quick change in tone made her sit up again.

'What is it?'

His face was instantly pale. 'There's been an accident in one of the diamond mines. An explosion.'

Gabrielle was on her feet in a second. 'How many?'

Franz was confused. 'How many what?'

She grabbed her jacket. 'How many casualties and what mine?'

Franz spoke again then stammered his reply, 'Around f-forty, mostly b-burns. It's the Pieper mine.'

She headed for the door as thoughts flooded through her head. Burns. Sullivan was a surgeon. After working in Helmand Province he was bound to have experience with explosive injuries and burns.

She spun around. 'Someone find Sullivan. Tell him I'll need his assistance.'

Franz put down the phone. 'Princess Gabrielle?'

She was already walking back out the door but something about his anxious tone stopped her. 'What?'

'Dr Darcy. He's already there.'

'He's *what*?'

Franz gulped. 'He's helping co-ordinate the rescue effort.'

She didn't wait for a driver. She got into the nearest palace car and just floored it. At least she tried to. Arun stepped out dead centre in front of the car as she reached the palace gates.

'Move!' she screamed.

He calmly walked around to the driver's side. 'Move over,' he replied smoothly.

She blinked, then took a deep breath and moved over. He slid into the driver's seat and drove down the mountain as if an avalanche was chasing them. But Arun had the skill and expertise to handle the car at speed.

He pressed a button on the steering wheel, connected to his control room, and spoke in rapid French. A few seconds later, another voice came on the line. It took Gabrielle a few seconds to realise who it was. By the time she did, Arun had disconnected.

They reached the bottom of the mountain and, instead of turning right, towards the diamond mine, he turned left.

'Where are we going?' shouted Gabrielle. 'People need help.' She could hear the sound of sirens in the distance. 'Was that Sullivan on the phone?' Her brain was still trying to fathom how fluent his French had been.

Arun made the next corner on practically two wheels. 'We're not going to the mine. We're going to St George's.'

'St George's?' She was confused. It was one of the most prestigious hospitals in Mirinez—mainly for private patients. From what she could remember, it did have a fully functioning small emergency department that treated private patients.

'Why are we going there?'

Arun glanced at her as they turned down the main road towards the hospital. 'Because apparently Sullivan has taken over.'

CHAPTER SEVEN

SPEAKING NUMEROUS LANGUAGES in Mirinez was definitely a bonus. So far he'd used French, Italian, German, English and a smattering of Chinese.

He didn't normally contemplate the big picture—but fate had certainly played a part in his being there.

His reluctant security host Mikel had shown him St George's Hospital and introduced him to the director only an hour earlier. The director had made a few casual enquiries about Sullivan's availability as a surgeon and his areas of expertise. What he hadn't expected was for Sullivan to turn up two hours later with a number of casualties from the mine blast.

Mikel, who had spent most of the morning growling at Sullivan and giving one-syllable answers to his questions, had been surprisingly smart when they'd first heard the explosion.

The ground had shaken underneath them as they'd stood in the car park.

Sullivan had moved right into combat mode. 'What's that? Where did that come from?'

Mikel had looked around for a few seconds. 'It must be the mine.'

Sullivan had sped back into the hospital and shouted

to the director, 'I need a bag for emergency supplies. We think something's happened at the mine.'

He hadn't waited. He'd moved through the department he'd just been shown around and started grabbing gloves, wound pads, saline and everything else he could lay his hands on. The director had hesitated for a second, then shouted to another member of staff as he'd watched the pile on the trolley grow. Sullivan glanced over his shoulder. 'Do you have ambulances you can send? And give me a couple of members of staff too.'

It wasn't a request. It was an order. Military mode had washed back over him like an old familiar blanket, and thankfully no one had argued. A few minutes later he'd had a bag of supplies and a nurse in the back of the car as Mikel sped towards the mine.

The main gates were wide open. Smoke was spiralling into the sky. People were running everywhere. There was a huge cloud of choking dust hanging in the air.

It only took a few seconds for Sullivan to surmise who was supposed to be in charge. He ran over to a man in a bright yellow fluorescent jacket. 'Sullivan Darcy, doctor. Where do you need me?' He repeated it in French and Italian and the man replied quickly.

'Over there,' he said, pointing to a large grey cabin. 'That's where the casualties are coming up.'

'Who is bringing them up?'

'The other miners.'

'Are there still casualties below ground?'

He nodded. Sullivan thought quickly. 'Ambulances are on their way. I'll triage those in the cabin. Get a report from the mine. If they need medical assistance down there, I can go.'

He moved quickly. The cabin was obviously used for occasional first aid and minor injuries but the first-aid kit must have been used up within seconds of seeing the first casualties. He kept the nurse next to him. She was used to working in a calm hospital environment and he'd obviously taken her well out of her comfort zone. But to her credit she was cool and efficient.

There were a huge variety of injuries—penetrating wounds, head and eye injuries, breathing difficulties, a few obvious broken bones. But the majority of injuries were burns—something he specialised in. It didn't help that every single patient was covered in a layer of smudged dust.

He threw some bags of saline at the nurse. 'We need to try and keep things clean. Irrigate everything that's burned. Remove any clothing or jewellery if you can do it without causing any damage. See if the kitchen has cling wrap. If they do, just put a clean layer across any burn. And keep the burn victims warm—ask for blankets. We don't want them becoming hypothermic. If anyone has a penetrating injury, look at it and patch it. If anyone's bleeding profusely, give me a shout. Triage One, Two and Three. One for the people who need to go to hospital first. Two for those who also need to go but aren't in immediate danger. Three for those who can wait for a limited period.'

She nodded and got to work. Mikel appeared at his side. 'What do you want me to do?'

Sullivan paused only for a second. 'I'm either going to ask you to transport some patients who are stable, or to come down the mine with me. What's your preference?'

Mikel gave a quick nod. 'Wherever you need me.'

Sullivan smiled. He hadn't given Mikel enough credit. He suspected he was a former soldier too—he was obviously a team player. He hadn't panicked when the explosion had happened, and he was happy to take direction and go where he was needed. This man wasn't scared.

Ten minutes later, when he and Mikel descended into the mine, along with one of the engineers, he was glad of the company. Four men were trapped by falling rocks and equipment. No one had known if it was safe to move them to pull them out from where they were trapped and Sullivan and the engineer did a quick assessment of each casualty. Two were able to be slid out slowly once the debris above them had been removed or propped up.

Another was more complicated. He had a serious penetrating wound and burns. By that time, more emergency services had arrived and Sullivan must have used seven bags of saline to saturate wounds, as well as putting in lines to increase fluids and administer some pain relief.

Half an hour later the ambulance he was in pulled up outside St George's. Gabrielle was standing, waiting, in the ambulance bay wearing an apron and gloves. She pulled back as she saw him. 'Where have you been?'

He looked down. Every part of his clothes was covered in dust. He reached up and wiped his forehead, leaving his hand covered in a sooty black mess. He shrugged. 'Down the mine.'

She shook her head and moved into professional mode. 'What have you got?'

He jumped out and pulled the gurney. 'Rufus Bahn, miner. Serious penetrating chest injury.'

She pointed straight ahead. 'The resus room is waiting—once you've washed.'

He nodded and walked quickly. Gabrielle's hair was pulled up in a ponytail on the top of her head. She had on a dress and a pair of strange clogs. She caught him staring and shrugged. 'I didn't have time to change. One of the nurses loaned me her spare shoes.'

Two nurses were waiting in the resus room. Both looked frazzled. Gabrielle gave him a smile as she acknowledged what he'd seen. 'St George's has never dealt with a major accident before. We had to call in some staff from a few surrounding hospitals.'

'Any with trauma experience?'

She shook her head as she put a probe on Mr Bahn's finger, checked his airway and slipped an oxygen mask over his face. As Sullivan tried to wash the worst of the soot and dust off, she scanned Mr Bahn's body, found the cannula she was obviously looking for and drew up some drugs. 'What's he had?'

He pulled on a paper gown and some gloves. 'Just a litre of IV saline.'

'I'm going to give him some morphine for the pain and some steroids for the swelling around his chest area.'

He nodded in agreement. He wasn't quite sure of the last time Gabrielle had dealt with an emergency situation. Any medic working for Doctors Without Borders could experience just about any situation.

Gabrielle seemed calm and confident, that was good enough for him. She'd tell him if she was feeling out of her depth.

She looked at the penetrating chest wound as he motioned to the radiographer. The mobile X-ray machine was wheeled in and Gabrielle glanced over at him.

He pointed to the door. 'You go out, I'll monitor his airway. I don't want to leave him alone.' He slipped his hand into the proffered lead apron and one minute later the machine was wheeled back out.

He picked up the wires for the cardiac monitor. There was no way electrodes could be fixed to this patient's chest—parts of his skin were missing. He motioned to Gabrielle. 'Help me sit him forward and I'll put these on his back. I want to try and keep an eye on his heart rate as well as his blood pressure.

She shook her head. 'No, wait a second.' She jogged out of the room and he could see her heading to the stairs. He kept an eye on his patient as one of the nurses came in with a check list. He scanned the list. There were twenty-one patients, including their injuries and current status.

'Where did the Chinese worker with a leg fracture go?'

The nurse looked at him anxiously. 'They took the rest of the patients to Princess Elizabeth's—it's one of the other private hospitals. It has a few specialist eye surgeons and an orthopaedist. Princess Gabrielle arranged it.' The nurse glanced around at the quiet chaos in the surrounding department. 'She was worried we wouldn't have enough theatres or staff.'

Sullivan nodded carefully. She'd triaged the patients as they'd come in. He'd been doing it at one end—and she'd been doing it at the other. It seemed that in emergency situations Gabrielle Cartier kept a clear and rational head. He ran his eyes down the list again. 'Okay, we seem to have the majority of patients with burns and explosive injuries.'

The nurse bit her bottom lip. 'Princess Gabrielle said you would be able to handle those. She's arranged for two plastic surgeons to join you. I think they're familiarising themselves with the theatre arrangements.'

'Perfect.' She really had thought of everything.

The door to the stairs swung open and Gabrielle jogged back towards them, her ponytail swinging madly. She had a sealed surgical pack in her hands that she waved at him.

'They do a lot of cardiac surgery here. They have proper packs in Theatre. These leads can go on the patient's back instead of their chest.'

Of course. They were in a state-of-the-art hospital. They probably had equipment that he'd not even seen yet.

They placed the leads on the patient's back as the chest X-ray was slid onto the light box by the radiographer. She didn't wait for Sullivan's diagnosis. 'Large penetrating injury to the right lung. No wonder his sats are poor. He has a pneumothorax.'

The radiographer was right. Sullivan just wasn't used to people reading his X-rays for him. He glanced at the monitor. 'If we have a theatre available I'd rather deal with the pneumothorax in there. It makes sense to be next to the anaesthetist when our next step is to remove what's causing the lung collapse and then deal with the burns.'

Gabrielle's dark eyes met his own. 'That'll be a long surgery.'

He nodded. 'It will.'

She could see her biting the inside of her cheek. 'What is it?'

'We have other patients who will require surgery. I think we'll have enough staff to have two teams. Do you want to triage the patients?'

Ah. That was it. He got it. She'd felt confident enough to categorise the patients and send them to the most appropriate hospital. But she wasn't a surgeon. She didn't want to step outside her field of expertise. It was up to him to prioritise the surgical cases.

'Absolutely.' He looked down at their clothes. 'And I guess we should both find a pair of scrubs.'

This time she smiled. She was used to him joking when they were at work together. In fact, this was the most normal things had felt between them in the last thirty or so hours. He felt like a fish out of water in the palace. Here? Even though he didn't know this hospital, this healthcare system or the staff, he felt much more at home.

And even though this was an emergency situation, Gabrielle seemed more relaxed too. Being a doctor was second nature to her. She could adapt to any situation. It brought out the best in her. It was her home too.

Even though they'd barely been there a day, she'd seemed fraught with tension in the palace. As he looked at everyone hurrying to and fro in the emergency department he leaned over and put his hand on her shoulder.

'I have no idea just how much you've done here, or how many promises you had to make to get these two hospitals to take the patients from the mines, but, Gabrielle, without these facilities a lot of these miners could have died.' He took a long slow breath. 'I think your negotiation skills will have to continue. Lots of the people affected will have a long road to recovery. I have no idea how the healthcare system works here, but you could have a tough time ahead.'

'Not as tough as these patients.' Her voice was firm and determined. 'Let me worry about that.' She gave him a soft smile. 'I'm just glad you were here, Sullivan. Today needs a trauma surgeon and a burns specialist and that's you. I know these patients are in safe hands. That's the most important thing in the world.' She gave a nod of her head. 'Now, check over the patients for me, then go to surgery. I'll see you later.'

He bent lower and brushed a tiny kiss on her cheek. 'Proud of you,' he whispered, and as he raised his head he saw her eyes glisten with unshed tears.

It was the first time he'd kissed her since they'd got there. For the briefest second he could see a million things flashing in her eyes. Attraction. Sorrow. Worry. Then he saw her suck in a breath and move away quickly.

It only took ten minutes to review the other patients with one of the nurses. 'This man next, he has full-thickness burns to twenty per cent of his body. I'll take him once I've finished with Mr Bahn. This patient goes to the other team; he has semi-thickness burns that will require cleaning and a skin graft. This lady, Arona Jibel, put her on the other team's list too. She has multiple small penetrating wounds that all need to be debrided. Put a note she'll need X-rays in Theatre to make sure they've got everything. And this man with the hand injuries and burns to his thighs, I'll do him third. The two patients with facial injuries—cheeks and foreheads—put them on the list for the other team. I think Gabrielle said there are two plastic surgeons on that team. If I'm finished before them, I can take one of those patients.' The nurse nodded and scribbled notes furiously. Sullivan held out his hand towards her. 'And thank you. Everyone here today has been great. I know this isn't what you're used to.'

She gave him a smile and she shook his hand. 'Actually, it reminded me how much I liked to be challenged at work. I'd think I'd forgotten for a while. Now, get going, I'll organise everything else and make sure these patients are monitored.'

Sullivan glanced back out into the corridor and leaned back, stretching his back muscles. There was no sign of Gabrielle. But that was fine. For the next twelve hours he would probably be very busy.

The difference between the Gabrielle he saw here and the Gabrielle back in the palace had given him a lot to think about.

Fourteen hours later Sullivan finally left Theatre. Half of Gabrielle's personal palace staff had arrived at one point or another at the hospital. The director of St George's had been charm itself, and had invited them to use his own personal suite. But Gabrielle wanted to be near the patients that she considered under her care. She'd taken a quick car ride to Princess Elizabeth's and checked on the patients and staff there too.

A whole array of directors had arrived from the mining corporation. Gabrielle had directed her staff to deal with them. 'Find out contact information for all their workers—there's a huge variety of nationalities—and make sure the hospitals have the information they need. If we need translators, arrange that too.' She glanced at Franz Hindermann. 'There'll need to be an investigation into how this accident occurred. I have other priorities but I expect our government to act appropriately. Make sure the mining corporation know that they will be footing the bill for all expenses. *All expenses,*' she emphasised. 'They should have insurance to cover it—I'm not sure all their workers will. We'll talk about that later too.'

She'd finally managed to procure a pair of violet scrubs and a thick pair of socks. At least she felt comfortable here at work, but from the glances Franz shot her, he was far from happy.

'Shouldn't you change? The people of Mirinez will expect a statement from their Head of State. You can't do it looking like that.'

She glanced down and felt a little surge of anger.

'Why not? Their Head of State is a doctor. They should be proud of her.'

Sullivan's voice cut through everything.

She jumped to her feet and ran over to him. What she really wanted to do was wrap her arms around his neck but it was hardly the time or place. 'How are you? Is everything okay?'

He pulled his surgical hat from his ruffled hair. There

were huge dark circles under his eyes. He looked exhausted. 'First case took longer than any of us thought. Mr Bahn arrested in Theatre. He's in ICU now. I've just checked on him again before I came down here. I've also spoke to the other surgical team about their patients.' He gave a weary smile. 'I have to say, for a bunch of plastic surgeons they've done a damn good job.'

She tipped her head to the side. 'You didn't think they would?'

He shrugged. 'I hoped. Most of these guys have spent the last few years performing cosmetic surgery. Breasts, noses, lips and liposuction.'

She shook her head. 'Nope. We have plenty of those too, but I demanded the doctors I knew had worked on skin and facial reconstructions. I thought they would be best.'

He gave her an appreciative smile. 'Then you were right. The two patients who needed facial surgery couldn't have got any better in the US. I'm impressed.'

'And I'm relieved,' she sighed. 'I'm just glad everything came together.' She held up her hands. 'Shouldn't we have a national disaster plan, where everything just falls into place?'

Sullivan threw back his head and laughed. He'd worked in enough countries and with enough organisations to know just how difficult those things were. 'Good luck with that. You're right, you should. In case of emergency, there should be an agreement between all healthcare providers in Mirinez that they'll play their part.' He shrugged. 'I don't expect them to do it for free, but when was the last time you had an emergency like this in Mirinez?'

Gabrielle glanced at Franz then Arun, who was standing by the door, and back to Franz again. 'I don't actually remember if we've ever had an emergency before.'

Franz frowned. 'There was some trouble at the harbour once. An accident when a boat capsized. There were around ten casualties.'

'And who looked after them?'

Franz looked a little embarrassed. 'Your father asked the French Prime Minister for help.'

Gabrielle couldn't help but let out an exasperated sigh. 'We need to do something about this.' Then a horrible realisation swept over her. '*I* need to do something about this.'

Sullivan's arm slid around her waist. While the warmth and familiarity was instantly welcomed, a thousand other thoughts of country and duty pushed into her head. 'What you need to do—in fact, what *we* need to do—is get some sleep. I'm happy the patients are settled for now and we can check on them later.'

She didn't step away. Couldn't. She'd forgotten just how tired he looked. He'd been down a mine then on his feet in Theatre for the last fourteen hours. She was proving to be a terrible host.

'Of course, you're right. Let's go.'

Franz held up his hand. 'But what about the statement? The people will be expecting one.'

Sullivan's arm put a little pressure on her from behind, urging her down the corridor. 'Just write a press release,' he said over his shoulder.

Arun walked in front of them, holding open the door of one of the palace limousines. 'Arun waited too?' Sullivan asked.

She smiled. 'And Mikel. He went to Princess Elizabeth's to see if he could help—answering phones, wheeling patients about. He said he wanted to.'

Sullivan gave a strange kind of smile. 'It's amazing how a disaster can bring out qualities you hadn't noticed before.'

He leaned back in the seat, letting himself sink into the soft leather. His arm moved from her waist to curl around her shoulders. She followed his lead and leant her head against his chest, closing her eyes for a few seconds.

Next minute Arun was opening the door and the cool air swept around them. She rubbed her eyes and stepped out of the car, waiting for Sullivan.

The palace corridors were quiet. Half of the staff would no doubt be glued to the news channels and the other half would be answering phones and queries from all over the globe.

Her feet started to slow as she started to wonder if she should offer to go and help.

'No,' said Sullivan firmly.

She stared up at him from tired eyes. 'What do you mean, no?'

He kept her walking. 'You're not going to do anything else. You're going to rest. Take a few hours down time. Everything immediate has been dealt with.'

She knew he was right, but something inside her stomach coiled. 'But—'

He cut her off. 'But your staff haven't had a functioning Head of State in over a year. Do you think Andreas would have organised any emergency services? Would he have found other surgeons? Treated patients? Negotiated with the directors of the hospitals?'

Fatigue rested heavily on her shoulders. 'No. But he isn't a doctor. He wouldn't have been able to think that way.'

Sullivan stopped outside her doorway. 'But would he

have done *anything*?' The coil inside her stomach gave a little somersault.

She pushed open her door and looked inside. In her eyes, this room still belonged to her brother. It didn't feel like the most restful place to be—she'd spent most of last night tossing and turning.

She turned back to face Sullivan. His pale green eyes stood out against the dark night visible through her windows. 'Probably not,' she whispered.

She hesitated at the door again.

'What's wrong?' he asked.

She shook her head. 'I just don't want to sleep in there.'

He gave a half-smile. 'In that case, come with me.'

He slid his hand into hers. 'I can't promise you'll be safe.'

Her heart ached. He had no idea how her thoughts tumbled around her mind right now. One hint of impropriety, one mis-seen kiss and the weight of a nation that was currently around her neck would end up around Sullivan's too. She still hadn't heard from Andreas. She still didn't know why he'd left. Could it have been the pressure to start a family? They'd never discussed his family plans. But as soon as he'd married, there had been constant press speculation about a pregnancy—an heir to the throne.

In the blink of an eye the same could happen to her. Every sighting of her with a man would result in hints of an engagement then a wedding. Then the pressure to have a baby, to continue the line of succession for Mirinez.

How could she contemplate putting all of that on Sullivan? There were already tiny shadows behind his eyes. He hadn't told her everything. She knew that. But she respected his right to privacy. The press wouldn't.

She looked down the empty corridor. She felt entirely

selfish. And so physically tired. But still it was as though every cell in her body just ached for him. She pushed everything else aside. Gave him a smile. 'I think I will be. I could probably sleep standing up right now.' He raised his eyebrows and she added, 'I'd just rather do it next to you.'

He opened the door to his apartments. The bed was right in the middle of the room, the dark windows looking out over the city below. He pulled his scrub top over his head and kicked off his shoes before he was even halfway across the room. She sat down on the edge of the bed and wriggled out of her scrub trousers and pulled off her borrowed shoes and socks, hesitating at the bottom of her top.

A soft T-shirt landed sideways on her shoulder. 'Here, have this,' he said as he climbed into bed, wearing only his black jockey shorts. This wasn't exactly how she'd expected to spend her first night in Sullivan's bed, but for now it just felt right.

'Thanks,' she said, swiftly swapping the scrub top for the T-shirt and crawling into bed next to him.

He held out his arm and she put her head on his chest, her arm resting across his body.

For the first time since she'd returned home she felt relieved.

This was exactly how things were supposed to be.

CHAPTER EIGHT

IT WAS THE ideal way to wake up. A warm body next to his, their limbs intertwined, and soft lemon-scented hair under his nose.

Once his eyes had flickered open he really didn't want to move.

He glanced at the clock. It was only six a.m. So far he'd seen one a.m., two a.m. and five a.m. Thankfully he'd missed three a.m. and four a.m. Last night had been a good night and Gabrielle's steady breathing had definitely played a part in that. It was likely that Gabrielle's day was due to start any minute. He would dearly love to wake her up with the promise that had been hovering between them since they'd first met.

His *body* wanted him to wake her that way.

He gave a little groan as she shifted next to him and laid her palm on his bare chest. He wasn't quite sure how Gabrielle wanted to play this.

The palace staff would be looking for her any minute. Would Princess Gabrielle want to be found in his apartments, wearing only a T-shirt and her underwear? He didn't think so.

He gave her a gentle shake. 'Gabrielle, wake up. We have patients to check on and you have a country to run.'

She made a comfortable little noise as she snuggled

closer, her fingers brushing the hairs on his chest. 'It can't be time yet. It just can't.'

He smiled. The temptation to stay here was too strong. Things were changing. A few days ago he'd thought he was going to have a harmless fling with a colleague. He hadn't contemplated anything else.

But circumstances had changed. For both of them.

The attraction between them was still strong. He would happily act on it in the blink of an eye. But Gabrielle wasn't just thinking about herself now. Everything she did would be examined and watched. He didn't want to make the front-page news in Mirinez. He didn't want her criticised or judged because of a casual relationship.

It was clear Gabrielle was already going to have to bear the brunt for the work her brother had ignored. He'd abdicated just as things were about to come to a head—that much was clear.

Her soft hair tickled under his nose and she moved her leg, brushing his thigh.

He groaned out loud.

She sat up in bed. 'What time is it? Oh, no. They'll be looking for me.'

He smiled. Her hair was mussed up and one cheek showed a crease from the pillow. 'That's what I thought. That's why I woke you.'

She swung her legs around the edge of the bed then paused, her dark eyes fixing on his. 'You were pretty amazing yesterday. Did I even thank you?'

'You don't need to thank me. I'm a doctor, it's what I do. But I thought you were pretty amazing too. We make a good team.'

Her smile reached her eyes as she nodded. 'You're right, we do.' She sighed and ran her fingers through her hair, trying to tame it. 'I'll need to check up on what's happened with the directors of the mine. I'll probably need to give an update to Parliament.' She stood up and walked across the room. His pale T-shirt outlined her figure in the early morning light. 'And then I'll meet you back at the hospital and help review the patients.'

He pushed himself up in the bed. 'You won't need to do that. I'm sure there are enough doctors at the two hospitals who can help me review the patients.'

'You don't know what the private hospitals can be like. Some doctors only like to see their own fee-paying patients.'

'Well, I didn't meet any of them last night. Maybe the fact that Princess Gabrielle was front and centre in the whole affair helped them find their civic sense?'

She shook her head. 'I'm fairly sure that the cold light of day and the arrival of the hospital accountants will mean that today will mainly be about finances.'

He slid out of bed and started to search through his backpack for some suitable clothes. 'Then I'm sure you can find a way to deal with it. This was an emergency situation. It might be the first, but you have to plan ahead. Give the task to Parliament to deal with.'

She looked thoughtful then walked back over to him, putting one hand on top of his arm and reaching the other up to touch his cheek. 'I'm sorry,' she whispered. 'This wasn't exactly how I imagined us spending the night together.'

He shook his head. 'Me neither.'

She licked her lips. It was almost as if she was trying to stop the words that came to her lips. 'Then let me make it up to you. How about dinner tonight? We haven't had a chance to spend much time together.'

'I like the sound of that.'

She stood on tiptoe and planted a soft kiss on his

lips. 'Then let's make it a date.' She grinned as she spun around and headed to the door. 'And dress appropriately, Dr Darcy!'

It was odd. She'd worked with the guy at close quarters for two weeks. She was still sorry that their night at the bar had been curtailed and waking up in his arms this morning had felt much more comfortable than it should have.

The day had gone quickly. There had been legal requirements, more agreements to sign, a meeting with Parliament, then she'd shared the rest of the day between the two hospitals. By the time she'd got to the first, Sullivan had reviewed all his patients and gone to the second hospital to help with communication with the Chinese patient.

He'd been right. The hospital doctors had cancelled their theatre lists and reviewed all the accident victims. It was only the finance departments that had a whole host of queries, but she'd expected those.

She was only just beginning to get a handle on exactly how much work her brother had left behind. He still hadn't answered any calls or emails. He must have heard about the explosion in the mine but he still hadn't called home. It was probably just as well, because right now most of what she'd say to him couldn't be repeated.

She adjusted the straps on her black dress and gave a wriggle. She hadn't quite got used to wearing formal clothes again. Yesterday the scrubs had been a relief. And when she'd opened her wardrobe tonight to find something to wear to dinner, she'd felt strangely nervous.

The thoughts of the press finding out about Sullivan being in the palace with her still made her nervous.

Any man who decided to be with Princess Gabrielle

would need to know what he was getting into. Every inch of his life would be exposed to the press. Sullivan could be sparky. Sullivan could be fun. His doctor side was compassionate and expertly efficient. But there was part of him that was private.

She needed to tread carefully. When she'd woken this morning, for a few seconds she'd felt nothing but bliss. But as soon as she'd opened the door and walked down the corridor to her apartments her royal life had been back, front and foremost.

Something was blossoming between them, that much was clear. That had been the impetus for tonight's invitation. She'd spoken on instinct, wanting to reach out and find out what came next.

Later her stomach had churned. Her emotions had cooled and rational thoughts had filled her brain. A tiny little seed was taking root. She liked him. She liked him a *lot*. Make the wrong move and Sullivan could be scared off by the press.

He'd served two tours of duty. He probably wasn't the kind of guy to be scared off by a few photographers or articles. He didn't strike her as that kind of guy at all. But she just didn't know. And she was scared.

Scared enough to have spoken at length to Arun today. Everything about tonight was to be entirely private. Sullivan had insisted on organising everything, but she had made sure there would be no whisper about what they were doing.

Her black dress with sequins around the V-shaped neckline was a favourite. Anji, one of the palace ladies-in-waiting, gave her an approving smile. 'Your Majesty should wear your mother's necklace with that.'

Gabrielle gave a little start. She'd completely forgotten

about the family jewels. In a way, she was surprised that Andreas's wife hadn't taken them all with her.

'Where are they?'

Anji smiled. 'In the main safe. The diamond drop necklace would look perfect with that dress.'

Gabrielle stared at her reflection for a second. Anji was right. It would look perfect. But opening the safe and wearing the family jewels would be another step towards being the ruler, remaining the Princess. Her stomach flipped over. She still hadn't got used to the idea. This all just seemed so unreal. Almost as if she were living someone else's life.

Her mouth was dry. 'Okay, would you tell Arun I'd like to access the safe?'

It was ridiculous that she should be nervous. She'd already seen the administrative work that needed to be done for Mirinez. She hadn't even questioned that there were treaties to sign, deals to negotiate. But this was different. This was personal.

A few moments later Arun appeared behind her and led her down the corridor to the family safe. He gave her a nod. As Head of Security he knew every item in the safe. She sucked in a breath as it was swung open.

'I half expected the family jewels to be gone,' she joked.

Arun glanced over her shoulder. 'Some of them were. I had to make sure they were returned.'

Her eyes widened. 'You mean…'

He slid out a tray from the safe. 'Let's not talk about it now. The diamond drop necklace? This is the one that you wanted, is it not?'

The necklace was in a black velvet box. He flipped it open to reveal the ten-carat sparkling jewel set in yellow gold. Her hands shook as she lifted it from the case. 'Yes, this is it. Thank you.'

Her breath caught in her throat. At the back of the safe, in two glass cases, sat two crowns. One for a Prince, with a heavy gold underlay and adorned with rubies, diamonds and emeralds, and one for a Princess, a more elegant version, mainly with diamonds.

Arun caught her glance. 'Mr Hindermann is already discussing potential dates for the neighbouring Heads of State to attend the official ceremony.'

A little chill ran down her spine. She couldn't hold off any longer. Her brother's abdication had been announced as soon as they'd been able to contact her. The citizens of Mirinez would expect the official ceremony soon—any delay would raise questions.

She gave a little nod of her head. 'That will be all, Arun. Thank you for this and thank you for tonight. I trust the arrangements are in place?'

Arun gave a quick nod.

She gave a nervous smile. 'Good. I'll let you know when I want to return the necklace to the safe.'

'As you wish.' He sealed the safe and disappeared discreetly. He would appear again soon. He said that Sullivan had discussed tonight's arrangements with him.

Sullivan was standing outside her royal apartment, wearing a pair of black dress trousers and a white shirt. 'I wondered where you were,' he said as she walked down the corridor towards him. His gaze swept up and down her appreciatively, settling finally on the jewel at her throat. 'Wow, you could take someone's eye out with that.'

She burst out laughing. 'Who taught you your manners?'

He laughed too. 'Just calling it like I see it.' Then

he shook his head. 'My father would be horrified if he heard that.'

Something passed across his face. It was a fleeting expression but one that she'd seen for a few seconds a couple of times before.

She reached up and touched his arm. 'How long is it since you lost your father?'

It was almost as if she could see the shutters falling behind his eyes. 'Three years.' He waved his hand. 'It's been a while. Now, about dinner.'

She bit her tongue. It was clear he didn't want to discuss this. It made her curious. What did he have to hide? For the most part Sullivan seemed like a straight-down-the-line kind of guy. But, in truth, he hadn't revealed that much about himself. Their first two weeks together had been in part intense work and intense flirtation. The last couple of days had been chaotic. She hadn't even had a chance to ask him what he thought of Mirinez, let alone fathom out where they were with each other.

She gave a conciliatory nod. 'Okay, then what about dinner? It could be I'm all dressed up with nowhere to go.'

One of his eyebrows quirked upwards. It made her laugh. 'I have plans,' he said as he swept an arm around her waist and started along the corridor.

'Where are we going?' She was curious. It had been a few years since she'd visited any of the restaurants in Mirinez. She didn't even know which ones still existed.

He took her down the main staircase. Arun was waiting at the front door with the car engine running. As they slid into the back Sullivan gave her a smile. 'We've had to make special arrangements.'

'What arrangements?' She touched the necklace at her throat nervously. 'Is this about the necklace?'

Sullivan laughed. 'No, this is about the *person* wearing the necklace. You're Head of State now, Princess Gabrielle. It means you get to book out a whole restaurant for yourself—or, at least, I do.'

She sat upright as the car moved along the palace driveway. 'Really? I hadn't thought of that.' She frowned. 'I can't remember that happening with my parents.'

Sullivan gave her a careful look. 'I think Arun might have re-evaluated some safety aspects of your current role.'

'But I spent most of yesterday in the hospital, seeing patients. I have to be able to move around.' She gave a simple answer, but her stomach gave a few flips. Arun had taken her request for complete privacy seriously.

Sullivan nodded. 'I get that. But didn't you notice how many black-suited men were in your vicinity yesterday?'

She sagged back against the comfortable leather seats. 'Well, no. I didn't even think about it.' And she hadn't. She been so busy thinking about other things.

Sullivan held up his hands. 'That's because you don't have to. Arun does.'

It was almost like a heavy weight settling on her shoulders. If she thought about it hard enough, she could remember the security staff always being around—she'd just assumed they were there to help, it had been an all-hands-on-deck kind of day—she just hadn't realised they had actually been there to guard *her*.

'The world has changed since you were a child, Gabrielle. Arun has to take so many other factors into consideration now. Nothing is secret. One tweet and the world knows where you are.'

She gulped. Sullivan had been in the military. He was probably a lot more familiar with all the security stuff than she was.

But what about the privacy stuff? The press?

She looked out of the window at the darkening sky. It was almost as if Sullivan could sense the turmoil of thoughts racing through her brain and he slid his hand over hers and intertwined their fingers.

She closed her eyes for a second and took a deep breath. She couldn't remember ever feeling like this before, experiencing a real connection with someone that she wanted to take further. She'd had teenage crushes and her heart had been broken a few times along the way, but for the last few years she'd been focused on her work. The couple of passing flings she'd had didn't count. This was the first relationship that actually felt real. Actually felt as if it could go somewhere. But at a time like this was it even worth thinking about?

The car pulled up outside a glass-fronted restaurant that Gabrielle didn't recognise. The street was in one of the most exclusive parts of Chabonnex. Sullivan got out of the car and greeted the maître d' in Italian before holding his hand out towards her.

She'd hardly had a chance to even stop and think but right now everything was paling in comparison to the handsome guy before her. Did he realise how well he filled out those clothes? The white shirt was a blessing, defining all the muscles on his arms and chest.

Then she paused for a second—had Sullivan lost weight? He looked a little leaner than before. But the thought disappeared as the streetlamp next to them highlighted his tanned skin and the twinkle in his pale green eyes. The one thing that made her heart stop in her chest was his smile.

He was looking at her as if she was the only woman in the world and that smile was entirely for her.

Her heart gave a little flutter and she slid from the car,

putting her hand into his. The restaurant was empty and the maître d' led them upstairs to a starlit terrace. Arun and his security team positioned themselves as unobtrusively as possible.

Sullivan pulled out her chair and seated her then settled opposite her. 'So, tonight, Princess, we're having Italian.' He held up the wine list. 'What would you prefer?'

She waved her hand. The night air was mild and there was a heater burning next to them to ward off any unexpected chill. There was something nice about eating outside after the last few days of constantly being surrounded by walls. The soft music from the restaurant drifted out around them. 'Since my last glass of wine came from the bar in Paris…' she leaned forward and whispered '…where—don't tell anyone—the wine was on tap. I'll be happy with whatever you choose.'

He gave a nod and ordered from the maître d'. A few minutes later their glasses were filled, their food order was taken and she sat back and relaxed.

Although the restaurant was empty, there were still people in the street below them. It was nice, watching the world go by.

'Happy?' Sullivan asked as he held up his glass towards her.

She clinked her glass against his. 'You realise there'll be a scandal if I'm caught doing this. I'm quite sure it will be considered unladylike and won't be becoming for the Head of State.'

He shrugged. 'It could be worse—it could be a bottle of beer. Anyway, I thought you would live by your own rules, not the ones you inherit.'

She opened her mouth to reply automatically, then stopped. Coming back here, suddenly everything felt so ingrained into her. Her childhood memories of her mother and father. Discussions about conduct and acceptable behaviour. Of course, she'd never felt the same pressure that her brother, Andreas, had been under—it had always been expected that he would fulfil his role. And she was quite sure that her lifestyle had never been as strict as some of her royal counterparts in other European countries.

But these rules were still deep inside her. Almost as if they ran through her veins. She sat her glass down carefully. 'Being Head of State is a big responsibility.'

'I didn't say it wasn't. You seem to be doing an admirable job already.' Sullivan was so matter-of-fact, as if it was all entirely obvious. 'But who is here to tell you how to live your life? Your brother certainly isn't. You're a good person, Gabrielle, and you'll do your best to sort out the mess he's left behind, but you don't need to lose yourself in the process.'

She sucked in a breath to speak but changed her mind, picked her glass up again and took a hefty swallow.

She'd spent the last few years completely under the radar—not being a princess at all. If any one of her colleagues had started a conversation with her about not conforming to the rules of being a doctor, she would have happily had that discussion. She would have enjoyed the debate.

But this was so much more personal.

The waiter appeared and placed their entrées in front of them. Sullivan smiled and took the wine from the cooler and topped up her glass. She ran her fingers up and down the stem of the wine glass, contemplating his words. But Sullivan wasn't finished. He continued, 'I thought you royal children had something inbuilt into you all—a kind of thing that always said, *This could be me.* Life changes constantly, Gabrielle. You're a doctor. You know that better than most. Accidents happen. People get sick. Surely you must have known this could always have been a possibility?'

She shook her head. 'But I didn't want this. I didn't ask to be born into this life. I've spent the last few years running away from it—keeping my head down and doing the kind of work that I wanted to do.'

'And you can't do that now?'

She stared at her entrée. The jungle seemed a million miles away. Right now it felt as if she would never get back there, never get to lead a team on another TB mission, never to get dance in her tent late at night.

'I'm not sure I can,' she whispered.

Sullivan reached over and squeezed her hand as a shiver went down her spine. Saying the words out loud was scary. They'd been dancing around in her head from the second Arun and the rest of the security team had approached her in Paris.

She met Sullivan's gaze. 'I feel as if my life has been stolen from me.' She closed her eyes for a second. 'And I feel terrible about the thoughts I'm having about my brother.'

'Is he still incommunicado?'

She nodded her head. 'Why can't he even have the courtesy to have a conversation with me? I know things happen. But it wasn't as if anything in particular did happen here. Andreas left. He chose to leave. He could have waited until I was back. He could have told me he didn't want to rule. We could have come to some…arrangement.'

Sullivan took a sip of his wine. 'And what kind of arrangement could that be? Oh, just let me work for the next ten years, Andreas, and then I'll come back and take over from you?'

Indignation swept through her. 'What's so wrong about that? At least then there would have been plans, a chance to think ahead—anything but leave the principality in the state it is now.'

Sullivan picked up his fork. 'Could there be anything else going on?'

'You mean besides his wife?'

Sullivan frowned. 'You said he'd emailed you while we were in the jungle. It's obvious he hasn't looked after things well these last few years.'

'What are you implying?'

He looked her straight in the eye. 'Could Andreas be depressed, for example?'

She was stunned. It hadn't even crossed her mind. Not for a second. She had just been so angry with him for disappearing and not answering any calls, texts or emails.

She picked up her fork and started toying with her food. 'I have no idea. We haven't been close these last few years. His wife...his wife has been his biggest influence.'

Sullivan must have picked up on her tone. The edges of his lips turned upwards. 'You don't like her much, do you?'

'I don't have much in common with a TV actress whose idea of a humanitarian act is to donate her lipstick to the nearest charity.'

Sullivan almost choked on his food. 'Okay, then, I'll give you that one.'

Gabrielle finally managed to put some of the delicious smoked salmon into her mouth. After a few months in the jungle, some burgers at the bar in Paris and quick hospital sandwich last night and today, it had been a long time since she'd tasted something so good.

She leaned back in her chair and gave a little groan. 'Can we come back here every night?'

Sullivan nodded. His plate was half-empty. He was obviously already enjoying his food. 'Fine with me. I think Arun might have something to say about it, though.' He leaned forward and whispered, 'I think we caused him a bit of a headache tonight.'

She smiled and looked around, taking the time to pick out some of the familiar sights of the capital city. The cathedral, the old monastery, the brick distillery. All of these had been part of her daily commute to private school.

She could feel the tension start to leave her shoulders. Thinking about Mirinez generally tied her up in knots. She'd been so on edge since she'd got back she hadn't taken the time to think about the things she liked about being here.

The food. The people. The weather.

Too much of her time had been spent on all the things that made her insides twist and turn. She sipped at her wine as she tried to relax a little. The uptight person she'd been these last few days wasn't normal for Gabrielle at all, even when she was working as a doctor in a time of crisis.

The waiter came and magically swapped their plates and the smell of her langoustine ravioli made her stomach growl. Sullivan smiled and picked up his fork. 'Feeling better yet?'

She took her first mouthful. 'Yes. I'd forgotten how good food like this tastes.' She gave her stomach a pat. 'If we eat here every night I'll need a major workout plan.'

'You mean besides running a country?'

She nodded as his phone beeped. He pulled it from his pocket, looked at it and stuffed it back. Her heart gave a few thuds against her chest. 'The hospital? Is there a problem?'

He looked amused. 'No. Not at all. It was Gibbs.'

'Gibbs?' The name of their co-ordinator at Doctors Without Borders jolted her back to reality. Sullivan had agreed to come with her Mirinez—to offer her support—but she had forgotten there would always be a time limit.

'We've just got here. He can't be trying to send you on another mission already?'

Sullivan shrugged and didn't answer.

'He is?' She was indignant on his behalf. She knew he'd come straight from one mission to join hers. They'd only just arrived in Paris before they'd come here and then been thrown straight into the mine accident.

'You need a break. You need some down time.' Then she shook her head at the irony. 'And you haven't exactly managed to get any here.'

'It doesn't really matter. I like working.'

'But there are rules about these things. We're supposed to have a certain amount of time between our missions. You've already stepped into an emergency once, there can't be another already.'

He raised one eyebrow. 'Can't there?'

She put down her fork. It didn't matter how delicious the food in front of her, for some reason she'd just lost her appetite. 'What does he want you to do?'

Sullivan finished another mouthful of food. 'I don't know. I haven't phoned him back. And I won't—not yet, anyway. I want to review the patients I've operated on. I might take the miner with the injured hand back to Theatre. I'm worried about contractures. I'll need to stay for at least...' he paused for a second '...a week or so.'

She gulped. 'That's not enough of a break. Plus, you're actually working.'

'Not all the time.' There was a twinkle in his eye now. A little pulse of adrenaline surged through her body.

She picked up her fork and played with her food. That

glint was taking her places she couldn't go anywhere in public. She'd never met anyone who could do that to her with just one look, just one smile.

'Do you ever have a holiday, Sullivan?' she sighed. 'I get the impression maybe not.'

He took a sip of his wine. 'The last holiday I had was around four years ago. My father decided we should do some touring. We spent three weeks on the road. Started in San Francisco, then went down to Los Angeles, across to Las Vegas then on into Utah and some of the national parks.' He gave a sad kind of smile. 'We hired a camper, and after the first week of sleeping in the camper my father could hardly walk. He said it was hotels all the way after that.' He gave a sudden laugh.

'What is it?'

'That was until we hit Utah and the national parks. Oh, no, then he didn't want to stay in a hotel. Then he wanted to camp and stare up at the starry sky at night.'

'And did you?'

Sullivan waved his hand. 'Yeah. We bought the whole kit and caboodle. I've never felt ground so hard in my life and I've never seen rain like it. And by the next day? *Neither* of us could walk.'

Gabrielle started laughing. It was clear from the way that he talked he'd had a good relationship with his father. She wished she could have seen them together. But as just as quickly as the joy had appeared in Sullivan's eyes they shadowed over again.

She'd seen that look before, when he'd mentioned casually that he hadn't had a chance to pack up his father's things back home in Oregon. It hadn't seemed significant at the time, but now she was getting to know him a little better it felt a little off. Working with Sullivan had shown her he was incredibly organised.

But even now he didn't seem entirely anxious to go home. There had been no pre-booked flight to Oregon to cancel when she'd asked him to accompany her. And she got the feeling if he hadn't been with her now, he might have answered Gibbs's text about the next mission. How could she phrase the question that was burning inside her?

She never got the chance because Sullivan nodded towards the old-fashioned picture house opposite the restaurant. It had a small poster on either side of the main doors advertising the latest action movie.

'What's with the place across the street?'

She smiled. 'The Regal? It's a picture-house based in one of the oldest buildings in Mirinez. There have been lots of attempts to modernise it—all of them resisted.' She couldn't help but let out a laugh. She'd witnessed some of the fierce arguments about 'dragging things into the twenty-first century', but she had fond memories of the picture house. Even looking at it now spread a little warm glow through her body.

'And they've all failed?' Sullivan looked interested.

'More or less. The electrics and plumbing have been modernised. The screen has been changed, but it's still like walking into an old theatre rather than one of those cinema complexes. The chairs are original—a tiny bit uncomfortable and covered in dark red velvet.'

'Just one screen?'

'Just the one. And each film only plays for a week so if you miss it, you miss it.'

'It's kinda quaint.'

She laughed again. 'There's a word I never thought I hear on Sullivan Darcy's lips.'

'Quaint? My dad used it, quite a lot actually. He must have picked it up when we stayed in England for a while.'

He tapped his fingers on the table. 'I guess if we want to see the latest action movie we'd better go in the next few days, then.'

Gabrielle started to nod and then rolled her eyes. 'We might have a problem.'

'Why?'

She held out her hands. 'Look at this place. You said Arun had to book the whole place out so we could come to dinner. If he tried to book the cinema out for just us, the rest of Mirinez would probably riot.'

'How about a private showing—could we arrange that?'

She sighed. 'Probably. But then we'd need to go in the middle of the night or first thing in the morning. It kind of takes the joy out of going to the cinema. You know, filing into your seat with your giant bag of popcorn and waiting for the lights to go down and hear the theme tune before the adverts start. There'd be no atmosphere.'

Sullivan thought for a few seconds. 'What if we go incognito?'

'What?' She hadn't even thought of that.

'You never did anything like that as a kid?'

'Well, sure I did. But we only had one security guy and he was really for Andreas, not for me. I used to sneak out to places all the time.'

'So…sneak out someplace with me?' All of a sudden she felt around fifteen again. It was the oddest thrill. Sneaking out somewhere with the bad boy. But, then, Sullivan wasn't really a bad boy, was he? It was just the way he said those words, almost as if it were a challenge.

And she loved a challenge.

She glanced over at the cinema. She'd love to go back there. She would. But as she watched the people milling around outside, a horrible black cloud of responsibility settled on her shoulders.

It was automatic. The enormous list of things that still needed to be dealt with started running through her head. 'I'd love to, but I still need to meet the owners of the mine, I need to check a trade agreement with another country, there's dispute over a part of our boundary—our fishermen haven't apparently been following EU fishing regulations—there are issues around some of our exports. We have applications from six major new businesses that want to invest in Mirinez—'

'Whoa!' Sullivan held up his hand and stood up.

The background music had changed to something a little more familiar.

'What?' She looked around.

He turned the palm of his hand, extending it out towards her. 'Give me Gabrielle back, please.'

She frowned with confusion. 'What do you mean?'

He was giving her a knowing kind of smile. 'I had her. I had her right there with me, then you just flipped back into princess mode.'

A little chill spread over her skin. He was right. She had. One second she'd been enjoying dinner with Sullivan, contemplating some fun, and the next? She'd been sucked back into the wave of responsibility that felt as if it could suffocate her.

Tears prickled in her eyes. But Sullivan kept his voice light, almost teasing. 'When Gabrielle hears this tune, there's only one thing she can do.'

The beat of Justin Timberlake filled the air around her. From the expression on Sullivan's face it was clear he was remembering their first meeting—when he'd caught her dancing around the tent in Narumba.

'How can any girl resist JT?' he asked again.

'How can any girl resist Sullivan Darcy?' she countered as she slid her hand into his.

The security staff seemed to have miraculously disappeared into the walls. After a few seconds it was easy to feel the beat and start to relax a little. Sullivan pulled her a little closer.

'I thought you didn't dance?' She smirked as the heat of his body pressed up against hers. Apart from the night she'd lain in his arms, this was the first time since Paris she'd really been in a place she wanted to be.

'I thought you needed to let your hair down a little,' he said huskily. 'Remember what it is to have some fun.'

She swung her head. 'But my hair is down,' she argued, as her curls bounced around her shoulders.

'Is it?' he asked as he swung her round and dipped her. She squealed, laughing, her arms slipping up and fastening around his neck. He held her there for a second, his mouth just inches from hers. She glanced up at his dark hair, running a finger along the edges. 'This is the longest I've seen your hair. Is that a little kink? Does your normal buzz cut hide curls?' She was teasing. She couldn't help it.

This was the kind of life she wanted to live. She wanted to be free to work hard during the day and laugh, joke and flirt her way with a man who made her heart sing through the nights.

He swung her back up, so close her breasts pressed against his chest. 'Now, that, my lovely lady, would be telling. Isn't a guy supposed to have some secrets?'

She wrinkled her nose as a little wave of guilt swept through her. 'I thought we were kind of finished with secrets.'

He waved his hands as he kept them swaying to the beat of the song. 'Princess Schmincess.'

She blinked. 'Did you really just say that?'

'Say what?' This time he was teasing her. And she liked it. She ran her hands down the front of his chest.

'I think you've been holding out on me.'

He spun her around again. 'Really?'

'Really. You never demonstrated these dance moves in Narumba.'

She was trying not to concentrate too closely on those clear green eyes of his. The twinkle that they held practically danced across her skin. And that sexy smile of his was making her want to take actions entirely unsuitable for a public terrace.

He slowed his movements a little and traced his finger gently down her cheek. 'Maybe I was saving them for a private show.'

She groaned out loud. 'Stop it. I've got security guards around. If you keep talking to me like this we're going to have to skip dessert.'

He leaned down and whispered in her ear. 'I've always thought dessert was overrated.'

His lips met hers. For a few seconds her brain completely cleared. Tonight had been almost perfect. It was like some make-believe date. Dinner, wine, dancing and...

His hands tangled through her hair as he teased her with his lips and tongue. She didn't want to break the connection—she didn't even want to breathe. Any second now she might start seeing stars.

Sullivan Darcy knew how to kiss. He knew how to hold a woman and cradle her body next to his. He kissed her lips, down her neck and along to her collarbone. Then just as her mouth was hungry for more he met her again, head on. His smell was wrapping around her, clean, with a hint of musk, or maybe it was just the pheromones—

because right now she was pretty sure the air was laced with them.

His hand moved from her hair to her waist, sliding upwards, his palm covering her breast. Every part of her body reacted. Every one of her senses was on fire. And there was an instant reciprocal effect from his body.

A sudden gust of wind swept past them.

She jumped back, breathless and trying to regain control. There saw a dark shape shuffle back somewhere inside the restaurant. She felt her face flush. The restaurant staff and security staff would just have witnessed their moment of passion.

She glanced back to their table, the unfinished wine and plates still waiting to be collected. People were chatting on the street below.

For a few seconds she'd been in her own little bubble with Sullivan Darcy. She didn't need a reality check. Didn't *want* a reality check.

So she did the only thing that seemed entirely rational. She grabbed his hand. 'Let's go.'

CHAPTER NINE

THEY'D STUMBLED BACK to his apartments instead of hers. It seemed that Gabrielle wasn't comfortable in the royal apartments.

The morning sunrise was beautiful. From here Sullivan had part view of the mountain covered in patches of green and part view of the city beneath them, all swathed in oranges, pinks and purples.

It had been a long time since he'd had the time to watch the sunrise. And he'd never done it next to a woman like Gabrielle.

For the first time in a long time the night hadn't drawn out, like a continuing loop. He'd actually slept a little. Yes, his brain had still spun endlessly round and round, but there had been periods of calm. Periods of quiet. It seemed Gabrielle was a good influence on him.

She was sleeping peacefully now, the white sheets tangled around her body. Her brown hair was fanned across the pillow and for once her forehead was smooth and not furrowed with worry. From the second they'd reached Mirinez her beautiful face had been marred by a frown that he'd only seen once the whole time they'd worked together.

This was the way she should look. This was the Gabrielle he'd first met a few weeks ago. The woman he'd spent last night with.

His stomach curled a little. Part of him wished the Princess part and Mirinez had never happened. He'd liked it better when she'd just been Gabrielle Cartier, medic from Doctors Without Borders. A girl with great legs, even better shorts, a killer dance rhythm and sexy as hell.

Here in Mirinez Gabrielle seemed coated in layers. Last night had been about trying to peel them all back and let her have a little fun.

And, boy, had they had fun.

He'd spent the last three years only having short-term flings. When he'd first met Gabrielle, his brain had pushed her firmly into that category. But from first sight his body had reacted in a way it hadn't before. At just a glance, a smile, the spark from a touch, it knew. Gabrielle could never be a fling.

Last night had confirmed that in a way he could never have predicted. He could stay in this position, watching her sleep, for ever.

But the dark clouds were still circling above his head. Right now, Gabrielle was like a ray of bright sunshine trying to stream through. If he could believe the intensity of these emotions—if he wanted to act on them—he had to pull himself out of this fog. For the first time in three years he was actually starting to feel something. For the first time he was starting to question—wouldn't it be so much better to actually *feel* again?

There was a shuffling outside the door. Sullivan sat up in bed, frowning to listen a little closer. There were low voices.

He swung his legs out of bed and grabbed a T-shirt, opening the door of the bedroom. Franz, the palace advisor, was outside. 'Dr Darcy, I have a message for Princess Gabrielle and I couldn't find her in her apartments.'

Sullivan nodded. He was sure the whole palace knew exactly where she was. 'Do you want me to get her for you?'

Franz gave a brief nod of his head.

Sullivan closed the door again and crossed over to the bed, sitting on the edge and putting his hand on Gabrielle's bare shoulder. He gave her a gentle shake.

'Gabrielle? Wake up. Franz is looking for you. They have a message.'

Her dark eyes flickered open. It took her a few seconds to orientate herself. 'I fell asleep?' she asked, as she pushed herself up.

'Nope. I just kidnapped you and held you hostage.'

She pulled the sheet up to cover her breasts as she tried to untangle her legs. 'Oh, no.'

'What?'

'I've got no clothes.' She looked down at the floor. Her black dress was lying rumpled across the carpet, her bra hung from the arm of a chair, and as for her underwear...

Sullivan walked to the cupboard and tossed her a T-shirt. 'This is getting to be a habit. Maybe you should move some clothes in here.'

She looked a little startled by the comment. She pulled the T-shirt over her head and looked around the room again, colour flooding her cheeks as she picked up her dress and bra. 'Give me a pair of your jockey shorts too.'

He laughed as she scrambled into the shorts. 'Don't you have a robe—a dressing gown—in here?'

Sullivan shook his head. 'Why on earth would I need one of those?'

'To let me keep a bit of dignity?'

It was clear she was feeling tetchy. He walked through the bathroom and ran the tap, washing his face and hands, trying to wake up a little more. He flicked the switch on the shower to let it heat up. Coffee. He would find some coffee, then arrange to go back down to the hospital and review the patients.

Gabrielle appeared at the door, looking pale, a newspaper clutched in her hand.

'What is it?'

She lifted up the Italian broadsheet so he could see the headline.

He flinched.

Princess Gabrielle's affair with Delinquent Doc

He snatched the paper and started to read. Speaking Italian was different from reading it, but he could easily understand the gist of the article.

The trouble was, no matter what the article said, the picture told a thousand words. It was of the two of them on the terrace last night. They were locked together, his hand on her breast, her arms around his neck. There was no mistaking where the night was going.

He held up the paper, trying to temper the anger that was rising in his stomach. 'What's this about anyway? We're two consenting adults—we can do whatever we want.'

'Keep reading.' Her voice had a little tremor.

Sullivan's mobile started ringing. They both turned their heads, but he ignored it. He kept reading.

It was a hatchet job. It questioned Gabrielle's suitability to be Head of State. It questioned her competence. There was nothing accurate in the article. It didn't even mention the fact she was a doctor and had worked for Doctors Without Borders for the last few years, or the work she'd done to help stop the spread of TB.

As for the 'Delinquent Doc', it seemed that no one

knew Sullivan Darcy had served in the US forces. There was no mention that he'd just helped out with a national emergency in Mirinez. No. All that was mentioned was a minor caution he'd received as a teenager from the police—something that had only ever been reported on in the local paper back in his home town. There wouldn't even be a record of it any more.

There was one final press comment.

Is this the man Princess Gabrielle will marry?

It was like a punch to the stomach. One date. One kiss. One night in bed—and the press didn't even know about that. Was this what it was like, dating a royal? Facing constant presumptions about what would come next?

His blood chilled in his veins. He was only just starting to feel again after three numb years. And he wasn't there yet. He wasn't. He couldn't offer Gabrielle anything close to marriage yet.

She held up another paper. 'Apparently there was a picture of us the day before too. My team just missed it amongst all the mine reports.'

Sullivan squinted at the paper in her hand. There was a photo of him and her walking out of the hospital. He had his arm slung around her waist, they were both dressed in scrubs and basically looking like the walking dead. He read that headline.

Who is the mystery man with Princess Gabrielle?

He shook his head and threw the broadsheet he'd been holding on the unmade bed. 'Well, I guess they found that out,' he muttered. 'Why are you so upset about this? It's nothing. It's rubbish.'

He was ignoring the wedding stuff. She couldn't speak Italian. Maybe she hadn't read that part.

Her tanned skin was pale. He could still see the slight tremor in her hands. Gabrielle started pacing around the room. 'But it's not. If people lose faith in me, Mirinez's reputation will be damaged.'

'Won't it already be damaged by the fact your brother hasn't functioned for the last few years?'

She completely ignored his comment and kept pacing. 'I still have trade agreements and business deals to finalise. This could threaten them. If other countries don't trust me to lead wisely, why should they invest in us?'

He shook his head and walked over, putting both hands on the tops of her arms. 'Stop, Gabrielle. Just stop.'

The breath she sucked in was shaky. He hated seeing her like this. But he also hated the fact his photo was slapped across the front of a newspaper. He'd always been a fairly private person and the fact it was an intensely personal moment sparked a little fire inside him. He glanced at the paper again, trying to work out who on earth had taken the photograph. From the angle it seemed to have been taken slightly from above—none of the restaurant staff could have done that.

He pushed all thoughts away and tried to keep on track. 'Who deals with publicity for you? Release a statement saying your privacy should be respected. If you have to, give them my name, rank and serial number. I suspect they already know—that just wasn't interesting enough to report. There's nothing else to find out about me, Gabrielle. I'm a surgeon. I've served in the military. I've kissed you. That's it. They can spin it whatever way they like. What you need to do is tell them about *you*.

'Arrange an interview—tell the world what you've come back to. Tell them about the work you've been doing on TB. Tell them about how the mining accident has been handled and your plans for the future to make sure it doesn't happen again. Tell them you've been working in the hospital as well as trying to catch up on work your brother left behind.' He waved his hand. 'They've painted you here as some kind of lightweight socialite, someone who can't be trusted to make decisions. This isn't you. Show them who the real you is.'

Her voice cracked. 'I can't do this. I just can't. I never wanted to do this anyway. I just want to go back to being a doctor. *Just* a doctor. I'm sorry you've been caught up in all this. It's not fair. Newspapers are awful. Some reporters will spend their lives looking for something to splash on the front page. They hound your family and friends, as if invading everyone's privacy is their given right.'

Sullivan stepped back. Something about this felt off. Something he couldn't quite put his finger on. Yes, Gabrielle was embarrassed to have been caught in a compromising position but her reaction seemed about more than that.

His insides curled up. Was she embarrassed by him? Worried that the world might read more into their relationship than she'd like? The truth was, he didn't even know what this relationship was—so how could anyone else?

Was she embarrassed by the presumption they might marry? Did she think he might never be marriage material? He'd never had to think that way before. That he might not be good enough. It was a whole new experience.

Particularly when he was trying to come to terms with the fact Gabrielle seemed to be bringing him out of the fog he'd been in for the last three years. Was this just a fling for her?

But there was something in those dark eyes that looked like intense worry. She'd been brought up in the public eye. Maybe not completely under the spotlight like some of the other European royal families, but he would have thought she might have more experience of the media than someone like him.

He took her hand. 'Get dressed. Come with me to the hospital. We have patients to review.' It seemed like the most sensible suggestion. In the hospital Gabrielle was completely at home, confident in her abilities and could focus on the job. Out here she was floundering.

Her head gave a slow nod. The hospital must have sounded like a safe place. 'Once we've reviewed all the patients we need to, we can make a plan.' He gave a little frown. 'Franz should be helping you with this. I suppose you should either release a statement or give an interview.' He took a deep breath. 'I'll support you whatever you want to do.'

A tiny part of him wanted to walk away from all this. But Gabrielle needed support. And the selfish side of him realised that even though she didn't know it, she was supporting him too.

This was the first real relationship he'd been part of since his father had died. He'd always been confident with women. But his career choices had meant he was constantly on the move. It was difficult to form meaningful relationships when you didn't know where you'd be in six months. And the truth was—he hadn't wanted to.

But now? Something was different. Gabrielle was like a breath of fresh air just when he needed it. Just a glimpse of her dark eyes brought a smile to his face. He wasn't quite as ready to walk away as he had been in the past.

She gave a nod. 'I'll meet you back here in half an hour,' she said as she disappeared out the door.

Sullivan didn't even get a chance to reply.

He stared at the crumpled broadsheet on the bed. Why did that discarded piece of paper suddenly feel like his life?

Her brain was spinning. Her initial worry about being caught without any appropriate clothes had disappeared the instant Franz had delivered the news.

She ignored everyone in the corridor as she strode towards her apartments, opening the door and walking straight through and flicking on the shower.

The reports were bad enough. Doubtless by tomorrow others would have picked up the story and started digging for more dirt.

And that was what she feared most.

People knew that Andreas had abdicated. They didn't know about the mess he'd left behind. And they didn't know the rest of it. The missing million euros she'd just found out about.

When the investigative journalists got their hands on that news it would make headlines anywhere.

And she would be left to face the music.

She couldn't share this. She couldn't tell Sullivan.

He hadn't signed up for this. He hadn't signed up for *anything*.

Her skin was still tingling. Tingling from where he'd touched her.

She stepped under the shower and let the hot water sting her skin.

Everything about Sullivan felt so right, but how could it be, when everything else in the world was so wrong?

She was trying to come to grips with the fact that this would be her life now.

Head of State.

She should have been more realistic. She should have realised this could always be a possibility. But she'd been selfish. She'd only been thinking of herself and had run away, fulfilling her dreams and ambitions to be a doctor.

She tipped her head back, allowing the water to sluice over her face, grabbing the scented shampoo and rubbing briskly.

When Sullivan had taken her to bed last night everything else had flown straight out of the window. Her worries, her fears about her changing life. She'd only concentrated on him.

Her feelings about Sullivan were so tangled up she really couldn't think straight at all. That smile. The feel of his muscles under the palms of her hands. For her—nirvana.

And outside that, he was so grounded. So matter-of-fact. He'd stepped into a crisis situation and responded without question. She liked that about him. She maybe even loved that about him.

She hadn't contemplated how much last night would mean to her. The connection she would feel with Sullivan. How right everything could feel.

But reports like the ones in the newspaper might well scare him off. *Marriage?* Neither of them could even contemplate something like that right now.

She had to concentrate all her time on her duties, on running the country. That was where her priorities should lie right now. Even if her heart didn't feel as if it wanted that.

The thing was, she felt that if Sullivan was by her side she might actually be able to do this.

When she was with him, instead of being filled with worry, she could actually remember some of the things about Mirinez she'd always loved and had just forgotten about.

The people were great. In previous years the economy and business had been thriving. The number of celebrities who stayed here because of the principality's tax-haven status was rising all the time. Mirinez was considered a glamorous place to visit and because of the celebrities the tourist industry was thriving. In light of the bad news she'd heard about the missing million euros, she probably needed to use that to Mirinez's advantage.

She flicked off the shower and grabbed her robe, wrapping it around her as she towel-dried her hair.

Would Sullivan even contemplate staying here, continuing a relationship? Part of her didn't want to even consider it. Sullivan seemed to be a workaholic. He went on one mission after another. And there was something curious about that drive. It was almost as if she had to dig a little deeper. It was obvious he was still mourning the death of his father but Sullivan was too alpha to ever admit that. Did he even realise himself?

She sighed as she sat down in front of the mirror.

All she really knew was that she didn't want him to leave. But the private hospitals of Mirinez would never keep the attention of a surgeon like Sullivan. There would need to be something else. Need to be something more.

Her heart squeezed in her chest. She'd like it if that could be her.

But what were the chances of that?

As soon as they set foot in the hospital Gabrielle started to relax a little more. She instantly moved into doctor mode. Someone asked her to check an X-ray regarding a potential case of TB and she looked so enthused he could have cheered.

His patients were doing well. He scheduled surgery for the next day for one of the burns victims, then spent a considerable amount of time talking to the miner from China and his family to assure them that he was being taken care of.

Gabrielle was at ease here. He watched her talk enthusiastically to patients, offering comfort as she reviewed their conditions and making plans for the future. Just like in Nambura, patients seemed drawn to her. Gabrielle wasn't a princess here. She balanced being the ultimate professional while showing care and attention to her patients.

Every now and then their eyes met and she gave him the kind of smile that had multiple effects, some on his body and some on his mind.

One of the nurses gave him a knowing look as she noticed him watching. 'I hadn't met Princess Gabrielle before now.' She gave a little nod of her head. 'She's great. I wish she'd stay around as a doctor. Philippe, our director, has had a total personality transplant in the last few days.'

Sullivan looked at her in surprise. 'What do you mean?'

The nurse met his gaze. 'I've been here five years. I came from France. Private hospitals here are all about money. For as long as I've known him, Philippe has been so uptight, so focused on profit and being the first place to offer the next big surgery.'

'And now?' Sullivan didn't know whether to feel irritated or intrigued. What had caused the change in the hospital director?

She sighed. 'He's better. I think because Gabrielle told him that the government and mining company would cover the medical costs he can relax a little. I think Philippe usually spends half his life chasing down accounts that haven't been paid.' She held out her hand, gesturing. 'Sixty per cent of our beds are currently filled with patients from the mining accident.'

Sullivan had never really worked in private practice. He'd gone from training to serving in the military—to working for Doctors Without Borders.

It gave him a bit of perspective about the pressures others were under—including Gabrielle. 'Money makes the world go round. I hope the mining company comes through on its promises.'

The nurse waved her hand as she moved away. 'If they don't, Gabrielle has promised the government will pick up the entire tab.' She smiled and started walking backwards as she made her way down the corridor. 'If you can, try and persuade her to keep working here sometimes.' She winked at Sullivan. 'You too, if you like. The surgeons have been talking. They're impressed.'

Sullivan couldn't help the smile that appeared on his face. Getting praise from a patient was always the best thing, but getting praise from colleagues in a competitive business like this? That was pretty good too. 'Thanks. But, hey, who says I have any influence over Gabrielle?'

The nurse tapped the side of her nose as she disappeared around the corner. 'I can see it…' she interlinked her fingers '…the connection. You two light up the place like a Christmas tree.' She winked again. 'And you could cook sausages with the sizzle in the air between you.'

She disappeared around the corner, leaving Sullivan smiling and shaking his head.

Ten hours later Gabrielle had never felt better. This felt normal. This felt real. She'd reviewed ten patients at length, changing prescriptions, altering care plans and discussing their care with them and their nurses. That was just at the first hospital. She'd then left St George's and headed to Princess Elizabeth's to review another three patients there.

Franz had caught up with her at one point. There were more legal documents to be signed, a briefing from one of the European lawyers about a contract dispute, but he didn't mention the missing money again. He looked gaunt and she was aware he knew exactly where she'd been all day. She put her hand over his. 'Let's talk about other matters tomorrow,' she'd said quietly.

'Of course,' he'd agreed. He'd pursed his lips then added, 'Are you sure about this statement?'

She'd written it by email while in St George's, given it ten minutes of her time and no more. She had patients to attend to and wasn't here to court the reporter's interest. She gave a quick nod of her head. 'Send it as it is.' She would deal with any queries tomorrow.

She wanted to do something else this evening. Something else entirely. By the time the idea had fully formed in her mind she was practically running down the corridor. She threw off one set of clothes and grabbed another. Five minutes later she knocked on Sullivan's door.

'Come in.' He was trying to decide how to persuade Gabrielle she should find a way to keep working as a doctor.

The door swung open and Gabrielle stood there, leaning against the doorjamb. She was wearing the tight jeans that drove him crazy, a grey hooded zip-up top and had a red baseball cap pulled low over her face. 'Ready?' she asked.

He spun around from the desk. 'Ready for what?'

She sauntered across the room towards him. 'To play hookey with me, of course.'

He stood up and walked over to meet her. 'You want to play hookey?'

She laid her hands on his chest. 'What I want is to go to the movies, watch the best action film on the planet and eat my body weight in popcorn.'

Now he understood the clothes. He ran his eyes up and down her body then wagged his finger. 'Oh, no. You can't do that. It's a dead giveaway.'

'What?' She looked down and then from side to side. 'What am I doing?'

He folded his arms and nodded his head. 'You're not doing it now. That's better.'

He walked over to the closet and pulled out jeans and a T-shirt. 'Got a spare baseball hat? I didn't think it would be required clothing in Mirinez.'

She wrinkled her nose. 'What was I doing? What'll get me recognised?'

He fastened his jeans and slid his feet into a kicked-in pair of baseball boots. He rummaged through his backpack and pulled out a navy blue hoodie.

'Smiling.' He winked at her. 'Put that smile away. It's recognisable anywhere.'

Her cheeks flushed a little, but the sparkle in her eyes made him pull her closer. He breathed in, filling his senses with her light floral scent as he pushed her hat back and dropped a kiss on her lips. She wrapped her hands around his neck and whispered in her ear, 'Don't distract me, or we won't get anywhere.'

'Hmm…would that be so bad?'

She touched the side of his shadowed jaw, her nail scraping along the stubble he now wished he had shaved. 'Haven't you heard? You're the delinquent doc. You're supposed to be leading me astray.'

'Oh, I can do that, no problem.'

She pulled her hat back on. 'Then get me out of here. Let's go and watch a film.'

He rolled his eyes as he slid his hand into hers. 'This is crazy. I want you to know, you're the only girl on the planet I'd do this for.' He opened the door and glanced down the corridor. It was surprisingly empty. 'I'm assuming you know a back way out of here?'

She gave him an innocent expression. 'I might. Let's just say I didn't waste all my teenage years in the palace.'

'I thought you were a good girl. The study queen.'

She put her hand on his arm. 'That's what I wanted to the world to know. The rest?' She held up her hand and gave him a wicked look.

He shook his head. He liked it that Gabrielle had a rebellious side. He also liked it that she'd obviously learned a number of years ago how to manipulate the press. Maybe it was time to refresh those skills.

They crept down the corridor, looking both ways as they went. Some of the palace and security staff were talking at the top of the one of the staircases. He put his finger to his lips. Gabrielle gestured with her head to the right. 'This way,' she whispered as they ducked down another corridor. She took them into the library, checked over her shoulder and pushed against one of the panels on the wall. After long seconds, the wooden panel slid to the side.

Sullivan couldn't help it. His mouth hung open. 'You have got to be joking.'

'What?' She smiled.

He held out his hand. 'A hidden door, a secret passage? No way.' He kept shaking his head but couldn't stop smiling.

She shrugged her shoulders. 'The palace is hundreds

of years old. There are numerous plans. What you find depends on which set of plans you look at.'

'This is like something from a movie.' He stuck his head into the dark corridor and pulled it back out in wonder, squinting at the dimensions of the room they were in. The wooden panels were deceptive. He was still frowning as he walked back out into the corridor to check the overall size of the rooms.

'Stop it,' hissed Gabrielle, laughing and pulling him back inside. 'You can think about all that later. Now we need to go.'

He was still shaking his head as she led him down the twisting and turning dark corridor. *'Phwoff!'* he said, wiping the cobwebs from his face. 'I take it no one else has gone down here in years.'

She couldn't stop grinning. 'Probably not. Andreas used to sneak his girlfriends in and out this way when we were teenagers.'

He squeezed her hand. *'Just* Andreas?'

She gave him a smart glance. 'Can I pretend I'm an American and plead the fifth?'

He rolled his eyes as they turned a corner with a chink of light at the end. She pressed her hands up against the door and pushed. Nothing happened.

He put his hands next to hers. 'You'd better tell me now, are we going to end up in that place in the kids' story where they go through the back of the cupboard?'

She shook her head. 'No. Just Mirinez. But who knows? It might already feel like Narnia to you.'

'Narnia. That was it.' He pushed hard alongside her and the door creaked open slowly.

Long grass and a tall hedge were impeding the doorway. Gabrielle flattened her back and slunk along behind the hedge out into the palace gardens, Sullivan followed suit and looked around, trying to get his bearings.

'Where are we?'

'Opposite side of the palace from your apartments.'

He looked back at the hedge. The door was completely hidden. He put his hands on his hips. 'I honestly can't believe there's a door there. I also can't believe you just didn't tell Security you were going out without them.'

Gabrielle shook her head. 'Where's the fun in that?' She waved her hand. 'Anyway, do you really think Arun would let me get away with it?'

She skirted along the hedge until they reached a large security gate, which she opened with an old-fashioned brass key.

It opened out onto the road and they walked half a mile to the nearest tram stop. Gabrielle pulled her hat down. 'Hope you've got plenty of money. I eat a *lot* of popcorn.'

He patted his pocket. 'I think I can manage to keep you in popcorn.'

They settled into a seat on the tram. No one even looked at Gabrielle and Sullivan pulled his hood up. As the tram travelled through the city she pointed out different areas to Sullivan. 'This is Felixstock. It's one of the city suburbs. Houses are cheaper here and a lot of the locals stay in this area. There are a few community clinics as a lot of the residents of Mirinez don't have their own health insurance. Some get health insurance through their employers.'

'But the rest don't?'

She shook her head. 'No, it's a bit of an issue. I'd really like to do some shifts in one of the community clinics.'

Sullivan gave her a smile. It seemed that he wasn't going to have to persuade her to continue being a doctor after all. The seed was already planted and growing. 'I think, once you get over the chaos period you'll be able to balance things to your advantage.'

He could see her biting the inside of her cheek. She let out a long slow breath. 'Here's hoping. I can't imagine reaching that point right now.' Then she wrinkled her nose. 'The chaos period?'

He nodded. 'Sorting out the disaster your brother left behind.'

There was the oddest expression on her face and he knew instantly that there was still something she wasn't telling him. Something coiled up low in his gut. He'd thought they were getting closer. Thought that she trusted him. But there were obviously some things she still didn't want to share.

What did he know about running a country? There could probably be a million things that Gabrielle could never discuss with him. He shifted in the tram seat.

As the city passed by outside he sucked in a breath. Something was eating away at his brain. Thoughts of Oregon, going back home and his father. He'd ignored another call from Gibbs. A call that would doubtless have offered a chance for the next mission—another chance to avoid going home.

He pushed those thoughts away as Gabrielle tugged at his arm and jumped up. The cinema was at the end of the street. They walked hand in hand, past the restaurant they'd eaten in the other night, and joined the queue outside the cinema.

The doors opened and they filed in. Gabrielle tried to melt into the background as he bought the tickets and the popcorn and soda. The cinema was dark when they entered and the adverts were already playing. 'Where do you want to sit?' he whispered to Gabrielle.

She winked at him. 'How about the back row?'

'Your wish is my command.' He gave a mock bow and led her up to the back row.

They settled in their seats. He slung his arm around her and she settled her head on his shoulder. Two minutes later she pulled her hat off. Her soft hair was just under his nose. The aroma of raspberries drifted up around him. As the film progressed Gabrielle tilted her head up to him. 'What do you think?'

He leaned closer. 'I think I need a distraction.' She tasted of popcorn and lemonade as her lips parted easily against his and her hand slid up around his neck. Even fully clothed he could feel her curves against him, reminding him of their night together. He slid his hand under her top, her silky skin warm beneath the palm of his hand. He sensed her smile as they kissed. 'You make me feel fifteen again,' she whispered as his hand closed over her hardened nipple. Her kissing intensified, her hips tilting towards him and one hand running along the side of his jaw. Her other hand slid over the front of his jeans.

'Is this how you behaved in the cinema at fifteen?' he growled.

'Always,' she teased, before she pulled her lips from his and settled back to watch the film.

Sullivan glanced sideways at her and adjusted his position in his seat. 'Now, that's what I call a distraction,' he said as he glanced at his watch. 'This is going to be the longest ninety minutes of my life.'

'Here, have some popcorn.' She dumped it in his lap with a cheeky glance.

The next morning the papers seemed to have changed their mind about her delinquent doc.

There was a fuzzy picture of them locked in each other's arms in the cinema. It seemed her disguise hadn't gone unnoticed. Arun gave her a stern stare as he handed over the morning's papers. '*Don't* do that again.' He narrowed his gaze and raised his eyebrows. 'I wanted to see that movie.' He strode off down the corridor.

She smiled as she settled down to check the press. Her staff knew she wasn't particularly adept at translating languages so they'd translated all the headlines pertaining to Gabrielle and Sullivan.

This time they'd actually found out a little more about Sullivan. They named his father and his great service as an admiral in the US navy. They'd found a photo of Sullivan from a few years ago. She had no idea where it had been taken—but it could have been used for an action movie. He was in uniform with a desert background. His face was smeared with dust, but he was on the ground, attending to a patient. He was clearly focused on the job.

He was pointing to something in the distance and shouting. The sleeves of his uniform were pushed high up on his arms, revealing his defined biceps. The intensity in his face seemed to emanate from every pore on his body. He hadn't noticed the photographer—or he wasn't bothering with them. He was totally in the moment.

The photo would stop just about every woman in their tracks. And if the photo didn't, the words underneath might: *Hero Doc.*

The press had certainly changed their tune.

Beneath the article was the statement she'd released via the Palace press office yesterday.

Princess Gabrielle has arrived in Mirinez to take up the role of Head of State after the abdication of Prince Andreas. She is ready and willing to take up this position, serving the people of Mirinez to the best of her ability.

Princess Gabrielle makes no excuses for the fact that she is a doctor. Her experience served her well following the recent mine explosion, and she will continue to serve as a doctor, in a community setting, as well as carrying out her state duties.

Princess Gabrielle was accompanied on her return home by Dr Sullivan Darcy, a surgeon who has worked for Doctors Without Borders and served in the US military. His skills proved vital in dealing with the victims of burns from the mining explosion and Princess Gabrielle is grateful to have his expertise at this time.

Everything would be almost perfect if it wasn't for the slightly grainy picture underneath of the two of them locked in each other's arms. It made it look as if she were trying to keep him a secret. As if she was ashamed.

The hardest part of the statement had been the part about Sullivan. What should she call him? A friend? A boyfriend? A colleague?

In the end she'd taken the easiest way out and not called him anything. Just using the words that he'd 'accompanied' her.

She was so torn. Her heart was going one place and her head another.

She looked at the list of responsibilities that she still needed to tackle as Head of State. As time progressed it was gradually reducing. There were still a number of critical issues to be dealt with—not least the one about the missing money. There were also a number of duties she still had to fulfil.

Duties were always the things she'd hated most as a child. Being forced to dress up and behave at certain state events had never been her favourite way to spend time. But now her childhood days and teenage rebellion years had long since passed, she could look on them with adult eyes.

Tomorrow night there was a state banquet. It had been arranged when Andreas had still been head of state. With everything else that was going on, she hadn't even given it a moment's thought.

As she looked at the guest list now, she could see the names of dignitaries, members of other royal families and members of parliament. Several of the people on the guest list were also featured on her list of responsibilities as Head of State. Talking in person was always so much better than talking on the phone. There were a few essential conversations she could have that evening to mend bridges or smooth over troubled waters that her brother had created.

She licked her dry lips.

Maybe this was a good way to hint at something else. To the press. To the people of Mirinez. And to the members of staff in the palace. If she invited Sullivan to the event as her partner—officially—that would send a message.

Her heart fluttered in her chest. Was this the right thing to do?

She walked over to her closet and pulled open the doors, running her eyes over the clothes. It had been such a long time since she'd been to anything officially 'royal' that she really didn't have much suitable. Franz had arranged for a few suits and work clothes to be available to her as soon as she'd arrived.

A banquet was something else entirely. And Gabrielle didn't spend hours deciding what to wear. As long as it was suitable, covered everything it should, and felt good, she would be happy. She'd never been the type of girl that was a clothes horse. She picked up the phone. 'Franz, I'll need something to wear for the state banquet—can you arrange that? And can you let people know that Dr Darcy will be my guest and find something suitable for him too? Thanks.'

She put down the phone and gave a nervous smile.

Finally, she had something to look forward to.

The surgery had taken longer than expected. His back ached. It had been a long time since that had happened. In Helmand Provence he'd frequently been on his feet in surgery for sixteen hours at a time. But it was odd. The heat of the environment that normally caused so many other issues had seemed to relieve any muscular aches and pains.

He strode down the corridor towards his apartments. The surgery seemed to have been successful. He'd had to graft a large piece of skin onto the hand, ensuring there was enough elasticity to allow adequate movement and dexterity for the fingers. Hand surgery was one of the trickiest, particularly around burns. But he'd review how things looked in the morning to ensure the best outcome for his patient. Surgery was only the first step. This miner would have months of physical therapy ahead. It would be a long, hard road.

It was unusual. The palace seemed busier than normal. More staff. More cars in the courtyard. There was a buzz in the air.

He opened the door to his apartments and stopped. A few suits were hanging from the outside of the wardrobe, along with a variety of shirts and ties, a military dress uniform and a variety of shoes.

Was he going somewhere?

Mikel, the security guard, appeared at his shoulder. 'Dr Darcy, I was looking for you.'

'What's up, Mikel? Why has my room turned into a department store?'

Mikel smiled. 'There's a state banquet tonight. It had already been arranged before you and Princess Gabrielle arrived—it will be the first that she's officially hosted.' Mikel pointed to the clothes. 'Anyway, you are the Princess's guest. Arun arranged for a few choices of clothes for you.' He gestured towards the uniform. 'He wasn't sure what you would want to wear.' He gave a cheeky grin. 'And don't worry. This time everything will fit perfectly.'

Mikel turned and headed for the door. 'Banquet starts at seven. You'll be expected at Princess Gabrielle's apartments at six-thirty.'

He disappeared out the door and Sullivan sank into the armchair next to the window. He was exhausted. What he'd really like to do was lie on top of the bed and search TV channels for a baseball game—the one thing he actually did miss while away on all his missions.

There was a tray on the table next to him. With a pot of coffee and…he lifted the silver dome…his favourite sandwich, a Philly steak cheese. He shook his head as the smell drifted around him. The palace staff were completely obliging and had obviously read his mind. He poured the coffee and tore into the sandwich as he looked at the suits hanging outside the wardrobe. He didn't even want to think about how much they had cost.

His eyes flicked to the dress uniform. He moved over and fingered the gold braid on the navy jacket. The cap was sitting on top of the nearby table. Would he be comfortable wearing his dress uniform? He had an honourable discharge from the US Army. If he had permission, he could still wear his dress uniform. The question was—did he want to?

While his time in the military had been an intense but enjoyable experience, just looking at the uniform reminded him of his father. He had numerous photographs of his father in his own dress uniform. As his father's whole career had been in the military, his uniform had almost been like his second skin.

He dropped his hand and moved over to the nearest suit. The first touch of the fabric told him its quality. He pressed his lips together. He didn't need to deal with the other stuff tonight.

It was eating away at him. Things only seemed to be intensifying as his relationship with Gabrielle blossomed. They were always there, always burning away at his soul—probably creating an ulcer in his stomach—always letting him know that he had unfinished business. The wall he had created around himself was starting to be eaten away by little chinks. Chinks he still didn't know if he could accommodate. One of the black suits would be fine. He walked into the bathroom and flicked the handle on the shower.

What was a state banquet anyway?

She opened the door as soon as he knocked. 'Wow, so that's what you look like when you actually wear the jacket as well as the shirt and trousers.'

He smiled. 'Hey.' He looked down. 'This is actually a different pair of trousers and a different shirt from the other night. I did contemplate the jeans from the cinema.'

She gave him a gentle shove. 'Don't go there.' She stepped forward and pretended to straighten his tie. Anything to get up close and personal.

His hand went straight to her hip. She could feel the

heat from his palm instantly through the fine satin of her dress. He rubbed his palm gently up and down the curve of her hip and waist.

'If this is what we wear to state banquets then I'm all in.'

She gave a little groan. 'Behave.' She'd picked a demurely styled navy blue satin dress. The bodice was also covered in lace and scattered with sequins that showed the tanned skin on her shoulders and around the top of neckline hint through the lace. In her ears she had large diamond and sapphire earrings and her hair was pinned up.

'How can I behave when you look like this?' he whispered.

She was wearing heavier make-up than normal, a little glitter enhancing her dark eyes and a brighter red lipstick. She licked her lips as she glanced at him. 'You'll have to behave. Haven't you heard? You're my official date. One day a delinquent doc, the next day the hero doc.' She stood on tiptoe and whispered in his ear, 'Who knows what tomorrow will bring?'

'Am I allowed to use my imagination?' The brush of her hair, the feel of her soft skin against his was enough to send his senses racing. He wasn't sure at all what tonight would entail, but he was happy to be by her side.

Gabrielle was nervous. This was a big night for her. It was a big night for them. And she still really hadn't taken the chance to sit down and explain things to Sullivan.

Part of her wondered what he might say. Telling him that this invitation might mean…that she was telling the world she hoped he'd stay around seemed desperate. And she had never been desperate.

But then again, she'd never been Head of State of

Mirinez before. And as much as she hated it, any minute now the press would move on to the next stage. This time next week they would decide that, yes, Gabrielle would be marrying Sullivan and start contemplating a date... then speculating about a family.

She wanted to be back in Paris with Sullivan, spending long lazy days and even longer nights in bed, just waiting for a call for the next mission.

Chances were, at this point she would still be nervous. They would always need to have that 'conversation'. The one where they decided if their fling was over, or if it meant something more.

Truth was, she was falling a little in love with Sullivan. He made her feel safe. One look from him, one hint of twinkle in his eye and it felt as if a thousand tiny caterpillars were marching over her skin. Just the upward curl of his smile meant her blood would start to race around her body. As for the feel of his lips connecting with hers...

She didn't want to lose that feeling. She wanted to grab it and hold on with both hands.

But Sullivan seemed to have spent the last few years on a never-ending mission. She couldn't expect him to give all that up. She would never ask him to. But would he consider something else? Would he consider somewhere and someone to come home to?

She tilted her chin up to his and wrapped her arms around his neck. He met her lips eagerly. This felt like coming home. His lips parted against hers, his tongue running along the edges. It was easy to welcome his kiss. She inhaled his fresh scent. Probably pure pheromones. The guy had them by the bagload.

He eventually pulled back and rested his forehead against hers while she caught her breath. He smiled and lifted his thumb to her lips. 'Might have smudged your lipstick. Can't have you leaving here looking anything less than perfect.'

She lifted her fingers to his lips too. 'I might have left you with my mark.' She rubbed the remnants of her red lipstick from his face.

He gave her a crooked kind of smile. There was something in his eyes. Not the twinkle that she was used to—this time it was thoughtful sincerity. It almost took her breath away. 'I could get used to that.'

She stepped back. Should she speak to him now? Should she ask him how he felt about the future—the possibility of a future with her?

There was a knock at the door. Franz entered and gave her an approving smile. 'Perfect, you're ready, Princess Gabrielle. A large number of our guests have already arrived and are being entertained. I think it's time to join them. Are you ready?'

He looked between her and Sullivan. She couldn't help but notice that Sullivan almost got an approving glance too.

She quickly fixed her lipstick then slid her arm into Sullivan's, giving him a smile as her stomach did a few somersaults. 'Yes, we're ready, aren't we?'

He nodded in agreement as they headed out of the apartments. As they reached the stairs she could hear the noise from beneath them. The ballroom was buzzing. A string quartet was playing in the corner and palace staff was circulating with silver trays containing glasses of champagne and hors d'oeuvres.

She gave Sullivan's arm a little squeeze as they descended the stairs. This would be his first experience of what royal life could entail. She crossed her fingers, silently praying that everything would go well and he wouldn't be on the first plane out of here.

But everything went like a charm. Sullivan moved easily around the room. He was a seasoned professional and his language skills took everyone by surprise. He was also a fabulous advocate for Doctors Without Borders, engaging delegates from other countries in conversations about working across the globe and the type of health interventions needed.

She was trying her best too, working her way through a number of difficult conversations that were clearly overdue. In the end, the paths seemed smoother.

The royal dining room was set up in shades of gold and cream. As always, the staff had done an immaculate job. Franz had seated people carefully—always a challenge at a state dinner. But the wine flowed and the food was served quickly.

Sullivan was across the table and further down from her. She could see him talking to the people on either side of him, neither of whom she could place. But from time to time his eyes drifted off. Her heart gave a squeeze when the expression on his face was almost pained. But as soon as someone next to him started talking again, he smiled and gave them his full attention.

If she didn't know better she'd think he was feeling uncomfortable. But she'd seen that look on Sullivan's face before. It was always fleeting. Always almost hidden.

She'd been so busy thinking about herself and her country, so busy hoping that Sullivan would feel the same way she did and want to continue their relationship, that she hadn't even stopped to wonder about those moments.

Relationships should be a partnership. He was supporting her. But was she supporting him in return?

She shifted uncomfortably in her chair, the sequins on her dress digging in a little around her arm. The chancellor of a neighbouring country brushed her arm to start another conversation and she responded. But Sullivan was still at the forefront of her mind.

Why did she feel like a teenager again, instead of a Princess?

Dinner had been fine. The guests and company had been interesting. He'd had a number of conversations about health issues that Doctors Without Borders supported. He also had avenues to explore in future months.

But the table had been huge, filled at either side and accommodating more than three hundred people. It was impossible to know everyone who was there.

He'd watched Gabrielle. She was the perfect hostess. Beautiful, considerate, genuine and very, very measured.

It was almost amusing. If they'd been on a mission he was sure she would have told a few diplomats exactly what she thought of them, but the role of Head of State was vastly different from managing a team in the jungle.

But he'd watched the rest of the people around the table. As the night progressed he could see Gabrielle moving up in their estimations. For some strange reason it made his heart swell with pride.

Everything about her—her smile, the toss of her hair, her laugh—seemed to connect with him in a way that was deeper than anything he'd ever experienced before.

He should be singing. He should be shouting from the rooftops and he wanted to, he really did.

But something was holding him back.

For the first time in his life he really wanted to make a commitment. He wanted to sit down and have that 'what if' conversation. The one where he could tell her just how he felt and see how he could make things work.

For a few days he just wished the whole royal scenario hadn't happened. But this was Gabrielle's birthright. She had responsibilities and if he loved her the way he thought he might, then he had to accept that.

He knew that she was struggling. And he wanted to help. He did.

So why did he feel as if there was a rope around his waist, pulling him back? Stopping him from going where he wanted to be.

The truth was that he had personal issues to deal with first. He'd left part himself back in the house in Oregon three years ago when he'd buried his dad.

Grief was a strange and curious thing. It started as an overwhelming sensation that the world sympathised with for a few weeks.

Then it was expected to gradually disperse.

In all honesty, he'd expected it to disperse too.

But it hadn't.

Instead, it had stayed. And grown. Starting as a little seed, it had changed to a sprouting plant and turned into a vine that had crept up and wound its way around his heart and soul, telling him to deal with it as the blackness had clouded in the background.

He was a doctor. A medic. He'd seen things on his tours of duty that would haunt him for ever. But he'd accepted that part of his life. He was supposed to be tough. A delinquent even. A hero.

Those words actually sent a chill down his spine.

But most of all he was a man. Add all those things together—doctor, man, delinquent, hero—and he should be easily equipped to deal with the loss of his father.

His way of dealing with it was constantly being busy, of constantly having his mind and body focusing on something else.

If he really wanted to move forward and work out a

way to continue this relationship with Gabrielle then he had to find a way to put the past behind him.

It was the voice he recognised first. His head turned automatically to try and locate the source. Then it was the figure. The broad shoulders and familiar dress uniform. The last time he'd seen Admiral Sands had been at his father's funeral.

At the same time Joe Sands looked over and caught Sullivan's eye. The recognition took less than a few seconds before he lifted his hand, waved and started to walk in Sullivan's direction.

A tightness spread across Sullivan's chest, his mouth instantly dry. There was a buzzing in his ears, as if he'd just been surrounded by a swarm of angry wasps. Joe Sands looked as relaxed as always. Time had been kind to him. Sullivan knew he must be in his late seventies; he'd retired twenty years ago. He'd been one of first people to get in touch following the death of his father, and he'd made a few attempts since then to keep in contact with Sullivan.

He slapped Sullivan's arm. 'Sullivan Darcy. It's good to see you. How have you been?'

Sullivan gave the briefest of nods as his mouth tried to formulate a reply. Even though he'd had a dress uniform in his apartments and had chosen not wear it, seeing someone else dressed that way had caught him unawares. He hadn't expected it—not here, in Mirinez. He'd got out of the way of being in the company of men in US uniforms. His father had been buried in his dress uniform—as many military men were—and as the light glinted from Joe Sands's buttons the hairs on the back of Sullivan's neck stood on end.

He finally found some words. 'I'm good. Still working.'

Joe was as amiable as ever. 'I never expected to see

you here in Mirinez. And you're with Gabrielle? That's wonderful. She's a beauty. Smart too. Your father would be so proud.'

Would he? It was the oddest feeling. Sullivan suddenly felt very young. He'd always wanted his father's approval. He'd always had it.

But in the last three years parts of his life had played on his mind. He'd been as rebellious as the usual teenager and young man—there were a few things his father had found about, a lot he hadn't.

But he'd never really done anything serious. He'd respected his father and their relationship too much for that.

Now every decision he made came under his nighttime scrutiny of whether his father would have approved or not. Sleep had deserted him.

Gabrielle had proved the best distraction yet. There was nothing like the feel of soft smooth skin to chase away any other jumbled thoughts. But when she fell asleep first, her soft steady breathing filling the air, then the crazy thoughts would find their way back in.

Part of him knew what this was. He'd been a doctor long enough to spot the signs in other people so he'd be a fool if he couldn't recognise them in himself.

But a man wasn't supposed to be unable to deal with grief. A doctor even less so.

Life had moved on. He should have too. If a therapist had asked him a question, he couldn't even give an obvious answer. No, he didn't have unresolved issues with his father. No, there had never been any real conflict. Their relationship had been strong, cemented in the fact they'd only had each other.

And since his father had died, Sullivan had felt as if he'd lost his right-hand man. In a way he had. The effects of being an adult, real-life orphan had never occurred to him.

Perhaps it was much simpler than all that. He missed him. He missed his dad every day. So many times he'd gone to pick up a phone or write an email and stopped instantly, body washed with cold at remembering his father wasn't there. It was ridiculous.

Packing up the house felt final. It was like ripping away the last part of his father that still existed.

He couldn't talk about this to anyone. They would think it pathetic. Men weren't supposed to grieve like this. Men were supposed to get to work. And he had done exactly that—for three years—because work had been the only place he'd felt safe.

And seeing Joe Sands was bringing everything back. Any minute now he'd start regaling Sullivan with stories. Stories about the visit to NASA or Washington. Stories about arguments with generals. Joe Sands had worked alongside his father for the best part of eight years. He knew things that Sullivan didn't. And part of that made him angry. He hated the fact there were memories of his father that he didn't have.

He pasted a smile onto his face and he reached out to shake Joe's hand. 'It's a real pleasure to see you again, Admiral Sands. I'd love to talk but I'm actually on duty. I helped with the mining accident in Mirinez and I've just been contacted to go and check on a patient. If we're lucky, we might be able to catch up later.'

It was all lies. And he only felt the tiniest hint of regret as he saw the wave of disappointment on Joe's face.

'You've had a call?' Gabrielle's voice cut through his thoughts. He hadn't realised she'd appeared and certainly not that she'd overheard him.

She caught sight of his face and nodded smoothly,

sliding her arm into his. 'That's why I came to find you. I've had a call too.' She nodded her head. 'Good evening, Admiral. It's so nice to see you. I'm sorry we haven't had a chance to talk. Possibly tomorrow?'

The Admiral didn't seem to notice Gabrielle's cover-up, but Sullivan's insides felt as if they were curling up and dying.

The Admiral nodded. 'It would be my pleasure.'

Gabrielle steered Sullivan towards the open doors out to the palace gardens. Her footsteps were firm. She gave a few people gracious nods as they passed but didn't stop to talk. It was clear she was on a mission.

As soon as the colder night air hit him his breath caught in his throat. It was the oddest sensation. Like breathing in, without being able to breathe back out. He'd never felt anything like it.

Gabrielle lengthened her strides as they reached the gardens. They passed the fountain and moved away from the paved pathways and across the manicured lawn.

His heart was thudding against his chest, beads of sweat breaking out on his brow. He tugged at the tie he was wearing and struggled to loosen his collar. His skin was itching.

Was he having an allergic reaction to something? What had he eaten? That was all he could liken the sensations to.

Gabrielle led him through some trees and out towards a glass and metal-framed summerhouse. Her footsteps didn't slow until they were inside and she pushed him down onto the bench seat that ran along the inside of the summerhouse.

She knelt down in front of him and unfastened the next few buttons on his shirt. 'Calm down, Sullivan. Breathe. Slow it down.'

He pulled at his collar. 'S-something's…wrong.'

She locked her dark eyes on his, her fingers pressing on the pulse at his wrist.

'Sullivan, you're breathing too quickly. You need to slow it down. We're going to do this together.'

Sweat was trickling down his back between his shoulder blades. He shrugged off his jacket, desperate to get some air around him.

Gabrielle kept talking. Calmly. Slowly.

'I'm… I'm…'

She touched his hand gently. 'You're having a panic attack, Sullivan. That's why I've not called an ambulance or taken you anywhere else.' She held up her hands. 'It's just you and me. There's no one else around. No one else noticed anything.'

Her hand rubbed up and down his. 'Breathe in for two, and out for two. Come on, you can do this.'

His head was spinning. Was she crazy? He'd never had a panic attack in his life. But things around him felt fuzzy and he could feel his heart thudding against his chest. Pain was starting to cross his ribs. Any minute now he might throw up. Could this really be a panic attack?

Her voice got firmer. Still calm, but with a little more authority. 'Work with me, Sullivan. Come on. Breathe in for two and out for two. In for two, out for two. Do it with me. You can do this.'

She was persistent. She kept talking. Softly. Steadily. Until she started to sound as if she was making sense.

He sucked in a breath to the sound of her voice.

'That's it. Do it. Follow me. In for two, out for two.'

He started following her lead. Within a few seconds she changed. 'Okay, now in for four, out for four.'

His heart was slowing. He could feel it. And the pain in his chest was easing ever so slightly. She kept talking, looking up at him with those big brown eyes laced with concern.

His skin prickled as the perspiration on his skin mixed with the cold air. His shirt was open to his waist. He'd practically stripped.

Reality started to take a grip on his brain. He'd never had an experience like that before.

He sucked in a deeper breath and ran his fingers through his now-damp hair.

He was exhausted.

He was embarrassed.

He was confused.

In the dim light, Gabrielle's dark eyes were fixed on his. He could practically see the wheels spinning in her head.

She rocked on her heels as she watched him. Now she could see that he'd calmed down she was obviously contemplating what to do next.

This was a disaster. Not just for him, but for her too. She was Head of State, this was her first official royal banquet. She should be in the palace, attending to her guests—not out here with a man who was falling to pieces.

After a few minutes of silence she stood up and sat next to him on the bench. She rubbed her hands against her thighs. It was almost like she could read his mind. Like she knew he was already concocting a hundred reasons to explain what had just happened.

She took a deep breath and slid her hand over his, intertwining their fingers together. 'What do you need?' was all she said.

It threw him. He'd been expecting a whole wave of questions.

He looked up and out through the glass into the dark

night. The gardens were peaceful, immaculate. If he hadn't known the palace was just through the trees behind him, he could have sworn they were somewhere entirely private.

He said the first thing that came into his head. 'I don't know.'

Gabrielle pressed her lips together and nodded. She turned sideways on so she could face him and placed her hand on his chest. 'From the moment I met you I've admired your physique, your muscles. But now I realise that the six-pack comes at a price. You're too lean, Sullivan. And I know you don't sleep well. You think I haven't noticed, but you get up and pace around at night. Sleep is the one thing our body really needs. We need it to recharge. We need it to refresh ourselves. How long has this been going on?'

He swallowed, his mouth drier than he'd ever known it. She was leading him down a path, one he'd spent the last three years avoiding. Maybe not all the three years. But the symptoms had started pretty soon after his father's funeral. They peaked and troughed. Just like now. Whenever he actually tried to focus some thoughts about what actually might be wrong, the symptoms intensified. Just as they did whenever he was due leave and might actually have to go home. Taking a call from Gibbs was always a relief.

It was almost like getting a licence for a few hours' sleep again.

'I can say it out loud if you can't.' There was definite sadness in her voice.

He'd disappointed her. Her hero doc wasn't a hero at all.

He was just a guy who couldn't hold it together.

She touched his cheek and shook her head. 'But I don't

know if that will help.' She lowered her gaze. 'It was the Admiral, wasn't it? It was seeing him. If I'd known that you knew him…' Her voice tailed off.

'You wouldn't have invited him?' The words came out much angrier than he'd intended.

She jerked and looked back at him. 'I would have warned you,' she said softly.

He cringed and closed his eyes. She might as well take a huge banner saying *Sullivan is depressed* and hang it from the palace.

He stood up and fastened the buttons on his shirt, grabbing his jacket and shrugging it back on. 'I need some space.'

She stood up next to him and nodded, her expression hurt. He didn't mean to be blunt but he couldn't help it. There was no way he could go back into that room full of people. It didn't matter that they had no clue what had just happened.

He knew.

Gabrielle knew.

That was more than enough people already.

Gabrielle picked up her skirt and took a few steps towards the entrance of the summerhouse. She turned back to look at him and licked her lips. 'I'm here for you, Sullivan. I care.' It was almost a whisper. Then she turned on her heel and disappeared through the trees.

Sullivan sagged backwards against the glass. How could she care? How could she care about a man who wasn't really a man?

It didn't matter that he was a doctor. It didn't matter that he knew the fundamentals of depression. He'd recognised grief, depression, anxiety and PTSD in a number of his colleagues in Afghanistan.

He just couldn't apply the same principles to himself.

This shouldn't happen to him. This shouldn't be his life.

But even as the thoughts crowded his head he knew how ridiculous they were. Depression could strike anyone, at any point, at any age, under any set of circumstances.

Gabrielle had vanished through the trees. His heart twisted in his chest.

He loved her. He wanted to love her.

But in order to do that fully, he had to deal with his own issues. He had to face up to the fact he wasn't infallible. He wasn't unbreakable.

Otherwise he could let the best thing that had ever happened to him slip through his fingers.

CHAPTER TEN

BEING A PRINCESS SUCKED.

Gabrielle didn't want to be in a room smiling vacantly at visiting dignitaries and listening politely to their conversation. She wanted to be with the person who needed her right now.

The pain in his eyes had felt as if it had ripped her heart out of her chest. His struggle to accept he wasn't perfect. He wasn't the person who could do and be everything.

She didn't want that for Sullivan. She'd never gone looking for a hero.

But Sullivan was too proud. He needed time. He needed space. She couldn't be his doctor. She just had to be his friend.

And that was hard. She was used to fixing people.

But this wasn't something she could fix. She couldn't stick a plaster on his grief and magic it away.

He had to find that path himself. She only hoped he would let her walk it with him.

Sleep was becoming the invincible soldier. Too far from his grasp to really get hold of. When Arun knocked on his door after the break of day it was a welcome relief.

If he'd heard anything about last night he didn't show

it. 'Dr Darcy, I just wondered what your plans were for the day.'

Sullivan rubbed the sleep from his eyes. He'd glanced in the mirror when he'd splashed water on his face earlier and knew they were bloodshot, ringed with black circles. He looked as if he'd gone ten rounds with a champion boxer.

The trouble was, his body felt as if he'd done ten rounds too. 'I just planned on going to the hospital to review my patients. Nothing else. Did you have something else in mind?'

His answer came out automatically. He was a doctor. Of course he would go and review his patients. But was that really what he should be doing?

His mind had been haunted half the night with the sad expression on Gabrielle's face as she'd walked away. She'd said she cared. Cared. It was a cryptic word.

He could have told her that he wanted to be free to love her. He could have told her that he *did* love her. But he didn't want to go into this relationship damaged. He wanted to feel as if he could commit to Gabrielle. She deserved that. She deserved to have someone by her side who could support her in everything she did. Was he capable of that right now?

Last night, he'd had his first-ever panic attack when he'd came across someone in his father's old dress uniform. It was clear he had a long way to go. Even if he was only admitting that now.

Arun was leaning against the doorjamb, giving him a cheeky kind of grin. 'We chatted about the free clinics before in Mirinez. How would you feel about giving a helping hand today?'

His stomach did a kind of flip. He could find Gabrielle. They could talk about last night. He could sit for a few hours and re-evaluate his life. His plan. He could book a ticket home and spend some time—some real time—at the house he'd been avoiding. He could find another doctor—or a counsellor—to give him steps to help him deal with his grief.

Old habits were hard to break.

Work was always a welcome distraction. He gave Arun a nod of his head, reached for a T-shirt and pulled it over his head. 'Let me brush my teeth and I'm all yours.'

She couldn't interfere. She couldn't.

But every single cell in her body wanted to interfere in every way possible.

She knew people. People who could help Sullivan if he'd let them.

She wanted to take him by the hand and lead him to that first appointment. Or be the person who sat down next to him while he just talked. She wanted to look at Sullivan's face and not notice the dark circles under his eyes and know that he'd barely slept any of the night before.

She'd walked along to his apartments earlier and found the door wide open and the place empty. For a few seconds panic had descended. He'd left. He'd walked out.

It didn't matter that she knew she could never keep him here. The thought of Sullivan leaving without a word hurt more than she could comprehend.

She'd rushed into the rooms, glimpsed the rumpled unmade bed, a drawer hanging open, and felt as if a cold wind had just rushed over her skin. But his toiletries were still in the bathroom, his backpack still in the cupboard next to his kicked-in baseball boots. Relief washed over her. He was still here—somewhere.

She made a few casual enquiries via the security staff and found out Sullivan had gone somewhere with Arun.

St George's was quiet. The staff here were ruthlessly efficient. All the patients from the mining accident were well taken care of. Some were ready to be discharged. Her reviews took less than hour. In truth, these patients could be handed over to the care of the other doctors now, but she was enjoying her time here. She was trying to fathom out a way whereby she could keep working as a doctor, as well as function as Head of State.

Every day the list of urgent things to do seemed to diminish just a little. Several of the key issues had been resolved solely by hosting the state banquet and talking to colleagues face to face. Which meant that ultimately she would have time to take a breath and decide how to manage her life.

One of the nurses gave her a wave. 'There's a call for you, Princess Gabrielle. Do you want to take it here?'

She nodded and reached over for the phone, then paused, unsure what title she should use. She shook her head then went with her instincts. 'This is Dr Cartier, what can I do for you?'

Sullivan's voice washed over her like a warming balm. 'Gabrielle. I think you might need to come down to one of the community clinics. I'm almost certain I've got a case of TB for you.'

'You're working?' She couldn't hide the surprise in her voice and cringed as soon as the words came out loudly.

'Of course I'm working. What else would I be doing?'

She winced. She could almost see the expression on his face as he said those words. 'Nothing. Of course. Which clinic are you in?'

She scribbled down a few notes about the patient. 'I

can be there soon. Arrange for an X-ray in the meantime and I'll be there soon.'

'There's another thing. I've got two children who'll need some attention. One boy has symptoms of appendicitis. He needs scans and probably surgery today. And there's another with a previously undiagnosed cleft palate. He's almost four and has problems with eating and with his speech. It's not an emergency but this should have been picked up at birth. The family have no insurance. I'm not leaving a child like this.'

She could hear the frustration in his voice and instantly sympathised. She took a second, remembering where the clinic was situated, compared to the nearest hospital with facilities for children. 'Okay, tell Arun the kids will be going to St Ignatius's. I'll phone and make the arrangements. How sick is your first little boy? Do you need an ambulance to transfer him?'

She could hear a conversation going on between Sullivan and Arun.

Something inside her recoiled. That inbuilt ethic—a doctor instantly putting his patients first and treating them. She would never expect anything else from Sullivan.

But she was also aiding Sullivan's avoidance.

If she'd known he was going to work at the community clinic this morning she could have offered to go in his place. But then he would probably have been offended.

She just didn't know what to do. She just wasn't sure how to help. If she pushed him towards therapy or medication he might walk away. He might think she was interfering. And she would be.

Was that allowed?

All she knew was that she didn't want to see Sullivan suffer any more. But how did she help all that if she couldn't interfere—just a little?

She grabbed her coat and bag, signalling to Mikel that she wanted to leave. The Corborre clinic was only ten minutes from here. But as soon as she reached the car, a call came through from Franz.

'Princess Gabrielle, you're needed at the palace urgently.'

She sat forward in her seat. 'What's wrong? Something else at the mine?'

Franz hesitated. 'No. We've made some further...discoveries.'

'Discoveries?'

She had no idea where this was heading.

'About Prince Andreas.'

Her stomach rolled over. 'Has something happened to him? Is he all right? Do you know where he is?'

She heard Franz sigh. 'No. We still haven't tracked him down. We have heard some rumours he's in Bermuda.'

'Bermuda?' Why would he go there? 'So what's wrong, then?'

'It might be better to discuss that in person.'

Gabrielle felt her heart sink. She could only imagine what would come next. 'Actually, Franz, I'm on my way to see a patient at the Corborre clinic. Whatever it is that Andreas has done, just tell me.'

In her head she could hear the drum roll. Franz finally spoke. 'It seems that the one million euros wasn't entirely accurate. We've found another account with diverted funds. To a bank—'

'In Bermuda,' she finished. She leaned forward and put her head in her hands. Franz hadn't continued and the silence was ominous.

'What else?'

'We think there are a number of items missing from the palace.'

She wrinkled her brow. 'What do you mean?'

Franz cleared his throat. 'There's another safe—one that Prince Andreas used privately.'

Gabrielle nodded. 'Yes, it's in the study in my apartments. I haven't even looked at it. Was something in there?'

'The Moroccan diamond and the Plantagenet emerald.'

'What?' Beside her, Mikel jumped at the shrillness of her voice.

'But they're family heirlooms.' The Moroccan diamond was over thirty-five carats and the emerald over forty carats. They'd been part of the family collection for hundreds of years and had moved between royal sceptres and crowns.

'We think there might also be a missing painting and…some other items.'

She leaned back and put her hand on her forehead. She could only imagine what the missing items might be. The palace was full of gorgeous pieces that had been received over the last few hundred years. Fabergé eggs, Ming vases, medieval tapestries, Egyptian artefacts and even some of Henry VIII's armour.

'I want an inventory started immediately,' she said. 'And I want advice from the palace lawyers. This can't be kept secret for long. If I have to issue a warrant for my brother's arrest, I will.'

There seemed to be a stunned silence at the end of the phone. Gabrielle closed her eyes and shook her head. 'We'll talk later. I have patients to see.'

She finished the call.

She would give anything right now to be back in Narumba with Sullivan. Before she'd known she had to be Head of State. Before he'd known she was a princess. And before she'd known that the man she loved was crippled by grief.

It was selfish. She knew that. And the instant the thought appeared she pushed it aside. Things were just overwhelming her.

The brother she'd loved and grown up with had betrayed her and their country for purely selfish motives. She still couldn't quite believe it.

No wonder she'd spent the last three years in a totally different world. One where patients were the central focus, instead of the welfare of a whole country. She'd never wanted that life back more than she did at this moment.

She watched as the city streets flashed by her window. In an ideal world she'd tell Sullivan exactly what her brother had done. But he already had enough to deal with. He didn't need her problems too.

The transfer of the children went relatively smoothly. Sullivan was greeted by yet another hospital administrator who re-checked his credentials more times than entirely necessary and made him sign what felt like a billion forms.

Appendicitis was quickly confirmed with one of the boys and Sullivan scrubbed in with one of the hospital's regular surgeons to perform the surgery. The other little boy had some tests ordered and a review by an ENT specialist, who scheduled him for surgery the following day.

Sullivan waited until the little boy with appendicitis was in Recovery and had woken up before he left.

He waved off Arun as he offered to take him back to

the palace. 'I'm going to go back to the clinic. Let me walk. It will do me good and I'll see some of the city.'

Arun gave him a careful nod and disappeared.

Night was just starting to fall in Chabonnex. The streets were bathed in a mixture of orange lights and purple hues from the sky. People were moving around. It was easy to spot the tourists. Cameras and phones were permanently in their hands and most of them were talking loudly.

St Ignatius's was on the outskirts of the city centre. There were still some buildings of interest nearby, but as he moved along the street it was clear he was moving towards a less affluent area of the capital.

The buildings were just a little shabbier, houses more crammed together. Restaurants were fewer and the cars parked on the street were changing from ridiculously expensive to something that the average man might be able to afford.

His phone rang as he approached the clinic. He hadn't thought to check what the hours of the clinic were but as the lights gleamed in the distance it was clear that people were still inside.

He glanced at the screen as he pulled the phone from his pocket.

Gibbs.

His breath caught in his throat.

His finger paused over the green light. It would be so easy to push the phone back in his pocket and ignore the call.

It would be even easier to answer and just automatically say yes to the next mission. That's what he'd always done before.

After his panic attack last night he'd more or less left

himself open to scrutiny by Gabrielle. She would ask. She would pry. She would try to fix him.

In a way it was ironic. He'd come to Mirinez to support her. To help her in a difficult situation. He didn't like it when things were reversed.

He could jump on a plane right now and be in another country in a matter of hours. Forget about all of this. Pretend it had never happened.

His footsteps slowed as he pressed answer and put the phone to his ear. 'Gibbs, it's Sullivan. What is it this time?'

'Sullivan, it's great to get you. Listen, I know you're just back but I'm a man short for a specialist mission in Syria. We need an experienced surgeon and your language skills would be a huge bonus.'

Sullivan could feel an uncomfortable prickle on his skin, like a million little insects crawling all over him. His tongue was stuck to the roof of his mouth, his mind spinning.

Yes, yes, of course I'll go. It's just one more mission. I'm needed. I can make a difference.

A bead of sweat ran down his brow. He wiped it away angrily.

I can sort this other stuff out later. I'll take a proper break after the next mission. I'll take some time away then. I've lasted this long.

'So you would leave probably some time in the next twenty-four hours. No need to ask where you are. I've seen you in the press. Such a shame about Gabrielle. We hate to lose her. She's one of the best doctors we've got for TB. I'll need to find about flights from Mirinez. What's the name of the airport there?'

He stopped walking. He couldn't breathe now. He

wasn't having another panic attack, but saying no just wasn't in his blood—not in his nature.

He tried to breathe out, to get rid of the choked feeling in his throat. His first thought had been that his father would never say no to a mission. He may not have been a doctor but as a commander, captain, then an admiral the US military had been in his blood.

He'd already stopped walking but now his feet were rooted to the ground. A cold breeze swept over him, chilling him more than it should.

But his father had said no. Of course he had. When his mother had died his father had refused to be stationed anywhere without his son. It just hadn't really occurred to him before now what his father might *actually* have said no to.

Gibbs was still talking incessantly. 'Sullivan? Sullivan? Have we got a bad signal?'

Sullivan sucked in a deep breath. 'No.'

'No? You can hear me?'

'No, we don't have a bad signal. And, no, I'm sorry, I can't come. I'm not available.'

'You're not? But…' Gibbs sounded so stunned he just stopped in mid-sentence.

Sullivan still really, really wanted to say yes but he kept talking. 'Sorry, Gibbs. I've worked for almost three straight years. I need some time off. I need a break. I have a few things to sort out. I'll get back in touch with you when I'm ready to come back.' He closed his eyes as he kept talking. 'I will come back. I want to. I'll let you know when.'

He pulled the phone away from his ear and ended the call. He wasn't quite sure what else Gibbs would have said, but he knew he didn't need to hear it. He could claim a poor signal at a later date if need be.

What was important was he'd said no.

He stared at the phone for a second, then pressed the off switch. His hand gave the slightest shake. The urge to phone back was strong.

He looked over at the lights on in the clinic. He could see lots of people through the windows. Was the clinic usually this busy at night?

He strode across the road. He'd talk to Gabrielle soon. He'd tell her what he'd done, then figure out what came next.

For now, there were patients. And he was a doctor.

The waiting room was packed. She had two nurses working with her at the clinic. They were used to being here—she wasn't. The equipment in the community clinic was embarrassing, some so old it was falling apart. The prescription medicine cabinet only had the bare essentials. The computer system was antiquated. All things she would deal with.

It seemed that Sullivan had already had these thoughts. She'd found a list he'd started in the room he'd been working in.

It was long.

She'd worked in countries all over the world with less-than-perfect equipment—she just hadn't expected to find it here in Mirinez. A luxurious tax haven.

Her desk was covered with mounds of paper. 'What on earth are you doing, and who are all these patients?'

Sullivan was standing in the doorway, pointing out to the waiting room full of patients.

She ran her fingers through her hair. It had long escaped from the ponytail she'd tied on top of her head. She sighed and gave her eyes a rub. She was going to ask him for help. She had to. But was that fair?

'The case you thought was TB?'

He nodded as he walked across the room and stood at the other side of the desk.

She nodded her head. 'Oh, it's definitely TB. But when I took a history I realised I'd just opened a can of worms. I've found another five definite.' She rummaged through her paperwork. 'Twelve probable.' She held up her hand again. 'And about another twenty still to review.'

Her phone buzzed and she ignored it. He must have caught the expression on her face. 'Something else going on?'

She couldn't. She just couldn't tell him that. Probably because if he asked her a single question about her brother she was likely to dissolve into floods of tears. She had to be strong. She had to keep on top of things. How could she help Sullivan if she couldn't control her emotions?

She shook her head. 'Nothing I can't deal with.'

He picked up some of the paperwork. 'What do you need?'

Everything about this was wrong. That was the question that she should be asking him right now, not the other way about. But what was worse was that she had to accept his help, even though she knew he needed help himself.

'Patient histories. Detailed patient histories. Chest X-rays read. Chests sounded. Treatment decisions—and maybe even a few admissions to hospital.'

She winced. 'My language skills haven't exactly helped. My Italian just isn't good enough. I don't speak Greek at all. As for Japanese? I just don't have a clue.' She was embarrassed to admit it. 'I've got one of the security guards out there, taking a history, because he knows a bit of Greek.'

Sullivan just gave a nod. But something was different.

She could tell. When he'd been thrown into the breach in Narumba, into an area he'd been totally unfamiliar with, he'd been enthusiastic and motivated for the task. He hadn't worried about being a fish out of water. He'd just got on with things.

This time he just looked resigned to the fact he had to help. There wasn't the passion in his eyes. There wasn't the same cheeky glimmer.

She stood up and walked over, placing her hands on his chest.

'I'm sorry. I'm sorry I'm putting you in this position today. I know this isn't a good time.'

'What's that supposed to mean?' he snapped, then visibly winced at his own words and stepped back.

He looked wounded. 'Do you think I'm not capable of doing the job?'

She shook her head fiercely. 'Of course I don't. You're one of the best doctors I've ever worked with.' She couldn't hide the passion in her voice. She looked into his hurt pale green eyes. All she wanted to do was pull him closer, to wrap her arms around his neck and feel his heartbeat next to hers.

She lowered her voice. 'I want to keep working with you, Sullivan. I hope to keep working with you for a very long time.'

Her voice was trembling. It felt as if she was wearing her heart on her sleeve.

His gaze locked with hers. She stopped breathing. She just didn't know what would come next.

Her phone buzzed again and she could almost see the shutters coming down in his eyes. He picked up a pile of the paperwork. 'Let me deal with the Italian, Greek and Japanese patients. The histories and exams won't take long. I'll let you know if I have any queries or want to admit someone.'

The phone buzzing was incessant. Whatever it was, it wasn't going to go away.

He frowned. 'Is there something else?'

She shook her head automatically. 'No. Thanks so much for your help with this.'

He nodded and walked out the room.

Her heart squeezed inside her chest. Why did none of this feel right? She felt so torn. A country to serve. A man who deserved her support and love.

Why was it so hard to do both?

It was the oddest feeling in the world. He was talking to patients in multiple languages and taking patient histories. He listened to chests, reviewed X-rays, prescribed treatment regimes. He listened to their social problems around overcrowding and suitable housing and made multiple notes for Gabrielle.

He just had to look at her to know how much he wanted to be with her. But that only emphasised the numbness around his heart. It was almost as if it were encased with a wall of ice.

He wanted to think, he wanted to feel, he wanted to love. But now he'd realised how long he'd ignored his underlying grief, it had brought everything else to the surface. He had to move on.

He wanted to take the steps so he could plan for the future—plan for a future with Gabrielle.

He just couldn't find a way to put the words in his mouth. There were so many barriers. All his experience, all his medical training and he couldn't find the words. The weirdest thing of all was the fact that he knew that if he were the patient sitting in front of himself now—even though it wasn't his specialist area—he'd know exactly what to advise. It felt ironic that he actually had some insight into himself.

It was like everything had been brought to a head. Now he'd reached the point of realisation he had to act.

He signed his last prescription and checked the final set of notes.

He had to talk to Gabrielle. He had to tell her what he was going to do.

He loved her. He had to tell her that too.

But no. In order to feel free to love her, he had to deal with the things he'd pushed aside. The thought of going home made him feel sick. He'd avoided the place for so long and he'd built it up in his head so much that the thought of going back filled him with dread.

It was ridiculous—irrational—and he knew that.

How could he love Gabrielle when there was so much standing in his way?

And what if he couldn't shake off the aura that had surrounded him for the last few years? It didn't matter that he loved Gabrielle—was he truly worthy of her? Could he stand by her side and help her shoulder the burden of her role?

The truth was he wasn't sure. He had doubts. Not about Gabrielle, just about himself.

Was he really living up to the expectations that his father would have had of him? His insides coiled. He was letting down his father. He was letting down Gabrielle.

Right now, he couldn't give her any false hope, make any false promises.

The best thing he could do right now was leave.

He stood up and looked around the clinic. It was finally quiet.

He could hear Gabrielle's voice coming from the other

room. She must still have a patient with her so he would have to wait until she was finished.

He tidied his paperwork and walked along the corridor. But Gabrielle's room was empty except for her. She was pacing back and forth, the phone pressed against her ear. 'What? How much? Have you spoken to the lawyers? What about the draft press statement that I prepared?' As he watched, a tear slid down her cheek. 'What do you mean, I'm not allowed to talk about it?'

She brushed the tear away angrily as she continued to pace. 'Is that what this has come to? I can be sued for how much?'

She stopped pacing. Her face was pale. He walked across the room towards her and put his hands on her shoulders, his expression asking the question for him.

She looked stricken but as soon as she realised he'd been listening she turned her back and walked away.

It was like a door slamming, being shut out completely. The person he wanted to reach out and actually talk to was obviously overwhelmed by something else entirely.

She didn't need any more pressure. She needed someone who could support her in the role she was struggling with. The last thing Gabrielle needed was a weight around her neck like Sullivan Darcy. At least that was how he felt at the moment.

What did he know about running a country?

He stepped back. The best thing he could do right now was give Gabrielle the space she needed to feel out her role.

He wanted to be the person by her side, but he didn't feel ready to offer her what she deserved. And whatever it was she was dealing with, it was obvious she didn't want to share it with him.

He gritted his teeth as she stood with her back to him, talking quietly.

He wasn't angry with her. He was angry with himself.

He'd never felt like this about someone before and was almost overwhelmed by how much it took the breath from his lungs.

He wanted to be better for *her*.

She was still struggling with being Head of State. It could be that she'd decide this was a role she couldn't fulfil. He'd love her whatever her decision was. She wasn't Princess Gabrielle to him. She was just Gabrielle. And he'd take her in whatever form she came.

If she'd have him. But right now—this second? What could he offer her?

He took a deep breath.

It was time to take the steps to get better.

It was time to go.

The call took for ever. It seemed the palace legal advisors were very nervous about the outcome of the Prince Andreas situation.

She was furious. Frustrated. She didn't want to keep secrets. She hated being told that saying a single word about what had happened could lead to the palace being sued for millions.

She glanced over her shoulder. She felt so torn.

She wanted to deal with this. She wanted everything out in the open. She wanted Andreas held accountable for his actions. She wanted to be able to tell Sullivan what was going on.

Andreas should be punished. Those items didn't belong to him. Those jewels weren't his to take. And the money—the diverted funds—*definitely* weren't his to take. If she could climb on the plane to Bermuda right now and grab him with her own hands, she would.

But there was also a sinking feeling in her stomach. He could never come back now. The role of Head of State and Princess Gabrielle would always be hers.

It was a change of a whole mindset. A change of her life's ambitions.

But working alongside Sullivan towards the end of this week had made her realise that she could make the adjustments she needed. It might be tricky. It might be tough. But if she worked hard at the balance she should be able to work as a doctor as well as fulfil the role of Head of State.

But deep down she knew she wanted to do that with Sullivan by her side.

Working in the community clinic made her even more determined. She could see the holes in their current systems. She could work to change things and improve the healthcare for the general population. She didn't doubt Sullivan would want to help her with that. She would never ask him to give up his missions. Part of her ached that she wouldn't be able to do them any more.

But maybe he would be willing to combine time with her and time with Doctors Without Borders. If they both wanted to, they could make this work.

The lawyer was still talking incessantly in her ear. She couldn't take another minute of this. She needed to talk to Sullivan. She cut him off. 'Check into our extradition treaties. I have no idea about them—but we must have some. Bermuda is a British overseas territory. If we don't have one, see if we can request Andreas's expulsion or lawful return. Find a way to make this work. If you need me to speak to the Governor, I will.'

She hung up the phone.

She needed to deal with this as quickly as possible. She wanted to spend time with Sullivan. She wanted to show him the same support that he'd shown her. It was obvious he'd been pushing things away for a long time. He needed someone by his side. Her heart and head told her that should be her.

She walked out of the office, her footsteps echoing through the clinic in an ominous way. 'Sullivan?'

The space seemed completely empty.

She glanced into the empty consulting room opposite her and walked through to the waiting room. One of the security staff was standing at the main door. 'Do you know where Sullivan is?'

He looked over his shoulder. 'He left ten minutes ago.'

Her stomach clenched. Something about this seemed wrong. It was the picture she had in her mind. The expression on his face. One part hurt, one part blankness.

'Did he say where he was going?'

The security guy shook his head. She walked back through to the office and picked up her bag. She'd arranged to admit three patients to one of the hospitals. Her medical instincts were overwhelming. She should go and speak to the staff about treatment plans, review their conditions.

One of the patients had been someone Sullivan had assessed. It could be that he'd decided to go and follow up. But in her heart of hearts she knew he would have spoken to her if that had been his plan.

She climbed into the car outside the clinic. 'Take me back to the palace first. I'll go the hospital later.'

The driver nodded. She couldn't sit still. Her hands were shaking. She needed to speak to Sullivan. She wanted to tell him that she loved him. She wanted to tell him she would be by his side the whole time.

By the time she reached the palace she could barely breathe. She ran inside and upstairs to where his apartments were. From the end of the corridor she could see the open door.

Her heart thudded in her chest as she reached the bedroom. This time the cupboard doors were open. His suit and dress uniform were still hanging inside. The drawers in the dresser were empty, the bathroom bare.

Bile rose in the back of her throat.

Arun appeared at her side. 'Princess, is something wrong?'

She spun around. 'Where is he? Where has he gone?'

Arun winced. She could tell by one look that he knew everything.

He spoke carefully. 'He said he had something to deal with. Something he had to deal with on his own.' His voice softened. 'He's gone, Gabrielle. I'm sorry.'

She stepped back. It was the first time Arun had ever just called her by her name. He'd always used her title before.

She could see the sympathy on his face.

Tears welled up in her eyes. She couldn't do this without Sullivan. She didn't want to do this without him.

She clenched her fists. Andreas. This was all his fault. It wasn't enough that he'd tried to destroy their country. Now his behaviour could ruin her relationship with the man she loved.

She sucked in a deep breath.

No. No more.

Tears poured down her face. This wasn't really about Andreas.

This was about her.

She should have acted sooner. She should have told

Sullivan how she felt about him. Asked him how he truly felt about her.

But now she knew.

The love she had in her heart for him wasn't echoed in his. Or, if it was, he still didn't want to be here with her.

He'd left with no explanation. He'd known she was busy. He hadn't even taken the time to talk to her.

But was that true?

He'd seen her on the phone. She'd been so over-whelmed she hadn't realised that those were the few seconds she'd really needed to break the call and talk to him.

Whether she'd meant to or not, she might have pushed him away.

She looked out of the window at the city below her. How on earth could she rule all of this? Her heart had hoped that Sullivan would be by her side. All the insecurities she'd had before were now bubbling to the surface.

It was time for her to take stock. To take charge.

To prioritise. She had to sort out her country. She had to function and serve as Head of State. It was time to fulfil the role that she'd inherited.

She watched the movement in the view below her. In a city full of people she'd never felt so alone.

She rubbed her hands up and down her arms as the tears continued to flow down her cheeks.

Alone.

The ache in her heart would never lessen.

She couldn't walk away from her country.

It seemed she had to walk away from her heart.

CHAPTER ELEVEN

TWENTY HOURS LATER he was beyond exhausted.

Stepping off the plane at almost four in the morning, Oregon time, he couldn't figure out if he should be awake or asleep.

The drive from the airport took just over an hour. The suburbs disappeared quickly, replaced by the rolling hills, greenery and trees he'd been so used to.

His stomach lurched as everything grew more familiar. Even though the temperature in the car hadn't changed, all the tiny hairs on the back of his neck stood on end.

As he ventured down the long drive he closed his eyes for the briefest of seconds. He just knew. He just knew as soon as he rounded the corner what he would see.

The traditional detached five-bed house sat on the edge of the scenic three-acre lake. The Cape Cod styled home with its wraparound porch and large single deck had a panoramic view of the lake, its large windows glinting in the orange sunrise. A three-stall horse barn with tack room and fenced pasture was behind the house, leading off to riding trails. It didn't matter the stalls had been empty for more than five years; if he breathed in right now, his senses would remember the smell. On the other side of the acreage was an orchard. Even from here he could see that his neighbour had kept good care of it after their handshake a few years ago.

As the car got closer, the details became clearer. The fishing dock at the front of house. The fire pit with custom pavers. The traditional dark wood door.

Perspiration started to trickle down his spine as he swung the car up in front of the house. He didn't want to get out. He didn't want to go inside.

His hands clenched the steering wheel and he just breathed. In. Out. In. Out.

The last time he'd actually gone to the diner just down the road and sat there for hours and hours. He'd eaten lunch and dinner, then nursed a cup of coffee that hadn't even been that good before he'd finally taken the road home under cover of darkness. He was tempted to do it all again today.

Gabrielle's face flashed in front of his face.

It was enough to make him open his eyes. He stared at one of the windows in the house. The pale yellow drapes moved a little. Was someone inside?

Before he knew it he was out of the car and trying the front door. It didn't open. He rattled it. Then pulled the key from his pocket, turning it swiftly and stepping inside.

Silence. A waft of vanilla and peach. This wasn't the normal aroma of the house. Wood polish was what he remembered.

He looked around, holding his breath.

The sun was rising higher in the sky, sending a beam of light streaming through the window. Each window had a stained-glass inset at the top, and shards of shimmering green, purples and reds lit up the white walls around him.

Each footstep on the wooden floor echoed along the

hallway. His head flicked from side to side, listening to the silence.

He strode through to the main room, eyes fixing on the curtains. There was still a tiny flicker of movement left in the yellow drapes. The room looked untouched. Comfortable cream recliners and sofas with wooden frames. Familiar paintings on the wall. If he closed his eyes right now he'd see his father sitting in his favourite chair.

His skin on his right arm prickled. He felt air. A breeze, carrying in the smell of peaches and vanilla from the orchard outside.

He turned and strode through to the kitchen. There. A small hopper window was open at the back of the house near the orchard, letting fresh air into the room. His finger ran along the counter top and he frowned as he looked at it.

Clean. No dust.

What the…?

Something washed over him. A realisation. When he'd shaken hands with his neighbour about the orchard he'd handed over an emergency key, just in case of fire or flood. Matt's wife, Alice, obviously occasionally looked over the place. They were a kind-hearted young couple who'd moved here with their kids to build a new life. His dad had liked them immediately. He would have to say thank you.

He stared about him. The maple staircase was almost beckoning. Calling him upstairs. His muscles tensed. So many memories were all around.

He moved to the foot of the stairs and rested his palm on the hand rail. His body jerked. An involuntary action. As if someone had just stuck their hand through his chest and grabbed hold of his heart with an icy grasp.

I can do this. I can do this. I can do this.

He started whispering the mantra out loud that was echoing around his head.

He'd done this before. He'd been up the stairs in the house after his father had died. He'd spent the night here before. Had he slept? Not a bit.

None of these were first times.

But he'd been so shuttered. It was almost like walking around in a plastic bubble, storing all the emotions inside so tightly it was almost as if they weren't there.

Today his emotions were front and centre. There was no barrier. No camouflage.

His hand trembled on the rail. His feet started moving slowly and steadily up the stairs. There was nothing to fear up here. There was no bogeyman. No axe murderer.

There were just a million memories of a man he'd loved and adored.

A father who'd centred his life around his son. Who'd adjusted his career. Who'd told him a thousand stories about his mother to try and keep her memory alive. There had never been a step-mom. His dad had always said his heart belonged to one woman.

And Sullivan understood that now.

He'd met Gabrielle. The picture in his head was of her dancing in the tent in her cut-off shorts and pink T-shirt, shimmying to the music. Even now it brought a smile to his lips. He wanted to get to the point where he could tell Gabrielle what she was to him. That she was the sun, moon and stars—never mind a princess. He had no idea if she would find him worthy. He could only live in hope.

His feet were still moving, automatically taking him to the door of his father's room. It was wide open, inviting him in.

There was no aroma of peaches and vanilla up here.

He moved slowly across the room. His hand shook as

he reached for the handle on the wardrobe. He jerked it open and within seconds the smell hit him full in the face.

He staggered, not quite ready to deal with the overwhelming rush of feeling that flooded through his system.

There were all the clothes. Hanging there, waiting. Waiting for his father to reach out and pick something out to put on. The button-down shirts. The pants. The jackets.

And the uniforms.

He reached out and touched the blue sleeve. The feel of the fabric shot a pulse of memories straight to his brain. He could see his father's smile and laughing eyes as he'd proudly worn the dress uniform. If he went downstairs right now he'd find a hundred pictures of the two of them in uniform together. His father had once made it out to Helmand Province. His all-time favourite picture of them both was one that a friend had snapped with a phone. It was of the two of them sitting on a block of concrete surrounded by the dirt of Afghanistan, hats at their feet and laughing as if a famous comedian was putting on a private show for them both.

One snap immortalised their whole relationship for Sullivan. Fun, love and mutual respect.

He staggered backwards and landed on the bed.

And then he sobbed.

CHAPTER TWELVE

HER HEART WAS wound so tightly in her chest it felt as if it could explode.

Three weeks. Three weeks of hearing nothing from Sullivan. She was pretty sure that he'd turned his phone off.

Arun had tracked his flights. She didn't know how and she wasn't going to ask any questions but Sullivan had gone to the place he should have—home.

Sleep had been a complete stranger these last three weeks. The first night she could smell his aftershave on the neighbouring pillow. She'd swapped it immediately with her own then had spent the rest of night hanging onto it for dear life.

She was determined. She had a duty, one that she would fulfil.

But she had another duty, one for herself and the man she loved.

Her rigid stance and feisty personality had meant that for the last few weeks her palace staff had seen a whole new side to Princess Gabrielle.

The advisors and lawyers were now firmly in their places.

But Gabrielle had discovered skills she hadn't even known she possessed. She'd been determined Andreas was going to be held to account for his actions and, thankfully, the government in Bermuda agreed.

She strode through to the room that had been specially set up in the palace. Her dark curls were pinned back into a bun and she'd asked for her make-up to be heavier than normal. She wanted her appearance to reflect exactly how she was feeling. This situation was serious.

She nodded at Franz. 'Everything ready?'

A look of panic crossed his face. He turned to the director. 'Well, we have to practise lighting and sound checks and set-up and—'

Gabrielle held up her hand. She narrowed her eyes and looked at the director. 'I expect all of these things to have been carried out. I'm ready. Are you?'

The room was silent. She walked around to the desk set up in front of the camera and sat down, taking a few seconds to adjust the seat and microphone.

She looked straight into the camera. 'There's no rehearsal. I don't need one. Let's begin.'

There was a flurry of activity. People took their places instantly. She wasn't trying to be scary. She was just trying to be direct. Her patience was spent.

After a couple of minutes the director gave her a nod. 'Princess Gabrielle, if you're ready, we're ready. I'll count you down.'

She nodded. The director gave a wave and spoke loudly. 'Three, two, one and go.'

Gabrielle took a deep breath. Her heart was thumping wildly but everything in her head was crystal clear.

'Good evening, citizens of Mirinez. As you know, I'm Princess Gabrielle, your new Head of State. You are all aware that this role is new to me. I've spent the last three years working as a physician specialising in TB medicine for Doctors Without Borders in various places across the world. I never thought the role of Head of State in Mirinez would be one I would have to fulfil. However, with the abdication of Prince Andreas, I have been called into service—this is a role I take seriously and am fully committed to.

'On my arrival back in Mirinez I discovered that a number of duties normally carried out by the Head of State had been neglected. I want to assure you all that since I've arrived, all outstanding matters of state have been dealt with. Unfortunately, I also discovered that some funds had been misappropriated and some national treasures belonging to Mirinez had disappeared. A full inventory has been taken. I've also requested a full and independent investigation of all accounting irregularities. After taking legal advice, a warrant for the arrest and a request for the extradition of Andreas Cartier was made to the government in Bermuda.'

Gabrielle stopped to take a deep breath.

'The warrant was served a few hours ago, the request for extradition granted and arrangements are now being made for the return of Andreas Cartier to Mirinez. A number of items missing from state have also been recovered.'

She kept her back ramrod-straight and didn't let any emotion show on her face.

'Andreas Cartier will be held to account for his actions, just as any citizen of Mirinez would be.'

She licked her lips.

'When I returned to Mirinez many of you will know that I had a friend—a companion—with me. Sullivan Darcy, a respected surgeon and colleague at Doctors Without Borders, helped with this transition in my life. He also assisted at the mining accident, operating on a number of patients. It is my intention to continue working as a doctor, as well as functioning as Head of State. I think that the two duties complement each other and will allow me to keep in touch with our citizens in the most fundamental way—by serving them at one of our community clinics.'

She felt her muscles relax a little, her expression soften.

'I will be gone for the next few days. But I can assure you all matters of state are in hand. What I need to do now is personal. I need to deal with some affairs of the heart.'

She couldn't help but give a small hopeful smile as she ignored all the chins bouncing off the floor in the room around her.

'When I return I will make arrangements for my dual role. And perhaps I will have some other news for the citizens of Mirinez. I ask you all to have patience with me in my time of transition and know that I am committed to doing the best job possible.'

Gabrielle stood up and walked out. Questions raged all around her. But Arun was waiting at the door.

She had one thing on her mind. She'd more or less just worn her heart on her sleeve for the entire world to see.

But she'd meant every word.

It was time to put her heart first. It was time to reach out to the person she loved and be there for him. She'd no idea what he'd say when she got there. She'd no idea what she'd find. But it was time to find out.

Three long weeks. That's how long it had taken to get to this point.

And it had been the longest three weeks of her life.

All the arrangements were in place.

She met Arun's gaze and he gave the briefest nod of his head, and spirited her away.

CHAPTER THIRTEEN

HE'D STARTED TO appreciate the silence. He'd spent so much of his life surrounded by noise and confusion that the silence of the lake was washing over him like a soothing balm. He'd spent the first night sleeping in his father's bed. What amazed him most was that he'd managed a few hours of actual sleep. But he'd woken with the biggest crick in his back in the world. It was clear the mattress needed replacing.

Yesterday he'd managed to take a few things from the wardrobe and chest of drawers and pack them up for goodwill. That had been hard. Every cardigan, every shirt brought back a flash of memory. The uniforms still hung in place. He'd get to them. He would. Just not yet. He wasn't quite ready.

Last week he'd walked around the empty stables. He'd never had a horse. Horses had been his mother's love. But it seemed such a shame that perfectly good stables and paddock were empty.

He'd spent the afternoon nursing a beer, sitting near the orchard and letting the smells of the fruit drift around him.

Today he'd walked over to meet his neighbours. Their children had grown rapidly and it was clear they'd added another as a pram was parked at their front door. He'd welcomed the family's noise around him as they'd chatted about future plans for the orchard.

Tonight he was watching the lake. There were a few boats out there, a few people fishing along the shore. He'd never been much of a fisherman and preferred to just sit with his legs swinging from the dock, contemplating whether he should take a look at the fire pit.

He hadn't turned his phone back on. There was always the chance that Gibbs would call again. He was sure Gabrielle would have called and that made his chest hurt. He wouldn't hide from Gabrielle—not like he'd hidden from this. But a few weeks in Oregon wouldn't fix him. It was just the first steps of a process. The thoughts of a counsellor were now chasing around his head. Some people would classify not dealing with grief as a kind of depression.

Sullivan had thought about it and didn't want to go down a medication route—not even for his lack of sleep. He wanted to deal with this in his own way.

He turned around the looked at the house. The lights were on inside, giving it a warm glow in the dimming evening light. He liked it that way. Any minute now his dad would appear, fold his arms, lean on the doorjamb and ask who was making dinner.

His mouth dried instantly. He took another swig of beer from the chilled bottle in his hand. The memories would always be there. The last thing he wanted to do was chase them away. What he had to learn to do now was let them warm him, instead of leaving him feeling cold.

The emptiness that had been there the last three years didn't seem quite so hollow now.

Gabrielle.

His father would have adored her. He wouldn't quite have believed that Sullivan had not only met a beautiful, courageous fellow doctor but that she'd actually been a secret royal. His father would have spent a lifetime teasing him about that.

Would his father have thought him worthy of Gabrielle? Now he'd started the healing process he could finally be more positive. His father would have encouraged him to find love. Wherever it was.

He looked down at the water rippling around his feet. There was something so reassuring about knowing that the two people he'd loved most in this world would probably have loved each other too. He could picture them all, sitting around the neglected fire pit while his father told her stories of long-ago missions and his clashes with a few well-known characters.

This morning he'd found a black velvet box tucked inside one of his father's shoes. Another of his quirks. It held a ring—a square emerald with a diamond on either side. There had been a tiny folded-up piece of paper inside with his father's writing.

Sullivan—for whoever the next Mrs Darcy might be.

That was all it had said. Nothing more. They'd never had a conversation about his mother's engagement ring. He'd always assumed his mother had been wearing it when she'd been buried. His father had never mentioned it. Never asked if he was planning on having a wife, or a family. Never put any pressure on his son. But the thoughts had obviously been there.

He'd left the ring in the shoe for now. There was only one finger he'd ever want to put it on. And a princess like Gabrielle would probably have a huge amount of jewellery that would be worth so much more.

But when the time was right, he would use the ring to ask the question.

He just wasn't sure when that would be.

Gabrielle was beyond tired. The voice on the satnav was grating. Honestly, if she could meet the person who had that voice, chances were she'd close her hands around their throat. How could you take the next road on the right when it didn't exist?

She'd finally turned it off and just gone with her instincts. Oregon was so much bigger than she'd anticipated, the scenery unexpected.

Rolling green hills, deep valleys, lakes and trees— everywhere. It took some time to get her bearings. The road was lined with trees. There was a calmness about this country, something that just seemed so right.

After about a mile she could see the house ahead emerging through the trees. It was large but inviting, set on the shore of a lake. Her heart leapt in her chest. Even from here she could see the orange lights and the figure sitting on the dock, nursing a beer.

Everything she had ever wanted.

That was her first thought. That was her only thought.

But did he want her?

His head tilted as he heard the noise of the car. He didn't get up, just stayed where he was, smiling.

She pulled the car up outside the house and opened the door. The warm Oregon air surrounded her, welcoming her, while her stomach did huge somersaults.

In her head she would have liked a chance to change and reapply her lipstick. But the world had a different idea. So she pulled her wrinkled yellow patterned dress from her thighs and let the air drift around her.

She wasn't as terrified as she'd been before. Just being

near Sullivan had that effect on her. Even without a word being spoken.

She strolled over to where he sat.

'Hi.' She might not be terrified, but she was still nervous.

'Hi.' There was warmth in his eyes. Calmness.

'Got another one of those?'

'I might have.' He leaned down into the lake at his feet and pulled up another bottle of beer from the water, knocking the cap off on the side of the dock.

She smiled as she kicked off her sandals and sat down next to him, letting out a gasp as her toes touched the water.

He laughed. 'I keep it a special temperature—all for cooling beer.'

'I think you do.' Now she was here, all the great speeches and declarations she'd conjured up in her head seemed to drift up into the purple clouds above them, floating off and laughing at her.

'How are you?' It seemed the best way to start.

He went to answer immediately then stopped. She watched him while her heart played around in her chest. 'I haven't found out yet,' he answered.

She nodded and took a swig from the chilled beer bottle. It was a welcome relief after the long hours of travel. 'Neither have I,' she agreed.

He glanced at her curiously. 'What have you been up to?'

There was no animosity. Just curiosity. He'd obviously wondered what had been happening since he'd left.

She stared out across the lake, reflecting a myriad of colours from the setting sun above. 'You haven't seen the news?'

He gave a half-laugh. 'Haven't you heard? I've put myself in solitude for a while.' He held up his hands. 'Consider this a media-free zone.'

She looked from side to side. 'Seems you picked a prime location.'

He nodded appreciatively. 'I certainly did.'

They sat in silence for a few seconds. It was beautiful here. She hadn't really taken the time to picture this place in her head at all. There hadn't been time. But now she was here? It was like their own little private haven. Secluded from all but a select few.

She pressed her lips together and gave a kind of wry smile.

'I caused a bit of a stir.'

He raised his eyebrows. 'What now?'

His rich voice sent pulses through her body. She locked gazes with him. 'I might have declared that I love you on TV.'

His eyebrows rose. 'You what?'

She stared at her beer for a second. Talking into the camera had seemed easier than this. Impersonal. It wasn't impersonal now.

'I decided some things were worth fighting for.'

His eyes widened and he stared. 'I'm not sure I'm worth fighting for yet.'

She could see confusion in his eyes. Self-doubt.

She held up her hands. 'You're here. You've taken the first step. Let me take the walk with you.'

She could see him swallow. He took a long time to answer. 'I want to tell you something, Gabrielle. I don't have a single doubt in my head or heart how I feel about you. I love you, I know that.' He pressed his hand against his chest. 'But I've shut out some things for so long that I feel unreliable. I've spent so long *not* feeling that it seems as though I have to deal with myself first before I try to move forward.'

She nodded. He'd said the words. He'd said the words she wanted to hear. She should be skipping. She should be happy. And she knew he was sincere. But she also understood.

'Why now?'

He nodded and gave her a rueful kind of smile. 'I guess I wasn't ready before. I think I probably didn't have someone to fight for. I was too busy pushing things away, wallowing, I suppose. I hate myself for that.'

She could see the self-contempt on his face. But he wanted to fight for her. That made her want to sing and shout to the world. 'It's called grief, Sullivan. Don't hate yourself. I have something to fight for too. You. Us. This is where I want to be. I love you too.' She held up her hands and smiled. 'I've told the world.'

She slid her fingers through his, intertwining their hands above his heart.

He met her gaze with his pale green eyes. 'I'm here. But I won't feel better overnight. I have some work to do.'

She nodded. 'And I'll be by your side.' She smiled and tilted her head to the side. 'You saved me, Sullivan. You saved me when I needed it most. You saved me when I was ready to walk away and forget everything. You helped me see that I could do both jobs.' She closed her eyes for a second. 'Hopefully, well.' Then she shook her head. 'But I don't want to do either of them without you. The last three weeks have clarified that for me. I care, Sullivan. I want you to feel well. I want you to get the help you need to say goodbye to your dad.' She reached over and touched his cheek. 'And something you don't know about me is that I'm patient. I can wait.'

He raised his eyebrows. 'Patient? You? Since when?'

She was glad he could still joke with her. She kept her hand where it was. 'I won't pretend this will be easy. You may see a lot of tears. The news I couldn't tell you before was the other part of my speech. Andreas stole from Mirinez. Money, artefacts, who knows what else. After some negotiations he'll be extradited from Bermuda. I'll have to watch my brother be tried in court and sent to prison. I won't pretend with you that in private I won't be breaking my heart and be sobbing about it.'

'Why didn't you tell me?'

She shook her head slowly. 'I was trying to take it all in. I didn't want to believe it at first. The palace advisors kept telling me not to discuss anything. I didn't know what to do.'

'And now you do?'

She smiled. 'I'm starting to find my feet. I'm hoping someone else will be able to give me a bit of balance.'

He turned his head to watch the rippling lake. 'Do you really think we can make this work?'

She nudged him with her shoulder. 'I think this will be messy. I missed you. You've only been gone three weeks. What happens when you're away on a mission?'

It was reality. She knew that once Sullivan felt better he would want to return to work. She'd never stop him. But it would be hard. It was best just to lay it all on the line.

He nodded slowly. 'That's part of the reason my phone's still off. I'm avoiding Gibbs.' He turned towards her. 'There's work to be done in Mirinez at the community clinics. People without insurance will still need surgery. I'd like to think that I can work between Doctors without Borders and the community clinics.'

'You'd do that?' Her heart swelled up in her chest. If Sullivan worked between both, it meant they'd actually spend some time together. Missing him would be hard but knowing he'd be back to work with her would make it so much easier.

His expression was so sincere. 'Of course. If you want me to.' He gave her a smile. 'I can't imagine a day without you, Gabrielle. I just had to know that I had something to offer you.'

She moved, putting both hands around his neck. 'You saved me, Dr Darcy. How about you let me save you right back?'

He smiled as he slid her arms around her waist. 'That sounds like some kind of deal. But how do we seal it?'

She slid her hands through his hair, 'Oh, there's only one way to seal this.' And she tilted her chin up and put her lips to his as the setting sun sent the last of its orange and red rays spilling across the lake.

EPILOGUE

Two years later

'READY?' ADMIRAL SANDS looked even more nervous than she was as he tilted his arm towards her.

She straightened her veil and took a deep breath. 'Absolutely.'

He'd been the perfect choice to walk her down the aisle. With her own father dead and her brother in prison, her options had been somewhat limited. But Joe Sands had been a great support during Sullivan's recovery and he'd become one of their greatest friends. It was the first time in the history of Mirinez that someone had given the bride away and also played the role of best man.

He leaned forward and whispered, 'You look absolutely beautiful, Your Highness. I'm so proud of you both.'

She stood on tiptoe and kissed him on the cheek. 'Thank you, Joe.'

He signalled to the staff at the door of the royal cathedral. The trumpets sounded as the doors opened and they started to walk down the red carpet.

The cathedral was packed. So much for the quiet wedding they'd both wanted.

One of Mirinez's tiaras glittered on her head, as well

as the emerald and diamond engagement ring glittering on her finger. She'd been so touched when Sullivan had proposed with his mother's ring. It had made their closeness even more complete.

Her gown was traditional, covered in lace made by traditional lace-makers in Mirinez, with a long sweeping train. Thank goodness they'd chosen the cooler spring for their wedding instead of summer.

Sullivan was waiting at the top of the aisle. Breaking with tradition, he turned to watch her coming towards him. In his dress uniform, with his tan from his recent mission, she'd never seen him looking so handsome. His face had filled out a little in the last couple of years and she could see the gleam in his pale green eyes even from where she was. That man was so sexy.

She couldn't wait to be his wife.

It was almost like he'd read her mind.

He started walking towards her, ignoring the sharp intake of breath from the wedding guests in the cathedral.

Joe Sands started laughing. 'Never could tell that boy what to do.'

He met them halfway up the aisle. 'What are you doing?' she whispered.

'This,' he said with a grin that spread from ear to ear, putting his hands around her waist, tilting her backwards and putting his lips to hers.

It was a kiss that promised everything. And spoke of the journey they'd taken. Sullivan starting back at work. His ever-steady presence during her brother's trial and conviction. The new radical decisions she'd taken about developing Mirinez's own health service for its citizens. And the joy she'd felt waking up next to the man she loved. She pulled her lips back for a second. 'We're causing a scandal.' She couldn't help but smile.

'Just wait until they find out about the twins,' he whispered in her ear as he eased her back up and took her other arm.

She winked at him as she smiled at the men on either side of her.

'Gentlemen, shall we? I think we have a wedding to attend.'

All three of them laughed. And that was the picture that made the headlines the next day across the world.

* * * * *

*If you enjoyed this story, check out these
other great reads from Scarlet Wilson*

*A ROYAL BABY FOR CHRISTMAS
ONE KISS IN TOKYO
THE DOCTOR'S BABY SECRET
A TOUCH OF CHRISTMAS MAGIC*

All available now!

MIRACLE FOR THE NEUROSURGEON

BY
LYNNE MARSHALL

Published in Great Britain 2017
By Mills & Boon, an imprint of HarperCollins*Publishers*
1 London Bridge Street, London, SE1 9GF

© 2017 Janet Maarschalk

ISBN: 978-0-263-92645-3

Dear Reader,

One of the perks of having a romantic's world-view and getting to write books is taking a tough story but featuring the silver lining. When I put my hero Wes in a wheelchair I knew that was the focus I needed to take.

Wes—or the Prince of Westwood, as I like to call him—had it all…and then he didn't any more…and this book focuses on his journey after that. In walks Mary from the other side of the tracks, with her never-say-die attitude, her tiny house on wheels, plus a crazy bargain. And his current world, based on discipline and survivor's grit, gets turned on its head.

Doing research for this book was enthralling, and I was amazed by the leaps that have been made in dealing with spinal cord injuries. Of course this book focuses on Wes and Mary's love story, but I drew so much inspiration from my research and from the people who refuse to limit themselves because of where they sit.

I hope you enjoy the fireworks and the admiration these two meant-to-be lovebirds have for each other as they struggle through to their well-deserved HEA. As I mention in my dedication, I wouldn't have had the guts to bring this story to life without the encouragement of a truly gifted editor: Flo Nicoll.

I hope you enjoy the book!

Lynne

PS Visit lynnemarshall.com for the latest news and to sign up for my newsletter.

To Flo Nicoll, for giving me the courage to write this
story, then helping me make it all it should be.
Having you as an editor has been a blessing.

Books by Lynne Marshall

Mills & Boon Medical Romance

Summer Brides

Wedding Date with the Army Doc

The Hollywood Hills Clinic

His Pregnant Sleeping Beauty

Cowboys, Doctors…Daddies!

Hot-Shot Doc, Secret Dad
Father For Her Newborn Baby

200 Harley Street: American Surgeon in London
A Mother for His Adopted Son

Visit the Author Profile page
at millsandboon.co.uk for more titles.

CHAPTER ONE

WESLEY VAN ALLEN looked like hell in a shirt. Not even a shirt, a T-shirt. A worn and dingy old white undershirt, with holes, that would be better suited for dusting furniture than wearing. Plus, it was wet, and he was obviously sweaty.

On second glance he looked more like hell on wheels with that driven dark stare. The pride Mary Harris had always admired in him was still in fine form, and so was that glint in his gaze. From the looks of the bulging veins on his deltoids and biceps she must have interrupted his gym time.

Mary bent and lightly kissed his cheek. "Remember me?" Yeah, he'd definitely been working out.

"How could I forget a pest like you?" Looking surprised, he used the hand towel from his lap to wipe his neck, as he gave her a lazy smile.

When he'd first opened the door, she'd had to adjust her gaze downward to accommodate his being in the wheelchair. His nearly black hair was longer than she'd ever seen it, and she had to admit it looked sexy all damp in disarray. For a man who'd always been proud to a fault and strutted around, letting the world know it, his posture hadn't changed…from the waist up, anyway. But strutting was no longer possible.

Those once sparkling, take-on-the-world eyes Mary remembered as pale brown, coffee and cream, to be exact, seemed darker, more intense than ever. The way they examined her now, made her question why she'd dared to come here today.

She instantly remembered, he'd become a man who'd nearly lost it all. One who worked every day, far too hard, to regain his balance, or so she'd been told.

Mary fought every muscle on her face to hide her sorrow over the guy she'd once known versus the man she saw now, fearing her eyes would betray her. *Do not cry. Do not.*

She forced a bright smile. "I've come to see if I can be of any help. I am an expert, you know."

He could probably see right through her, but she was determined to pull this off.

Alexandra, Wesley's sister, had contacted Mary when the accident had first occurred nine months ago—the shockwave had hit so hard she could barely walk the rest of that day, her chest felt caved in, crushing her heart for the man she'd never gotten to know like she'd once dreamed she might. Mary had just signed on for a six-month hospital physical therapy position in Bangor, Maine, when he'd had his waterskiing accident. Far across the country, she couldn't get home to see him. But she'd mourned his loss, and had worried about him every day, until Alexandra had assured her he was out of danger. Though he would never walk again.

How many times had she wanted to pick up the phone and call Wes, or write him a card expressing her truest thoughts and feelings, but had chickened out because in the end she'd felt she'd had no right? She was just a girl he'd once known. Nothing more.

Alexandra had called again last week, out of desperation, and Mary had heard the panic in her friend's voice. Wes had fired the third home health physical therapy assistant in as many months. "He's taken independence to new heights. No one can stand to be around him!" Alex hadn't known what else to do, so she'd turned to her longtime friend for help.

Though about to sign a contract for another job, this one in New Mexico, Mary had rearranged her work schedule on the spot to get here. That was the beauty of being a free agent, an interim employee, getting to call the shots while traveling the country. But since that phone call, and after not being there for Wes in the beginning, nothing could stop her from helping the man she'd had a crush on since she was fifteen.

"Seriously, what are you doing here?" His unwelcoming tone stung like a paper cut. He rolled his wheelchair backward to allow her to enter. At least that was something.

"I already told you, I'm here to help." She followed him, hiding the hurt from him brushing her off.

"I don't need any help. I've got this." His suspicious gaze seemed to hunt for pity, and if he found it, she knew he'd attack.

She adjusted her over-bright expression to one of questioning. "Really? A guy who's fired three physical therapy aides in three months doesn't need help? I beg to differ." Did she honestly expect him to welcome her when showing up out of the blue?

He *harrumphed* and made a U-turn and continued toward the opposite door in the large and beautifully furnished beach home living room. The ceiling-to-floor windows looked out onto the Pacific Ocean. At the moment it was teal and silver blue, covered with glitter from the sun, and she couldn't avoid noticing. Yet the house felt shut down, dark and lonely, and she wasn't sure if she was supposed to follow him or not. She did anyway, through opened double doors into a huge hallway where a wraparound staircase looked like open arms. Because of his accident, that welcoming entrance would forever be off-limits to him. How awful to be reminded every day in such an in-your-face way.

"I'm serious, Wes, you can't fire the world. It won't bring back your legs." She'd always been one to name the elephant in the room head on, that was if she knew what it was, and in Wes's case she knew exactly why he'd become this guarded and fiercely independent man. He'd become a paraplegic and was dealing with his disability by working too hard, beating the life out of it. And apparently everyone else. No one could keep up with his breakneck schedule, according to Alexandra.

"I don't need you." He spat out the words, reacting to her dose of reality, sounding nothing like the successful neurosurgeon who'd known the course of his life since he'd reached puberty. Who could've predicted this part?

"Alex doesn't agree and she's asked me to help out for a while." When he immediately opened his mouth to protest, she held up her hand to stop him. "Because she loves you."

"Alex needs to mind her own business. She's got her husband and kids to worry about. Tell her I release her of all sisterly responsibility. And you can leave now."

Crushed, Mary laughed, surprising herself. She hadn't seen Wesley in ten years, the day Alexandra had gotten married. The day they'd claimed their second mind-boggling kiss and far more, blamed completely on sharing too much champagne. "Not so easy, Wes. I've taken two months off work to come here. I literally picked up my home and drove from New Mexico to California."

"Why ever would you do that without asking first?"

"Because that's what friends do. Show up to help."

"My friends always ask first." Dismissed.

Another paper cut, this one slicing deeper, drawing more blood. *Do they ever get invited in?*

He might still think of her as a charity case, a stray kitten his sister had once dragged home from public school, but she'd risen above her poverty and all the odds stacked against her. She didn't deserve to be spoken to like that.

"You used to call me kid sister number two. I practically lived with you, Wes. You can't deny you were *all* like a second family to me." She tried to make eye contact, but he didn't co-operate. "Your parents gave me shelter, and you, you insisted I make something of myself." He'd told her that the night he'd *been volunteered* to take her to the prom. She stepped closer to him, hoping with all of her heart she could get through to him. "Well, I have. I've got a freaking PhD, and now I'm here for you, one doctor to another." Funny how life worked out that way.

"So this is payback?" He looked directly at her, taunting her with hurtful insults to give up and leave him alone. "I don't need your help. Thank you, though."

He rolled toward a wall unit lift to take him and his wheelchair upstairs, intent on leaving her standing there, openmouthed. But the snub only gave enough time for fury at being dismissed like a servant to form into words.

"I've been told you're being a total jerk." *Have proof of it firsthand now.* She'd also spoken to his parents before coming. They'd thrown up their hands and moved back to their retirement home in Florida after spending the first six months of recovery with him. "Someone's got to snap you out of it."

"Have you been talking to my parents? Dear old Dad,

who blames me for what happened? I don't need toxic people like that around."

His father may had been the pusher in the clan, but certainly his mother had never been anything but supportive.

"And I'm not like that. Toxic." Had his father actually blamed him for the accident? Shameful. She'd always known Mr. Van Allen had expected the world of both of his children, but most especially from Wes. He'd raised hell when Alex had changed majors from pre-med to become a dietician, which only required a master's degree. If Wes had ever dared to venture off his life path, who knows what Mr. Van Allen would have done? Somehow, even back then, she'd sensed that failure was not an option where the Van Allen kids were concerned, but to blame his son for a life-altering accident? Unbelievable.

"Can't you see I'm doing fine?" He staunchly defended his shutting out the world.

It was time to double down. She knew, though on the surface Wes looked like he was in fact *doing fine*, he needed assistance from daily PT in ways he didn't even think about, and not just on the parts that were working, but also the muscles and joints in need of passive range of motion. That was something he needed to learn to do for himself, too. And even in the gym, which she presumed from the looks of his upper torso, chest and arms, he did rigorous workouts, someone needed to be standing by in case he got hurt, possibly further injuring his spine. No. She wasn't going anywhere. At least not today. "Have you ever performed surgery without consulting another neurosurgeon first?"

"What's that got to do with this?"

"Everything. You may think you know what you're

doing but, whether you know it or not, you need a second opinion."

They shared a ten-second stare down, and he was the first to look away. "Get used to it, Van Allen, I'm not leaving." She waited for him to turn and look at her again. "For the next two months, anyway. In fact, regardless of what you want or think, I'm the best person in the entire world to show up on your doorstep today." Pure bravado. *False bravado.* She caught up to him and placed her hand on his arm to make a point, her knees nearly knocking with insecurity as she did. He jerked at her touch, but didn't yank the arm away.

"There's no doubt you're doing great, but you can't do it all by yourself. You need some supervision with the process. I'm only temporary, but I'm necessary for now. You're a smart man. You know that. So let me help you." To hell with the anxiety summersaulting through her stomach over the possibility of being rejected, his long-term health was more important than her nerves… or her ego. Yet if he told her to leave one more time, she wouldn't be able to justify sticking around.

He shook his head, looking irritated. Something told her to intercept his thought before he said it, to state her case one last time, this time pulling out all the bells and whistles.

"It's because of you that *I'm* the perfect person to help." She tried to keep eye contact, even though matching his resolute stare made her ankles wobbly. "Wasn't it you who told me to make something out of myself? To not let my parents and poverty hold me back? Well, here I am, a bona fide physical therapist, with a doctorate degree, at your service. I understand it may come as a surprise, but I just might know a little about what you need at this point in your recovery. And I don't intend to leave before you're back on your feet." Damn, she'd said the wrong thing! She saw his jaw twitch. Without intending to, she'd delivered her own paper cut. "Metaphorically speaking." It was too late—she couldn't retract the stupid and insensitive phrase.

"For a second I thought you were selling yourself as a miracle worker." He let out an exasperated huff of air, like she'd solicited a service he didn't want or need— subscribe to this magazine or donate to this cause—but felt obligated to take anyway. "If this is your sales pitch, I suppose I have to pay?"

"No!" She was making a total mess of everything, but couldn't back down now. "Let's get that straight from the start. *I don't work for you.* I'm here as a *friend.*" *That way you can't fire me!*

"And where do you expect to live?"

"I've got that all taken care of."

He sat quietly, offering a dead stare in her vicinity, along with a sigh. "Suit yourself," he said, as though he couldn't care less, and continued on toward the wheelchair lift. "I'm going to the gym."

Dismissed again. *Well, not so fast, buddy.* "I'll be back at eight o'clock tomorrow morning to begin your therapy. In the meantime, do you have a groundskeeper? I need some help with something."

He tossed her a quizzical glance, then propelled himself out of the room, calling a woman's name as he did so. "Rita!" His housekeeper? Once she'd come out from the far recesses of the kitchen, making Mary wonder exactly how big the house was, he gave a quick instruction for her to find someone named Heath, as he rolled his chair onto the lift and began ascending the stairs.

Rita tipped her head at him and passed an inquisitive gaze at Mary. "I'll call him now."

"Thanks. I'll be on the porch."

She stepped outside the front door, her hands shaking, her body quivering. She leaned against the wall biting her lip, blinking her eyes, until sadness overtook her. The man she'd idolized as a teenager was sentenced to a wheelchair for the rest of his life. She'd known it in advance, of course, but seeing him—the same yet so changed—drove the point home and deep into her heart.

The ocean blurred, her skin flushed with heat, and her pulse jittered, forcing her to let go of the threatening tears. To stop fighting and release them before she choked and drowned on them. It had been a long time since she'd cried, and they pricked and stung the insides of her eyelids. She buried her face in the bend of her arm, smothering the sudden keening sounds ripping at her throat, thankful the screeching seagulls overpowered her mourning.

Wesley took a break from his demanding workout routine and peered out the upstairs window, not believing what he was seeing. Heath, his groundskeeper, directed Mary as she backed a tiny portable wood-covered house, complete with porch—if you could call that a porch—onto the graveled ground beside his unattached garage. *So that's how she'd taken care of living arrangements.* She drove the pickup truck like a pro, threw it into park and jumped out to check her handiwork. Clearly satisfied with the parking job, she dusted her hands and went about releasing the house from the towing hitch.

This wasn't her first time at that rodeo.

His guess was that the RV-sized house couldn't be more than two hundred square feet, tops. Sure, Mary was petite, no more than five-three and a hundred and ten pounds wringing wet, but it had to be snug in there. Why would she want to live like that for two months?

She smiled, and from all the way upstairs he could see the self-satisfaction in her expression. Determination had always been her saving grace, and he'd admired it. Until just now when she'd trained her grit on him and weaseled her way back into his life. He didn't need anyone—didn't his family get it? He shook his head, frustrated yet amused. That same tenacity had always been the key to her survival. Could he fault her for not letting him send her away?

He moved further into his gym and grabbed some free weights.

Mary had gotten a lousy start with her parents stumbling their way through life, blaming everyone and everything else on their failings, rather than taking a good look at themselves. Fortunately, she hadn't picked up their lax habits. In fact, she'd done exactly the opposite— she'd taken a long look at her parents and had become convinced she could do better for herself. Then she'd set out to prove it. And prove it she had. She held a doctorate degree. Could work anywhere she wanted. And at this point in time she'd chosen to work here. Lucky him.

When Alexandra had first brought her home, Mary had been scrawny and had worn clothes from thrift shops. They'd been assigned to work on a science project together, and instead of judging Mary on her appearance Alex had been raised to be open-minded. She'd treated Mary like all of her other friends, though those friends had all been rich. Without passing judgment, Alexandra had quickly zeroed in on how bright Mary was—beyond how nice and sweet she was—and their team project had taken first place. She'd also realized that Mary couldn't always depend on meals at home so she'd quickly become a regular guest for meals at the Van Allen house. Soon Mary had become best friends with his big-hearted sister.

Back then, he'd also been taken in by Mary's upbeat spirit, and secretly by her waist-long strawberry blonde hair, which she wore only shoulder length these days. Her shining inquisitive green eyes had stood out like a newly discovered gem in a household of brown-eyed people, and he'd been drawn to her from their very first meeting. Plus, he'd seen something else in that wide and intelligent stare of hers—admiration. Admiration for him. He'd enjoyed knowing his sister's new best friend had a huge crush on him, accepted it with pride, even fed that crush from time to time.

But she'd been innocent and vulnerable and, with parents like hers, hungry for love and attention. With a father like his, who had unwavering expectations for him, well, Wes had been wise enough to play gently with Mary's heart by keeping her at arm's length, knowing his future would take a far different direction from hers. Still, selfish eighteen-year-old that he'd been, he'd strung her along, given her enough attention to keep her hopeful.

Damn, he'd been mean even then. Or careless? Egotistical for sure. Hadn't the *Prince of Westwood* been his family nickname? Especially the one time he'd slipped up and let his—what should he call it—curiosity or desire get the better of him.

Long before *everyone* had had a cell phone—especially kids like Mary—and social media had taken hold of the entire world, she'd appeared on their doorstep, breathless and excited. Alexandra hadn't been home—come to think of it, no one else had been either—but he'd invited her in anyway. When he'd seen her disappointment at not having Alex to share her great news with, he'd offered to listen and to deliver the information personally to his kid sister.

Mary had made the principal's list, which would ensure she'd be able to continue on at the Magnet school for the next year. She'd only been admitted the prior year on that contingency, and because, like most private schools, the school held a certain number of slots for marginal teens like her. Her joy had been contagious and swept up by her beaming smile—the same one she'd tried to flash at him just minutes earlier in his entryway—he'd let down his usual barriers where Mary had been concerned, crossed the line and kissed her.

What had started out as a congratulatory kiss had soon changed into one packed with typical teenage male need and longing that he'd kept hidden since the first day he'd met her. And she'd been a very active participant in that kiss, a kiss so heady he remembered it clearly to this day. If his mother arriving home from her charity meeting hadn't abruptly broken things up, being young and driven by hormones, not to mention dumb enough to let desire take over back then, who knew what might have happened?

He traded in the first weights and lifted two heavier weights and began vigorously trading repetitions, like a locomotion locked in place.

He'd always been lucky that way, saved from his wandering, kept on the straight and narrow if not by himself then by outside forces, especially by his father, because he was meant to be a doctor. And not just any doctor, a neurosurgeon. He'd planned his entire life around it, and a young, pretty and fresh face like Mary's couldn't get in the way. Yes, his parents were open-minded about many things, but getting mixed up with a girl literally from the wrong side of the tracks would never have been tolerated by dear old Dad. Alexandra having Mary as a friend had proved to be charitable enough for the Van Allen family.

Until her prom two years later. When no one had invited Mary the first week after the school prom kick-off announcement, Alexandra had begged Wesley to invite her. He'd fought it at first, knowing there had to be several guys who'd love to take a girl like Mary, unless they were snooty and let her being poor get in the way of good taste. By the end of week two Alexandra had gotten her mother involved, and what had seemed beneath him as a twenty-year-old university student had been foisted on him. Two-three years older than all the others attending, he'd been volunteered to take Mary to the prom.

If he'd let himself look deep down, he wouldn't have been able to deny he still had vague feelings for her. He'd become a sophisticated pre-med student and a seventeen-year-old woman was not only jail bait but socially undesirable. The Prince of Westwood had taken her to the prom anyway, just so his family could wear the "aren't we good people" badge.

His worldly-wise self hadn't expected to be knocked off his feet when he'd seen Mary that night in the dress his mother had bought. Not as pricey or special as Alexandra's dress, of course, but perfectly suited to her. His conscience had been dealt its first blow when he'd picked her up at the ratty mobile home park she'd lived in, her parents not even bothering to make an appearance. Maybe they'd been embarrassed? Regardless, he'd taken Mary back to his house where Alexandra and her friends had waited to take before-prom pictures, wondering how such a lovely flower had grown in such bleak surroundings.

Then he'd spent the entire evening keeping her at arm's length, being a boorish cosmopolitan-minded university

man, The Prince of Westwood lecturing her on making
something of her life. Explaining to her how insignifi-
cant something like a high school prom registered in the
course of a lifetime. *So why was he still thinking about
it now?*

While on his soapbox that night, he'd warned her about
guys—like himself—who'd love to take advantage of her.
So wise. So stupid. So moved by her poverty. So protective of her. Out of obligation, he'd asked her to dance
and when holding her he'd made the mistake of looking into those eyes, a shade darker than her pastel green
dress. Innocent and beautiful and calling out to his soul.
To love her.

He'd known he couldn't. He hadn't been nearly enough
of a man to risk that. When he'd taken her home, out of
gratitude she'd thrown her arms around his neck, and he'd
nearly kissed her the way he'd wanted to all evening. But
he'd known it would change everything if he did, and he
couldn't stray from his calling. Nothing could keep him
from medical school, and surely getting involved with
a girl like Mary would change his life. For the better?
Who knew?

How pompous he'd been, lecturing her on making
something of her life. To do it for herself because no
one else could.

He stopped the repetitions and stared out the gym window down to where her crazy little house stood.

Wes had seen the disappointment in Mary's gaze after
their chaste kiss the night of the prom, yet her sweetness
had remained. She'd dutifully thanked him and promised not to let him down, playing her "kid sister" role
perfectly. Before he'd left, he'd told her how beautiful
she looked and even in the dark of night she'd beamed.
So princely. Such power. All the more reason to save her

from him. Yet he'd walked away wondering who between them had the most power over the other and sure he'd left a piece of his heart behind. Forever.

The least he could do was let her share her expertise with him now. Who knew, he might learn something, and if that helped his recovery and goal to get back to work again, it would be worth all of these memories bombarding him about his unwanted guest.

He'd had enough of the free weights and trained his sight across the room, out of that blasted window…to her house.

Returning to university that next afternoon, it had been easy to brush the moment—their special night—under the table and move on. Not really, but he'd worked at it at least. Truth was he'd carried those memories around with him for a decade until they'd been replaced with an amazing kiss they'd shared at his sister's wedding several years later.

He rolled under the pull-up bar and grabbed hold, lifting himself out of the wheelchair, pressing his chin to the bar, over and over, until sweat rolled down his temples and his arms trembled.

Still on the fast track to success back then, he'd been about to become engaged to Giselle, a young woman of his social standing, with all the proper credentials and diplomas to be a rich doctor's wife and a doctor herself. Plus she'd been vetted by dear old Dad. Yes, the decision had been cold and calculated, but it fit in with his future. To this day, long after his engagement had fallen apart, his medical practice had taken off and his bank account had doubled—but what did success matter anymore?— he'd recalled that champagne-inspired kiss he'd shared with Mary at Alexandra's wedding with a longing smile.

He let go of the bar and landed with a plop in his waiting wheelchair—his special, no-choice buddy for the rest of his life—remembering the night of his sister's wedding.

Mary had changed at twenty-four. She'd become a woman who knew herself and how to tempt a man. She'd taken control of her life just like she'd promised the night of the prom, and she'd radiated confidence and inner peace because of it. Always reaching for that next step on his ladder to the pinnacle, Wes had wanted that. A taste of her secret recipe for contentment. She'd also happened to look amazing in the strapless maid-of-honor dress. It had been ice blue, he vividly recalled, enough to make him smile.

A forgotten sensation tickled down his spine until it reached the location of his spinal cord injury and stopped. He glanced out the window again, watching her sweep her tiny porch as he experienced phantom tingles in his toes. What was that about? Maybe he'd pulled something during his workout?

He'd always known Mary deserved a family of her making, a place to call home. A shot with a decent guy. He'd also had the wisdom to know that they were never meant to be together, so he'd never followed through on his "what if" thoughts. BP—before paraplegia. Useless, silly thoughts, meant only for thinking, savoring even, but never acting on. Until it was too late… AP—after paraplegia.

He wiped his face with the towel, searching the room for another form of man-against-machine torture to take his mind off these wandering thoughts. What was the point? He chose the cable machine, first lowering the sides of his specially made workout wheelchair, then grabbing the bar to begin a series of triceps cable extensions.

Was this how she lived now? Dragging her mini-house

with her everywhere she went like a mega-sized back-pack? What kind of vagabond life was that for a woman like Mary? She'd been raised in a trailer park by inattentive parents. He'd always pegged her as a girl who wanted to set down roots, who wanted a family more than anything else in the world, the kind she deserved, not the one she'd been born into. Though he could never picture a guy worthy of her, he'd still imagined her settling down, raising children. Now, apparently, she traveled the country alone. In that thing. A house suited more for a mouse.

The irony didn't take long to sink in about *him* wondering about what kind of life *she* led. *Take a look at yourself.* More money than one person could ever use, living alone in a fortress made of the latest building materials, a ten-million-dollar view of the Pacific Ocean out his front door, yet completely alone.

The last thing he needed to do was examine his own situation. Nope, he was determined to ignore that.

He shook his head. He wasn't ready to think about the AP future. Not after failing miserably when he'd tried to go back to work prematurely three months ago. How the humiliation had burned like a branding iron when his department head had suggested he'd come back too soon, telling him to take more time off to get a better handle on balancing his demanding job with being in a wheelchair.

His father's words to live by had infused his way of thinking. *Failure is not an option.*

The problem was, he already had. Failed. Big time.

He glanced out the window again, catching sight of the back of Mary as she pushed into her doll house.

One finger skimmed the area on his cheek where she'd bussed him when she'd first entered his house. He hadn't had the chance to dodge it. Oddly enough, her touch had produced a sweet warm feeling, as she always had for

him, and had unleashed his wrath for catching him off
guard, for daring to make him *feel* something. Because
these days he, like his legs, refused to feel a thing, other
than pain from working out too hard and too long. Which
he believed was strength. As crazy as it seemed, physical
pain reminded him he was still alive, not locked away by
his own choice in this castle by the sea.

He guided his top-of-the-line workout wheelchair
down the hall, past the specially built elevator to his bedroom, where he would have slammed the damn door if
he could've only figured out how to get the right amount
of leverage to do it.

This was his truth now. He was a guy stuck in a chair.

Mary went about the business of settling her home after
another long journey. For the last two years and over a
half-dozen moves, she'd lived in the tiny house she'd
helped design and for which she'd paid cash. Another
lesson she'd learned inadvertently from her parents.

She'd chosen to bring her house along with her wherever she got assigned, rather than stay in cold, short-
term rentals or soulless extended-stay hotels. This was
home. She'd carefully chosen the floor plan to meet her
every need, yet using the smallest amount of space necessary. That had turned out to be two hundred and fifty
square feet. She'd gone the woodsy cabin route, yet the
repurposed materials they'd used to build the house were
surprisingly light, making it easy to travel, as long as
she was willing to drive a pickup truck. Which had cost
nearly as much as the house!

Her living room space came complete with a large
enough mounted flat-screen TV. The kitchen had been
a bit trickier, yet she'd made it state-of-the-art enough
to make do, since she enjoyed cooking. She'd settled for

a two-burner gas stove, minimal counter space but with a built-in table that folded down and opened up when it was time to eat or if she needed a place to knead bread dough or cut out cookies. The half-sized refrigerator kept her eating fresher and healthier, since she didn't have much storage. Yes, the kitchen sink had to double up for face-washing and tooth-brushing, but for payoff she'd managed a nearly full-sized shower, with a stackable mini-washer/drier nearby and a petite toilet, all at the back of the ground-floor living space.

She chuckled, thinking of her mini-house as two stories, but her favorite spot in the entire tiny house was her loft bedroom. That counted as a story, didn't it? Plus, the permanent wood ladder she needed to climb to get to the loft doubled as a small A-framed bookcase downstairs. No space went to waste, and she liked living like that. Unlike the ratty tin and Formica filled trailer she'd been raised in, this was truly a home. Cozy. Warm. Filled with life. Her life.

She might not be able to stand up straight in her bedroom but, whichever city she set the house up in, each morning she could peer out of the small "second story" window at the head of her bed to greet the day. The view changed often, and so far she liked it that way. This time, she had the luxury of parking on Wesley's grand Malibu estate, and she was guaranteed to see the ocean first thing every sunrise. If she hadn't been so depressed about seeing him, she'd be excited about living here for the next two months. What she needed was a serious attitude adjustment.

She sat on the long pillowed and comfy couch, which doubled as a storage bench, with a cup of tea, and thought about Wesley. His situation broke her heart and she'd proved it with her meltdown on his doorstep earlier. He'd always been her hero, the guy with the world at his fingertips. The Prince of Westwood! *Invincible.* He'd made her want to be better than who she was, to build a dream then follow it to the end. Because of him, she'd pursued a doctorate after her post-graduate P.T. degree. She took a sip of hot black tea, thinking of his intelligent eyes, hers welling up again as her heart pinched.

The man might be considered disabled by everyday standards, but he was also a skilled neurosurgeon, and the world still *needed* him. She couldn't allow him to hide away in his gym day in and day out.

It seemed he had to relearn how to *be* himself. The confident, outgoing guy he used to be. That was a task far beyond her physical therapist's pay scale. All she could hope was for their once shared friendship and mutual respect to pull him back to what he'd been before the accident. Not the gym rat he'd become. Didn't he know that true strength came from inside, not from muscles?

Her phone rang. It was Alexandra. "How'd things go?"

"A little rocky at first, but he's agreed to let me stay for now."

"How does he look?"

Great! Sexy as ever. "Determined, and obviously buffer than I've ever seen him."

"If anyone can get through to him, I know you can."

"I'll do my best."

"Promise?" *Mommy! Mommy!* Mary heard children's voices in the background. With three kids, Alexandra never seemed to make it through a phone call without interruption.

"Promise."

"I'm going to have to cut things short."

"I understand. I'll keep you posted. Give those kids a hug from me, and two for Rosebud, okay?"

"Can you believe little Rose is one now?"

"Unreal." She'd missed her birthday from being out of state, but had seen videos, and had also had face time with her on the computer when little Rosebud had opened the gift she'd sent—a small rocking horse that talked to the rider. Rose had loved it and the grin on her face when she'd opened the package had managed to wrap around Mary's heart and change her life forever.

They hung up, and Mary remembered the day she'd first held Rose when she was less than a week old. The tiny bundle, completely helpless, had still managed to get her needs across with grunts and stretches, cries and flailing pink spindly arms. And the newborn had felt more amazing than anything Mary had ever held in her life.

Her education and traveling had kept her away from the births of Alexandra's first two children, Oliver and Bailey. But she'd been given the honor of becoming Rose's godmother so she couldn't very well miss out on meeting her right off. That meet and greet had changed her life.

A loving warmth fanned over her skin as she remembered how deeply she'd been moved by holding her goddaughter. How the tiny baby had reached into her heart and planted a need she'd never dared to dream of before.

As she stared out of the two decent-sized windows of her tiny home, looking out toward the beach, she thought of her own situation. She was at a crossroads in life and, at nearly thirty-four, she finally admitted what she really wanted. More than anything. A child.

It was little Rosebud's fault. And Matthew's, the sturdy little six-month-old she'd held just last week. Her patient, his mother, had been instructed to do some exercises and the baby had needed to be held. Mary had thought nothing of helping out until the sturdy boy with those chubby dimpled hands, two chins and a Buddha belly had looked into her eyes and squealed with joy. She'd never wanted to cuddle, squeeze and kiss a baby more in her life. Oh, yeah, she wanted one.

Now she dreamed of having a child. Illogical, yes, with no man in her life. Living completely without roots. An inconsistent job that took her all over the country. Yet she'd finally heeded the whisperings of her body that had been building for years, and with the recent help of two little ones, that whisper had turned into a scream. She wanted to be a mother more than anything. To have a baby all her own…before it was too late.

Finishing off her tea, she stood and walked the few short feet to her kitchen sink. How exactly did a woman go about such a task on her own?

She glanced at the mansion up the walk, which may as well be a prison for its current purpose of shutting out the world for Wesley Van Allen, M.D. Then she put her yearning for a baby aside. Wes needed to be her first priority for now.

She was adamant about setting a time limit with him, though. Two months. Tops. She'd allowed for the lapse in a paying job into her annual budget for exactly that amount of time. If she intended to pursue her dream of having a child on her own, she'd need to change jobs to one where she could settle down in one place in order to be a stable parent. It was her chance to provide for her baby what she'd never had herself. Permanence, unconditional love, protection and opportunity. And, father or no father, she wanted it with all of her might.

She washed her teacup, deciding to take a walk on the gloriously beautiful beach. Maybe when she got back she'd crack open that bottle of wine she'd been saving, sit on her cozy front porch, have a toast to her latest post, and lift a glass to her future plans. Truth was, she could spend the entire evening daydreaming about becoming a mother, but…

Right now, her long-ago—but never forgotten—first crush had to come first.

CHAPTER TWO

THE NEXT MORNING, Rita met Mary at the door and escorted her as far as the stairs, which Mary took two at a time, priming herself for a fight when she reached the gym. Instead, she found Wesley dressed, freshly shaved, and with his hair tied up, waiting for her. Surprise.

"This is a change." She smiled, entering the workout room, but Wesley, dressed in a black T-shirt and grey sweatpants, didn't exactly return it. At least he didn't scowl.

"The sooner we get on with this, the sooner..." He stopped himself.

But she had a hunch what he'd planned on saying was, *the sooner you'll be gone.* "Two months. Remember? Give me two months and you'll be a different man."

Now came the deadpan stare. "I already am a different man."

She refused to take the bait. "You may be buffer than I ever remember, but there's more work to be done, though the outcome will be less obvious..." she held up her index finger "...but necessary." Without giving him a moment to protest, she grabbed a stool on wheels by the nearby wall in his top-of-the-line equipped gym and rolled over to his wheelchair. "I need to do a complete evaluation of your muscles and reflexes."

He pulled in his chin and his brows pushed down.

"You didn't think I was going to start you on exercises without first evaluating your motor and sensory status, did you?" From her large shoulder bag she pulled out a multi-paged form. "Let's get started."

"I've already been through this."

She'd learned from his online records—which she'd been approved to view—that he'd had sufficient occupational training for activities of daily living. She'd also learned about his past and personal medical history, which, to be honest, prior to the accident had been uneventful. But if there was any health issue, she'd leave that part up to his primary physician. He certainly seemed independent from the looks of him, all dressed and ready to go so early in the morning.

"Yes, but you haven't had a thorough examination in several months, and I need to compare your current status with the last one."

Her plan was to measure muscles, grade their power, tone and level of flaccidity. She'd test modalities of sensation, both superficial and deep, above his injury and compare them to the American Spinal Injury Impairment Scale. He'd nearly severed his spinal cord at T11-12, which made him paraplegic but able to sit on his own, which he obviously handled like the Prince of Westwood, and that definitely helped with breathing and the ability to deep cough. Both important for general health and well-being.

After the first part of the evaluation, which took a good half-hour, though impressed with his upper body strength and the fact he'd increased muscle mass since his last evaluation, she was most concerned about the decrease in the use of joints below his waist. With him being a doctor, she'd have thought he would have cared about such things, but she hadn't taken into account his mental outlook. He was an achiever and worked like the devil on what he could change, in his case developing strength and muscles like a regular Adonis, while ignoring the part he had zero control over—his hips and lower extremities.

She continued with her examination and as she used her hands to feel and measure his thighs, she sensed his discomfort and decided to lighten the mood. "Hey, it's not like you haven't had women groping and crawling all over you before, right?"

"They were usually naked."

He'd actually tried to make a joke—or a snide remark, but she preferred to think of it as a joke—and she couldn't let his effort lie flat so she played along. "Are you asking me to take off my clothes?"

She pinned Wesley's caramel eyes with her own, wondering where she'd gotten the nerve to be so bold, but rode it out in spite of her inner cringing. Acting this way felt completely wrong. He didn't look away and it sent a subtle shudder right down her middle.

"That's a thought," he said, his voice a rough whisper that definitely wasn't snide.

She'd never pull something like this with a patient, and as long as she was here to help she'd expect nothing less from herself. "Excuse me, Wes. That was uncalled for. I apologize for crossing the line. You being an old friend shouldn't make a difference."

He didn't let her off the hook but studied her, his head tipped just so as he did. Inside, she squirmed, wishing she'd never pretended to be bold, waiting to see if she'd offended him and if he was going to let her have it.

"I'm still considering your first offer." His were now the eyes doing the pinning…and the teasing. The internal cringing doubled. He was testing her. She may as well be naked since she couldn't hide the total body goose-bumps.

"Gah! You win. I had no business acting all vampy with you. I'm the least sexy person on earth."

"Says who?"

"Oh, trust me, I am. Anyway, you win. I bow to your poker face." She went overboard, taking the ditzy route, hoping to keep him from realizing what she instantaneously had. He was paralyzed from the waist down. She felt safer with him. It was a sad truth she'd have to face herself with later in the mirror. She'd judged him without even realizing it, putting him in the "safe" male category, becoming gutsier as a result.

For that one instant, she understood how he must feel about the rest of the world judging him as a man. She'd inadvertently labeled him as less of a threat and had acted differently than she would've with any other male patient, simply because he was a friend sitting in a wheelchair. Inwardly, she shook her head. Ashamed.

He was an incredibly smart man, and intuitive, and, well, with friends like her, no wonder he'd become a recluse and an overachieving gym rat. Barbells didn't judge!

She took a deep breath and continued the examination using only the most impeccable professional skills from then onward.

And her heart broke again as she discovered how stiff and nearly locked his hips, knees and ankle joints were. She had to get him back on track as this weakness would eventually impact on all the strength he'd developed above the waist. Not to mention his circulation and oxygen uptake. He might feel like "half" a man these days, but half of him was a lot, and the best parts, his brain and those strong shoulders and arms, would help keep the rest of him going. As long as he was willing. But he couldn't ignore the parts that didn't work.

She glanced at him. He still stared her down, keeping her feeling naked without a place to hide.

"So here's what I propose." She sat back on the rolling stool, and met him as close to knee to knee as she could get with his feet on the wheelchair footrests. "We work on a regimen to improve your lower body strength with passive range of motion exercises at first."

In response she got a blank stare.

"We need to preserve your joints—your hips, your knees, your ankles. Heaven forbid you should develop foot drop."

"Why?"

"For a better quality of life." That went over like a conk on the head. "You know that." More staring. "Or how about for when they finally figure out how to help paraplegics walk through nerve innervation." Still no response. "Come on, Wes, you're a neurosurgeon, you crack open people's heads for a living and do all kinds of things to their brains. Surely you've thought about the future, right?"

He shook his head. "These days I only think about the present." End of topic? Not if she could help it. Besides, she detected his defense mechanism in full force.

"Baloney. I believe there are hundreds of patients you've helped and saved who need you back on the job. I believe your future is still bright."

"Anyone ever tell you how annoying you are?"

Wesley was impressed with Mary's thoroughness, and also with her positive attitude, but wasn't about to let her know that. Why give her the upper hand? His personal doctor had promised him a much rosier recovery than he'd had, and as far as he was concerned he'd done his part to get as strong as possible. Yet he'd never get out of this damn wheelchair.

"I'm annoying?" She mocked surprise. "Yeah, all the time. I'm a physical therapist, what can I expect, I tick off all my patients. It's part of my strategy." Her expression went serious. "I know I'm bothering you, but I'm doing it because it's important. And speaking of important, where's your stationary bike?"

He screwed up his face. "In case you haven't noticed, I can't use my legs."

"You need the aerobic exercise to enhance circulation and increase oxygen. Let me show you." She dug into her shoulder bag and shoved a catalogue at him. "This is expensive, but from the looks of your house you can afford it."

He took a look, but wasn't the least bit enthusiastic about what he saw. The bicycle strapped the legs and feet in place and stimulated the muscles as the patient rode it, or so said the product description. *Completely high tech and necessary for paraplegics,* according to some Norwegian study.

"Since they did this study, I've recommended this bike to all of my paraplegic and even quadriplegic patients."

He tossed her his best "so what" face, straight out of the teenage contrarian handbook. It didn't faze her.

"You might think it does all the work, but this little baby will keep you in tip-top shape." She stopped herself from saying more, but he understood she was about use the "D" word—"deteriorating", and take the broad-brush approach for life expectancy in paraplegics.

"Look, I get it, Mary. My tough-love doc showed me a video early on when all I wanted to do was shut down."

That notorious video, which he could tell from the

change of expression on her face she knew of, used time-lapse photography to document a young man's demise. Hell, she probably carried around a copy of it in her bottomless shoulder bag, to use on uncooperative patients like him.

The patient in the video had been eighteen at the time of his skateboarding accident and had quickly given up on himself. The photographer had crunched ten years down to one minute. The brutal video transformed a young generally healthy man into a shadow of his former self and had shocked the defeat right out of Wes. Mission accomplished. From that day on he'd worked at his rehab with a vengeance. Never wanting to quit, even when hospital personnel pleaded with him to slow down, he'd refused to give up. Since he'd been home, if the rehab PT didn't like his work ethic in the gym, he'd fire him or her. He didn't care which gender they were, out they'd go.

"So I don't have to paint that graphic picture for you, right?" Little Miss Sunshine returned.

"Right. I've seen it and I never want to go there." The thought terrified him; his worst fears had been laid out before him by that video. Never, ever, did he want to wind up like that. Not without a good fight.

"So I can order this for you, then? It says they can have a rush delivery here in a week to ten days."

The room went thick with silence as they carried out a staring contest. Why was she pushing this bike so hard? Did she have stock in the company, or know something he didn't?

She used her thumb and forefinger to pull back the hair above her forehead, a frustrated gesture, for sure. His stubbornness had gotten to her. "You're still a doctor, Wesley. It's completely possible for you to go back to being one *and* performing surgery again."

"Ha! That's rich." He let his honest reaction slip through the cracks. Been there, done that. Failed! Now he didn't believe a word. She may as well be selling snake oil. "I've already tried to go back to work and it was a miserable failure. My department head sent me home."

"Because it was too soon. How can someone as smart as you be so dense?" He saw determination in her eyes as she sat straighter, and he let the slur slide. Maybe he needed to listen to her. "As long as we keep your motor skills intact and your mind alert, there's nothing to stop you from going back when you're ready. The key phrase being 'when you're ready'."

Mary went back to her large bag, which apparently held the world in it from everything she kept taking out. She lifted a stack of medical journals and handed them to him. "Here. Why not catch up on the latest in neuro-surgery?"

"Look, I appreciate your enthusiasm and concern, but I've got my own plan for getting back on the job."

"Sheer will and body sweat isn't a plan, Wes. My plan can't make you perfect again. No. But I guarantee it can and will help you improve and increase your chances of performing surgery again."

"How can you guarantee that?" He dug in, because he wanted what she preached so badly it hurt, but what if her promise never came to be? So far his Neanderthal work-out-until-you-drop approach hadn't panned out. Sure, he was buffer, but ready to go back to work? She was right. Not yet.

She pushed her face right up into his, those daring green eyes seeming to have X-ray vision over the battle going on inside his head. He tensed, shutting down a little, but he didn't look away.

"Prove me wrong." She put the journals on his lap.

"Prove it. Give me a month and you'll see and feel the difference, then give me another month and you'll be amazed. I know it and totally believe it, and you'll just have to prove otherwise. Of course, all things considered, I'd rather you co-operated."

He couldn't deny the determination in her stare, or the genuine look of caring. She gave a damn. About him and his situation. And from the fire in her gaze, she wouldn't give up.

Then he felt it, that tiny flash of hope that throughout all of the trauma and disappointment and pain he'd suffered had refused to die. That pinpoint of faith in modern medicine and optimism for the future suddenly beamed brighter, because of *her* enthusiasm, and he found his mouth moving before he could stop it. "I doubt that I'll be amazed, but I'll take your challenge. Hopefully, you'll win."

Her eyes widened, she was obviously as surprised as he was, a sweet beam spreading across her face. She clapped her hands then pumped the air with a fist as if she'd just scored the winning point. "Yes! So does this mean I can order that stationary bike?"

"Order the damn bike," he said, rolling himself out of the gym.

The next morning Mary arrived with a mug of coffee, and found Wesley waiting for her in a halfway decent mood. She chose the stairs, two at a time once again, as he took the elevator to the second-floor gym.

"The first thing we need to do today is get you loosened up." She pointed to a thick floor mat beneath the workout bench. "Can you lower yourself to the floor?" She didn't have a clue how much he could or couldn't do for himself, so today would be one of discovery.

"Sure, but I don't make a habit of it."

"You should, you know. You have perfectly good arms, so I'm sure chair presses are a cinch for you."

"Let's find out."

She laced her fingers, stretched her arms and cracked her knuckles, then rolled her shoulders and stretched her neck side to side, like she'd be the one to do the lift and lower. He got a kick out of it, but didn't let her know. Then he put his hands on his locked chair wheels and pushed up until his hips left the seat. She stood back and let him move himself forward, repositioning his legs on his own, using his arm and shoulder muscles to their capacity as he lowered himself as close as possible to the mat and plopped down.

"Great," she said, helping him lie down and straightening his legs for passive range of motion. "Okay, you know what I'm going to do, right?"

He tipped his chin upward. "Yup." Reminding himself to be tolerant, that she wanted to help.

Positioning herself beside Wes, Mary took his right leg, carefully lifted and bent the knee and pressed the leg toward his chest, noticing how tight he felt. How long had he been ignoring the parts that didn't work? She ran him through several basic exercises to loosen his hips and knees and then concentrated on his ankles. He watched her intently as she repeated the same exercises on the other leg.

"Once I loosen your joints, I'll show you how to do all of this for yourself."

"Sounds like a plan."

"Yeah, so why haven't you been doing these?"

He shrugged, and she would have given anything to know what was going on inside his head. It didn't make sense to work himself to the limit with weight training, then ignore the fragile part that needed equal attention. "Okay, I'm done here, for today anyway. You can get yourself back in that wheelchair, and we'll do your favorite part."

She sat back on her heels and watched with admiration as he bent his own knees then put the other arm on the wheelchair seat and essentially did a one-arm press to push himself back in. Impressive. And for someone who'd avoided doing this regularly, he made it look damn easy, too.

As they worked through Mary's planned program of weight exercises, Wesley was struck by how intent she was on balancing his training. She'd forced him to remember he had a lower half where circulation was just as important as the top. Where bad things could happen if he didn't take care of all of himself. Like a child, he'd been playing a game—*Maybe if I ignore it, it will go away.* One thing was sure as the sun, paraplegia didn't go away.

Halfway through the second set of butterfly presses with free weights, he focused away from himself, and watched Mary in all of her earnestness as she studied his technique like a perfectionist, adjusting his elbow here and his shoulder there. He liked the attention.

Later, when he shifted from his chair to the bench for some chest presses, Mary leaned over him, like a life coach, motivating him to keep pushing. He didn't need motivation, being determined as he was to be in top-notch shape so he could go back to work again—the upper half of him anyway—but he appreciated her interest and help. Which surprised him. All the other PTs had seemed like pains in the butt and he'd treated them all accordingly. But Mary was different.

"Let's up the weight," he said, testing her ability to let him call some shots.

"Sure." She put more weights on the bar and he went right back to work. Okay, so she was fine with him pushing himself.

In amusement, he watched her facial expressions mimic what he assumed were his as he lifted the heavier weight, and it made him lose concentration. He pressed the bar above his head, then laughed and lost ground. Spotting the weights, she had to move in quickly to catch the bar before it slammed onto his chest. Though he was perfectly capable of doing it himself, since he'd had to many times on his own, and had the bruises to prove it, he admitted he liked having her there, on point.

"You okay?"

"Fine. Just wondering when you turned into a slave driver."

"You're the one who wanted more weights."

"And you're the one who loaded them on." He got a kick out of goading her, and she fell for it every time. Just like she used to. And unlike the other PTs she was willing to push him as much as he wanted to go, not slow him down.

"So are you saying you want to take a break?"

"Could use some water."

She lunged for a bottle. "Five-minute break."

He gulped a drink. "I take it back. You're not a slave driver, more like a dominatrix."

"What?"

It felt good to tease and smile, like a lost and forgotten part of himself had suddenly shown up again. "All you need is some little leather get-up and a whip."

Her cheeks flushed and she stepped back. So he'd rattled her. Excellent.

"You'd look hot in skin-tight leather."

"Okay, the break's over. Finish your water, and let's move onto the back exercises."

Wesley caught her gaze. He'd definitely gotten to her. Good. "See what I mean?"

Her gaze shot up toward the ceiling, just like it used to do when she was a teenager and he'd frustrated and bothered her.

He pulled himself into a sitting position and she separated his legs on either side of the narrow bench with the weight bar just out of reach above his head. She straddled the bench in front of and facing him, and used her legs as support beside each of his knees, with her feet guarding his, keeping them in place.

"We'll start with fifty pounds, and go from there."

"What do you mean, 'we'? Seems like I'm doing all the lifting here."

"As you should be," she said, with a serious as hell expression.

She squeezed his shoulder and it took every last bit of his attention away from the teasing. Her hand on his shoulder woke a bundle of nerve endings, and warmed the skin all the way up to his neck. He couldn't deny he'd missed the touch of a woman these past nine months.

Her touch made him think of the last time he'd seen her. It had been at his sister's wedding, where they'd played a dangerous game of getting high on bubbly champagne and acting like they didn't know what they were doing. Then they'd kissed, teasing each other with their lips and tongues, crossing the line with their touches. He glanced at her chest then quickly looked away, needing something to get his mind off those thoughts.

"So I'll do these exercises, but you're going to have to entertain me by bringing me up to date on your life." He didn't need her help to hold him in place on the bench.

He balanced himself every day and used sand bags to keep his feet from straying, but he liked having her this close so he kept it to himself. Now he needed distraction from her nearness. "The last time I saw you, you'd just gotten your Master's degree. Oh, and your hair was a lot longer than it is now." Though he definitely liked this more cosmopolitan yet sexy look. He pulled down the weighted bar and did repetitions. Fifty pounds was nothing, but she'd find out soon enough.

She watched his every move, ready to jump in and catch him if he lost his balance. Again, unnecessary, but he'd let her do it since it probably made her feel useful.

"Well, I went on to get my PhD, then passed the boards and became a physical therapist."

"I get that part. I want the juicy bits. How many hearts did you break? Love affairs. The good stuff."

She gave a short laugh. "That'll take all of two minutes."

He raised a brow in mid-pull, hands spaced wide on the bar working the neck, shoulder and trapezius muscles. As always, it felt great. But her personal assessment of what he thought was a damn important part of a person's life—interactions with the opposite sex—felt all wrong. Two minutes? "I don't believe that for a second."

"I was totally focused on my career and it was hard to meet nice guys."

"So tell me about the rotten ones, then. Come on, I've been living in a cave. There must have been someone." He challenged her to dig deeper, just like she'd been doing to him. "I need some dirt."

She sighed, hands on her hips, her legs in a hip-wide stance. For a sex-starved man, even that looked sexy. He gripped the weight bar tighter.

"I got engaged when I was twenty-nine. I think it was

more out of panic for my upcoming birthday. The first big one after twenty-one, you know?"

"Do women still let that bother them?"

"You do live in a cave. Wes, some things never change. Like right now, I'm almost thirty-four and I'm re-evaluating my life. If I wait too long, it might be too late."

"You don't look a day over thirty. In fact, I don't see much change at all since my sister's wedding and that's, what, ten years ago now?" He stopped in mid-press. "And too late for what?"

"My eggs are getting old."

"Eggs? Oh, for crying out loud, get a dog or a bird or something. You can have a pet in that traveling house, can't you?"

"I could, I'm just not sure it would be fair to a dog or cat."

"A bird would be in a cage, what difference would it make?"

She shrugged, then stared off into the distance. That made him curious. "So why didn't you marry the guy you were engaged to? You could've had a bunch of kids by now."

Her prior open expression closed down. She paused. "It was the other way around. He decided not to marry me."

"That's harsh." Who in their right mind wouldn't want to marry Mary?

A wistful breath laugh escaped her lips. "Let's just say it took me by surprise." She kept staring toward the ocean, and he wished he hadn't picked at an old wound by being curious. "I guess he wasn't the one."

Wes wanted to guffaw at such a silly notion, but he could see she was still hurting, so he trod lightly. "You honestly think that? The 'one' bit? Hell, I figured that out after my first engagement."

With all of her attention now turned back on him, she'd clearly moved on and it relieved him. "How many times have you been engaged? Sheesh, Alex obviously didn't keep me in the loop."

Having successfully captured her interest, he sat straighter, ready to boast like the jaded man he'd become. "When I first graduated from medical school I thought I was in love. Didn't work out, though, when I caught her in bed with my roommate. Then, after Alexandra got married, I guess I was feeling a little pressure. I proposed to my girlfriend of the time, a fellow doctor, and we set a date. With my neurosurgery fellowship and her pursuing thoracic surgery, sometimes the relationship felt more like a competition. Anyway, we were both extremely busy and we wound up not having enough time for each other, and whatever we'd had going on before kind of fizzled out."

"Why didn't you bring her to Alexandra's wedding?"

Ah, so she hadn't forgotten their time together. Their second world-class kiss and more? To be honest, he'd purposely opted not to bring Giselle that weekend. When he'd found out that Mary was the maid of honor, and he'd also be in the wedding party, he'd wanted to go solo. He'd been planning to ask Giselle to marry him, but had put on the brakes at that point, deciding to wait until after he'd seen Mary again. He wasn't even sure why, but he knew for a fact that it was what he'd needed to do to be fair to Giselle.

"The wedding interfered with her schedule." Conveniently.

It felt weird, realizing how he'd intentionally set that

up. No wonder his second engagement had been doomed from the start.

Quiet now, Mary directed Wesley into a new position and had him work one arm at a time with a dumbbell. As usual it burned and hurt, but in a good way. A challenging way that made him feel alive. Lately it was the only way he felt alive.

"So what was dumb schmuck's name?"

"Who?"

"Your ex-fiancé."

She laughed, obviously liking what he'd called her ex. "Charles. Chuck."

Now he guffawed. "Oh, hell, no. There's your proof right there. No way should you have married a guy named Chuck."

It made her smile and he was surprised how good that felt.

"What was your fiancée's name?"

"Giselle."

She made a funny face. "Of course your fiancée would be named something like Giselle."

Well, he had been a prince back then, according to his mother anyway. But he needed to bring the subject back to Mary. "You've got to have more to tell me about the last ten years than that." He strained out the words as he worked up a sweat. "By the way, Chuck rhymes with schmuck."

After he'd made her laugh, which again felt great, she set off telling him about the six places she'd lived in over the last two years, how she'd decided to design and commission someone to build her tiny home to her exact specifications. How she'd had to learn to drive a pickup truck, and how happy she was jumping from assignment to assignment, and loving the freedom of being completely self-sufficient. Yet he didn't believe for a minute that she was over her broken engagement with the guy with the unfortunate name.

Something else nagged at him. Her freedom. For the first time in weeks he focused on what he missed more than anything. The loss of his independence clawed at his chest and he nearly dropped the dumbbell.

"Woah! You okay?"

"I think I've had enough for today."

Surprisingly, she understood, and didn't push him. "You've done great. I can tell how hard you've worked over the past months. Once we get your lower extremity joints fine-tuned you'll be feeling great. I promise."

He zeroed in on those eyes that reflected the teal of the afternoon sea. "I'm going to hold you to it. Just so you know."

"And I'd expect no less."

Some twisted kind of mutual respect arced between them, until he got back on task. Once back in his wheelchair, he rolled himself toward the door. "Don't let me down."

"I won't, and that's why I'll be back later this afternoon to do more passive range of motion."

"Can't wait."

He'd suspected, like him, she'd only touched the surface of her life today. He'd skimmed his personal life so lightly she'd walk away not knowing an iota more about him. He wanted it that way, too. When he'd lost the life he'd taken for granted for almost thirty-seven years, he'd nearly given up. All that had gone before simply didn't matter anymore, because everything had changed. Sometimes it was too painful to remember what he'd lost. Sometimes he'd wake up in a panic at night, forgetting he couldn't use his legs anymore, freaking out while trying to get out of bed to use the bathroom. Then it would hit him. *I'm paralyzed.* He was living in the AP world now, he couldn't just get up and walk anywhere he wanted anymore. *After paraplegia*, everything had changed.

He used the towel she'd handed him on his way out to wipe down his face and arms, as always liking how exercising made him feel alive. Vital.

From the waist up.

He headed for his room and thought about Mary wearing those yoga pants with a midriff-showing workout top. Her body went in and out at all the right places, and he liked those curves. She had muscular legs, and not many women could boast deltoids, triceps and biceps on the arms like that, without coming off masculine. On her they were sexy.

Which brought him back to his unlikely ongoing attraction to the woman he'd always known had a crush on him. He'd taken that knowledge lightly back when he'd taken her for granted. Back then he wouldn't let himself explore the protective feelings he'd harbored for her, so he'd kept things superficial. What an egotist! Now, clearly, everything had flipped, and he felt edgy being around her, giving her carte blanche with his physical well-being. Hopeful, yet not knowing how much to expect in results. *Prove it, Mary. Please.*

Why had his mood taken a nosedive since seeing her again? Because she reminded him of everything he'd never have again? If that was the case, why had he started looking forward to spending time with her? Like right now, knowing she'd be back in a couple hours to push his legs to his chest. Something he'd been trained to do by himself months ago but had refused to keep up.

Nothing made sense since she'd popped back into his

life. Before, he'd lived for his routine, worked like a fiend in the gym until exhausted, so he could sleep. And forget.

Now she was here and he'd started remembering. The problem was all he wanted to do was forget. What was the point in remembering?

It was too late. He lived in an AP world. Everything had changed.

So why was he still looking forward to passive ROM later today?

CHAPTER THREE

MARY ATE HOMEMADE granola with milk, preparing for another day of getting Wesley Van Allen back to where he should be. Physically, anyway. As she did so she sat on her front porch and took in the view of the thickly overcast morning and the sound of a cranky sea. Strangely, it calmed her.

Since spending so much time with Wesley the past week, she'd been inundated with memories of him at eighteen. The year she'd met him. Tall, tanned, athletic in a tennis player kind of way. Not nearly as buff as he was now, but he'd definitely looked fit. Hair nearly dark as midnight, with light brown eyes softening his otherwise commanding demeanor. Not your everyday brand of handsome. Back then he'd seemed so worldly and independent, so sure of himself. It had also been evident his parents had treated him like a prince. Alexandra had nicknamed him the Prince of Westwood and had snickered with Mary every time he proved it.

She could only imagine how shocking his becoming paraplegic had been to all of them, but most especially to a guy who'd never met a challenge he couldn't take on and win.

Was that why he'd agreed to give Mary two months?

Because she'd stared into those unwavering eyes and dared him to?

Instead of graduating high school and heading off to university in another state, like most of his high-achieving friends, Wes had elected to attend U.C.L.A. Even though less than ten miles down the road from his West Los Angeles family house, he'd taken a dorm room, probably to feel some independence, but had still gone home every weekend. His mother had lavished attention on him, and his father had exuded paternal pride, feeding his princely calling. Neurosurgeon. Who'd want to move away from that? Alexandra had used to confide in Mary that she resented it. When she'd called after he'd first had his accident she'd sounded devastated and, more recently, desperate to help him.

Luckily for Mary—the teen who had seen Wesley as nothing less than a heartthrob—he had often been home for weeknight dinner. She'd kept her little secret from Alexandra, worried it could impact their friendship and she'd think Mary only came around because of him. Mary had loved Alex for accepting her for who she was. She'd found an amazing second home and hadn't wanted to risk losing it.

"Why eat cafeteria food when I have Sarah, the best cook in L.A., fixing dinner?" Wesley had once answered succinctly, when Mary had gotten up the nerve to strike up a conversation with him, using dinner as the "fascinating" topic, so flummoxed by his presence that it was the only subject she could think of. With her living in a trailer park, they'd shared so little of anything else.

Mary had never tasted such delicious food in her life before going to dinner at the Van Allens'. Her parents' idea of a home-cooked meal was a microwaved frozen dinner. If she was lucky that frozen meal hadn't started out with freezer burn. Eating at the Van Allens' had opened up a whole new world of culinary delights, and tastes she'd developed on her own all the years since.

She took another bite of the granola, which she'd baked in her own tiny oven until the honey glaze had been just right on the almonds and walnuts. She especially liked the addition of fresh coconut, now roasted to perfection and scattered throughout the nuts, seeds, and oats mixture. She'd definitely make this recipe again. Maybe she should take Wes some.

His attractiveness had improved with time, giving him character. She liked the hint of gray at his temples, and the fine lines accentuating his brown eyes. It seemed the high-stress workouts made them grow darker. Probably the hell-bound determination mixed with adrenaline was the reason for his dilated pupils.

When she managed to make him smile, which happened more and more often as they worked out together, she loved the grooves on either side of his mouth. She could tell an authentic smile, which brightened his entire face, from the obligatory ones that never reached those eyes. But most of all, since she'd first arrived a week ago, like boards getting ripped from a wall, their barriers had started to come down.

Yesterday he'd even invited her to watch a video with him, some crazy movie about an unlikely group of men and animals who guarded the galaxy. Who'd have thought he liked silly movies like that, and it had felt wonderful to laugh with him as they'd shared a bowl of popcorn. Also his suggestion. Had he always been an everyday guy, but she'd never noticed, or had his accident been the cause? And could she call a man stuck in a wheelchair for the rest of his life an everyday guy?

Her heart clutched hard over his situation, but she refused to let it bring her down. She'd treated patients in far worse situations, and she'd learned there was something special, a certain ingredient that made the difference between giving up or carrying on—and that component resided in the human spirit, something called hope. Medical reports said Wes would never walk again, but it didn't mean his life was over…just the life he'd always known. She didn't want to get dejected all over again about his current state, so she focused back on that silly movie they'd watched together yesterday. The popcorn. The laughs. And she smiled.

Mary thought hard. Had they ever laughed together when they were teenagers? Surely, if they had, she would have remembered how robust his laugh was, how it infected her and made her giggle right along. Once yesterday, while laughing, they'd glanced at each other. She'd tried to take a mental picture, because he'd looked like a man who didn't have a care in the world. Of course it wasn't true. Everything had changed. Still, there had been that moment. If she had to leave tomorrow, she'd carry that memory with her the rest of her days. That and the way he'd looked like an honest-to-God prince in a tux on the night of her prom when he'd told her he thought she was beautiful. And maybe that sexy dark gaze he'd unveiled after their hot make-out session at his sister's wedding reception. His pupils had definitely been dilated then, too.

Okay, she'd ventured too far down memory lane, leaving her tensing her inner thighs. She checked her watch. Geez! She was running late. She crammed the last bite of cereal into her mouth, rushed inside and rinsed the bowl, then brushed her teeth at the same sink. Today she planned to up the repetitions—progress—and the thought made her smile.

Hmm, maybe she *was* a dominatrix in the making, but would one bring a client granola?

That was the second time she'd grinned that morning, thanks to Wesley Van Allen.

"You ever get lost in that thing you call a house, Harris?"

Two hours later, Wes gritted his teeth and spit out the words in mid chest press. She'd increased the usual weight by twenty-five pounds, and he handled it like nothing, even making small talk as he lifted and pressed. She liked it that he'd reverted to referring to her like he used to. *Harris.*

"It's plenty big enough, Wes. I have everything I need."

He glanced over, looked her up and down. "I suppose living in workout clothes helps with closet space."

"I've got plenty of regular clothes."

"You can't tell me that if I invited you to Geoffrey's for dinner you'd have something special to wear."

"You mean glamorous? Does anyone even do glamorous anymore? Are we talking shoulder pads and glitter? Come on, we're in Malibu, isn't this the home of casual?"

"You've never been to Geoffrey's, have you?"

"Uh, no, but any woman worth her salt owns a little black dress, including me."

He stopped in mid-press. "Key word being 'little' with your living situation, I suppose." He smiled over his snappy reply.

"And when's the last time you went out to dinner?" She decided to press him on getting a normal routine. Why couldn't and shouldn't he go out to dinner?

"Is that dress sexy and does it show off your curves?" He'd obviously chosen to ignore her prodding him on living a more normal life, instead turning the conversation back on her.

She decided not to push it, and gave him a skeptical glance. "I've got curves? Since when?" She tried to brush off the topic, but he kept staring at her, making sure she knew he thought so. A whisper tickled through her with the promise of goose-bumps on the way, and there she was, tensing her inner thighs again.

"So tell me about your house." Thank goodness, he was letting her off the hook just as she had him, a moment before. Had he noticed her reaction? His eyes were back on the weights, his concentration on working his muscles.

And she liked what she saw popping up on his back and shoulders. "It's everything I ever wanted."

"I guess that means you never wanted much, huh?" This came through gritted teeth. So she *had* challenged him.

She playfully kicked his foot. "Come visit. You'll be surprised."

"I doubt my wheelchair would even fit inside."

"Of course it will. Hell, I'll even have Heath help me build a ramp. What time do you want to come?"

"You're serious, aren't you?"

"I'll even throw in dinner. That is if you tell me where a girl can grocery shop around here first. What do you say?"

She saw the battle ensuing in his thoughts, his troubled eyes giving him away. Of course he wouldn't accept her invitation, he was still too intent on punishing himself for the rest of his life for going water skiing and having an accident. Just like his father had insisted, he'd accepted it had been his fault. Well, to hell with that!

"Why not? Okay."

His surprising response stole some of the ire she'd worked up on behalf of his father. "Seriously, you'll come?"

"Sure."

Well, there you go. Now all she had to do was think of something spectacular to cook.

Seven o'clock sharp, Wesley made it up Heath's makeshift ramp to Mary's front porch in his ultralight sports chair. Small and compact, it was perfect for her house. He'd put on a pair of chinos and a button-down shirt for the first time since the accident. He'd been shocked at how loose fitting those chinos were since the last time he'd worn them, which had been before the accident. Earlier, he'd made a rash decision and used electric clippers to buzz cut his hair, military short. A Samurai topknot really wasn't his style. He ran a hand over his scalp, liking the fine prickly feel and the fact he'd let go of the confirmed recluse look.

Her door was open, and he had to admit that on first sight the lighting and wood-planked walls looked warm and inviting, though snug.

Her back was to him at the far end of the single room in the designated kitchen area, her hair was down and shining extra blonde under the soft glow of the indoor lights. Smooth jazz music played over speakers. She'd put on leggings and a gauzy sleeveless tunic top that billowed around the outline of her hips and upper thighs. She was literally barefoot in her kitchen, preparing dinner for him. Bohemian and sexy—not to mention showing off her toned and sexy arms—and he didn't need to feel from the waist down to notice that the sight of her turned him on.

Damn, it had been a mistake to come here. What was the point? A wave of claustrophobia swept over him at the thought of going inside, being stuck in his wheelchair. He clumsily attempted to turn around on the mini-porch before she noticed, so he could go back home and forget the whole thing. He'd call and say he'd developed leg spasms or something. He didn't fit in anymore and had already proved that by trying to go back to work three months ago. What a catastrophe.

"Hi! Come in. I'm so glad you came."

Hell, she'd caught him in mid-turn. He couldn't get out of it now.

"What'd you do to your hair?" Her smile was genuine and welcoming and his frontline, prepared-for-action defense cut him some slack. For that moment her appeal overcame his resistance. Maybe it had something to do with those dangly copper and gold earrings that sparkled and played peekaboo with her strawberry blonde hair.

"I figured since you're putting me through boot camp, I may as well do the military thing."

"Wow, what a difference."

You think? He hadn't bothered to look at himself closely in the mirror and was now curious. A buzz job was a buzz job, right? He rolled in front of a small mirror on her wall and took a look. Yeah, it was short all right. "Uh, thanks?"

"The grunge look was never your style."

True, he'd always taken pride in his appearance, but since the accident he hadn't given a flying whatever about the way he looked.

He saw her reflection standing behind him in the mirror. Right now her opinion mattered a lot, especially with her looking so damn good.

He turned. Rather than stare at each other, a million ideas winging through his brain, he rolled his chair around her, needing to distract where his thoughts were going and to fight off another surge of claustrophobia. "So show me around. Wait, I guess I've already seen everything."

"Ha ha. There are subtleties you've never imagined here, my friend. Let me point them out."

She showed him around a room that felt more spacious than its actual square footage, even with a whole lot of wood—knotty pine planks covering the walls, a peaked roof in the living room, laminate nearly black wood flooring. A Tyrolean mountain cabin on wheels. He noticed she'd rolled up a colorful area rug and tucked it by the wall, probably in preparation for his wheelchair. There were no less than four good-sized windows bringing in what was left of the daylight, which helped his subtle but unrelenting panic over the tiny space.

To break up all the wood, she'd hung a bright and busy oil painting on canvas above a pull-out desk, next to the bench covered in upholstered pillows. The couch? Okay, he'd buy that. A large-sized TV was mounted on the adjacent wall, and was currently turned to the jazzy saxophone and bass stuff, accompanied by a slideshow of beautiful nature pictures. *Not bad.* It helped smooth out his unease.

"Something smells great."

"Thanks. I found some free-range chicken cutlets at the Malibu Ranch Market. I'm trying a variation on chicken Parmigiana but with homemade pesto sauce instead of marinara. Oh, and since they had such a great assortment of wines, I chose a Pinot Grigio. Would you like some?"

Where were his manners? He'd shown up at her house without bringing anything, because he'd refused to think of this—being sociable with an old friend—as anything other than obligation. She'd challenged him. He'd taken the dare.

He'd had enough awkward encounters with old friends after he'd first had the accident. Everyone had tried really hard to act like everything was the same as always between them. Even his doctor friends. Except it wasn't. He sat in a wheelchair and couldn't pick up and do anything he wanted. Ever again. That had reminded each of his friends how much had changed between them, and had caused their visits to dwindle off. But this was Mary, not just an old friend but a physical therapist. She knew about people like him, treated him like she always had, and he felt bad about skipping a basic courtesy, like bringing wine or flowers when invited for dinner.

"So would you like some?"

Damn, he'd tuned out, a habit he'd gotten good at since the accident—going deep into his thoughts. "Oh. Yes, thanks." The old and forgotten part of his personality nudged him. "Sorry I didn't bring you any wine. I suppose the least I could do was bring dessert." It felt kind of good, too.

"Nonsense. I invited you. All I wanted was for you to come for dinner. See my place." She put the wine on a narrow counter beside the refrigerator and opened it. "To prove you'd fit."

"What's back there?" Curious, he pointed to a door frame with a sage-green burlap curtain. "Your pantry?"

"My bathroom and laundry room." She stepped aside so he could peek in.

Everything was smaller scale than normal, pushing down on him. Even the toilet wasn't the usual size, and there wasn't a sink. Tension made him clutch the armrests of his chair. The glass door on the positively one-person shower gave the room—if you could call it that since it was about the size of a normal pantry—a sense of being larger. Yet he still sensed heaviness with each breath in the tiny room. The stacked front-loading, stainless-steel washer and dryer couldn't have been more than a third of the normal size. More like Ken and Barbie-sized. What could he expect in a four-foot-by-four-foot area? But he could see for a single person on the road this would definitely do the trick, as long as Mary parked in a place with hook-ups for electricity and water. In other words, for a person who liked to go camping all the time. And definitely not for a person in a wheelchair.

"Compact, for sure, but surprisingly functional, I suppose." He scrambled for something positive to say.

"Absolutely." She opened the table lying flat against the wall, stabilized it with a latch, and placed their two wine glasses there. He rolled over and parked as she poured for both of them.

Taking another hint from his old sociable self, he offered a toast by lifting his glass. "Of all the strange places your travels have taken you, I'm surprised..." he tipped his head in acknowledgment of her efforts "...and pleased you arrived here. Cheers."

He took a sip, but she stood looking at him, dumbfounded. "You're glad I'm here?"

"Don't push it, Harris. Just take a drink."

She did, but smiled the whole time and he wondered how the wine kept from dribbling out the sides of her mouth.

As he took another drink, his eyes glanced upward to the loft. "Now, that's a bedroom sure to keep a guy like me away." The irony—both practical and sexual—struck him. Had his joke been tasteless or merely true and to the point?

She laughed good-naturedly, bearing with his crude-on-so-many-levels joke, then stepped forward and ran her hand over his head. It made him feel like a dog and he hated her for that for one second, until he saw the sweet tenderness in her peaceful green eyes. She'd meant no harm. It'd been a gesture of affection.

A word he refused to remember.

"With your upper body strength, you could probably take that ladder, or any ladder, without breaking a sweat."

He laughed, wondering if she'd just subtly come on to him. Hoping a little she had. "It's the getting down that will be the hard part." Yes, he'd intentionally skipped over the down and dirty bits on the loft mattress, knowing that probably wouldn't be part of his life again. Especially not with her. The previously fruity Pinot Grigio went sour on his tongue. "Don't you hit your head on the ceiling when you sit up?" Speaking of harsh reality.

"I used to, but I've adjusted now."

"You're nuts, you know that, right?"

"One person's *nuts* is another person's happy. I'm content here." She swirled the wine around in her glass and smiled at him.

He couldn't deny that she looked happy. "Even though it feels like a tree house?"

"Best damn tree house I've ever seen." She preened that silky hair with those earrings slipping in and out of view, and it hit him full on in the center of his chest.

Her happiness, her freedom, she nearly took his breath away. "One big gust of wind could have this place on its side." He deflected the feeling using one of his favorite defenses, being snarky.

"Look, I know it's small but, like I said, I have everything I need, and I'm happy here."

He glanced out the window up the driveway to his huge and lonely house. "That's more than I can say for myself so good on you. I'm happy for you." Why hold a grudge over his predicament against an innocent victim like Mary? She'd come to help him and as much as he'd wanted to kick her out at first, he was grateful she was here.

The oven timer went off and Mary rushed to take out the mouth-watering chicken, pesto and cheese scented meal from the toy-sized appliance.

Dinner was served and at first they sat in amicable silence as he savored the food, tasting pinenut-flavored chicken in a way he hadn't enjoyed a meal in nine months. He'd turned half the lights off in his life since the accident, and Mary was insisting on being his generator. The light may be dimmer than it used to be, but it had become so much brighter than before she'd arrived. He needed to thank her properly one day soon.

Over dinner and more wine, him more than her, they opened up and talked about old times, carefully avoiding the most significant moments—their first kiss, a mind-blower—and their one date at her prom, the night he'd realized she was the most beautiful woman he'd ever seen, and had wanted her with everything he'd had. Not to mention the second life-altering kiss ten years later.

During the course of dinner, including seconds and followed by a spectacular apple crumble with vanilla ice cream for dessert, he felt human again—like a guy with feelings and passion and experience, and a surprisingly huge appetite. Nearly admitting that nostalgia was far better than isolation and bitterness.

His hands clutched the armrests on his wheelchair, remembering he'd never walk again. She'd almost tricked him into forgetting that detail.

He ground his molars and went quiet. Damn reality.

"Are you okay?"

"Sure." He hadn't fooled her. She homed in on his restless eyes, forcing him to meet her gaze. He needed to get out of there. The moment seemed like an eternity, which she made up for by crossing the short distance between them, leaning in and kissing his cheek. The exotic flowered scent in her hair nearly overpowered him.

"I know it must be unimaginably hard to deal with all you've had to, but I want you to know that you're the one guy in my entire life I'll always look up to. You're my life-changer. Nothing will ever alter that."

Moved by her words, maybe a little dumbstruck, he held her earnest stare, thankful for her honesty, unaware as she angled her lips on top of his, settling so gently before slipping away, leaving him craving more, more than he'd dared to want since he'd lost half of himself.

He left her house that evening scraped, bruised and frustrated emotionally, though his stomach was filled with good wine, food and dessert. On so many levels it had been torture, reminiscing about the past, knowing he'd never be that person again. That reality always managed to cut deep and suck the joy from a room, and it had happened so much faster in a treehouse-sized place like Mary's.

He'd enjoyed her company more than he'd cared to admit, but he wasn't that guy anymore. Her life-changer. He'd grown comfortable in withdrawing, it had become his default program, and he a computerized robot who only liked to work out in the gym. But Mary was making that escape route more and more difficult to navigate.

He'd been a complete gentleman when he'd left, not grabbing her shoulders and forcing her mouth to stay with his, as he'd wanted with all he had. Why not take what he wanted? He'd already lost everything else. But he'd chosen not to cross that line and had made a quick exit, so she'd never have a clue how torn up and mixed up he felt. Maybe he overrated his acting ability and she saw right through him—who knew?—but she'd seemed fine with his abrupt departure. He simply couldn't take another moment of what she offered—life, optimism, sexual desire. He'd let go of those feelings long ago.

Once home, after undressing and getting ready for bed, he remembered a promise. Mary had asked him to take ownership of his bedtime range of motion exercises, and he'd said he would. So he transferred from his chair to his bed and gathered his leg, bending the knee and pulling it toward his chest. It went so much easier than the last time he'd tried to do it a month or two ago. He had to give credit where credit was due, so he thought about Mary. Again. Probably a bad idea while lying on the bed after her tender kiss.

He'd acted like he thought she was crazy for choosing to live in a movable tiny house but, in truth, he'd gotten a kick out of her unusual living arrangement. Even envied her being able to pick up and move house wherever she took a job. The freedom. Independence. No strings attached.

He manually rotated his ankle around the socket, then flexed and pointed his foot, and thought how Mary had once been a caged bird living with those parents yet had always managed to be a free spirit. He'd admired that about her way back then, even though it'd forced him to take notice how much he depended on *his* parents. Had he ever been a free spirit? Why hadn't he chosen a university farther away from home when he'd had the chance, with several to choose from?

With his eyes closed, he grimaced. *Because of her.* Even then Mary had made an impact on his life. Sure, she was his sister's best friend, but she'd reached somewhere new inside him, a place that had never been touched, and he wanted to watch over her. Not in a big brother kind of way either. Hell, if he'd gone to Harvard, like his parents had wanted him to, he wouldn't have been there for her when Alexandra had sworn Mary needed a date for the prom. If he hadn't encouraged her to think big and go after her dreams, would she have had a different life altogether? She'd called him her life-changer—could it be true?

How could he ever know for sure?

His thoughts wouldn't let up and he suspected he wouldn't be getting much sleep tonight.

Over dinner, she'd told him all about her job with the medical agency, how she'd specifically chosen it in order to see the country. She could have made three times as much money signing on with a large hospital and staying put. Then she'd reminded him that, unlike him, her family had never, ever taken a vacation. She had a lot of territory to cover to make up for that. Staying put had never been an option.

These days, staying put was his only option. My, how things had flipped.

That was another thing he'd always admired about her, she never complained about her lot in life. Nothing seemed to get her down. She'd been wise enough, even back then, to know that one day she'd be in charge of her own future, and since then, rather than blaming any failures on her parents, she'd done wonders with it.

He lay back and rolled to his side, adjusting the pillow under his neck, noticing that he could already sense the difference in hip rotation from consistently doing ROM.

There had always been something else he'd dug about her—she'd been crazy about him. Sure, it had just been a teenaged infatuation, and that usually faded over time. But somehow he'd known that, coming from Mary, even a crush could turn into forever. Back then he hadn't been anywhere ready for forever…but still the small one from the trailer park had called out to him. And then he'd kissed her.

Why hadn't he ever done anything about those in-stincts when he'd had the chance?

Adrenaline leaked into his chest, making his heart speed up and an anxious feeling spread like a flash flood throughout his upper body. The first kiss had knocked him for a loop, and *forever* hadn't seemed like such a bad idea at the time.

Bad idea. Really bad idea.

Fortunately, he'd come to his senses before he'd acted on his most basic of all instincts. He'd had big plans for his life, so had his father, and getting mixed up with his kid sister's friend couldn't be a part of it. Dear old Dad would have hit the ceiling if he had gotten involved with Mary. The man could only take charity so far.

He rolled to his other side, reaching down to adjust his legs again. Then he admitted something else—that first kiss had been for curiosity and had shaken him up, but in a good way; the kiss ten years later had been a test to see if his feelings had changed. The truth had shown up that evening at his sister's wedding—he'd never stopped wanting Mary.

But what the hell did any of that matter now, when everything else had changed?

Seeing her again, spending time with her every day, now that he was who he was, sometimes felt like rolling in ground glass. Yet being around Mary was still worth it. He might never be the guy she'd look up to again, but he knew she still valued him, no matter what he'd become.

In the beginning, after the accident, he hadn't wanted to live anymore, but over time he'd found a reason to go on. He still loved his family and wanted to see them all have good lives, even though his father had been out of line insinuating he had been to blame for the accident. He had knowledge that a dozen years of medical training had taught him. Hell, he'd saved lives. Regularly! That had to account for something.

He'd discovered the gym and full-out body building. Well, upper body building, anyway. It had saved him and had given him false hope for getting back to work. He'd tried it his way before and it had backfired. He hadn't been ready to go back to work, mentally or physically. Having full-out leg spasms in front of a shocked patient had proved it. Now he had Mary in his corner, and even though she mixed him up with forgotten feelings, she was his one big hope to get back on the job.

Prove it, she'd challenged him, and he hoped with everything he had that he would.

She'd given him a second chance, and right about now that meant everything to him.

CHAPTER FOUR

MARY STARED AT the very close ceiling in her loft bedroom. She'd always felt cozy and protected up here, yet tonight she couldn't sleep. It definitely had something to do with spending the evening with Wesley Van Allen, and drinking wine. And what was up with the kiss?

Wes had looked rugged with that short haircut, and had seemed more his old self, and, well, she'd gotten carried away, once again proving his being in a wheelchair leveled the playing field in her head with a guy who'd always been out of her league.

Shame on her, but he was right there, easily accessible, and it had felt really great to kiss him. And she could tell he'd liked it, had seen the slight flare to his nostrils and a glint in his eyes afterward.

As hard as it was, putting thoughts of Wesley aside, she lay in the dark, staring at the ceiling and thinking about the topic that had captured her heart for the last year—having a baby.

She wanted a baby of her own so badly it hurt. She'd be turning thirty-four soon, and she couldn't exactly hold out for finding the right guy first. What if she never did? She wanted her own child to love and hold and cherish. She'd never felt cherished in her life, but she knew, after bonding with little Rose, it would be easy to do with a baby of her own. The older she got the more complications there could be with giving birth, too. Of course she'd love her baby, no matter what, but it would be challenging enough being a single, working mom. Why take any added chances by putting off what she could feasibly accomplish now? Maybe she should blame the urgent feelings about getting pregnant on all the Kegels she'd inadvertently been doing lately, thanks to Wes.

Which reminded her, she really needed to get going with her plans. Should she go with an insemination clinic or do it the old-fashioned way? *Ha-ha, with who?* She squinted to avoid the image of a certain handsome man with a new haircut.

Not exactly putting yourself out there, are you, Harris? She could practically hear Wes's snarky retort, that was, if he had a clue what was on her mind. Then it hit her.

She sat bolt upright and conked her head on the loft ceiling. After seeing a burst of stars and rubbing out the pain, she lay back down but not before admitting her crazy idea might just work.

The bigger question was—would Wesley Van Allen consider being a sperm donor? Think of the phenomenal DNA! Smart. Handsome...so out of her league.

The idea was further proof she'd had too much wine to drink. Now with the bump on her forehead, at least she wouldn't feel a hangover.

Hitting her head had also knocked some sense into her. This crazy idea was asking too much, and Wes would throw her out of the house if she dared bring up the subject. Heck, he'd probably think she'd set up this whole *"Hello, I'm just popping in to help you get back on track"* for the sake of getting what she wanted.

How awful would that be! Even though it had honest-to-God never occurred to her about Wes until just now. He'd never believe her. She couldn't dare betray his trust.

She needed to drop it. Drop the subject right now.

She rolled onto her side with one tiny thought waving its hand far in the back of her mind. *Maybe?*

Wesley had been co-operative over the past few days since their dinner, but today's workout had seemed extra hard for him. Yet he'd kept pushing himself, getting frustrated when he didn't get the results he'd expected.

"Your head's not into it today. That's to be expected from time to time," Mary said.

"I feel like I've hit the wall." He dropped the free weights and they landed with a loud thud on the workout mat.

"Don't get discouraged."

He glared at her. "Don't give me that."

"Okay, you can keep pounding your head against a wall if you want. I'm just saying today might be a good rest day." She tossed him a towel.

He grabbed it and wiped his face, agitation tensing his eyes.

She drank some water, then offered him his own bottle.

He shook his head.

He wasn't about to be appeased. It was clear all he wanted to do, besides work himself too hard, was sulk.

"If you overdo it, you may regress. Take a break today. Watch some movies." *Why did she suddenly hope he'd ask her to join him?* "Get outside for some fresh air."

"I'll make my own decisions. Thanks." He made his point grudgingly.

She paced the gym, putting some distance between them. He'd seemed tenser the last few days of workouts since their dinner together, and she'd hoped he'd get over it, but he clearly hadn't. What a bonehead idea it'd been to kiss him. *Don't take all the blame, there could be dozens of things bothering him that I have no idea about.* But whatever was getting to him sure had a tight grip.

While standing behind him, she saw the incredibly fit man in the wheelchair gulp down the entire bottle of water. Everything he did lately was extreme. He tried too hard, expected too much of himself, insisted on pushing, pushing, pushing.

The guy needed an outlet beyond the gym. "I have an idea, why not use that beautiful Jacuzzi sitting out there on your patio, empty and lonely?"

He thought for a moment, his brows smoothing as he did. "That's not a half-bad idea. Maybe I do need a break."

She clapped. "Great."

"Come with me?"

"I thought you were sick of me."

"That's not the issue."

"What is it then?"

"Do you have to make such a big deal about everything? It was your idea, wasn't it? So come with me. That's all I'm saying." He spun his wheelchair toward the door. "I'll meet you out there in fifteen minutes."

"Deal!"

Twenty minutes later Mary showed up at the patio Jacuzzi. Wes was already in it, his arms outstretched along the tastefully patterned tile, the picture of a man of leisure without a care. From this vantage point, no one would know he needed a chair to get around.

She felt self-conscious taking off her bathing suit cover-up in front of him, because he didn't look away, just sat there grinning the whole time. It made her suck her stomach in tight and tense her inner thighs.

As quickly as possible, she slipped into the soothing water and sat across from him. Looking disappointed, he patted the spot beside him so she complied. He greeted her with a little splash, and she returned the favor. Smiling at each other, they settled down, submerged in the hot water, soaking in the sun and feeling completely relaxed.

"This feels great," she said, leaning her head back on the rim.

"I know. I should use this more often."

"I told you!" After a few seconds of silence she couldn't resist asking. "Why don't you?"

"It's not something I enjoy doing alone."

"Is it a safety issue?"

He shook his head, lapping up some water with his palm and dropping it on his head, wetting his face. "No. It's just with all these seats it's meant to be a group activity. Not solitary."

"True. But it's also therapeutic. Good for your circulation."

"Could you stop, just for one minute?" He lifted his hand out of the water to warn her. "Everything we do doesn't have to be about my rehabilitation. Can't we just sit here like a couple of old friends enjoying a soak?"

"I'm sorry, Wes, I wasn't aware that was how I came off."

"I get that you showed up to help me, but honestly, Harris, I've got it covered. Now that your wonder bike has arrived, everything is all set up. I've got everything I need."

"Are you saying my services are done here?"

"No." He scooted closer on the underwater bench they

shared and whispered in the vicinity of her ear. "Start thinking of yourself as my guest."

"Not your dominatrix?"

He laughed, as she'd hoped he would. "If you want that job, it won't be in the gym." He winked, and she couldn't very well blame the warm water for the chill that ran along her spine. "Here's the deal. Things have been out of balance. Since you showed up, you've been running things. I get it that you want to help me, but I liked a lot about how I did things, too."

"You want more teamwork?"

"That's a start. I guess what I'm saying is we've got this time together, so why not enjoy ourselves?"

"Wow, this hot tub really has mellowed you."

He smiled, looking more relaxed than he'd been since she'd arrived two weeks ago. "Maybe we should do this more often."

Rita appeared with a tray of sandwiches and lemonade. "Thought you might like some lunch," was all she said, before putting everything on the nearby glass-topped table with an umbrella at the center, and heading back to the house.

"Thank you!" he called out, helping Mary understand he didn't take his ghost-like cook for granted. It meant more than he could realize.

The sky was cornflower blue, the water the perfect temperature, the buff guy next to her looked *hot* as hell, and he'd just invited her to think of herself as his guest. Could her day get any better?

She closed her eyes and sighed, and was quickly surprised by the arms that gathered her near, and the inviting mouth that landed on hers. Under other circumstances she would have tensed, but not here. Not now. Because everything felt too perfect. Especially the seductive kiss Wes had just planted on her.

Was this a dream? Making out in a hot tub with an even hotter guy? She opened her eyes just as Wes's fingers strayed from her shoulder and traced across her chest to the other side before he nuzzled her neck with more kisses. She hadn't thought it was possible to get goosebumps in a Jacuzzi, but his touch had set off every last one of them.

"This was what was on my mind all morning."

"Kissing me in a spa pool?"

"Can you blame a guy for being grumpy?"

She stopped from asking if it had been a long time, since she knew chances were he hadn't ventured back into an intimate relationship with a woman since his accident. "Are you sure that's all that mood was about?"

His arms dropped from around her. She'd broken their "moment" and immediately regretted it.

"I focus too much on my condition, but I can handle it. Then here you are, doing the same thing. I've just felt under a microscope in the gym lately, and all I wanted to do was feel like a regular guy for a while."

"And here in the hot tub we can do that?"

"I'm just a guy sitting in a spa with a good-looking lady, enjoying myself." He splashed her full on in the face.

She squealed but retaliated, pushing water his way with both hands.

He laughed and doubled down, covering her with water, and she fought back. Soon they tired of acting like unsupervised kids and settled down, though still laughing. And damn if it didn't feel great.

"I'm hungry," he said.

"Me too." She climbed out and found two large towels

draped across a lounge chair. She tied one around herself and before she could bring one to Wes, he'd already gotten himself out of the tub and was sitting along the edge of the small pool.

"Can you bring my wheelchair?"

She looked around and saw it subtly tucked away under the cabana and brought it to him, first spreading the towel on the seat cushion, with the sides open and waiting to cover him. With ease and muscle he hoisted himself into the chair. Soon they were sitting at the table under the umbrella, enjoying sandwiches and fresh lemonade.

She wasn't sure what had just happened back in that spa, but was really glad they'd taken the afternoon off. He'd gently reprimanded her for being too focused on his condition instead of seeing him as a whole person exactly as he was. She'd just had a good glimpse of that guy, too, and really liked what she'd seen. The trick would be keeping the balance from here on out.

Why did she suddenly feel like she walked a tightrope over her profession and her true feelings?

After lunch they went their separate ways, saying nothing about their shared world-class kiss in the hot tub earlier.

The next morning Mary showed up in the gym to find an even grumpier Wesley.

"I thought we'd just work out alongside each other today," she said in response to his unspoken gloom. "Is that okay with you?"

He harrumphed.

She'd thought long and hard about what he'd told her yesterday about not wanting everything to focus on him. She'd realized how he must have seen things, her showing up out of nowhere, sweeping into his life to, what, save him?

The idea made her cringe. "Hey," she said.

He pressed a huge amount of weights in response.

"Everything okay?"

He grunted.

Then it hit her. She'd spent a fair amount of time thinking about the issue between them last night—the unspoken attraction that was definitely still there—especially after their wonderful kisses shared in that Jacuzzi. "You know what this is about, right?"

"What what's about?" he said, after dropping the pulley weights and making a loud clank when metal hit metal.

He looked at her as if she'd become a talking mutant. Like she'd dared to read his mind and she'd better not get it wrong. Not a sound passed between them for several seconds as she got up the guts to hit him with the elephant in the room.

"Sex. This is about sex."

He continued to glower, squinting for emphasis.

"You miss it. You need it."

"For flipping hell's sake, get off my back."

Whammo!

His brush-off only made her dig in her heels. "I'm not the one pushing myself within an inch of my life. You're obviously trying to work off your pent-up sexual energy, and you've failed…"

If he could have exterminated her with the white-hot anger flashing in his eyes, she'd be toast.

"Miserably." She wouldn't back down. He needed to hear the truth and get some facts. Now was as good a time as any, plus it might break him of needing to overwork himself.

"Thanks for reminding me, Harris," he said, putting a dreadful emphasis on *Harris*.

It hurt to see him focus his anger on her, yet she refused to break eye contact. "You can have normal sex."

He went still, seething, nearly fitful, clearly using every ounce of restraint to keep from verbally attacking her. "In case you haven't noticed, there isn't anything that's normal about me anymore." He'd lowered his voice, yet every word shouted, *This is a warning. Back off!*

She opted not to listen to the unspoken message. "You're a neurosurgeon. You know it's possible. Just not the way it was before."

The fire in his glare showered her with restrained anger, making her face go hot.

"Then what's the point?"

The rush of exasperation hit her by surprise. She was a professional, had had this conversation with several male patients over the years, yet Wes had gotten to her. He'd won. Shut her down. For now she'd give up on the topic. She picked some free weights and went to town with curls. "You'd be surprised."

He rolled the chair toward her, challenging. This conversation was far from over. "What do you mean?"

Oh, hell, was he thinking she'd just made him an offer? That wasn't her intention at all, it was the subject that needed defending, not her talking specifics. What should she say?

Act professionally. "There are many wonderful women around the world who are devoted partners of paraplegics."

Though buffer and stronger than he'd ever been in his life, he was still fragile. "You know I've always had a crush on you, Wes, and no matter how you are now, that hasn't changed. Your wheelchair doesn't factor into the equation. At all. You're an impressive and appealing man."

Emotions ruled his thinking. Now he'd gone from red-hot anger to sizzling need in record time. Very moved by what Mary had just said, Wesley took her hand, pulled her down to his eye level and, letting the barrage of desire take over, he kissed her. He forgot about where he sat or why they'd been spending so much time together over the last few days. All he saw was a woman he'd never gotten out of his mind, who'd just admitted she still had feelings for him. And he went for it.

As they kissed, every obstacle in his head stepped aside. He freely explored the lips he'd reacquainted himself with yesterday in the hot tub. He did what he wanted, took what he wanted, and she met his rough kisses with sweet music in her throat. Her reaction turned him on even more. As his tongue slid over the velvet of her lips and inside her mouth, he remembered what it was like to be a man.

She'd ignited fire inside him, and the heat of it, after all this dormant time, shocked him. "Prove it," he said over her mouth, mid-kiss. A moment later he stared into her fully dilated pupils, cluing him in she'd been as much into that kiss as he'd been. "Prove that I can still have sex."

Wes's dare sent a disturbing chill down Mary's spine. Shaken back to consciousness, she pulled away, fully aware of his clutch on her arms. He'd laid down the gauntlet, challenged her, and she was nowhere ready to prove anything!

She stood, but his hands went to her waist, keeping her near, staring at her like the commanding man he'd always been.

It took everything she had to stare deeply into his hungry eyes. She saw raw need there—*Help me be whole again.* He needed her help and, to be honest, with her recent craving to have a baby, she needed his. The next thought sent a lightning-bolt reaction through the center of her chest. Could they strike a bargain?

Her stomach twisted at the possibility. That would be all wrong.

And completely unprofessional.

She gingerly pushed back from his grasp, which had slipped to her hips, frantically thinking of a way to smooth over this huge shift in power. In the course of a minute of hot and heavenly kisses, she'd managed to annihilate all the trust she'd worked so hard to build in Wes. He'd found out her weakness, and now she had to take back her role as physical therapist. "I think we both know that would be a huge mistake."

"Was yesterday and the day before a mistake, too?"

"I'm sorry if I gave you mixed messages. I have such fond memories for you, and it was so nice to have you in my house, and yesterday in the hot tub… I overstepped my bounds. I'm sorry." Oh, God, would he buy it? It was partially true.

"*Fond. Nice.* Such tepid words. That's not what I felt yesterday or just now."

She swallowed the dry lump that had lodged in her throat. "Look, I felt what you felt, but that doesn't matter." She forced herself to stop wringing her hands. "I came here as a friend, to help you get back…" Oh, damn, her fingers kept interlocking and unlacing, and here she was about to stumble over her words.

"On my feet?"

His transparent fury cut deep, and hurt to the point of knocking the air from her. In a few short seconds everything had fallen apart. She had to fix this, and it was time for her to plead. "You know that's not what I meant." Regret washed over her in bucketfuls, throwing his own sentence back at him, but she couldn't figure out how to make things right. How to keep things in balance. Because her mind had been jumbled by that kiss.

With muscles twitching on both sides of his jaw, he made a jerky movement and rolled his wheelchair away. "I'm taking the morning off. Doctor's orders."

Mary decided she had blown it big time. She jogged along the beach, her toes digging little holes into the wet sand, thinking she should probably pack up and leave. An overcast day, it seemed to accentuate the scent of seaweed, and the downcast mood that had overtaken her. Unintentionally, she'd humiliated Wesley, a man whose pride had always ruled the day. A man who now sat in a wheelchair, and who'd somehow gotten up the nerve to ask her to have sex with him.

As she ran, the rhythmic sound of waves crashing tons of water onto the shore helped her calm down. Everything seemed mixed up. She'd never encountered this kind of problem with a patient before. Because they had a history, being around him had forced her to realize she still harbored feelings for him. The moist air soothed the tension that had built up in her throat.

The crazy thing was, her wish to have a baby and have Wesley donate the sperm had planted itself in her head and wouldn't go away. She needed to shake it out, because he wouldn't even talk to her now, let alone offer to donate sperm.

Every time she looked at him from now on, she'd know his thoughts, because he'd asked her to prove he could have sex again! It had to take a lot of nerve to ask it, and she'd brushed his wish aside, humiliating him further.

The scariest part of all was how much she wanted to go for it, as in, with all of her heart! There was no way she could discuss her proposition with him. If she didn't word things perfectly, he could feel used. So would she. That could make a wonderful thing seem icky. No, she needed more time to work things out.

Who knew how long he'd go back to being a hermit after their blow-up?

Should she leave? Had she blown it that much?

Her cellphone rang and she saw it was Alexandra. "Just checking in to see how things are going."

"They've been going pretty well, but today was bad."

"Don't let him bully you, Mary. He's done it with every person we've had work with him."

She wanted to say it was more than that, that she'd had a lot to do with the problem. And she wasn't sure she could fix things. "It's not that easy, Alex."

"Please? Oh, I'm begging you. Don't give up on him. He may not act like it, but he needs you, Mary. Please."

How could she let down the person—her first best friend—who'd always accepted her as she was and had changed the course of her life by bringing her into her home? "No need to beg, Alex. I said I'd come for two months, and I promise to stick it out."

She hadn't come here as a physical therapist—she'd come as a friend first. He never would have tolerated her staying around if they hadn't had that connection. She'd played with fire by kissing him, now she had to deal with the consequences. He wanted her to prove that he could have sex and enjoy it with a woman. A really big deal to every man. No, it wouldn't be exactly the way he'd experienced sex before, but from all the reports and studies she'd read, it would definitely be satisfying. Just different.

Her strides got longer, her breathing harder. She pushed aside her desire to ask him to consider being her sperm donor to not confuse things between them any further. Yes, she was here as a friend, but she needed to step up on the PT side and help Wes return to a full and fulfilling life. Getting him strong enough to go back to work. Enhancing his dexterity so he could perform surgery again. His rehabilitation was reason enough to sacrifice her secret wish.

As for sex, well, she had another idea, but first she needed to get in touch with one of her prior patients. Soon. She'd been here just shy of three weeks, she knew her menstrual cycle, and time was running out. Great, just what she needed, to put more pressure on herself.

She'd run herself ragged on the beach, which had been her plan. Now she'd shower and crash in her house for the rest of the afternoon. If she were lucky, she might actually have some clear thoughts. But when she reached her door she saw a note tucked in the seam.

It was from Wes.

Have dinner with me. Since you won't accept a salary from me, the least I can do is feed you.
W.

This had to be his way of apologizing, yet she wasn't ready to face him again. Not before she'd done more research. She opted to skip the shower. She'd also call Rita, not Wes, since she presumed she'd be the one to cook dinner. She'd tell her she couldn't make it tonight.

Coward's way out, yes, but it would serve her purpose. She had to get things back on track between them.

Two hours later, after a thirty-minute conversation with her former patient, Sean, the busiest bachelor in a wheelchair she knew, her laptop was open to the ultimate guide to dating paraplegics. While deep into research on products, there was a tap at her door.

Still in jogging shorts and tank top, her hair a mess, through the window in the door she saw the outline of a man in a wheelchair. Wes.

She jumped up and opened it, recognizing that look of chagrin, and because of his humble attempt to make things right by inviting her to dinner earlier, she was more than ready to forgive him for pressing things earlier.

"Are you not having dinner with me because you're still mad at me?"

"Hi. No, actually I'm working."

"But you're still upset."

"I took a long run and fixed that."

He glanced over his shoulder. "I haven't been down to the beach in a long time. Had Heath build an access for me ages ago, but have rarely used it."

"That's a shame."

"Take a walk with me?"

He'd come in his sports chair, light and maneuverable, clearly ready for the packed-down sand on the beach at low tide. Considering how messed up things had been earlier between them, and the fact the man came all this way to ask her for a walk, how could she refuse?

"Let me put my shoes on."

Twenty minutes later, they'd spoken minimal words, choosing to enjoy the gorgeous ocean, the light pale tone of evening after the sun had set, taking the burst of bright colors with it. Cruising along with the tide in the twilight, she sensed a softening in him. He hadn't come to apologize or to prove anything, he'd come to…come to what?

To court her?

"So, I guess I shouldn't have expected you to have dinner with me after my outrageous request earlier."

"You certainly surprised me." Yet she understood how much he needed to prove. How much that meant to his personal identity.

"I'm sorry."

"No need."

"I was out of line."

"Okay, apology accepted." She shrugged. Hell, she knew firsthand the need to prove something just out of her reach. Since that moment of holding newborn Rose when she'd been hit with the deep unwavering need, with all of her heart and every other part of her, she wanted to be a mother. A most basic function for a woman, and something she couldn't do by herself. Of course she knew how he must feel about a man's most basic function—sex—so she'd cut him some slack for pushing a topic neither was really ready for.

"So I was thinking how much I enjoyed having dinner at your house, and thought we should take meals together. All I do is watch the news and get indigestion. It would be nice to have someone to talk to."

"Or, in our case, to argue with?"

That got a good-natured laugh out of him, and it touched her more than she'd expected. He was really reaching out to her, and she needed to be careful not to hurt him.

"That, too."

"I'd really like that, Wes. I get bored eating alone every night."

"Great. Tomorrow I'll fix you my go-to meal."

"Let me guess, it's the one great thing you know how to cook to please the ladies?"

"Nah, I always have Rita fix those meals."

It was her turn to laugh, and it felt good to let go of all the tension between them.

They'd started back toward the house since it was quickly growing dark. Though Heath had thought of everything, lining the long wooden path from Wesley's yard to the beach with solar lights. It looked like a mini version of an airport runway.

"Now I'm really intrigued what that dinner will be."

"You'll have to show up to find out." He took her hand and tugged her close, then put his hands on her waist. "Come here."

She sat on his lap, wrapping her arms loosely around his neck. Eye to eye under the moon, his were dangerously dark. He lifted his chin and they kissed, natural as breathing. He kissed her well, but didn't linger for more. Just a simple kiss good-night. But nothing was simple with Wesley Van Allen, and she felt that kiss all the way down to her toes.

He rolled the chair with her on his lap for the last few feet on the wooden planks. She took a deep breath, enjoying the ride, glancing up in time to see a shooting star. "Look!"

He saw it too. "Too bad you won't be here in August during the Perseid meteor showers. They put on a great show."

It hit her then that their time together was limited, and as light and airy as she'd felt a single moment ago, the sudden weight of leaving Wes was like a punch in the gut.

They'd made it all the way back to her tiny house in silence, and rather than take the ramp up, Wesley stayed put, so she got off his lap and strolled to her porch.

"I'll see you at eight tomorrow morning," she said,

leaning against the rails. "I've got some new things to show you."

"Now *I'm* intrigued." As darkness settled, all she could see was the silhouette of his body and head and the white of his teeth. "It had better not be more rehab exercises."

She smiled in his direction. "You'll just have to show up to find out."

"You're a tease, Harris," he said, turning his wheel-chair and heading back toward his house. Leaving her wondering if that had been an intentional *double entendre*. "By the way," he said over his shoulder, "I've been doing some research myself and have something to share."

"Really?"

"Yeah, you'll just have to show up to find out." He kept rolling.

"Who's calling who a tease?" she called after him.

That night Mary made a huge mistake and let her mind wander. She imagined what it would be like to become Wesley's lover. After the kisses they'd been sharing, the way her body had come alive around him, those sensations were fresh in her mind.

The bittersweet thought was supposed to be positive and uplifting, but knowing she'd be leaving in a little over a month, it left her with mixed emotions. She tossed and turned in bed.

Besides sex, there was another gap in his life. A huge one. He was a specially trained doctor, who needed to work again.

Rushing to sit up, this time she stopped short to avoid hitting her head. Her laptop was on the mini dresser—a former regular dresser that had had the legs shortened to fit the loft A-frame space—so she reached over and grabbed it then sat in the center of her bed, the one spot where she could sit straight. Booting up the computer, she surfed to an occupational therapy website that promised to enhance digital dexterity, something a guy only pumping iron for the last nine months may have lost.

In order to feel whole, Wesley needed two things— neither of which was his legs—one: to be gainfully employed again, and, two: a gratifying sex life.

Yeah, she certainly had her work cut out for her before she left.

CHAPTER FIVE

THE NEXT MORNING, Wesley detected an extra sparkle in Mary's eye when she showed up in the gym. He hoped it had something to do with all the kisses they'd been sharing, but he was on task and didn't wait to find out.

"Let's skip the gym exercises for now, okay?" he said. "I've got some things I want to show you."

That totally captured her interest and, instead of disappearing, the sparkle brightened. "Such as?"

"Get out your laptop."

She pushed a small table toward his wheelchair, then brought a chair to sit on. Digging into that overgrown shoulder bag, she dug out her laptop.

"I want you to have a look at this." He took charge, booting it up, and soon clicked on the video he'd discovered about a doctor who'd become a paraplegic and designed a special wheelchair so he could continue to perform surgeries. The accompanying article showed how the electric wheelchair could elevate to a standing position with support around the chest and on the legs above and below the knees.

Mary studied the contraption carefully.

"I wondered how healthy it might be, staying in that position for long hours performing brain surgery. How it might affect my breathing and circulation. But the idea of being able to do procedures is a game changer." For emphasis, he played a short video with the guy doing an orthopedic procedure.

"Amazing what someone can do with motivation," she said.

He took it as though she'd just questioned his, and immediately got defensive. "I went back to work too soon, there wasn't a contraption on the earth that could've helped me." He'd had the misfortune of running into Giselle his first day back and what he'd seen in her eyes hadn't been sympathy but pity. She'd wanted to help push him down the hospital corridor, and he'd hated her for it. He'd miscalculated so many things about returning to work, like leg spasms and patients caring more about his condition than their own. Even the logistics of performing a simple examination had tripped him up.

The week-long experience had been humiliating and he'd never felt that way in his life before. He'd hated every second of it, had gone home and never wanted to open his door to the outside world again. Good thing he was a guy who got bored with wallowing quickly, and buried his feelings behind barbells and weight machines.

"Wow. With something like this, nothing can stop you from picking up your career and carrying on with your life."

He understood why she held him accountable for his future, it really was all up to him. Her belief in him felt hopeful, and he was grateful for that, so he smiled. "I know."

"And we're on the same page!" Instead of gloating, which he'd expected her to do, she reached back into her bag of goodies and produced a deck of cards. For some crazy reason her doing something so off the wall tickled him, but he donned a poker face until he could figure out where she was going with the prop.

"We've been working your large muscles but overlooking your fine motor skills. So here's the deal; if you want to go back to doing surgery, which after seeing that video I know you can do, you need to start working on your fingers and hands."

Would she stop at nothing to get him back to work? At a loss for how to respond, he let his mouth drop open.

She moved her laptop and edged the deck toward him. "So shut up and deal."

After he'd gone back to work too soon, and couldn't even handle seeing patients, he hadn't let himself think about ever performing surgery again, especially neurosurgery, which often required hours in the OR, and total focus on fine details, often so minute it required special headgear with magnifying glasses. One false move and someone's life could be changed forever. He'd never been too confident to forget that, but these days, sitting in a wheelchair, he found it much harder to wrap his brain around. Yet his finding the video of the standing wheelchair opened up his world and proved there was something out there to accommodate his logistical problem. He could stand upright in the OR again. And potentially perform neurosurgery! All he had to do was order one.

For an instant, he was overcome with fear, but he fought it off and instead focused on the pretty lady holding out some cards.

He dutifully took the deck, shuffled and dealt, soon realizing, if push came to shove, he'd never qualify for a job as a dealer in Las Vegas.

"Try it again, but faster," she said.

Like a character actor, he needed motivation. "What game am I dealing for? And don't say, 'Go fish'."

She made a cute thinking face, glancing toward the ceiling, distracting him and ruining any chance of his impressing her with his dexterity skills.

"How about gin rummy? Ten cards."

Fair enough. He could handle ten measly cards, so he dealt.

"Again," she said, ripping away the deck—along with his instant of pride for counting out the right number of cards in what he considered a reasonable span of time—tidying the stack and handing it back to him.

Again and again he shuffled, not making much progress on the speed. But he tried, in a sorry sophomoric attempt to impress her. "Are we ever actually going to play this game?"

"Keep dealing." Total dominatrix. And he liked it.

After a few more deals she gathered the cards and put them away.

"Not good enough?"

"Not bad, but there's more to do."

The day was sure to go downhill from here. He fought the urge to make the sign for loser and posting it on his forehead. *Failed at card dealing.* Still, it amused him.

She didn't give him a chance to think for long before she produced something else from that huge bag of hers—a quarter. "Can you roll a quarter through your fingers?"

"Wait. We're through playing cards? I was just getting the hang of it."

She ignored his taunt. "The quarter roll. Ever tried it?"

"Never." He had to admit he'd started liking her bossiness, but only because she looked so cute doing it.

She handed him the coin, then opened the laptop again. "Watch this little video first."

She brought up a well-known video site and a tutorial

on coin rolling. Tricks. She'd sunk to teaching him common sleight of hand tricks. But he liked her undivided attention, so he co-operated.

"If I do this, you have to kiss me."

"The joy of victory isn't enough?"

"Not for me. I need some lips." He pointed to his mouth. "Yours. Right here."

Her devilish angel expression nearly knocked him out of his chair. Now he really needed to kiss her.

"You're on." She tipped her head. "Make that quarter roll."

He positioned the coin just below his knuckles on the back of his hand and tried rolling it, using each preceding finger to prod it along like the video had shown. Slow but steady, with Mary's encouragement, he attempted the task without complete success. But he wouldn't give up. She'd laid down the gauntlet, in this case a quarter, he'd bargained for a kiss, and he was damned if he'd fail. A half-hour later, he finally perfectly advanced the coin from finger to finger on his right hand. Yes!

She applauded, but the big bonus was her smile. It made him stop and take it all in, bright, beautiful and sweet, and he called in the kiss. She willingly obliged, taking her place on his lap first. He glanced into her eyes, enjoying the little thrill, knowing she was about to kiss him, and let her deliver the kiss her way.

She was definitely out to impress, planting her hands on either side of his face and her mouth soft and warm over his. He tried to hold back but couldn't. Every kiss they'd shared had only made him want more and more of her. Their tongues soon found each other's and just on the verge of deepening their kiss she was done.

"Now do it on the left side." Back to that seductive impish expression, and him definitely wanting to kiss her again. He did what he was told, but not before bargaining for more.

"And if I do, you have to kiss me again, but this time I get to use my hands."

"This is starting to sound like a new kind of strip poker."

"I'm hoping for a lap dance."

She sputtered a laugh. "You'd be so disappointed."

"I doubt that."

"I don't have a vampy bone in my body."

"Now I know you're lying."

With Mary still sitting on his lap, he stared into her darkening green eyes, liking the desire buzzing beneath his skin. She'd been bringing him back to life step by step since showing up on his doorstep. He thought about kissing her again, but had waited too long since she scooted off his lap and stood, handing him back the quarter.

Since the left was his non-dominant side, it took thirty minutes to accomplish what his right hand had done in twenty. But he'd done it! Yeah!

More applause, with the addition of a high-five, accompanied by another broad grin from the lady with the buff arms, and Wes felt odd, admitting Mary's approval was almost as good as her kisses.

He gestured for her to sit again, and she eased onto his lap, looking a little wary. "How much 'hands' are you planning to use?"

"You'll have to kiss me to find out."

Raising a brow but taking his dare, she tilted her head the opposite way from the last kiss and started a slow, seductive kiss that had his hands wandering around her back and down her arms in record time. She nibbled his lower lip and a low growl escaped his throat. His hands shot down to her hips and grabbed hold, kneading her firm skin and pulling her closer. He wanted her. All of her.

Shocked by the revelation, he was the one to break the kiss. Wouldn't taking this any further just be frustrating for both of them?

"That was nice," she said, dreamy-eyed.

He bit back his first thought—*That's about as far as we can go. Ever.* Logically, he knew it wasn't so, but he didn't have a shred of proof from his own body. Still, making out with Mary was a hell of a great way to pass the day. "I thought we were just getting started."

"Sorry to break it to you, but we've got more work to do." She got off his lap again, but not before he could see the tightened tips of her breasts through her clingy workout top. So he hadn't lost his touch.

He'd woken up grumpy and frustrated, as he did many mornings, and had planned to work it off with dumbbells, but now he'd accomplished some death-defying acts of sleight of hand, and been paid in kisses and a quick feel up of his rehab coach. What else would this day bring? So he grinned, and as far as he was concerned, if Mary kept kissing him, they could sit there all afternoon rolling coins through fingers.

But now what was that mischievous twinkle in her eye about? The day just kept getting better and better, and he didn't have to wait long to find out.

In the next second she produced another small box from her shoulder bag, and he was sure the thing had a trapdoor inside.

"And what's this?" Admittedly, he began to feel excited, like a kid on Christmas morning with a special trapdoor stocking. Especially if he kept bargaining for kisses.

"Chinese exercise balls. They're meant to improve finger dexterity."

He spurted a laugh at the explanation, the first he'd laughed in days. What would she think of next? As the old saying went, *If my friends could see me now.*

She opened the box and showed him how to hold the two balls in the palm of his hand and rotate them over and over. "The goal is for the balls not to touch. Eventually. It takes a lot of practice, but we've got time."

He dutifully took the balls, getting a feel for them. "And you just happened to have these lying around?"

"I go to PT conferences for continuing education. You'd be surprised what the vendors give out."

From first-hand experience, he knew about medical conferences and product vendors, and bought her story without question about how she'd acquired the Chinese balls. He worked them in his palm first with one hand then the other, liking the slick metallic feel of them. They seemed cold and slippery and he had to be careful not to let one drop. He also realized his hands were getting tired from all of the dexterity tests that morning, which meant she'd been right—he was out of shape in the hand department.

"Work on those this afternoon and tonight. Both hands."

"Yes, ma'am."

"Tomorrow we're going to thread tiny beads."

"Why do I suddenly feel like I'm ten again and back in summer camp?"

"It's just part of the process, Wes." She smiled, and it lit up the room again.

An ordinary expression shouldn't be that noticeable, but coming from her—plump lips parted over naturally spaced teeth, lips he'd tasted and liked, the smile easily infecting her eyes—it was extraordinary. Everything she did for him seemed larger than life, yet humble and sweet, and always forced him to get too close to her, her kisses the prize he wanted to keep winning.

"Well, if neurosurgery isn't in my future, maybe I can get a job as a sleight of hand magician somewhere?"

And there was that beam again, as if it was a beacon showing him the way to happiness, touching his heart and a whole lot of other places. He juggled the metal balls in his palm faster and faster, looking forward to the rest of the day, and especially their dinner that night. Alone. With Rita banished once she'd set everything up for the meal.

For a guy who'd woken up grumpy, things were definitely looking up.

For the first time since his accident he believed he might be able to pick up the skills he'd once honed, and continue with his professional life again. Before now, he'd refused to consider it, especially after attempting to return to the hospital too soon, and experiencing full throttle failure. Not to mention humiliation. No longer able to juggle patients with ease and conviction, he'd fumbled with simple things like holding a laptop on his lap and wheeling himself into an examination room. He'd had to face colleagues feeling less than their equal. When he'd bumped into an examination table and set off leg spasms, he'd had enough. His ears heated with the memories. After a few days of denying the truth, he'd had to admit defeat and return home feeling lost.

Never a quitter, that's when he'd gone even more manic in the gym, and for his efforts he'd never felt physically stronger in his life. From the waist up. Yet he was still so insecure about returning to his life's vocation. The job he'd felt called to do since he was a teenager.

Now, here he was with news about a special stand-up wheelchair, and Mary with a deck of cards, a quarter, some odd little balls, plus a promise to string beads tomorrow. The crazy thing was, every little part of the day's equation had made him feel anything was possible again. Looking at life through new eyes, he felt ready to say, *Why not?*

He watched her across the room, setting up for their passive range of motion session, and took a moment to marvel over how she'd opened up his world to the possible again. It wasn't sleight of hand magic she peddled either. She spoke the truth. Honest and practical. And for that he'd always be grateful.

Like a spear to the chest, it hit him. She'd signed on for two months, and one had already passed. He'd miss her when she left. A sensation he'd compartmentalized for months forced its way out—giving a damn. He cared about her, looked forward to seeing her every day, and would definitely miss her when she packed up that tiny house and moved on.

With her help he'd go back to work and become part of the living again, even though he wasn't at all sure he was ready to join that group.

Mary showed up on time for dinner, worrying about her choice of clothes—her best black slacks and a clingy blue patterned top that might show a little too much cleavage. After their kissing game earlier, she didn't know what to expect from Wes. One thing she did know for sure, though, she liked it!

She'd called out once she'd gotten to his front door.

"It's open. I'm in the kitchen."

She didn't want Wes to think she was trying to seduce him with her choice of clothes, but she wanted to look nice, and this top came with a definite dip of cleavage. From the appreciative gaze in Wesley's eyes when she walked into his kitchen, she figured she'd made a good choice.

"Wow, something smells delicious!"

"I owe my amazing cooking skills to Rita, who had the good sense to prepare all the ingredients for our meal and take off, leaving me with the easy cooking part."

Hadn't he said he used Rita when he wanted to impress his date? Was she considered a date or an old friend? And did old friends find multiple excuses to kiss each other? Man, she was confused.

"Must be nice." She could only imagine what it would be like to have a personal sous chef. She'd never been in his kitchen and was blown over by the huge marble-topped island, all the high-end appliances and a breakfast nook large enough to throw a party in. Heck, it was the size of her entire kitchen! This for a guy who lived like a recluse.

He led her to the dining room, just around the corner from that breakfast room. He had a casserole dish on his lap as he rolled the wheelchair, and she worried it might be burning his legs and he didn't know it. "May I take that for you?"

"I've got it."

Dumb question. She needed to learn to let him be independent without rushing to his aid. If her hope was for him to feel whole again, she shouldn't interfere with his process. *Let him be a man.*

The dining table nearly took her breath away. He'd chosen a cozy area with a splendid view of the ocean, with light naturally stained table and chairs, making her think of beach chic, whatever that was. The dishes were brightly patterned and she picked one up to see where it had been made.

"Got those on a trip to Spain."

Oh, the life he must have led BP. Before paraplegia. "They're beautiful." The yellow patterned dishes with dark blue highlights picked up the midnight blue drapes bracketing the long line of windows.

"Come, help me bring out the rest of the food. All that sleight of hand stuff makes a guy hungry."

After a couple more trips back and forth to the kitchen, their table was set, but before he took his place at the head, where she'd noticed no chair had been placed, he opened a drawer in the sideboard. Soon he rolled from candle to candle placed all along the buffet and at several stations across the expansive table, as he used the candle lighter. Once done, he turned off the overhead lights and gestured for her to sit next to him, but not before he fiddled with something on the wall, next to the electric switch. *Voilà!* Music. Soft, strings and piano. Perfect.

With chills across her shoulders she sat, watching the man she'd seen every day in the gym for the last few days, and who she'd recently started kissing for pure pleasure. He was on his own turf and he looked nothing short of handsome and confident, and for that she let fly a quick, secret dream. *What if?*

He opened a bottle of red wine and poured each of them a glass, then removed the lid from their appetizer dish.

"Wow, that looks great."

"Good, you like shrimp. This is my version of shrimp cocktail. I sauté them and serve them warm. Help yourself." He handed her the platter and she dug right in.

"You made this?"

"Spent the last hour and a half getting everything ready for us."

"What about Rita?"

"She bought everything I'd need and had all the ingredients right where I wanted them."

"That's great. So you like cooking?"

"Sometimes. If there's a lady I want to impress."

She stopped, shrimp midway to her mouth. Their eyes met and she saw the flash of interest. She'd felt it earlier when they'd kissed too. The chills returned and she knew tonight was going to be different. "Well, thank you, then. I'm definitely impressed."

Over spinach salad with pancetta and feta cheese Wes seemed to relax. "I used to do all the cooking when I was with Giselle."

"Your ex-fiancée?"

He nodded and took another bite.

She wondered why he'd brought Giselle up, especially since they'd been seeming to slip into something more serious the more time they spent around each other. She worried she was setting herself up for a fall by thinking a few kisses meant something to Wes. According to Alex, he'd never been without lady friends.

"I forget, was she fiancée one or fiancée two?"

He ignored her dig, but went serious. "My fiancées never stood a chance, I suppose, not with how work was my total world and all. Emma found someone else to make her happy and Giselle married her job, just like I did." He'd jumped off on a subject that nearly made her drop her fork.

"Are you saying you think it was your fault?"

He served New York steak strips with smashed potatoes, and the heavier food seemed compatible with the topic of conversation. "I feel like I squandered any chance of being in a solid relationship, you know, that *one* you mentioned the first day we worked out, that 'special one'. I never believed in it before and now it's too late."

"Why do you say that? You're talking like your life is over, and that's just not true." Why couldn't she get through to him?

"It would be really tough to get involved with a guy like me. I'm a special needs guy now."

"You're the same person inside you've always been. That's the part that attracts people."

After two failed engagements, Wes was hell bent on never opening his heart again, had his excuses lined up and waiting, and she didn't have time for him to figure things out. Besides, she'd already been through that with her one and only fiancé, Chuck. From him she'd learned if a guy didn't want you, he simply didn't want you, and there was nothing she could do to change that. Yet, foolishly, she had tried.

Like Wes focusing on his job back when he'd been engaged, these days all she wanted to focus on was becoming a mother. Holding a baby of her own in her arms, loving and protecting it was her number one goal, and she couldn't let anything stand in the way. Especially not a guy unwilling to accept there was life after paraplegia.

"I'll give you this, Harris," he said, forking a piece of steak and mixing it with potatoes before eating it.

She waited as he chewed, taking a dainty bite in case she needed to prod him along.

"You've brought life back into this house. It had gotten dreary and lonely, but now things have changed. That's all thanks to you, and don't choke on your steak but that means a lot to me."

He'd been refilling his glass with dark red wine, and she was sure he'd never broach this topic if it wasn't for the magic of vino. She was so grateful he had, because he'd just paid her an amazing compliment.

"And that means a lot to me, too, Wes. I came here because I'm an old family friend and I wanted to help."

"And my sister begged you to come."

"And *I am* a family friend, did I mention that?"

He winked at her, and damn if that didn't give her a quick thrill. She almost forgot what she was going to say. Oh, right. "So we got off to a rocky start, but I'm super happy with where you're at now."

"Cheers." He raised his glass and smiled, his eyes showing the effect of the couple of glasses he'd enjoyed, as he charmingly ignored what she'd just said.

She drank more and admitted he'd chosen the perfect wine to complement the steak and potatoes. The wine warmed her insides, and also loosened her lips. He was opening up, why shouldn't she? So she decided to be supportive of his reaching out by giving her a huge compliment. Coming from him, that was a big deal. "Just so you know, I can totally understand how you feel about it being too late. I've given up on finding the right life partner, too. But here's the crazy part. I've always prided myself on being a free spirit, you know, independent and self-reliant. Heck, I never had anyone to depend on until I met your family." She took another sip of wine, choosing to hold the glass nearby rather than put it down. "But guess what, since meeting your youngest niece, Rose, this free spirit wants more than anything to have a baby."

There, she'd finally admitted it to someone, and it didn't sound so crazy, did it? She took another sip of wine just in case it did seem like a whacky idea, and watched the expression change on his face.

Wes stared at her for a few seconds, digesting what she'd confessed, looking so serious she chose to think he was treating her secret with great care, and she deeply appreciated that. So she drank more wine to give him time to mull things over.

Before she realized it, he rolled his wheelchair over to her and took both of her hands in his. "So is this our secret?"

She nodded.

"Crazy, isn't it? Neither of us ever expects to find 'the one'. I don't have a clue if I can have sex, and you want to be a mother. Does that sum things up?"

Put that way, she had to laugh. "I know. Crazy, right?" But it felt good to finally tell someone.

"It's not crazy, Mary, if that's what you want. You'd be a great mom, too." He pulled her close and kissed her gently, then reached around her shoulders and hugged her.

The hug felt like home, so she kissed him back. He hesitated briefly but soon his lips complied and a simple kiss suddenly turned into much more. Then it ended far too fast.

He stared seriously at her. "So it seems we both have something to prove. Me going back to work and you putting your uterus to work."

"Something like that." She grinned and was grateful he hadn't laughed her out of his house, though her thoughts were still hung up on the far-too-brief make-out session from the moment before.

He stared at her for a long moment, and she projected that he was thinking the same thing she was about the ramifications of his last statement. He wanted to have sex again and she wanted to have a baby. They both had something to prove and she was helping him so maybe he should help her? Or maybe she was reading far too much into his sympathetic expression.

He backed his chair away. "Are you ready for dessert?"

"There's more?"

"How about some grilled peaches with ricotta and honey?"

"Yes, please."

"Great. So come into the kitchen and let's get cooking."

"I'm making dessert?"

"No. You're watching me make dessert. I just want your company."

They'd both drunk enough wine to open up on topics they'd kept close to their chests until tonight. They definitely didn't need to drink anymore. "How about I make some coffee?"

Wesley worked diligently grilling peaches then spreading them with the sugar and cinnamon mixture as he thought what a total disaster it would be to try to make love to Mary. It would be a total clinical trial and humiliating, so humiliating, and it was the last thing he'd ever want to face. Yet, putting his pride and wheelchair aside, the thought of being with Mary made his head spin. What he'd give to go back in time and take her the way he wanted to now. He'd had the chance, was sure of that, back then. Now she needed someone to help her get pregnant, not someone who didn't even know if he could still function in that department.

In a far less festive mood now, he served dessert with the coffee she'd made, and they ate in silence. The sweet-tasting peach hardly registered with his brain, because he couldn't get the thought of helping her get pregnant out of his mind. After all she'd done for him, why shouldn't he volunteer? Maybe he couldn't take her to bed like he'd prefer, but he sure as hell could still be a sperm donor. The ramifications of fathering a baby he'd never be involved with didn't sound appealing. He'd never really thought about being a dad, but he sure as hell knew if he ever became one, he'd want to act like one. Not some donor with no say.

"We've got an early start tomorrow," she said, out of the blue. Probably because he'd gone missing with his thoughts. "I'd better get home."

Damn, he'd really blown the mood he'd so carefully set earlier. He'd wanted tonight to be special, he'd even started to open up to her about his failed engagements, then he'd let insecurity hold him back. Now she'd taken the "all business" route. "Ah, yes, tomorrow we make jewelry from tiny beads."

"Yup. Can I help with the dishes first?"

"Nope. That's the beauty of Rita. She'll take care of everything in the morning."

"So that's how the other half lives. Must be nice." She strolled and he rolled toward the front door.

"Hey, don't knock my life of privilege until you've tried it." He knew she'd grown up the hard way, but never felt she'd held a grudge toward him about it. Now that he spent his days in a wheelchair, he figured the playing field was level. Who could envy him?

"Tomorrow we'll work on strengthening your abs, to get you ready for that standing wheelchair I see in your future."

She never gave up, and that endeared her to him all the more. "Yes, boss. It sounds nuts, but I can almost see myself performing surgery again."

"You will, Wes. I know it."

He tugged on her hand and brought her closer. "And I see a baby in your future."

"Do you?"

The excitement on her face nearly broke his heart. He

promised something he had no business getting mixed up in, but it didn't stop him. "I'm sure of it."

"Thank you."

"I'm going to tell you something, but don't let it go to your head, Harris. I like having you around."

She gave a flirty gaze. "Then don't let this go to your head either. I like being around."

He brought her face down to his and kissed her, because he couldn't stand another second without touching and tasting her. Wishing he had that standing wheelchair right now, he'd give anything to be on her level. Eye to eye. Mouth to mouth. Her breasts mashed against his chest and his hands wandering anywhere they liked.

But kissing her from this angle wasn't half-bad. In fact, right now, since she sat on his lap, he couldn't think of any place he'd rather be, as long as they were sharing a kiss.

Where were they going with all these kisses, anyway? What did it mean that they couldn't seem to keep their lips apart? Was it a promise of good things to come? The thought of getting his hopes up sent a shudder through him. Or maybe it was the sensation of her tongue slipping over his that set that off.

He'd gone off at the deep end, imagining all kinds of miracles happening between them, and drinking three glasses of wine had to be the reason.

Yeah, that had to be it. The wine. Because there was no way he'd let a sexy, exciting and wonderful woman like Mary Harris get hooked up with him.

She deserved far more than a guy stuck in a chair.

CHAPTER SIX

TWO DAYS LATER, Mary and Wesley worked side by side on the high parallel bars. He used the strength of his arms to move forward, and had just made it along the bar.

"Can you turn and go back?" Mary asked, dropping off the bars to watch. "I'll spot you."

Obviously unsure of this bright idea of hers, he passed her a warning look. "Like hell you will. If I let go and fall, I'll be dead weight and bring you down with me."

"You won't let go."

"And you know this how?"

"I know you, Wes. You've got this. You're the strongest guy I know." *And the best looking and the smartest and the sexiest.* Her encouragement must have given him the last bit of confidence he needed because he pressed upward in stiff arm gymnastics style, swung and switched hands to face in the opposite direction, then walked his hands back to the other side. When he got to the end he dropped to his armpits on the bars and let out a yelp.

"What's wrong?"

"Cramp. Got a cramp."

She rushed to his aid, and with her helping him balanced against her she eased him to the mat. He grimaced and grabbed his shoulder near his neck. She massaged the area, feeling the golfball-sized knot. It didn't let up.

"Lie down. Wait right here." She rushed to the pile of gym towels, ran one under water in the kitchenette in the corner of the gym, wrung it out and popped it into the microwave for a quick heat up. Once done she whirled it round and round to cool it off a bit, then placed it on Wesley's shoulders. "Still tight?"

He clenched his teeth and continued to rub the area. "Yes."

At the top of his head, she leaned over him and again massaged his neck and shoulder muscles with a deep and intentional touch, finding the unchanged knot, as tight as before. He groaned, but in a good way, so she continued until she felt the muscle on the right side loosen and finally let go. But she didn't stop. She made fists and rolled her knuckles round and round on his trapezius muscles to keep the spasm from returning, then switched back to the deep massage. Finally, she slid her flattened hands beneath his upper back and pushed in and out, locating a nerve bundle on each side below his scapula and pressing her fingers upward. He moaned, sounding in ecstasy. She pressed and released several times until she felt him relax completely.

"I let you down, Harris."

"No, you didn't."

"When I was up there, I pretended my legs still worked, and I got a little cocky trying to swing myself like a real gymnast. That dead weight put a quick stop to that fantasy." He rubbed his forehead. "Never realized how strong those gymnast guys are."

"Could have fooled me. You were the master of those bars from where I stood."

He made a pained laugh. "Yeah. I won all right."

She sat back on her heels, let her hands slip from his shoulders.

"Don't stop," he whispered, then reached up and grasped a wrist, pulling her forward until her face was above his. She continued to gently massage both shoulders for several more silent moments.

"Come and lie down with me."

The invitation was too deliciously inviting to resist. She scooted beside him and curled toward his torso, and now that his cramp was gone he wrapped his arm around her, pulling her close. Oh, how wonderful it felt to be skin to skin, finally getting to explore all of his hard work with the touch of her fingertips. "You looked incredibly sexy up there."

"Yeah? How do you like me now?"

They laughed gently together and seeing him devoid of his usual defenses—vulnerable and open—turned out to be the most powerful aphrodisiac she'd ever experienced. Off and on she'd gotten peeks at this part of the formerly borderline arrogant and commanding man, and she definitely liked this side of his personality best.

A wicked thought popped into her mind. What she'd give to straddle him, then watch him contort from the feel of her, this time in a pleasurable way, not in pain.

Her thoughts worked like a bellows on the fire that always seemed to simmer between them. Surely he felt it too? She rose up and planted a full-on kiss on his welcoming mouth. He pulled her down on top of him, she stretched like a cat and deepened the kiss, showing him what she wished they could do with their bodies.

"This is highly unprofessional," she said over his lips after a particularly mind-boggling make-out session.

"You don't work for me," he said quickly, pulling her mouth back on target.

After that she stopped thinking and went with the feeling whirling inside her, heating her, making her super sensitive to his every touch. Minutes and more minutes slipped by as they kissed and she squirmed over him. He scouted her tightened breasts with his fingertips, soon taking them into his hands. She fought the urge to throw off her gym top, but something held her back. She really shouldn't be doing this, yet she could kiss him all day. She grew damp between her legs, and he must have sensed they were nearing a point of no return.

He broke off the heated kiss, the fire in his darkened eyes turning to anger. "What's the point of getting all worked up when I can't—?"

Damn, she'd crossed the line with him. "What we were doing felt great. What's wrong with that?"

He thinned his lips, shutting down right before her eyes. "I've worked enough today. Shoulder's still acting up. I'm ready for a break."

The snub stung deep, making all the wonderful sensations she'd just enjoyed disappear. "Okay." She rolled off him, grateful she hadn't shed her top when she'd wanted to, thinking how exposed she would have felt sitting half-naked in front of him. He didn't want her. That was clear. "Let me help you into your chair."

"I can do it myself." He sounded defensive, or tired of her not getting the point he was independent. He didn't need her help. Every barrier they'd broken down quickly got put back in place.

She rolled his chair to him so he could do his thing and put himself in it from the floor. The stunt always amazed her, especially how easy he made it look. "So that's it for today, then?"

"Yeah." He didn't make eye contact. "See you tomorrow."

And he left.

At a loss for what to say or do, and especially how

to feel, she stood there and watched him roll away. She needed to get out of that gym where just moments ago she had nearly been in heaven, kissing and loving the man she wanted with all her might to help. The man who'd have nothing to do with her beyond his comfort zone. He liked to call her the dominatrix, but he was the one in complete control. Over the past couple of weeks they'd ventured into showing their affection for each other with kisses. Each session got more daring than the next. Today they'd taken a huge leap forward—she'd straddled him!—and now several steps back. She'd pushed her desire too far. He obviously wasn't ready for the next step.

Her stomach twisted and her hands fisted and opened several times while she stared at the closed door. She needed to get out of here now. It was time to pay the beach a visit. Maybe fighting with waves would help get her mind off Wesley, the guy who turned her on but wanted nothing to do with her.

What a mess.

Wes had showered and now dried himself, remembering the feel of Mary's hands on his shoulders, massaging him, easing his tension. Then she'd taken his mouth and driven him mad with her insistence. He'd fought every thought, and the desire to have her, but had given in. She'd felt incredible, and her breasts had nearly done him in. She'd made him forget how he'd changed, and all he'd felt had been desire. With everything he had, he'd wanted to take her, to be inside her. Then he'd remembered who he was now, how he had no idea how to take a woman, and their sexy moment had vaporized.

Any woman would get tired of that unfulfilled promise soon enough. She'd deny it until the day she died, too, because that was the way Mary Harris was. No way would he tie her—or her free spirit—down.

From the bathroom window he glanced out at the ocean. There she was, jogging toward the waves in a tiny bikini, her slender, toned legs displaying the muscles from all her hard work. With nothing but a towel across his lap, he rolled into his bedroom for a better view. She dove into the water, swimming past the first few waves, then, like the female warrior she was, fiercely swam to catch the next, successfully catching and riding it nearly to the sand.

Had she been as tied up in knots as he'd been when they'd wrapped their bodies together? He watched her stand up on the beach, turn and watch the waves, kick some sand, then head back in. He couldn't help but notice how her swimsuit had tucked itself into her high and tight rear end. His hands had felt that fine curve the day they'd played their racy little game of quarter roll. Damn, she looked sexy. An odd flickering feeling circled low in his abdomen.

Enjoying the distant sensation somewhere below his belly—his groin?—he watched her swim out and take another wave, body surfing, getting lifted and dumped onto the sand. She laughed, standing covered in caked-on sand, wiping some away from her chest, skimming the tops of her breasts above that string called a top. The breasts he'd finally felt and longed to taste earlier. Unfazed by getting beat up by the water, she swam out again. It made him smile. After a few false starts she caught another swell that lifted her and carried her as she perfected her swimming strokes, all the way to shore until she stood and walked the rest of the way in. That was the woman he'd known since she was a teenager, she never gave up. Obviously satisfied with her accomplishment, she rolled out her towel and plopped on top.

Damn if he didn't want her more than anything he'd ever wanted in his life. Beneath the towel he felt himself, surprised by what he found—a full erection.

He'd never admitted to anyone the real reason he'd broken his engagement with Giselle. Aside from her having a sexy name, she wasn't the woman he'd hoped she'd be in bed. Once a week had never been enough for his voracious appetite, yet their schedules had dictated every facet of their lives. She'd seemed satisfied. He hadn't been in the least.

He'd gone to his sister's wedding and had had his overpriced socks knocked off, making out with Mary. Half-tipsy or not, they'd known what they were doing, and she'd turned him on like Giselle never had. How could he marry her after that?

Taking one last glance at Mary on her beach towel, Wes longed to be there beside her.

He rolled into his bedroom and opened his laptop, typing into the browser and searching. A list of websites came up. One in particular held his interest, and within minutes he placed an order for some things that would accommodate positions for sex and also enhance natural movements during intercourse for a paraplegic. A gliding chair and an extra bouncy cot. Who knew two such practical-looking items could turn a guy on? But they did. He was on fire. Not that he needed any help at the moment, with Mary's bikini-clad image burning behind his eyes.

Still revved up, he explored the plethora of information out there on the web about paraplegics and sex, and spent the rest of the afternoon engrossed and admittedly titillated by the provocative reading.

* * *

The next morning, Mary wasn't sure what she'd find when she showed up at Wes's gym. Drawing on extra courage, she popped her head out the door to the hall-way. "Wes! Are you there?" Nothing.

She ventured down the hall toward his room. "Wes?" It was a long hallway, huge like the rest of the house, so she kept walking, worry creeping its way under her skin. What if he'd gotten sick last night, or had injured himself? Surely he had emergency pull cords in strate-gic areas? Or maybe he'd just had it with her? Her nerves twisted at the thought.

"Wes?" Though her pace slowed, she continued cau-tiously onward, worry working its way through every cell. She thought she heard conversation coming from his room, so she stopped and listened harder. Not conversa-tion. The television. She stepped up and knocked on his bedroom door. "Wes? Are you in there?"

"I'm busy," he called out.

"You're not sick or injured?"

"No."

The conversation on the television seemed to have stopped. She listened harder. Heavy breathing and moans had taken its place. *What the hell?* Was someone in there with him?

Antonio! Antonio! Oh, ah, ah, ah.

Okay, wait minute. What was going on in there? A big fat wave of adrenaline coupled with jealousy washed over her as she knocked and pushed her way through the door. She had no clue what she'd find, but she needed to see.

Obvious sounds of a couple going at it emitted from the laptop he watched from his bed. He wasn't sick or in-jured, there was that, so her nerves settled the tiniest bit.

But he hadn't gotten out of bed yet, and he was obviously watching… "Porn? You're watching porn at this hour?"

His eyes never left the screen. "Didn't realize there was a designated viewing time."

"You know what I mean."

"Look at this. Come look at the size of…"

"What are you doing, Wes?"

Finally, he broke away from the computer and cast her a defiant gaze. "You mean, what am I not doing, as in not going to work out."

"Why not?"

"I'm taking the day off. Even you said I should do that once in a while." The woman's squeals of ecstasy made it impossible to follow his conversation. "Join me?"

He'd staged quite a dramatic way to tell her he'd had enough of their "friendship-workout partnership", especially after yesterday when she'd tried to seduce him. Could she blame him? She certainly had some making up to do.

Against her better judgment, she took the last few steps toward his bed. "Holy Long John Silver, Batman, that *is* big!"

He slanted a sideways glance her way, the corner of his mouth twitching just the tiniest bit. Good, she'd gotten through to him. She wasn't the enemy. She really was here to help him step back into the life he'd left behind. Why couldn't she get that through his head?

Seriously, the guy was one thing, but how did a woman ever lie on her stomach with an enhanced chest like that?

"You did tell me I could still have sex."

"No one can have sex like that! That's impossible. Geez, I think that position has been computer generated or enhanced, or whatever it is they do these days."

He laughed outright. "I used to do that all the time."

It was her turn to laugh as she shifted toward him with a huge questioning gaze, and thank God it lightened the tense, for oh-so-many reasons moment. "You did?" She tried to mix deadpan with a hint of interest.

He cracked a genuine smile. "Maybe not exactly like that." Yay, she'd won! What, exactly, she didn't know, but he didn't feel nearly as belligerent as when she'd first walked in. Progress. "I'm just saying you did promise me."

"Absolutely, but within reason."

"Oh, so now you're backtracking."

"No. No, I'm not. You *can* have sex."

With those piercing coffee-tinted eyes he stared at her then shut down and closed the computer, all the while watching her. Once the soundtrack had gone quiet he reached for her wrist, lightly grasping her flesh. "Show me."

Do not chicken out now. It was the second time he'd asked her to prove to him he could have sex. Gratifying sex. His dare had everything to do with a plea for help, and it was her one opportunity to help him cross that huge barrier keeping him from feeling part of the living. Or, more specifically, a complete man. Getting back to work would only solve half of the problem. This, the most personal of all issues, could possibly be more intimidating than performing neurosurgery again. She needed to tread lightly, and make sure she got right her one shot at proving him wrong.

She needed to buy herself time to gather her thoughts. "I don't intend to prove a damn thing with you lying in bed in your pajamas. Once you've showered and dressed, meet me in the gym." And off she trotted as though she knew exactly how to handle this most unusual request.

At the door, she turned to find Wes was the one with a dumbfounded gaze. Good. It gave her an idea. "While you're getting ready, I want you to think about one important thing. Don't ever forget the brain is by far the biggest sex organ." She walked out the door. "Even bigger than those things on that woman's chest."

She hoped she'd left him smiling instead of scowling.

Twenty minutes later, Wes rolled into the gym where she'd done some quick research on top of her searches in the past and set up her own laptop.

He looked determined, with his computer on his lap. Good, he was here to do some serious work on a very serious issue. It gave her courage to bring up the new techniques she'd learned about from talking to her former patient, Sean, the other day. Fortunately Sean was a guy who had zero inhibitions about his personal life. After their long conversation, she felt well schooled on the subject of paraplegic sex.

"I'm ready if you are," he said.

"You certainly look better." And once he was closer she kept her next thought to herself—*You smell great, too.*

He smiled easily, and reached out to touch her hip, an intimate gesture that helped her realize they were both adults and she liked it when he touched her as much as she hoped he liked her to do so. Her free arm dropped around his shoulders. Hey, if they were about to get down and dirty, theoretically speaking, they may as well be comfortable with each other.

He opened his laptop and clicked, then turned it her way. "Read this."

She opened the blog titled "Confessions of a Paraplegic's Girlfriend", and found the author had written in detail about the various ways she and her boyfriend pleased each other. She read silently, with obvious interest, how oral sex for both partners was a great start, how her partner was able to have an erection watching her give him oral sex, and how she was able to keep him firm with her hand and then mount him and bring herself to orgasm. How her pleasure turned her boyfriend on to the point of experiencing fluttering in his lower abdomen as she orgasmed and he swore he could feel her tightening around him, and how eventually her undivided attention to him brought about ejaculation.

Mary swallowed quietly, turned on, her mouth having grown dry reading the exquisitely intimate and thorough descriptions.

She'd call the writing erotic since reading the blog had aroused her, and she assumed it had done the same for Wes.

"I told you," she said, finding it difficult to meet his eyes, and immediately flitting away when she did. Only then did she realize her nipples had hardened and he'd noticed through the thin fabric of her bra and white top.

He took his time lifting his gaze from her chest to meet her eyes. "You did. But I found this. And more."

"You've definitely got my attention." Suddenly feeling winded, she inhaled.

"Good," he said, latching on to her stare, which arced between them and with it traveled sexy vibrations that dove and zinged throughout her upper body.

He subtly lifted his brows and toggled to another website. "This one is less erotic but very practical."

She clicked on what looked like a small canvas cot divided into two parts—an open-sided, low sitting chair, which glided, and a cot which was far less cumbersome than a bed, and allowed a paraplegic's partner easier maneuverability and access, with built-in natural bounce.

"It's called the glide rider with extra bounce," he said, serious as hell.

Mary pulled in her chin, needing to take another deep

breath while he explained how the contraption might work and the number of positions it could allow.

Her face went hot. She was definitely turned on, but for the sake of science she went along with him as he explained step by step the sexual process using the gliding chair. Their heads were nearly touching as they both studied the computer screen, Wes using the mouse cursor like a laser light on the various parts of the contraptions. His lime and spice aftershave invaded her nose, and she hoped her tropical garden shampoo excited him half as much as she tried to concentrate on the website.

He'd certainly been doing his research.

He lifted her hair and kissed her neck, surprising her. She sat straighter, acutely aware of his lips tripping down her neck, igniting the length of her spine. She inhaled then held her breath to fight off a flood of shivers. Unsuccessfully.

"This is turning me on, you know that, right?" he said in a low husky voice.

His whiskey-tinged voice was turning her on, too, not to mention those feathery kisses on her neck. "I thought it was the other way around," she said, trying not to sound breathy.

"Something's obviously working." He glanced at his lap, where his arousal was in full form beneath his jeans.

Surprised and happy, she smiled softly at him. "I told you."

He continued playing with her hair. "Normally I hate it when you say that, but I'll forgive you this time."

"Gee, thanks."

He nuzzled her neck, sending more tingles across her skin, and she involuntarily clenched her inner thigh muscles.

"So how do we order it?"

"I already have." The man was definitely taking the lead on a new version of his sex life.

She let her grin stretch from one side of her face to the other, like a kid unable to keep a secret. "A two-day delivery?"

"Sorry we have to wait that long, but yes."

We? Seeing the hunger in his eyes, feeling it herself, knowing his need to prove he was still a complete man, she quickly sorted through their situation. She was his friend, but they'd moved way beyond that now. In his own way, he'd been courting her, and he definitely wanted her. If she was honest, she'd admit how much she wanted him, too.

How would they make things work? She traveled. Would leave in a few weeks for another state to be determined. He planned to stay put. To resume his medical career. But this one thing, this pure desire arcing between them right now, was the one exact thing—if it worked out the way she hoped—that could unite them for life. Even if they never saw each other again.

He needed her to help him prove he was still a man.

And she needed him for an equally touchy task.

A baby.

Nothing ventured, nothing gained. Why not go for it?

She swallowed away the dryness in her throat in order to speak. "You're the smartest and best-looking man I've ever known. You want to have sex." Her voice started to tremble. "And I want a baby."

From his wide open stare, just short of going slack-jawed, she knew she had his attention so she plunged ahead.

"Will you consider making a bargain with me?"

CHAPTER SEVEN

MARY'S OFFER OF striking a bargain sent all the sexy feelings flying. His need to hold her in his arms? Gone. His erection? Also gone. He'd never given a thought to becoming a father. Not without a wife, and with two unsuccessful engagements he'd yet to find the right woman. Once he'd become a paraplegic, to be honest, he'd never given parenting another thought.

A business deal. Was that what she'd just suggested?

Wes sat staring at Mary, considering how far they'd come and how so suddenly off track they'd gotten. He needed to clarify. "A bargain as in signing a contract? 'Must have X number of sexual encounters and produce one offspring. Or all prior encounters will be null and void'?"

With an earnest expression, taking his hands into hers, she said, "You know that's not what I'm talking about. There could never be anything so cold and hard between us." She glanced at his lap, where he hadn't disappeared nearly as much as he'd thought. "Well, cold anyway. Wes, come on, we have an opportunity to each provide something life-changing for the other. It's a proposition only people who trust each other can make, and I trust you. Will you think about it?"

The tips of her ears had gone red and he understood

how difficult this must be for her to bring up. As tough, if not more, than it had been for him when he'd asked her to have sex with him—just so he could prove he could. Why hadn't he thought about the procreation part? She'd been straightforward about wanting a child before since she'd hit some magical age, and he'd understood how she might want that, but right here and now? With him doing the honors? She asked far too much. He couldn't just impregnate and go. If he had a kid he'd want to be a part of their life.

"I've definitely got to think this through." He sent her a warning glance for changing the serious topic of having sex into an even more serious subject of making a baby.

"I understand, but if you agree, please know I'd never hold you accountable for my child."

"What kind of man do you think I am? Of course I'd want to be involved." He scrubbed his face in frustration. "Look, we're not even sure this pregnancy can be produced, but you know as well as I do how surprises pop into life all the time. Like me having an accident. Something could happen to you. I wouldn't want a kid staring me in the eyes, asking why he or she never knew I was their dad."

"I know I've taken you by surprise."

"Far beyond that, Harris. Bargaining for a baby?" Though initially appalled by her request, Wesley couldn't hide the part of him that found the deal sexy as hell. It must have shown in his eyes because she gave a demure smile—one that attempted to hide the obvious adult-woman-bargaining-sex-for-personal-reward-who-has-just-blown-potential-partner's-mind. The sweet expression didn't come close to covering the truth—she'd sleep with him—and damn if he didn't find that sexy. As hell.

"I'm not trying to trap you into anything, Wes, and I'll sign any document you want to prove it."

Was he ready or willing for the rest of her bargain? He needed to give becoming a father at this stage in his life some serious consideration.

Playing the "cool" card, he rolled his chair backward. *Yeah, he did stuff like this all the time, bargained for sex. Further proof how worldly he used to be. Not!*

"I'm going to think about this today, and I'll be in touch." Off he went to his office in hopes of wrapping his mind around what she'd just suggested, and trying really hard to keep his mind from imagining the possibilities. In front of her, anyway.

Having sex again would be great, but the thing that struck him the hardest was the possibility of becoming a dad. A crazy sense of hope frightened him. He'd let go of so many dreams after his accident, but here was Mary pushing her way back into his life, forcing him to feel alive again, filled with desire, and now daring him to consider making a baby. Was he ready for that?

After thirty-seven years, one thing he knew about himself—once he put his mind to something, nothing could stop him.

Mary's cellphone rang around two in the afternoon while she sunbathed on the beach. It was Wes. Immediately her pulse tripled. "Hi. Worked things out yet?"

She held her breath in anticipation of his answer, praying he wouldn't say no. But also scared to death he'd say yes, because it would change everything between them, and she'd really gotten to like being Wes Van Allen's friend.

"Have dinner with me tonight." It wasn't a question but a statement, and suddenly she could breathe again.

"We'll go to Geoffrey's. I'll pick you up at seven." After a pause when she expected him to hang up, because a guy in control of her future didn't need an answer knowing how much this meant to her, he said, "Oh, and wear something sexy."

She couldn't be sure what he'd decided about her proposition, but with that request her heart thumped in her chest, and something both frightening and hopeful thrummed throughout her body. She wanted to help him feel whole again, though knowing that once she left what they'd intimately shared, he'd be free to do that with other women. Jealousy cramped her stomach. But she'd known from the instant she'd held newborn Rose that she was meant to be a mother. She wanted that with all of her might. She also knew everything in her life came with a cost.

"Okay," was all she managed to get out before he disconnected the call.

She lay back on her beach towel, her face under the umbrella. A whirlwind of hope and desire made it impossible to relax. Anticipation of what might or might not play out later kept her on edge. Knowing from Alexandra the kind of women Wes was used to keeping company with, her one LBD would fall far short of the mark. At least she'd had more time to tan her legs so she wouldn't have to wear stockings to dinner. Hopefully he'd find that sexy enough.

At seven, Mary heard something hit her front door window, like maybe a small bird had flown into it. Since it was more of a thump than a knock, she ignored it and put the finishing touches on her hair and lipstick. She'd worn the one and only little black dress she owned and strappy sandals with lots of fake bling on the straps.

"Harris!"

Why was he yelling for her instead of knocking? She rushed to the door and when she opened it there he was in his huge electric wheelchair on the small plot of grass near where she'd parked her mini house. Several small rocks were on his lap. "Why are you yelling?"

"I tried the old pebbles-on-the-window trick but it didn't work. I didn't want to break your window."

She gave a confused stare.

"Too big for the ramp and it won't fit on your porch. I can't get there to knock." He made a bowing gesture, using only his hands to indicate his wheels. "You look great, by the way."

"Thanks. You're looking pretty good yourself." She opted to play down the fact he looked dashing and scary as hell. Then gave an approving nod after checking out his stylish peach and sage plaid shirt—it complemented his dark eyes—and slim-cut navy blue chinos. Had he been shopping online? "Let me get my purse."

Once she met him on the grass, without another word, he put the electric wheelchair in motion and took off. "Come on, I'm driving."

She had to jog to keep up.

He'd never given her any indication that he was independent enough to drive, yet here he was looking like a guy who did it all the time. What else had he been holding out on her?

They arrived at the three-car garage where someone had already backed out a custom-made candy apple red van. Wes directed Mary to the passenger side and opened the door for her to get in. He steered himself toward the rear hinged doors where he mounted a hydraulic lift, then rolled into place on the driver's side.

"And here I thought you weren't able to get around,"

she said as he locked himself in. "Turns out you've just been antisocial."

"My prerogative."

"Well, I'm glad you've made the exception for me."

"Don't let it go to your head, Harris. I go to Geoffrey's all the time."

"Since when?"

He acted nonchalant, like they went out to dinner all the time together, definitely making it hard for her to figure out what he'd decided about her offer. Was it too soon to ask?

"Maybe not recently, but I used to be a regular."

Using hand controls and steering knobs, he drove with confidence, even cussed a couple of times when someone cut him off. Within ten minutes they'd arrived at the restaurant, and again she was surprised by the fact the parking attendant seemed to know him. So he had been a regular there BP.

He waited on her side for her to get out of the van and made no effort to hide how he watched her bare legs in the short dress. She was glad she'd painted her toenails bright pink. Was that sexy enough for him?

"Dr. Van Allen, wonderful to see you again," the maître d' said, as though nothing monumental had changed about him at all.

The restaurant was able to accommodate his request for a table on the main floor balcony with and a gorgeous view of the ocean. As she relaxed and took everything in, a steward brought wine for Wes to approve—again giving her the impression it was the same wine he always ordered—and Wes ordered an appetizer to share. Like always?

Insecurity put her in competition with any woman he'd ever brought there, and she was suddenly more than a little envious of his prior dates. The thoughts she'd admitted earlier about leaving him, knowing he'd find someone else to fill her place, only ratcheted up the jealous feelings.

"Prawn and scallop ceviche all right with you?"

Snapped out of her thoughts by food, she smiled, hoping she looked more confident than she felt. "Sounds great." She sipped the freshly poured, cool and crisp Sauvignon Blanc. "Wow, this is good."

"It's my personal request whenever I come here."

She'd been right! "So you actually do come here a lot?"

"Not in a while. I brought my parents here after I got the van, but they made such a big deal out of everything I haven't been back since."

"Your parents or the restaurant?"

"Both. I think they got the point when I left abruptly. I called and warned them I was coming and they're doing much better this time. Before the accident, I was a regular on Saturday nights."

She made a note not to make a big deal out of anything, which she'd just been about to do over the full ocean view. *Play it cool. Don't blow it. He may look cool as a cucumber, but he's feeling insecure, too. And my future could be on the line.*

She'd been right. He'd probably been here with loads of women, a new one every week, before the accident. And after she left, the same routine would probably start back up. He'd be working, meeting new people, living a full life. Though that made the green demon rear its ugly head again, in a crazy way it also gave her hope that he'd think nothing of granting her desire to become a mom. With the way things had always been in her life, she couldn't get her hopes up he'd agree to her terms.

"I don't mean to seem eager, but have you made up your mind about what we talked about earlier?" So much for playing it cool. She couldn't help herself.

"Not here, Harris. Let's just have a nice dinner out."

She took his cue and toned it way back. All her hopes and dreams were put on hold while she quaffed light, fruity white wine and enjoyed a chicken roulade she simply couldn't pass up because the spinach bread pudding seemed too interesting to miss. It didn't disappoint.

From time to time, Wes met her gaze, seeming to notice little details about her hair and earrings with his comments. "Between the ocean and those aquamarine earrings, your eyes almost look blue tonight." And another time, "I like how you've done your hair."

Hell, all she'd done was twist it and pile the ends on the top of her head. No biggie. But if he liked it, she was glad she'd gone for something different.

Under any other circumstances—no bartering for sexual favors and pregnancies—she'd have considered tonight a wonderful date with a handsome and bright guy, one she'd hope to go out with again. In or out of a wheelchair.

But this was Wes, the man who needed to prove he was still a man, and she was a soon-to-be thirty-four-year-old who wanted to be a mom with all of her heart—to know how it felt to grow new life inside her body. To give birth to a baby with half of her DNA. *But no pressure.* She fought the urge to blow her wispy bangs off her forehead.

She opted to skip dessert, instead having another glass of wine. Yes, she'd had more than she usually allowed herself, but she wasn't driving and if things went in her favor tonight, she'd be expected to make good on her bargain. Yikes! A little liquid confidence was definitely in order. She took another sip and pretended to watch the sea, knowing Wes was studying her. She chanced a glance his way and found admiring eyes, and a mischievous smile she recalled from his sister's wedding. The night they'd made out like teenagers in the back of the "just married" limousine under the guise of decorating it for the newlyweds. Her face went hot. Dark and sexy thoughts invaded her mind, and feelings like she'd felt when she'd straddled him the other day. So she drank more wine.

"Are you ready to go?"

Maybe once they got home he'd tell her his decision. "Yes," she said, sounding far too eager.

They were oddly quiet the entire drive home, and she chalked it up to the life-changing plans that might or might not be carried out. *Would she be signing a contract tonight?*

Once there, he again asked her to wait so he could help her out of the car. A true and extremely appealing gentleman.

"Come inside with me."

It wasn't a question. And the commanding delivery excited her. She followed, nearly holding her breath.

Rita had left wine chilling in the living room. In all the weeks Mary had been coming to the house, she'd yet to sit in this huge and beautifully furnished room. She sat on the edge of a modern and comfortable couch, so he could roll his wheelchair next to her and serve her another glass of wine. She'd had enough at the restaurant, but sipped to be polite, while he enjoyed his drink. He'd only had one with dinner, no doubt because he was driving. Now they were on his turf, he could relax. And if they were about to have the conversation she hoped they would, maybe he'd need a little something to loosen him up, just like she already had.

Why did she suddenly feel like she needed more?

Surprisingly, they never broached the topic in question for the next hour.

"Remember that time you and Alex snuck Dad's car and came to visit me at UCLA?"

"And we ran out of gas halfway there and had to beg you to come save us? Oh, how could I ever forget? You were so pissed off."

"I was, but I was still glad to see you."

"Could've fooled me. All I remember was you huffing around, scowling, cussing and lecturing us."

"I was worried about you. Both of you. By the way, whose idea was it?"

She went coy, but honestly couldn't remember whose bright idea it had been. "Alex's?"

He obviously liked it when she left him dangling, never knowing for sure if Mary had wanted to see him that night, or if Alex had just wanted to test out her new driving skills. He took her chin between his thumb and index finger.

"Look at me. Tell me it wasn't you."

She tossed her gaze toward the ceiling. "I honestly don't remember."

He'd had his ego stroked enough by that stage in his life, why add to the once but never forgotten Prince of Westwood's inflated pride? Besides, she preferred the humbler man she'd come to know these last several weeks. By far.

Giving up on ever knowing the truth about the UCLA caper, he moved on. So they continued to reminisce about old times, laughing and teasing each other with embarrassing stories. Letting each other know they'd never forgotten the times they'd shared. She decided it was his way to court and woo her, and for his efforts she felt very grateful. The other—the bargain—would feel so cut and dried otherwise.

Out of the blue she leaned over and kissed him. Yes, she'd had another glass of wine and felt bold, but it was more because of how sweet and attentive he'd been over dinner and was continuing to be back home. "Why don't you scoot out of that thing and join me here on the couch?"

He flashed a dashing smile with a hint of danger, his cheeks touched pink from the agreeable wine. "Why didn't I think of that?"

He made the transfer with ease, and she snuggled into him, his hand resting on her thigh, lightly rubbing and kneading her skin.

"So we've got an agreement to discuss."

"That we have," she said, her heart picking up its rhythm at the mere mention of the topic. With his hand on her leg, she already felt he'd staked his claim for his bedroom.

He traced his middle finger from her knee to her upper thigh. "The terms boil down to the proverbial—you scratch my back and I'll scratch yours."

Aside from the fact his finger drove her wild, the absurd wording made her laugh. *Scratching each other's backs?* "I didn't expect you to get so technical about it."

He joined her laughter. They'd put themselves in an astoundingly awkward position, but neither, so far, had backed out. With his head resting comfortably against the back of the couch next to hers, the last bit of tension seemed to evaporate.

He turned toward her, smiling, watching, making her feel special.

"You know I could pay someone to do what I need, and you could pay a sperm bank, right?"

"True."

"But what would be the fun of that?"

"Also true, but a little scary." She took his hand and squeezed.

"I'm the one who's got the most to prove," he said. "What if you don't get pregnant?"

"Nothing ventured, nothing gained."

His hand broke free and he squeezed the muscles just above her knee. "We seem to be tossing around banal sayings tonight. I hope that isn't an omen for how things go in there." He pointed toward the ceiling, letting her figure out his bedroom was the one upstairs above the living room. Her stomach flip-flopped over the possibility of what might come next.

"So I've made my decision, and I'll accept your bargain under two conditions."

Her head popped off the couch. He'd finally gotten to the good part—helping her have a baby. "Yes? What's that?"

"You move into the house with me, so we can spend the rest of your time here, in Malibu, together."

She should have known he'd never go for such a cold and calculated plan as she'd offered. Honestly, she couldn't imagine how things would actually work out—work out in the morning, sex in the afternoon. Back in the gym the next day.

His compromise was a gentleman's way of making their arrangement personal. Her pulse flittered at the possibility of becoming a bigger part of his life, which made her feel extremely turned on. This was her chance to finally get to know Wesley Van Allen in a way she'd only dreamed of before. Who needed to think about that?

"And if you get pregnant, I want to be the dad. A real dad."

She almost slid off the couch. "You mean like sharing the responsibility? That's exactly what I promised you wouldn't happen."

"I couldn't live with myself otherwise."

"But we won't be together."

"And I don't want to be written out of my child's life."

"We don't even know if I'll get pregnant."

"Or that I can actually have sex."

"True. Maybe we should quit talking."

"Less talk, more action?"

They laughed, realizing they'd resorted to yet another cliché.

"It's a deal."

Obviously happy, he leaned into her and they kissed. Soon passion heated the way, their kisses growing frantic, his hand, which shifted from her knee to the inside of her thigh, sending a thrill straight to her core. As he delved deeper with his mouth, hers welcoming him, his fingers found a way beneath the lace of her underwear, and soon their make-out session took on a whole new dynamic.

And Wes knew exactly how to make this woman like putty in his hands.

CHAPTER EIGHT

AN HOUR LATER, Wes had proof the brain was definitely the biggest sex organ. Seeing Mary naked, knowing he'd made her come using his hands and his mouth, seeing how she still wanted him until they'd joined together, made every worry evaporate. He was a man who wanted a woman, and by some magic she'd shared with him he'd made love to her. Completely.

That paraplegic girlfriend blogger had been right. The sex had been gratifying in ways he'd never imagined, and Mary had been the number one secret ingredient. He'd thought he'd known her body from working out with her every day with her wearing skimpy workout shorts and tops. But seeing her nude, feeling every inch of her satin skin, tasting her, inhaling her special scent, discovering what she liked and what she *really* liked, had been completely different from what he'd imagined. Damn, she was gorgeous, and sexy, and he'd sent her over the edge. Him, a guy who couldn't use his legs or hips.

She'd also made him feel something he'd never thought he'd feel again. When she'd orgasmed over him, he could have sworn he'd felt her tightening around him—whether it was his imagination or had been real didn't matter because he'd "felt" it, thanks to that huge sex organ called his brain—and he'd been as hot with desire as he'd ever been. That last special sensation of her rhythmically gripping him as she'd come had sent a message shooting straight up his spine. There was no denying that part. Then she'd assured him that he'd ejaculated.

He'd never expected anything like that to ever happen again. Not because it wasn't possible but because he'd snobbishly assumed it would never be good enough, so why settle or even try?

Now they snuggled in his bed and, closing his eyes, holding and feeling her next to him, breathing his scent all over her, he remembered what a major part of being a man was. He'd made her his, and she'd willingly given him all she had. Nothing in the world felt better than that.

He smiled into the darkness, stroking her shoulder as she curled into him.

"That was nothing short of amazing," she whispered.

To hell with being humble. He'd done it for her, and she'd just told him it had been amazing. Yeah, that definitely got a grin out of him.

Mary couldn't believe the way this day had wound up. She'd been bold enough to state her case and ask the most brilliant man she knew to father a baby with her—a guy who wasn't sure if he'd ever have another intimate relationship again—and now she'd had the most astounding experience in her life.

They'd always had sexual chemistry, had just never acted on it. Well, never completely acted on it, though they'd come pretty darn close at Alexandra's wedding.

The important thing now was to keep her head on tight, not let her thoughts float up to the rainbow-colored clouds that seemed to have appeared since Wes had said yes. Though he'd thrown her a curveball about wanting to be actively involved as her baby's father; that was, if she actually got pregnant. She felt closer to him than she'd ever dreamed and realized she was in a precarious position. She'd helped him prove he could still be sexually active, which was great, but the down side was she'd have to leave soon, and now that he knew he could, a man like him would easily find someone else to carry on with.

Jealousy threaded around her heart again, as it had so many times already that day.

Why hadn't she thought about that part of the deal when she'd gotten her bright idea about him fathering her child the old-fashioned way? Or his insisting he'd want to stay a part of her life if she got pregnant.

Suddenly a seemingly straightforward plan had gotten surprisingly complicated. Maybe they should forget the whole thing.

Too late. Things had changed between them now, in a major way. For the next few weeks it would be up to her to make sure the main reason she'd come to Malibu stayed in focus. To help Wes step back into his old life.

He lay beside her, a contented expression on his face, the most relaxed she'd ever seen him. She put her chin on her hands that rested on his chest, and studied him.

"What?" he said.

No way could she let him know her true thoughts. That she loved being here with him. That in a sense it had been a dream come true. Boy, if she could only talk to her fifteen-year-old self right now—*Just wait, one day you'll be with him*. She chuckled inside, and hoped he couldn't read her mind from her delirious expressions. But being with Wes was so much more than that. The portion of life they'd staked out together in his gym had come to mean more than she'd ever hoped. Especially now. And she needed to put the kibosh on these useless, fanciful thoughts. "Don't expect this to get you a free pass in the gym tomorrow."

"Slave driver." He tightened his grip around her and kissed her forehead. They definitely had something good going on.

And coming to Malibu to help an old friend could be the most dangerous thing she'd ever done in her life.

Of all times for Alexandra to call! Wes had sent Mary home early to pack up and move in with him. At least she didn't have to lie when Alex asked what she was up to.

"Just doing some straightening up around the house." She used a damp paper towel from the kitchen and mindlessly wiped up dust on the counter in the kitchen so as not to be a liar.

"Your house. Yes, that's right, your tiny house. How's that going?"

"Great. Remember I sent you some photos when I first bought it?" Two years ago.

"Vaguely. I'd assumed you'd be living in the house with Wes."

Was she a mind reader? "Why do that when I've got my lovely little house, and all that privacy?"

"I guess you've got a point, but he's got that gorgeous estate. But, oh, hey, I'll get to see your house tomorrow in person."

"Tomorrow?" Mary's casual cleaning motions quickly turned into a tornado of wiping and scrubbing.

"Yes. I've just gotten off the phone with Wes and told him my plane arrives tomorrow at nine. Will you come get me?"

She glanced at her phone, only then seeing the text slide in from Wes—*Alex is coming!*

"Of course. Can't wait to see you! How great. It'll be

like old times with the three of us together." And no more "hot" nights with Wes until after Alex left, even though Mary was entering her ovulation period. "How long are you planning to stay?"

"A couple of days."

Damn! "That's wonderful." Mary hoped she'd kept a cheerful tone in her voice, even though Alex's visit would seriously mess with her and Wes's plans. Between the sheets!

Adjusting her attitude, Mary remembered Alex was, after all, her best friend for life, but her showing up at this crucial time of their bargain—and her cycle—would be challenging to say the least. She'd need to keep a poker face where Wes was concerned, but how could she hide her true feelings from her best friend? Freaking over the moon with the chance to get pregnant by the guy she'd had a crush on since she was fifteen, and now that guy had become the man who'd blown the roof off her sex life on their first encounter.

"How's my brother doing?" Alex asked, in a decidedly serious tone.

Mary suppressed her cough. "Well. He's doing well. Made a lot of progress." Boy, had he ever! Did she mention he'd blown her mind sexually last night and had given her an incredible wake-up call just an hour ago? Not to Alex, she wouldn't!

"Mommy, Mommy." Two tiny voices demanded their mother's attention.

"I'm going to have to go now. You'll have to tell me all about Wes's progress on the ride from the airport tomorrow."

"Are you bringing Rose?" Even now, frantic and surprised, Mary wanted a chance to hold that toddler who'd turned her world upside down the day she'd been born.

"Not this trip. You'll have to come here soon. Promise?"

"Mommy!"

"That's a promise."

"I can't wait to see both of you."

"Me too! I'll meet you at baggage claim tomorrow."

Mary disconnected the call and closed her overnight case, since it would be a waste of time to pack it now. Her moving in with Alexandra's big brother would have to wait a few more days, until after she'd gone.

The next afternoon, Rita had put together a lovely spread of appetizers. Wes, Alexandra and Mary sat on the front patio, all taking in the sun, drinking sangria and snacking.

"I've never seen you look so relaxed, Wes. I think Mary is a good influence on you." Alex tucked her nearly black hair behind one ear. She wore it stylishly straight at chin length with Cleopatra bangs and looked much younger than thirty-five, especially with the midnight-blue highlights. Her long, narrow nose and coffee-brown eyes, so similar to her brother's, gave nothing away if she was by any chance suspicious about why her brother was so relaxed.

"We've gotten into a good routine, that's for sure."

Mary nearly spewed her drink over Wes's loaded response, but coughed and choked instead.

"You okay?" Alexandra tapped Mary's back a few times until she settled down.

"Went down the wrong way." She glanced at Wes, that mischievous glint in his eyes sparkling in the sun, and sent him a warning, though stealthy glare, then quickly looked away.

He popped a shrimp into his mouth and chewed vigorously. "We'll have to show you the gym later. This crazy lady has me cycling and doing gymnastics workouts."

"Well, you've never looked fitter."

"He's also thinking about going back to work again soon, right?"

She'd caught him off guard, and it showed by the way he stopped reaching for the avocado dip. "Yes. I guess I am. Gonna get measured for this special wheelchair that can help me stand for surgery."

"Wow, that's fantastic."

"I almost couldn't believe it when he showed me the video of the doctor doing surgery in this futuristic-looking contraption," Mary said.

"I knew I'd done the right thing, begging you to come."

"Oh, we had a rocky start, but Wes is a reasonable guy." *And a maniac in the bedroom!*

Alex started giggling. "Oh, gosh, remember that time I stole my Dad's car and we went to see Wes, but ran out of gas first?"

They all laughed, Mary and Wes more so because they'd just been talking about that last night, BS—before sex.

"How could I forget?" he said. "So whose idea was it anyway?"

Mary's eyes went wide. Damn.

"Mary's, of course. Come on, you must have known about her huge crush on you back then."

A Cheshire cat grin accompanied the "busted" stare coming from Wes. Her ears went hot.

Over the two days of Alexandra's visit Mary and Wes passed meaningful, though surreptitious looks when they all went to the movies that first night. Another thing Mary hadn't realized Wes still liked to do. And after Alex and Mary had gone to the beach the next afternoon, Wes met them at the hot tub for a long and relaxing group soak.

Dying to be with him, Mary found ways to touch him, and he did the same. "Oh, excuse me," he'd say, after reaching across her and grabbing a sneaky squeeze on her thigh. His mere touch set off a path of thrills straight to her center. Or she'd lean over him, managing to brush her chest against his while reaching for a spa towel. When Alex wasn't around, they'd grab quick kisses, filled with excitement and promises for make-up time soon. She'd done a lot of clenching by the end of day two.

"You haven't seen my house yet. Come, let me show you," she said to Alexandra, mainly to break up the torture of being so near yet so far from Wes.

"Yes. I'm dying to see how you manage there."

Once Mary had given her introductory tour, and Alex had given the obligatory compliments along the way, she nailed Mary with a no-nonsense stare.

"What's going between you and my brother?"

"Is it that obvious?"

"I almost didn't know where to look watching the two of you make love with your eyes over the dinner table last night!"

Mary felt heat rise all the way to the crown of her head. "It's not what you think."

"I think it's definitely what I think. Now, are you going to tell me or do I have to ask him?"

Mortified that Alex actually would go to her brother, Mary spilled some of the facts but left out the part about everything starting with a bargain.

"I knew you guys always had chemistry. Pity it took his accident to finally bring you together," Alex said with tears brightening her eyes.

"In a way, getting to know Wes has been healing for me."

"And for him! My God, his attitude used to be unbearable. Now he seems like his old self again." She took Mary's hands and squeezed. "I can't thank you enough."

How should she respond? *It's just part of my job?* "Like I said, we're healing each other."

Later, it was time to say goodbye to her brother. "Something told me Mary was the only person who could help you. I'm so glad you've found each other."

He looked perplexed, but accepted her good wishes. It seemed Mary held her breath until Alex was finally gone and she and Wesley were alone again. Turned out to be for a good reason, too. Because he'd shut down a little. And had withdrawn.

Had letting his sister know something was going on between them ruined what they'd salvaged from their relationship? Had her stepping over the line with her bold bargain proved to be nothing more than craziness?

Mary shook her head, her face dropping into her hands. How badly had she screwed things up?

Wes worked like a fiend in the gym over the next few days, and as he did so he remembered all the things Mary had said to him about picking up his old life again and working as a doctor. Because of her, he wanted to live each day to the best of his ability and believed he could once again achieve a life he actually enjoyed. Just different. She'd believed in him when he'd given up. He'd gotten sick of feeling like a victim anyway.

Why should he be uncomfortable with his sister knowing he and Mary had become lovers? Why hold that against Mary? It didn't make sense, and he certainly hadn't stopped having sex with her because of it, he'd just held back some of the confusing feelings that arose along with the great sex. He was sure Mary sensed him pulling back, too. Ah, hell, what was the point of overthinking their bargain? Enjoy it while it lasted. It would take a miracle for her to get pregnant. He pushed the negative thoughts away. Wasn't it time to seize the day again?

"You're going to injure yourself if you keep up those repetitions with that amount of weight," she said, chiding him, but the expression on her face said otherwise. He'd impressed her, he knew it and he liked it.

"I could go on all day."

The light touch of her fingers tickled across his neck. "Save some of that energy for later."

Thanks to the devices he'd ordered to help make intimacy easier and more satisfying, their last few days had gone by in a crazy sexy haze as they tried them out. Making up for the lost time during Alexandra's visit, he'd wanted her often, and she'd complied. So different from Giselle, Mary seemed perfect for him.

He couldn't fool himself into thinking it was totally him. He understood she had an ulterior motive, and the fact was her fertility cycle ruled the day. Still, lucky him.

Following her PT regimen had made him stronger than ever, after having reached a plateau with his own workout before she'd arrived. Wasn't that what she'd promised? Give her two months—that was how she'd tried to sell her brand of healing.

He finished another set of repetitions, thinking the upper half of his body had never been stronger. His thoughts circled back to Mary. A disturbing thought popped into his head. Was he falling in love? Then another—was he even capable of being a father?

She'd be leaving soon, and he needed to get on with life, not get stuck in a rut of wanting someone he'd never have. "I'm going to call the head of neurosurgery this afternoon to let him know I'm ready to come back to work."

She wasn't able to hide the surprise, and he saw it

clearly in those ocean-green eyes. "They'll be thrilled to have you, too." *Great cover, Harris.* The fact she'd poorly hidden one moment of...what, sadness, fear, loss, encouraged him that she might have feelings for him, too.

He grabbed her and pulled her onto his lap. "Thought I'd venture back a little at a time. See some patients. Watch some surgery. See where that leads."

"Order that special stand-up wheelchair now." She'd clicked into PT mode. All business. Was that her defense?

"I already have."

"Someone will need to come and measure. Who knows how long it takes to make one."

"That's been arranged too, Harris. Besides, going back to work sooner or later doesn't matter, just as long as I get there." He'd surprised her again, going all Zen. He'd surprised himself, too.

"This from the impatient man I found in your gym six weeks ago?"

"You've changed me. I give credit where it's due."

She hugged him. "Thank you. But you've done all the hard work."

"That's because I've had a relentless slave driver as a coach."

His face was close enough to see flecks of gold in the kaleidoscope of green and amber in her irises. He'd miss those eyes. Overcome with feelings he wasn't ready to sort out, he kissed her, his mouth melding with the lips he'd come to want and need more than he'd ever imagined possible. She'd fought her way back into his life, and now had conquered him. He opened the kiss and plunged his tongue inside in a desperate move. She matched his urgency, pressing her body tight against his chest. His hands roamed her back and hips as if he'd never touched her before, frantic to find what he needed. Her. All of her. She rocked over his lap, taking his breath with her kisses, and he knew he'd found home.

Whoever had designed that glider chair and the cot with extra bounce was a flat-out genius. Mary plopped back on the cot completely sated. Wes had so much upper body strength he'd stayed on top as she'd utilized the rebound of the special fabric beneath, her legs wrapped around his waist as the cot enhanced their timing, moving them piston-quick. When his strength faltered briefly, her arms held him where she needed for those last crucial seconds. Wow, had that been worth it. What teamwork! Though on her back, she'd controlled the rate and rhythm, and when Wes had once again held strong in a push-up above her, she'd gone for it and had quickly found her golden ticket to heaven.

He'd started reacting to her orgasms as if they were his own, and she believed he felt what she felt, just in his own way.

Now that she'd settled down, he collapsed beside her. Still unable to talk, all she could do was shake her head. *Wow! Just wow.* He gave his self-satisfied look, which she loved, but pretended otherwise.

"This is crazy," she said after several more seconds of basking in the post-sex haze.

"Not nearly crazy enough."

Her head bobbed up. "You're already tired of me? Am I going to have to do that impossible position from that horrible porn movie?"

"No way. I'm just saying I'm happy to oblige, no matter how often."

"With all the times we've been together, I'll be shocked if—" Damn, she hadn't meant to bring the passion they'd just shared down to the mere function of a bargain they'd made. *Get me pregnant. That's the point of all this.*

Because it wasn't. Not anymore.

"Don't get your hopes up too much," he said, breaking into her thoughts. "I've been reading up on this and apparently paraplegic sperm motility isn't always up to par."

Funny he hadn't mentioned that before now, after two full weeks of mating like bunnies. "All it takes is one good swimmer."

He spanked her once and pulled her closer on top of him. "Then here's to one good swimmer."

He kissed the top of her head, and for some reason that chaste and tender kiss felt more special than all the fiery ones that had preceded it, sending a cascade of tingles down her neck and fanning over her shoulders.

Wesley Van Allen held the magic touch for Mary… but their days together were numbered.

Two days later Mary assisted Wes with passive range of motion to warm up. His hips, knees and ankle joints were flexible and healthy, and she'd managed to stop the progression of atrophy of his leg muscles. But the credit wasn't all hers. "Okay, onto the bike."

"Yes, boss."

Using his superb upper body strength, he shifted from the workout wheelchair onto the stationary bike designed especially for paraplegics. In her quest to help Wesley live a long, vital life, she knew from the beginning his circulation had to be addressed. Since money was no object with him, shortly after she'd come to help, she'd ordered the amazing stationary bicycle designed especially for him.

Since its arrival a month ago, they'd utilized the bike as part of his daily routine. She strapped his right leg in

the holder and his foot to the pedal. He insisted on doing
the same for the left leg. Next, she attached electrodes to
his right thigh and gluteus maximus muscles.

"Here, let me do that," he said, setting himself up
on the left side. She intended to flip on the switch on
the control panel, but he stopped her. So she stood back
and let him set up the bike for his proper daily workout.
He chose the high-intensity mode, which involved four
minutes of hard exercise with an equal interval of easier
training. Four sets.

He knew as well as she did that this exercise demanded
energy that increased his blood flow and pulse, with the
benefit of accelerating oxygen uptake and enhancing the
heart's pumping volume. Once he'd read the Norwegian
university study on this very subject, he'd become a be-
liever. This style of aerobic exercise would add years to
his life. And if Mary miraculously got pregnant, she'd
want the father of her baby to hang around for a long
time. All for the baby's sake, of course.

"Remember to check on that order for the arm cycle,"
he said during the second repetition, hardly winded.
"When I go back to work I won't have time to spend
hours in the gym."

That was a fact. He'd need exercises that maximized
the workout in minimal time. Using the bike, along with
a similar contraption for his arms, would buy him precious time as well as multiple physical benefits.

As she watched him tear up the imaginary road on his
bike, one more thought came flying at her and landed
right between her eyes. He didn't need her anymore.
She'd come to help get him back on track, and now he'd
taken off at a sprint on his own. Her job here was done.

Then another thought landed, this one weighing heavily on her mind. The fact that she'd accepted her next as-

signment and would have to leave for Astoria, Oregon, in another week. Was she ready to say goodbye to Wes? More importantly, would she ever know if he felt the same way about her as she did about him?

She'd made the biggest mistake of her life and had fallen in love with him. That old insecurity of her teens had her thinking that if she dared to stay, he wouldn't want her, and she was afraid to find out.

Chuck had left because, after all they'd shared between them, she hadn't made the grade. It had cut her to the core, having opened her heart to love, only to have it tossed aside as her lover had set off for parts unknown. Why would she think a man like Wes, the once Prince of Westwood, a brain doctor, who knew where she'd come from—had seen the trailer park first hand—would ever see her as an equal, or good enough to love?

No, it was better to leave things as they were, he going back to work and she, well, just going. But if she was lucky, she'd be taking something special along with her. A part of Wes. His baby.

The Prince of Westwood had granted her that wish. And she'd certainly lived up to her part of the bargain. The guy was an amazing lover. He'd also said he wanted to get involved with the baby's life if the unlikely occurred, which would be tricky if they lived in different states. But she wouldn't deprive him of that. Maybe she should find a job and settle down here.

A baby *and* a relationship with Wes was too much to hope for. Wasn't it?

Three days later, Mary began packing up the house and hoped she'd be prepared for her thousand-plus-mile drive to her next job in Astoria by the weekend. When she'd first arrived nearly two months ago, she hadn't expected leaving to be so hard. She'd broken a professional car-dinal rule, never to fall for a patient. Up until now that had never been a problem, no matter how cute some of them had been.

But she and Wes had set things up differently. She hadn't been employed by Wes—she'd come as an old friend. He might not have considered her a friend at the time, but they'd worked through their differences and had quickly skipped from friends to lovers. Who had time to fall in love? Yet she had. Her bargain, an offer that only a true friend would make to a man like Wes—to help him understand he could still have sex—had turned out to be a huge mistake.

What had made her think she could keep their love-making clinical? He'd needed something. She'd needed something. It had made sense at the time. Now she was left with a wadded-up mess of love clogging her heart.

Hell, they'd used each other, and while thinking how civilized she was, she'd accidentally fallen in love. Stu-pid. Stupid. Stupid. She could only speak for herself, of course, but from the way Wesley seemed to be moping around these last couple of days, she suspected he might have his regrets, too.

What could have been a disastrous attempt to help him understand that sex was doable as a paraplegic had turned into a profound experience, one that had changed her life forever, too.

And there he was, at her tiny house door, the man she could never admit her true feelings to because he had far too much on his plate already. And her chest squeezed with that unique sensation she wasn't supposed to feel.

"I've been thinking, Harris."

"Oh, that's always dangerous." She gave her best shot at being upbeat and fun.

He gave a tolerant smile, watching her with warm brown benevolent eyes. "I've been thinking you should look for a job closer by so we can keep in touch. See each other."

She nearly lost her balance, but blamed it on the cardboard box underfoot, then recovered as quickly as she could.

Wes understood Mary fiercely needed her independence, and she'd never settle for only being a live-in girlfriend, catering to him and him alone. Sure, it was a nice fantasy, but one that would never work. Under those circumstances, he'd soon lose respect for her, as she would for him. Yet that was all he really had to offer her. She'd be miserable, strapped down with him. So the next best thing would be for her to work in Los Angeles. And the best way for him to convince her that she wouldn't be completely trapped in a life with him was to show her he could live a regular life. Wasn't that what she'd been hammering home since she'd gotten here?

"I know you're busy packing, but let's take the day off tomorrow and go to the Getty Museum. There's a smaller one right down the road in Pacific Palisades, the Getty Villa."

Surprise brightened her face and the sweetest unassuming smile followed. "I could use a break." She gestured to the several cartons and boxes lining her mini living room. "I'd love to."

"Great, I'll order some tickets online right now."

Once he'd used his phone to secure entrance to the museum the next day, he stuck around. The least a man could do was help her with her packing, so they spent the rest of the afternoon putting her dishes in boxes and securing anything else that could break in drawers and inside the tiniest closets he'd ever seen.

"What about the bed?" Yeah, he was a guy, always thinking about beds. Especially where Mary was concerned.

"That's pretty much secured up there, but I still put up a plywood barrier to keep the dresser from sliding around. Oh, that reminds me, I need to pack away the mirror from up there."

She had a mirror in her bedroom? Hmm, that sounded promising. Yet he'd never get to see the bed or the mirror since the only way to her loft was up a narrow ladder. *Paraplegic stopped by climbing device.* The metaphor of not being able to make it over that never-ending hill AP— after paraplegia—seemed especially appropriate for their situation. He'd also been hit with a wave of claustrophobia like the first time he'd come to visit, so he thought up a reasonable excuse and made a quick exit.

The next day, he displayed all his independent skills by driving, parking, and using his electric wheelchair to get around the Roman-styled architecture of the museum. As they strolled along the side of the main Grecian-styled pool and the central courtyard gardens, and later the gallery within the villa, he didn't notice a single sculpture. Instead, he spent the entire afternoon admiring her. How her strawberry blonde hair brushed her face when she turned too quickly. How she pursed her lips when she concentrated while using earbuds and the self-guided tour to study the collections. How delicate her hands were, even though she could pump iron with the best of them. How she glanced at him often, making sure he was enjoying the Greek and Roman antiquities as much as she was. He fudged and pretended he was.

She was his museum, the person who knew his past, who was the one woman who had seen him completely vulnerable in all his paralyzed glory, yet who'd still seen something worth wanting in him. With her around, he felt confident and alive. He could see his future. The question was, how would he get along without her?

He had to. Otherwise all her efforts would be for naught and she'd have failed. He owed her his success. And so much more. She'd reawakened his sleeping soul. She'd showed him step by step how to flourish. He'd even learned a magic trick or two thanks to her unorthodox approach to rehab for fine motor skills. But most of all, with her PT regimen, she'd ensured he'd have a long and healthy life as a paraplegic. He couldn't let her down.

He'd go back to work and pick up where he'd left off. He'd already ordered the special stand-up wheelchair, and expected to be doing neurosurgery again within the next few months. He'd prove to her, his family and the world he could go on, and quit hiding out in his comfortable cave. He'd join the living again and make a life for himself. That was the only way he knew how to repay her.

"I'm done," she said, clicking off the self-guided tour and removing the headphones.

"Did you enjoy it?"

"Totally. I'd like to come here again sometime."

"I'd be happy to bring you. Just say when."

She caught his gaze and he thought he saw a hint of longing in hers but knew he'd probably read into that look out of wishful thinking.

Instead of replying, she took his hand and squeezed. All the answer he needed.

"I thought we could have an early dinner out, if you'd like?"

She glanced around thoughtfully, as if searching for the best way to say what she needed. "You know what I'd like? To go back to Malibu and cook dinner for you.

I've been here almost two months and only cooked for you once."

"If that's what you want."

"You'll be dessert." She winked and walked ahead, leaving him grinning and forgetting to push the forward button on his chair.

CHAPTER NINE

HOURS LATER, AFTER Mary had prepared a simple meal of chicken in lemon and herb sauce, quinoa and salad, because that was what he had handy in his kitchen, they took a stroll on the beach. He used his workout wheelchair that rolled easily along the wet, packed-down low-tide sand, like a bicycle would have.

The chill of the night had Mary hugging herself, but she didn't complain. The lapis lazuli sky was thick with stars, and frothy fluorescence-tipped waves rolled one after another to shore. Wes had to move quickly to avoid getting his chair wet more than a few times. But they carried on because the ocean always brought peace, and Wes needed peace of mind with that damned ticking clock hanging over his head, and the barrage of thoughts plaguing him. The foremost was that Mary would be leaving soon.

Back at his house, Wes took Mary's hand and kissed it. "Come with me." He pulled her along the path to his porch, across his living room and into his private elevator. When the doors closed he grasped her hips and tugged her near, hugging her tight around the waist and resting his head on her breasts. "I've wanted you all day."

She ran her fingers over his freshly buzzed hair. "You must have read my mind."

Once in his bedroom, fighting the passion that threatened to take over, he helped her undress, taking time to lightly stroke and touch her skin as the layers of clothing came off, rather than ravish her as he longed to. When he removed her bra he tasted the velvet of each tip as she tensed and swayed under the touch of his mouth. His mind swirled with hunger for more, yet he held back, instead settling for the sensation of the bud as it peaked against his tongue.

He edged her onto the bed, spreading her legs, running his fingers over the satin-smooth skin of the inside of her thighs, then leaned forward, mesmerized by her heady scent. He covered her with his mouth, at first only flicking his tongue, teasing her, hunting for that tiny nub, then using long strokes to soothe her into submission. She let loose a long quivery sigh. Her sweet taste made him feel drunk with desire. She purred for him, and he kept her floating in that special state of bliss for as long as she'd let him. This was all about her, and his need to show how much he wanted to make her happy. Hoping she'd never forget him.

Soon she arched her back and he delved deeper and flattened his tongue, rubbing and licking, enjoying the whimpering sounds and squirming under his touch. He clutched her bottom and went deep, bringing her to the brink then pushing her over with a cadence of stiff strokes and one endless swirl. She gasped and her belly quaked. Unrelenting, he drove her to bucking and crying out, until she'd gone completely, lost to his wizardry. And even then he hadn't begun to come close to showing her the depth of how much he needed her.

Morning broke through the edges of the window and Mary tried to open her eyes to the glare.

"What time is it?" She sat up, searching for the nearest bedside clock.

Wesley slept peacefully beside her. They'd made love like the world had been ending last night, and she was sore to prove it, but in a wonderfully contented way. She stroked his cheek and he began a long, meandering journey toward waking up. Then it hit her. She was leaving in two days. She'd never have the chance to see him like this again, and her chest gripped like a vise.

His eyes now opened, obviously not having clicked in with the living quite yet, Wes smiled sleepily and blissfully at her. She wanted with all of her being to stay with him, wished it was possible, but knew better. If he realized how much she wanted him in her life, he might think she'd trapped him with a baby bargain. Why further complicate his life with her mistake of falling in love?

They'd risked it all with that crazy bargain—first proving he could have satisfying sex again, and, boy, oh, boy, had they proved that beyond any doubt, and, second, trying to get her pregnant. Well, half of the bargain was better than nothing. And life would be far less complicated this way.

"Let's skip the gym workout today and stay right here," he said, stroking her arm.

It would be so easy to do that, to get lost in his body, to hold him close, but she might never want to let him go and, worse yet, she might tell him how she really felt.

That wouldn't be fair, and would be far beyond what he'd bargained for. He'd call it sabotage. She couldn't do that to Wes, not when his life was just beginning to get back on track.

"Sounds great, but to make up for taking yesterday off, I've got to finish up my packing. And don't you have a meeting with the head of neurosurgery later?"

"Ah, damn, yes. But that's not until noon. Let's stay here a little longer, at least."

She couldn't get lured into making love with him again. After last night, giving him everything she'd had, and he still hadn't uttered a word about loving her, she needed to start protecting herself. It would be hard enough to leave. Why set herself up to rip out an even bigger piece of her heart? No. She had to toughen up, accept that where men were concerned she'd yet to measure up. First with Chuck, who'd walked away from her, and now with Wes, who was letting her leave. Yeah, she needed to harden her heart, and it may as well begin right now.

"I'm pretty sure I've met my end of the bargain. I proved you could have sex. Great sex, may I remind you."

He grabbed her hip and rolled her closer. "Since we're talking about our bargain, then your half hasn't been met. I promised to make you pregnant. I don't think you should leave until we've achieved that goal."

She laughed with him, keeping things light yet seeing something careful going on behind his casual mask. *Oh, yes, aren't we so grown up and worldly with our bargain.* "Theoretically, that sounds great, but I hate to remind you I've got a new job to start on Monday, and it's going to take me the weekend to drive to Oregon."

She was probably reading into his look, but she could have sworn she saw panic flash inside those caramel-tinted dreamy eyes. "All the more reason to take the morning off. Let's give it one last try. I owe you. Right?"

It certainly wasn't a flowery proposition, but he was being honest. She wanted a baby, had risked her heart for it, so shouldn't she do whatever it took to know she'd done her best? Taking cold, hard logic into consideration, how could she refuse?

She moved into his open arms, loving the heat of his

body and the feeling of home she'd recently found in his embrace. Maybe this time he'd admit how he really felt about her. Should she be the first to say the L word?

Mary had been wrong. Yes, they'd made love like they hadn't seen each other in weeks, but Wes hadn't confessed any special feelings for her beyond, "Wow, was that as good for you as it was for me?"

She'd let herself down, too, by not having the guts to tell him how she felt. What was the use? She was leaving. Telling him she loved him would ruin everything they'd worked so hard on the last two months. All it would do was prove to Wes that he should never have let her in his house in the first place. Damn, she'd fouled up.

They weren't meant to be together, or they would have taken that chance ten years ago, at his sister's wedding. Everything had been perfect then. She could have taken a job near him as he hadn't yet been officially engaged. The timing had been perfect. Yet they hadn't even had the nerve to find out what it would be like to have sex. That said it all, didn't it? And things were so, so different now.

She had a life to go back to. Her own little home. He was still picking up the pieces of his, but it was a start, and his future, once again, looked bright.

"Just to let you know, I'll be sleeping at my place tonight," she said, beginning her exit strategy, if she could call it that. Because she was nowhere near ready to say goodbye to Wesley Van Allen. "I want to get an early start on the road, and—"

"Wait a minute. What? You're leaving tomorrow? I thought—"

"I've changed my mind. I'd like to get there a day early so I can set up my house and be ready to start the job full out on Monday."

He shook his head, not looking in the least bit pleased. "I've got this meeting this afternoon, and you're messing with my concentration. Can't you leave on Saturday, like you originally said?"

She let hurt and an aching heart speak unedited for her. "It's not always all about you, Wesley. Sorry, I can't accommodate you this time."

She turned to leave his bedroom, after having taken only a minute to put on her clothes.

"Harris, that's not what I meant."

Too late. Instead of looking back, she strode to the door, knowing he couldn't catch her.

Mary stood her ground and refused to rush back to Wes that night. He owed her an apology. But he hadn't come crawling to her door, like she'd expected. Beyond the argument, she'd been dying to hear how his meeting had gone, but figured if he wanted her to know, he'd come and tell her.

It turned out he was as stubborn as she was, but she already knew that. So why did it hurt so much?

As she lay in her loft, still angry but realizing she could have spent one last night with Wes if she hadn't gone all emotional and let hurt do her talking, she broke down. Feeling raw, hormonal and completely mixed up, she cried until her eyes swelled shut.

Her gut assured her she really never had been good enough for him. Even now, with their playing field somewhat leveled. Because he was still rich. He'd been raised like a prince, the Prince of Westwood—it was in his blood to be proud. In his parents' eyes, the universe truly did revolve around him. They'd convinced him of it, too. She'd come from a trailer park, not one of those upscale versions around these days but the last-ditch, park-what-

you've-got kind of place. Starting humble like that, everything else was a step up. Now she lived like a vagabond,
traveling around the country in her tiny portable house.
Owning that house was the best she could do for herself
and, damn it, she was proud of what she'd accomplished
after starting from nothing. And yet she still didn't feel
good enough for Wes.

He'd sat there stoically in his bed, like the world owed
him something, like she owed him something. Her early
departure hadn't worked for his timeline. Seriously?
Well, to hell with him!

But she loved him. Damn it. She picked up her cellphone and brought up his number, ready to call and tell
him everything she felt. Why not? She was leaving. Say
it and go. Let him figure out the rest. But the next second
she stopped and, chickening out, she never pressed "call".

The next morning, after several rounds of cold com-
presses on her eyes, feeling she finally looked decent
enough to face him without giving herself away, she set
out to say goodbye. And pride be damned, a swarm of
butterflies seemed to take over her stomach.

Wes had hardly slept. His meeting at the hospital had
gone well, and he'd be returning to work in two weeks,
but the way things had been left with Mary yesterday
morning had nagged at his peace of mind all night. She'd
acted out of character, surprising him about leaving early,
then had gotten all moody and snide when he'd blundered
his immediate response. He'd given a knee-jerk reaction
and an equally adolescent reply—"You're messing with
my concentration. Can't you leave on Saturday?" Good
Lord, what an ass. It had come off like a hurt child taking his toys and going home.

In other words, he'd blown it. Big time. He should have

apologized on the spot, but his damn pride had tripped him up and, having a deep grasp on him, that same pride had kept him from going to see her last night. Instead, he'd waited for her to come to her senses.

And he considered himself a fairly well-adjusted adult, how?

Today he'd woken up with a double helping of remorse, but couldn't for the life of him figure out how to make things right. Though he knew one thing, he needed to go to her and apologize.

In the kitchen, Wes put together something to eat. His stomach was in knots and he wasn't even sure he'd be able to get anything down. Then the doorbell rang. Over the last two months, Mary had made herself at home, coming and going any time she wanted. He'd made a point to leave the door unlocked for her today, too.

But the doorbell rang again.

He wheeled himself to answer, wondering if it might be someone else, but there she stood, looking beautiful and heartbreakingly sad.

"I'm all packed and ready to go," she said. Her hair pulled back in a ponytail, without a stitch of makeup on, wearing cut-off jeans and an old T-shirt, she looked like he remembered her at fifteen. He detected some puffiness around her eyes, and they looked far less clear than usual. Knowing he'd been responsible for that made his gut twist tighter.

"Come in. Don't stay on the doorstep. Let's have a proper goodbye." He moved back, making room for her. She hesitated, then cautiously stepped inside.

He tugged her hand and pulled her close, wanting nothing more than to kiss her. She resisted. So he bussed her cheek. No, they couldn't separate under these circumstances. "What have I done, Harris? I apologize for being a jerk yesterday, okay? Why are you acting this way?"

She shook her head. "You haven't done anything, Wes."

Why did he get the distinct feeling there was a whole lot more to that answer? "Yes, I have. I've made you angry, and I can't stand you leaving under these circumstances."

She studied her feet. "Well, it's not like we have the gift of time to work things out, right?"

For a lady who always named the elephant in the room, she was sure dodging the issue. Since he might never see her again, he needed to say what he'd been thinking all night, beyond giving an apology. "I know we agreed to use each other, but this leaving on such bad terms seems so cold."

"Use each other?"

Damn, he'd chosen the wrong words again. "You know what I mean."

"We made a bargain."

"Yes." Sadness enveloped him, topped off with old anger that still managed to trip him up when he wasn't careful. "I foolishly thought we actually had something." A devastating thought landed like a hatchet to his chest. He'd hoped she'd get pregnant because he knew without a doubt that if she had, he wouldn't let her walk away. It had turned out his slow sperm hadn't done the trick after all, and he felt sorry for himself. "I get that it's time for you to move on, that I'll always just be another guy in a wheelchair that you've helped."

"Stop it right there!"

He'd obviously hit a sore spot.

"First of all, it's unlike you to feel sorry for yourself, so quit it. Second, how dare you make all these assumptions about me?" She'd given up staring at her feet and now impaled him with anger he'd seen often enough in the mirror. "How could we have *something* when you've never once told me you love me?"

Was that the problem? He didn't think they'd been in this bargain for love, so he'd kept his feelings at bay, and now she was blaming him? "I never heard those words from your mouth either," he fired back, feeling far too defensive, and immature, and knowing it was a pitiful comeback. Nevertheless, it was how he felt.

"You wouldn't have believed me if I'd said them," she said, so quietly he almost couldn't hear her. "You had things all wrapped up long before I arrived. You'd never trust anyone who dared fall for you in that chair. Why would I be so foolish to beat my head against that wall around your heart?"

In other words, he was the one who needed to have said it first. "I knew it was stupid to make that agreement. We played with fire, and now we've both been burned."

"You're the one who challenged me to prove it. Remember?"

What could he say? He'd challenged her—begged her, actually—and she'd given in to his demands. *Show me I'm still a man.* She'd asked for something in return, and he'd foolishly thought that would make their deal acceptable. All for sex. They'd owe each other nothing beyond the terms of their agreement. Wrong! Now he'd hurt her, and his mind was so messed up he didn't have a clue how to make things right. Yet one thought held firm. If she were pregnant, everything would be different. She watched him as he sat there without a single word to say beyond "I'm sorry, Mary."

"I can't stand the thought of these last two months being ruined by a silly argument."

"It's not so silly, is it?"

She sighed. "Like I said, it's not like we have another month to figure things out."

"True." He hated this moment, knowing she'd say goodbye and it could be another ten years before he saw her again. He reached for her hand and she let him take it. "Will you call me when you get there?"

"Sure."

He knew in his gut she wouldn't. They'd reached a truce. Nothing more. The word "love" wouldn't be uttered. For better or worse, they'd settled that.

She leaned over and kissed him. Unlike any of the other times, this was a parting kiss, and it tasted unbelievably bitter.

Then he sat there like one of those sculptures at the museum, and foolishly let her go.

CHAPTER TEN

One month later...

WES HAD FINISHED a thirty-minute procedure for carpal tunnel repair in outpatient surgery. He'd just successfully released the ligament over the affected nerve in the forty-year-old female patient's left wrist. If all went well, she'd soon be pain free, and the one-inch incision would heal and look like part of her "lifeline" on the palm.

Since returning to work, the head of his department, Ram Ramanathan, had suggested he cut his teeth with the shorter procedures. Thrilled to be back in the OR on any level, he'd agreed to start slowly and work his way back to the more complicated and time-consuming surgeries. The wrist nerve repairs were the perfect first step.

Even with the new "standing" wheelchair, he'd found being strapped into an upright position difficult to tolerate for long periods of time. Three to four carpal tunnel repairs were about all he could tolerate in a day. As most neurosurgeries took several hours, he was content to build up his tolerance, right there in day surgery. Most importantly, since returning to work he had distraction from his twenty-four-seven thoughts about Mary and how completely wrong he'd played his hand.

Returning the specially made wheelchair to the sitting position, he took a deep breath, and, glad to relieve the pressure around his chest, he rubbed the area, then released his legs from the thigh and shin straps. Though he couldn't feel his legs, he knew it was important to do some quick passive ROM exercises to help with circulation. After stripping off the dirty OR gown and gloves, he rolled into the post-surgical room and washed his hands.

A few minutes later, fresh scrubs donned under his white OR coat, he'd returned to his office for a few remaining appointments. As often happened, his mind drifted to the one who had got away, Mary. Instead of calling when she'd arrived in Astoria, like she'd promised, she'd merely mailed him a card. He still kept the envelope with her new address in his office desk drawer just to look at her writing, knowing her fingers had once touched it. Damn, he missed her.

In the card, Mary apologized for how things had turned out, then told him briefly about her new job. She'd stepped in as lead PT in a small hospital situated in a beautiful town tucked beside the Columbia River called Astoria. He could imagine her tiny house fitting in perfectly there, but hoped she didn't plan to stay there beyond the six weeks she'd agreed to in her work contract, while the regular lead PT took a cruise around the world.

Not wanting to mess up her plans, he'd kept his feelings to himself about how much he missed her, and wished beyond hope she'd come back. Instead, he'd sent a cordial yet contrite text message in response.

I'm sorry too. Glad you made it there safe and sound. Keep in touch.

What a jerk. He didn't deserve a great woman like Mary Harris. Not because he was in a wheelchair, but because at the age of thirty-seven he still didn't know how to love a woman the way she deserved. He wanted to. Was pretty damn sure Mary was the one person he could learn with, too.

He shook his head, remembering how he'd teased her about waiting for "that one special person". What had he known at the time? That had been before he'd finally gotten to know the most amazing woman in the world. Regardless, their relationship was out of his hands now. She worked in Oregon and he in California.

His computer lit up with an odd jingle. A video call. He considered ignoring the computer call—he'd explain later how busy he was—until he glanced at the monitor. Mary's name flashed.

Shaken, he quickly accepted the call, adrenaline suddenly perking him up. In a flutter of nerves he knocked the computer mouse off the desk. He quickly bent to pick it up, hoping he hadn't accidentally disconnected the call before it'd started. But when he sat back up, there was her beautiful face, on his computer monitor screen. She took his breath away, and he didn't have a second to prepare, yet there was so much he wanted to say.

No. She made the call. Let her talk first. See where it leads.

"Harris, how are you?" He did his best to sound casual but, with his pulse fluttering in his throat, he came off as anything but.

"I'm great. Beyond great." She definitely looked ecstatic, her eyes bright, shining with tears. Happy tears. "I wanted you to be the first to know, Wes."

"What? Is everything all right?"

She nodded vehemently. Some hair fell across her eyes, and she quickly brushed it away. "Couldn't be better. Perfect, in fact." She took a moment to compose herself. "So here's the news—you've held up your end of the bargain after all."

What? Now he really couldn't catch his breath. "You're...?"

"Yes," Again she nodded like a bobble head. "I'm pregnant!" She held a home pregnancy test strip, colored pink for positive, close to the computer camera for proof. "It's positive. I've tested two mornings in a row before calling just to make sure. We did it!" She pulled back the strip, her face coming into view again. Those bright green eyes broke into tears, though she grinned happily. "Thank you, Wes." She swiped at some of the tears making their way down her cheeks, but it was a futile gesture.

He wanted to touch her, to hold her in the worst way, to comfort her, hating the miles and the computer screen between them. Though frustrated with their separation at a time like this, tingles descended down his spine as he took in the significance of what she'd said. He'd fathered a child. He was going to be a father! A miracle, or meant to be?

Remembering their cold and calculated bargain, he kept cool. "One good swimmer, hey, Harris?"

She laughed, though he swore he could see a hint of sadness in her gaze. "Yes. All it took."

"Th-that's fantastic." What was he supposed to say? The woman he loved was pregnant with their baby. She'd bargained for that baby. Remember? She'd fallen in love with his niece Rose, and suddenly couldn't live without one of her own. He couldn't let her down by showing his true feelings. That he loved her and missed her and didn't know if he could go on without her. Or their baby.

Some strange yearning started building slowly, but he didn't have time to figure it out.

The new information certainly put an added spin on

things, which had been complicated enough *before* her getting pregnant. Though shaken to the core, he pasted on his best happy face. Something he was sorely out of practice on. What the hell was he supposed to do now? *That's great. Carry on without me. Have a good life.* Damn it all to hell.

"I don't want to interfere with your work," she said, "but I've been bursting to tell you."

"You're not interfering." *Hang on to her as long as you can.* Though he did have an afternoon of appointments waiting. "I'm so glad you called."

"And I'm so happy you're back working. I was told you were in surgery this morning when I first called your office. That's wonderful. Everything we worked for we've accomplished."

"Even getting you pregnant." The biggest and most confusing shocker of all. That odd feeling seemed to be snowballing.

"Yes! Everything. Well, I won't keep you. I'll call again soon, though. I—"

Don't let her say it. Because then you'll have to be honest and tell her how you feel about her, and everything will change. Am I ready for that? Lover. Father. Husband?

"Uh, me, too, Harris. Me too."

Keep her wondering what I mean, and keep guessing what she was about to say.

"I love you" would have been his top choice. He'd had more than enough time to think about that unspoken phrase. Though long overdue, under the new circumstances, a baby, everything had changed!

She disconnected and her beautiful face disappeared from the screen. The room felt immediately empty, though the news had certainly knocked his socks off. She was pregnant!

He sat transfixed for several moments, considering his options. Theirs had been a bargain, both had gotten what they'd wanted. That should be that, right?

Not on your life. Everything had changed. He'd sworn the day she'd left that if she were pregnant everything would've been different. He wouldn't have let her leave. He wanted to be a father to his baby, not a long-distance parent but a dad every single day of his child's life. And because he'd fallen in love with her. When he finally told her, he needed to do it in person, not on some computer screen phone!

Wes picked up his work phone. "Ram? It's Wesley. Listen, I know I've only just come back to work. What's that? Yes, things are going very well, but I do have a problem. I need to take off a few days. I have some pressing business to take care of. No, it has nothing to do with my medical issues. I need to make a quick trip to Oregon. Could you ask Beverly to clear my schedule for the next few days?"

Once he'd hung up the phone, between seeing his afternoon patients he went online and booked the first flight to Portland, Oregon, for early the next morning. Then, when a patient failed to show for an appointment, he took advantage of the time to find a car rental that could accommodate his special need for hand controls. Because it was his first flight since becoming paraplegic, he decided to use the electric wheelchair to navigate the airport for greatest ease. But first, because he was back working and took his responsibility as a doctor seriously, he finished his remaining afternoon appointments in the clinic.

There were many obstacles complicating his getting to

Mary the next day, but now that he'd come to his senses about what he needed and wanted to do, nothing would stop him. He grabbed the envelope in his desk with her new address, shoved it in his briefcase and rode out the office door.

Mary had had a particularly busy day and felt exhausted. The early pregnancy seemed to drain her of all her energy. And this was only the beginning. How would she handle it by herself when things got really tough?

Insecurity gripped her as she drove home. Could she do everything alone? Wes had said he wanted to be involved, but how involved would that be? And he hadn't said a peep about any of that yesterday when she'd called. Maybe she'd made a mistake. Not on her life. She wanted this baby with every cell in her body. Knowing life was growing inside was the most thrilling sensation ever. She couldn't wait to hold her newborn in her arms. This bout of uncertainty had everything to do with hormones and nothing to do with her bold plans. She'd overcome a heck of a lot worse things in life. Having a baby would definitely take getting used to, but she'd find her support system and make it work. She had to.

She honestly didn't know what she'd expected when she'd called and told Wesley the news yesterday. A part of her, way inside her heart, had hoped he would propose on the spot. Stupid, wishful thoughts. She'd bargained for this baby and he'd certainly enjoyed his part of the process. Then she'd left abruptly. Hell, he could already be dating some new woman and moving on with his life. Either the thought or the hormones sickened her in a quick wave.

She pulled the pickup truck into the secluded driveway that led to a small man-made pond next to which she'd been lucky enough to park her tiny house. As she neared the cement pad where she hooked up to water and electricity, she saw an unfamiliar van. She parked on the opposite side of her house and when she got out she heard the other vehicle's doors slam shut.

Mary walked around to the front of her house and nearly stumbled and fell when she saw Wesley in his electric wheelchair, waiting for her. Her circulation took a dive from head to stomach at the sight. She needed to hold on to something, so she grabbed the porch railing to her house for support.

His coffee and cream eyes were guarded yet determined.

Still in shock, she managed to squeak out some words. "Wes! What are you doing here?"

"I love you. I need you. Figured it was about time I told you."

Positive she wouldn't be able to take a single step on such shaky legs, she clutched the wood tighter and stayed put.

He moved his electric wheelchair, covering half the distance between them. "You need me. Our baby needs us." He managed a smile, his lips trembling nearly imperceptibly, but she could tell he was as nervous as she was. "Since you left I discovered there's something much worse than being paraplegic. Loneliness. I don't want a life without you."

She swallowed against a paper-dry throat. Was she imagining this perfect moment?

"Let me be a real father to our child." Her gaze shot upward, hardly able to believe what she was hearing. She tried to take a breath but could only manage a pant. He waited until her shock wore off and her eyes settled back on his. "Please."

Wes had just said the fantasy words she'd been waiting and dying to hear all her life, but especially for the last two months. Oh, hell, she'd blame the sudden onset of tears on the hormones, as she knew too much information was about to flood out from her heart. She took a trial step toward him, still not trusting her legs. "I've loved you since I was fifteen, Wes."

"Why didn't you ever tell me?" He reached out for her, his eyes softened and full of emotion but still stunned over what he'd just said, and she couldn't make herself move.

"I was afraid." Her hand flew to her stomach and her gaze dropped to the ground. "I never dared dream you could love a girl like me."

"A girl like you? You mean the most wonderful woman in my life?"

She looked at him again, unable to believe this moment was really happening. He'd shown up out of the blue from another state, which took some planning for a guy like him. He'd obviously been waiting for her. Now he'd confessed he loved her and wanted to be a part of her life.

How much more goodness could she take? Afraid she'd crumble if she let go, she held fast to the porch railing.

He studied her, an understanding expression on his face. Then he must have realized he hadn't said enough, even though he'd told her he loved her and wanted to be with her. Yes, she was that insecure where he was concerned.

So he began. "You were the first girl to ever take my breath away. At my sister's wedding, you looked more beautiful than the bride, and all I could think about was wanting to get you out of that dress. I was supposed to be engaged, but I couldn't think straight around you. What if, I thought, what if I went for it with Mary? Would she even want me?"

Her head spun with the information that would have changed the very course of her life back then. Why hadn't they gone for it?

"I've always been selfish, Harris, you know that. If I'd reached out for you then, if we'd gotten together, I would have blamed you for anything that went wrong." He dug fingers into now longer and fuller hair from the last time she'd seen him. She stood quiet, barely breathing, but taking in every word her spoke. Someday she'd want to savor these moments again, so she needed to memorize his face and what he was saying.

"Hell, I might have been like my father and blamed you for my becoming a paraplegic. Who knows? Because I didn't know how to open my heart up and love someone back then." He moved closer, dividing their distance by half again, until she could see the self-doubt in his eyes and the longing to make her understand. She began to relax, her fingers letting go of their death-like clutch on the wood railing.

"The point is, Harris, I've changed, and you're the one who changed me. You showed up uninvited and wouldn't take no for an answer, and I couldn't for the life of me understand why you stuck around. I was horrible to you, because you mixed me up, made me remember old feelings. Hell, I was in a wheelchair, what good were old feelings anyway? But you wouldn't let me get away with excuses. I started waking up every morning looking forward to seeing you, to getting to know you all over again.

"I was shocked how much you'd changed. How confident and skilled you were. How beautiful and sexy. My God, I couldn't quit thinking about you, and it bugged the hell out of me. What was the point? Why fall for the most lovable lady on the planet when nothing could come of it?

"You led me back to the living, and we made our pact with the devil, and, heaven help me, you made me feel like a man again. You may have thought I wasn't man enough to tell you how I really felt but the truth was I didn't want to trap you or tie you down with me. What did I have to offer you?"

She whimpered, sadness draining her, remembering their tragic and complicated story, the one she'd thought through a thousand times but had never come up with a satisfying ending to, until today. Until right now.

"The point of all this is everything has changed. I finally realize I love you with all my heart and soul, but only because you taught me how to love in the first place." A tiny ironic laugh slipped through his lips. "You once called me your life-changer. Well, it's you who changed me, and I love you for it, and I want with everything I have to be a real father to our baby, not just some sperm donor."

She drew her fist to her mouth, trying not to sob. He was for real. There was no doubting his intentions or sincerity.

"But the big question is, since you're still hugging those railings and I'm laying my guts on the line for you, will you have me? For better or worse?" He gestured toward his legs and the wheelchair. "The future won't be easy with me, but I want to go there with you. If you'll let me."

She broke free from her hold and rushed to him, then melted into his arms and folded herself onto his lap. "I love you more than you can ever understand, because I've never stopped loving you since the first day I met you. There's no changing a young girl's heart." She kissed him, getting his cheeks as wet as hers. "I love your stubbornness and your pride and even your arrogance. I love your resilience and intelligence, but most of all I love you being a big enough man to admit you didn't know how to love."

She threw her arms around his neck and squeezed tight. "I'm so happy to be the one to teach you, because you helped me, too, to love like I never believed I could. We ventured into that wilderness together with our crazy bargain, and, man, what a shocker. I love you, not because you're the best lover I've ever had but because you're the best man I've ever met. Sitting or standing. You're the one, and I don't ever plan to stop loving you, because I never have yet, and you've given me plenty of good reasons."

They laughed together, him being self-deprecating, further proof he was a changed man. Then they kissed again, this one not full of fire but more like a solemn vow, a sweet promise of all the great things to come.

Wes's fingers stroked her cheek. "You said I could still have it all, and I want it all, but only with you…and our baby." He tenderly planted his hand on her stomach. "Let's prove it, Harris. Marry me."

How could she not take him up on his dare? "I'd love to."

His confident smile soon turned cocky. "Aren't you going to invite me in?"

She lifted a brow, then slipped off his lap and took him home.

EPILOGUE

Eighteen months later...

"WHOA, WHOA, WHOA!"

Henry Van Allen was the spitting image of his father, with dark hair and shining eyes, and at ten months he was determined to prove he could walk. He tottered, breaking away from the coffee table in the waiting room, and took four drunken steps toward Wes in his wheelchair. Then stopped.

Mary clapped her hands, egging him on. "Come on, come to Momma." She bent forward and held out her hands while walking backward. Henry stood still, as though considering his options, then went for it and made a dozen more steps in quick order across the doctor's waiting-room carpet before landing on his diaper-padded bottom. He pouted and cried, and Mary rushed to pick him up.

"Do you know how proud I am of you? You can walk! Such a big boy." She hugged him then put him on his father's lap.

"Trying to show up your old man already, huh?" He proudly squeezed the boy, who always ate up any and all attention from his dad.

A physical therapist appeared at the door and invited

them all in to the therapy room. "Are you ready, Dr. Van Allen?"

"As ready as I'm ever going to be."

"Have a seat right there."

A regular chair awaited him, but on the chair was something that looked like a jet pack, and extending down, connected to the back apparatus, were serious-looking leg braces. They called it an exoskeleton and it had cost as much as a new sports car, but with Wes, money was not the object, walking was.

Once he transferred from his wheelchair to the other chair, the PT assistant helped him slip the straps over his shoulders. He snapped them tight at his sternum. She moved down to his thighs and then around his knees to two other sets of braces and fasteners. Once secured, she handed him two long rubber-tipped canes with braces for his elbows and hands, the hand sections with sensors.

The PT held a small box of controls in her hands. "Once you get the hang of walking again, you'll be able to control your steps all by yourself."

"I'm ready."

Mary had never seen her husband look more determined in her life. She snuggled a squirmy Henry and held her breath as Wes prepared to take one small step for himself, but a huge step for his future.

The PT stayed close behind him and fiddled with the control panel and, to her amazement, Mary saw her husband stand. Soon he was taking natural-looking steps, with his knees bending and heels touching the floor in a perfectly normal gait.

Henry squirmed to get down so he could go to his father. Mary held his pudgy hands to keep him from falling.

"Once you're more familiar with the technology,

you'll be able to control your walking using the sensors in the canes."

Wes glanced up at Mary with an amazed expression. "Can you believe it? I'm walking!"

"Daddy's walking!" She watched excitedly as Henry tagged alongside him. "You and Henry have a lot in common."

He laughed good-naturedly, as that sweetest part of his personality had grown exponentially since they'd married and he'd become a father. "I think Henry might already be doing a better job of walking than me, though." He truly had become a new man, starting first from the inside out, and now, with his standing and walking the length of the PT room right before her eyes with the help of the robotic skeleton, proved it.

"You're doing great, Dr. Van Allen. How about once more around the room then we'll let you try it out all by yourself."

Wesley looked at his wife, walking beside him with their wavy-haired, chubby and sturdy boy, and had never felt prouder in his life. He and Mary were eye to eye for a change—without being vertical on a bed. Actually, he was a good foot taller than her now that he was standing. He'd spent the last couple of years looking up at people's chins and nostrils and, to be honest, he'd gotten sick of the view. But not tired of looking at Mary, he'd never get tired of looking at Mary. Or Henry.

A couple of months ago he'd found an online video of a lady taking her first steps after being paraplegic for over twenty years. With Mary's eager blessing, he'd soon been measured for his very own exoskeleton. Now here he was, showing off for his kid, who had taken a break and sat down, now playing pat-a-cake and gurgling as he watched his dad take his first steps around the room.

Once Mary had told him she was pregnant, and she'd wrapped up her contract in Astoria, he'd convinced her to come back to Malibu and marry him immediately.

Within the month they'd had a small wedding in his living room for family and a few friends, with the Pacific Ocean as a backdrop at sunset. He'd never forget for as long as he lived how beautiful she'd looked in a simple white Grecian-styled satin gown, her shining hair flowing free over her shoulders, with a delicate wreath of baby's breath flowers around her head and holding white roses. He'd hardly been able to believe she would be his from that day forward.

Wearing a white tux and sitting in his special standing wheelchair, he'd flipped a switch and, thanks to a smooth hydraulic system, he'd literally risen to the occasion to take their wedding vows upright. Eye to eye.

He wouldn't have believed their lovemaking could have gotten any better after saying *I do*, but that night, making love as man and wife, he'd been overcome with emotion, fully understanding the precious gift he'd been given in the form of Mary Harris. Wondering why it had taken him twenty years to figure it out, but finally understanding how transformative love could be. All he could say was that he was one lucky guy.

And their life together had only looked up. Within a few short months he'd happily picked up his full career as a neurosurgeon, and he was back to his prior booming practice. Surgery and all. Meanwhile, Mary had quickly found a part-time job nearby, which had also given her plenty of time to plan, paint and decorate the nursery. And soon, as the good book his grandmother used to read to him at Christmas said, she was great with child.

In fact, she'd looked fantastic pregnant. In her case,

she'd truly glowed and beamed with life. He'd taken all the birthing classes with her and had been at her side through a long and grueling labor. When she'd become exhausted and about to give up, their boy had finally popped out his head, already crying before the rest of his body had even been born. And if marriage wasn't adventure enough, parenting had been the toughest yet most rewarding thing he could ever imagine. The kid was theirs! Plus he loved the fact his genes were clearly dominant in the boy.

His son, so far, only knew him as being in a wheelchair, yet today he'd stood and walked. He might look like an astronaut on the moon with the computer-directed steps, but it was a start. He believed in scientific innovation and had read a few successful studies using functional electrical stimulation to restore muscle movements. These were all temporary fixes, but he believed in the power of neuroscience and robotics and figured it was only a matter of time before they'd be able to implant a tiny computer with sensor-stimulators along the injured sections of the spine.

Until then, his job was to keep himself in good shape. With a wife like Mary, he had no doubt he'd be in top-notch condition for the rest of his life.

For now, though, he'd settle for this clunky walking suit.

"Are you ready to try it on your own?"

He looked at Mary and winked. "Hell, yeah, let's get on with it. I want to dance with my wife on our second anniversary."

Wes grinned, full of bravado, then, showing off for his wife and kid, he used the hand sensors on the canes and took himself for a slow but steady stroll for the first time in nearly three years.

And the best part of all was hearing his baby boy say, "Yay. Dada. Yay."

* * * * *

If you enjoyed this story, check out these other great reads from Lynne Marshall

WEDDING DATE WITH THE ARMY DOC
HIS PREGNANT SLEEPING BEAUTY
A MOTHER FOR HIS ADOPTED SON
FATHER FOR HER NEWBORN BABY
HOT-SHOT DOC, SECRET DAD

All available now!

MILLS & BOON®

MEDICAL ROMANCE™

THE ULTIMATE IN ROMANTIC MEDICAL DRAMA

A sneak peek at next month's titles...

In stores from 1st June 2017:

- **Healing the Sheikh's Heart** – Annie O'Neil
  and **A Life-Saving Reunion** – Alison Roberts

- **The Surgeon's Cinderella** – Susan Carlisle
  and **Saved by Doctor Dreamy** – Dianne Drake

- **Pregnant with the Boss's Baby** – Sue MacKay
  and **Reunited with His Runaway Doc** – Lucy Clark

Just can't wait?
Buy our books online before they hit the shops!
www.millsandboon.co.uk

Also available as eBooks.

MILLS & BOON®

EXCLUSIVE EXTRACT

Can a miracle surgery prove to cardiologist
Thomas Wolfe and his ex-wife Rebecca Scott that
it's never too late to give love a second chance?

Read on for a sneak preview of
A LIFE-SAVING REUNION

DON'T MISS THIS FINAL STORY IN THE
PADDINGTON CHILDREN'S HOSPITAL SERIES

The silence that fell between them was like a solid wall.

Impenetrable.

It stretched out for long enough to take a slow breath. And then another.

They weren't even looking at each other. They could have been on separate planets.

And then Rebecca spoke.

'I should never have said that. I'm sorry. It was completely unprofessional. And…and it was cruel.'

'I couldn't agree more.'

'It's not what I believe,' she said softly. '*You* know that, Tom.'

It was the first time she'd called him Tom, since he'd come back and it touched a place that had been very safely walled off.

Or maybe it was that assumption that he knew her well enough to know that she would never think like that.

And, deep down, he had known that, hadn't he? It had just been so much easier to think otherwise. To be angry.

'So, why did you say it, then?'

'You've been so distant ever since you came back. So cut off. I don't even recognise you anymore.' There was a hitch in Rebecca's voice that went straight to that place that calling him Tom had accessed. 'I guess I wanted to know if the man I married still exists.'

His words were a little less of a snap this time.

'I haven't changed.'

'Yes, you have.' He could feel Rebecca looking at him but he didn't turn his head. 'Something like what we went through changes everyone. But you...you disappeared. You just...ran away.'

There was that accusation again. That he was a coward.

The reminder of how little she understood came with a wave of weariness. Thomas wanted this over with. He wanted to put this all behind them effectively enough to be able to work together.

He wanted...peace.

So he took another deep breath and he turned his head to meet Rebecca's gaze.

Don't miss
A LIFE-SAVING REUNION
by Alison Roberts

Available June 2017
www.millsandboon.co.uk

AND IF YOU'D LIKE TO CATCH UP WITH ANY OF THE OTHER BOOKS IN THE PADDINGTON CHILDREN'S HOSPITAL SERIES THEY ARE ALL AVAILABLE NOW:

THEIR ONE NIGHT BABY by Carol Marinelli
FORBIDDEN TO THE PLAYBOY SURGEON by Fiona Lowe
MUMMY, NURSE...DUCHESS? by Kate Hardy
FALLING FOR THE FOSTER MUM by Karin Baine
HEALING THE SHEIKH'S HEART by Annie O'Neil

MILLS & BOON®

are delighted to support
World Book Night

Georgie Lee

The Secret Marriage Pact

www.millsandboon.co.uk

B0517_2